Invisible Rider

Kathleen Summers

Lynora David
Old friends - good friends

K Summers

Copyright © 2022 by Kathleen Summers

All rights reserved.

No part of this publication may be reproduced, distributed, or transmitted in any form or by any means, including photocopying, recording, or other electronic or mechanical methods, without the prior written permission of the author, except as permitted by Canadian and U.S. copyright law. For permission requests, contact the author.

This book is a work of fiction. Any references to historical events, real people, or real places are used fictitiously. Other names, characters, places and events are products of the author's imagination and any resemblance to actual events or places or persons, living or dead, is entirely coincidental.

Book Cover by Brandi Doane McCann

First edition 2022

To Maisy, my dear friend. Thank you for prodding and reading and reading and reading. You kept me on task.

Chapter 1

JUST ANOTHER SUNNY DAY IN PARADISE

It slithers swiftly and silently across the continents and the seas, into the crevices where living things hide, taking every beating heart with it. No one sees it coming.

The blowback from the howling wind and rain rattles and breaks against the windows and fabricated steel house siding. The house is built for this, and they're safe, but they never get used to the ferocity of the spring and fall storms. Alex feels like she's on a ship at sea, and they could go down in the waves. Princie, their old dog, is unsettled and sitting up between their heads, panting nervously. They try to calm her, to no avail. She looks wildly at the windows. A colossal crash hits the roof, Princie yelps and Alex and Sam think it must be a tree branch from the old willow out back. They know the roof will be okay. It's impervious to anything. Still, they'll have to call the grounds service people tomorrow to remove the tree branch. They're not crazy about the guy, Peter, who comes around. He seems angry at the world and unresponsive when they try to engage him. They stopped trying and left him to his work.

Alex feels a knot of anxiety in her gut with this storm. An uneasy dark mist drifts into a far corner of her mind. She can't name it, but it's there. Her skin prickles and she snuggles in closer to Sam. He stirs in his sleep and draws her close. They toss and turn throughout the night, with an ear to the wind outside.

Once the noise of the rain stops, Princie returns to the bottom of the bed and sleeps. At six, she paws Sam awake, and he gets up to take her out and check the roof. The wind is still blowing so hard he keeps her to the lea of the house while she pees and poops. To her indignity, she's been blown over on her side a time or two. She's an efficient little pooper and doesn't make him wait. A very thick branch lies across the top of the back of the house. The old willow lost an arm.

They have an eccentric neighbor who lives in a dilapidated bungalow next door with a decaying old shack beside it. He's not all the way to a hoarder, but he keeps things, like old cars and boats, none of which will ever operate again. They predate solar vehicles. He's been broken into many times. His cooler is padlocked. He has nothing of value other than food. He seems to survive despite that. All the local wildlife use the crawlspace under his shack to safely give birth to their litters and introduce their kits and pups to the world from the broken concrete basement opening. Little masked raccoon faces, groundhogs, possums, and baby skunks launch from the bottom of this old shed. Their host is a small, sleek, black feral cat. He's the grand old man who welcomes them into his safe spot. The comings and goings of all the mothers and little ones do not bother this cat. He sits in the sun in the backyard, cleaning his shiny coat, the benevolent king of his territory. Their neighbor feeds him twice a day. The cat shows up for meals, but he's untouchable. He's his own cat. He often stands back from the bowl and shares it with another feral cat, who also visits the shack, but doesn't live there. Alex and Sam aren't sure who has the upper paw here. The cats have worked it out. Too many people haven't. At the very least, the menagerie is safe from the ever-prowling coyotes. Sam and Alex enjoy their miniature zoo next door.

At dawn, the birds wake up and have a tweet party in all the trees and shrubbery. It's a cacophony of avian conversations, sharing bird gossip, food sites, and flirtatious messages to the bird next branch over. I'm a hot robin. Check me out. Whatever, they're having a great time.

It's April 2092. Long before Alex and Sam were born, scientists devised a way to miniaturize batteries and solar panels, significantly extending their longevity and scope. Everything in the world now runs on solar and doesn't need a lot of sunlight to feed it. There were huge lobbying efforts by all the old power drivers and great political strife for decades. Free accessible clean power won out. It changed the planet's chemistry and people stopped talking about global warming for a change. All governments provide free Nutri biscuits to those that can't feed themselves. No one goes hungry anymore. Housing is also provided to all. It's not pleasant, but everyone can have walls, a door, and privacy. You'd think all society's problems had been fixed. Not so fast.

Unfortunately, rising seas stole houses, land, cities, and entire countries from too many. The homeless refugee populations became completely unmanageable around the world. The fast changing technical world also left billions of people unemployed with no hope for gainful employment. They would never have those skills and couldn't keep up. The haves and have nots were so deeply divided. The world was unsafe. Traveling gangs of the disenfranchised broke into homes and businesses, stealing everything and murdering indiscriminately. People weren't safe on the streets. Smart Homes were developed, with their own solar sources of heat and air conditioning, water, and sewage handling. Their exteriors were made of a steel composite and impervious to bad weather and bad people. People have adapted to this way of living. It's normal. Life goes on.

The planet still walks on a tightrope of recovery and collapse. There's no safety net. Alex and Sam live well and stay safe in an angry world. Too many still don't. The passage of time changed the world in a million ways, and yet, not at all.

Alex is a professional researcher and works late most nights, digging deep into the bowels of the Newnet, gleaning scraps of information related to her research contracts. She's a talented hacker and can often get past security walls others can't. She sleeps late and wakes to the sun streaming in across the floor. The storm has passed; the wind has died down, and it'll be a beautiful day. She and Sam might get out for a run before they head next door to the Kracker's for dinner tonight. There's a guarded running track nearby. Not perfect, but at least they're outside.

Princie's asleep at the bottom of the bed, odd for her. Sam takes her out first thing, and she usually stays downstairs with him. She struggles climbing stairs now, but she scampers down lickity split when they come home. She takes great pride (Alex has assigned her this feeling) in still jumping up on their bed at night. If they help her, she looks insulted. She takes a long run at it and doesn't slip off... most nights.

Alex gives her a tummy tickle and gets nothing, no response, although her body seems to move as it sinks into the covers. It's a strange vision Alex can't somehow absorb. Princie's eyes are glassy and staring straight ahead, but her body is moving. Alex knows immediately Princie is dead, but what's with the moving body? It appears to be flattening in front of her eyes. She was 16 years old, so no surprise she's gone. No. It's still a big surprise. Alex's heart is bursting. Life without Princie. An enormous hole in the space in the house. She must tell Sam. Princie is a daddy's girl, and he'll be a mess. Alex twitches slightly at the sight of the dog's body still subtly moving, but her brain puts that aside for later. She heads downstairs to tell Sam.

Someone is screaming in the street, and she hears an alarm going off outside. What the hell? She checks the exterior cameras and sees nothing. She wonders why their security guard hasn't dealt with this. Their screens show empty news sets, empty desks, backdrops, and notices of interruption, but no people, no news, no sound. Very odd.

   She reaches Sam's office on the lower level and sees the top of his head lying on the desk, his hands on the keyboard. They look peculiar. She calls his name but knows in her core he's also dead. Her heart pounds: she's shaking uncontrollably and can barely stand. She can't take this in. Running in the back of her mind, behind all the noise of Sam, dead Sam, is the question. "Is it food poisoning? Did Sam and Princie eat something she didn't? What's in this house that killed them?" Sam's body is also moving and fast dropping to the floor, decomposing. No. He's disintegrating before her eyes in the strangest way. He's turning into a pile of sand. Something is so wrong, her mind can't grasp it. Standing there, watching this, she calls their security guard. No answer. She then calls their emergency line. It rings on, no answer. Not even an answering service clicks in. She kneels beside this strange sight of her husband's body, falling to the floor inside his clothes. It's a fast process. Within an hour, he's a pile of sand on the floor, with no bones, teeth, or moisture. His hair is as intact as it can be without a skull underneath. She's now shuddering, truly in shock.

   She needs information and help. Going outside may be dangerous, with no responding security guard out there. Still, she steps out onto the street. She needs answers. There are rarely any safety issues in the daytime, anyway. There's a big safety issue now. Their neighbor Cora is out on the street repeatedly screaming, "Help me!" She's in her early forties, with badly dyed red hair, grey roots showing, and one of those waistlines that drops from her bust to her ass in one bulging blob under her t-shirt. She's not bright. She's collapsed in the middle of the road, legs splayed.

   Cora and Alex share a cancer past, so they're more in touch than most neighbors. You live tight and close in this world. They share house security codes with her and their neighbors, the Krackers. Cora gets up and runs to Alex. "Fred is dead and is turning into a strange pile. I can't get security or emergency to respond. Our screens are dead. What's going on?" She's beyond consoling, sobbing in great gasps, ugly cry face. She's in a complete gasping panic. A crazy thought passes through Alex's mind. She wants to slap her and tell her to "Snap out of it." There's nothing too crazy today. Instead, she says, "I don't know what's happening. Sam and Princie are in the same state." They ring some doorbells. No one answers. The street alarm has stopped. There's no birdsong. This is big. Their neighborhood has gone silent. Is it an explosion nearby in one of the canal freighters? A gas leak? What?

Alex needs time to think this through and escorts Cora to her house with her arm around her back. She does not want to go in with her and says, "I know it's awful, but I need to see who else might still be messaging out there. I'll check in on you later with any news."

She can't do anything for her right now. She's a mess.

She returns home and checks on Sam, hoping this is just a nightmare. *Time to wake up,* she thinks. He's now completely flattened out on the floor, his hair is gone, and his clothes are still sitting on top of the pile of sand. She has two brains. The sensible one says, *well, at least I don't have to deal with maggots and flies.* How could she have that thought? This disintegration of his body and Princie's is the strangest phenomenon. What killed their husbands, the dog, the birds, and maybe their silent neighbors and spared her and Cora?

She calls all their friends and her mother in Victoria. Nothing. Why isn't her mother picking up?

She returns upstairs to Princie, who's now nothing but a pelt at the bottom of the bed, covering her pile of sand. Her fur is fast disappearing. She had such a beautiful, thick white coat. Alex thinks she should do something with Sam and Princie's remains. Maybe keep them in case the world rights itself and someone can explain what happened to them.

She gets a garbage bag for Princie, moves her remains into it, and knots the bag. What's left of her beautiful coat falls away from the remaining sand and breaks into individual hairs. She returns to Sam. Alex doesn't want to put him in a garbage bag, but can't think of anything else. She shakes out his sand from his clothes and has to turn his socks inside out to do this. Two hours after finding her husband dead, she's shaking him out of his socks as beach sand. Her world is spinning. She folds all his clothes and stacks them, trying to stay sane by doing something normal. Now she's left with his pile of sand. Her husband, lover, and best friend aren't there. As they always did, they had kissed goodnight before falling off to sleep last night with a tossed-off casual "I love you." No need to worry. See you in the morning. Thousands of those ahead of us. She puts him into a pillowcase. Somehow nicer than a garbage bag.

Cora is back ringing the doorbell and frantically banging on Alex's door. She's not to be ignored. Alex feels like the world has flipped on its axis. She suggests to

Cora they deal with Fred's body, and they walk back to Cora's house with Alex barely holding her up. Fred is now a large pile of sand on the couch in front of the monitor. He's still in his sweats and t-shirt, never a dresser, even for death. He was overweight and flew bush planes. Alex could never put those two things together, but he had no problem getting licensed every year, so not his problem. Alex asks Cora if she has a container suitable to put Fred in. Together they shake out his sand from his clothes. Cora comes up with an old game box, and Alex suggests they might want to put him into a plastic bag to contain him first. Cora robotically obeys Alex's suggestions. This cleanup tedium gets them through the next few hours. At least Fred's body disintegration isn't such an affront to Cora's sanity. Alex suggests Cora eat something, but Cora says she has some sleeping pills, and she just wants to knock herself out for a few hours and make this all stop.

Alex is frozen in this nightmare, still processing it, and has yet to cry.

She scouts the neighborhood to see if she can learn anything. At the end of her street, a guy stands alone, staring out into the road, stunned, not moving. She doesn't know him. He could be dangerous, but danger's now everywhere. She approaches him. He's mid-fifties, thin, with a bit of a gut. He's unshaven and partially bald on the top of his head, with some patches still on the side. His hair is half-gray. He's not yet an old man, but he's heading there early. His nose is long, thin, and red across the bridge where his sunglasses sit. He has no lips and a receding chin. He's not blessed with good looks. He's in a long-sleeved blue cotton plaid shirt with stains on the front and is wearing jeans and sandals. If she had to give the guy a color, it would be ash grey. As she approaches, she takes all this in and asks, "Everything okay?" Knowing it's not. Without looking at her, he says in a monotone, "I overcame leukemia this year with the vaccine. Our life was ahead of us. Now she's a pile of sand up in our bedroom." It dawns on Alex the only people still alive in the neighborhood are those that got the Libertas1 cancer vaccine.

She tells him she and her neighbor have experienced the same thing and don't know what's happened. He mumbles, "Maybe poison gas." She doesn't have a response. She doesn't have an answer. She realizes the three of them have somehow been bypassed by something lethal. That might not be permanent. Alex suggests to the guy they all retreat to their homes for safety. She can't deal with more grief than her own, anyway. She tells him she'll knock on his door later. Alex has no intention of doing this and leaves him standing there.

Alex returns to her house, not knowing what to do. She calls her mother again. She had the vaccine and should be alive. There's no answer. She repeatedly calls for hours, desperate to talk to her, maybe get some advice. She wonders, "Could this have hit the entire country, or perhaps the world?" She can't believe something in the air could selectively take out the world. One of the research topics on her desk, but not yet started, was toxins being used as weapons. It was a government contract. She wishes now she knew more. Not that it would have saved anyone. What bastard government lab has let this out? Was it one dumb fuck who left the lid off while he had a sandwich, as simple as that, or ...intentional? "You can't eradicate us because we'll take you out first." There are always crazy bastards with a suicide bent. "We have nothing left to lose. We all go down."

One of those crazy bastards waits for her in the shadows of her future.

She risks a ride around the city, stopping at all their friends' houses. They should be home. There's no response when she rings their doorbells. She doesn't want to face the image of them all dead, piles on their floors where they fell. Particularly the kids. She moves on. The service cars just continued to their booked destination and stopped there. No smash-ups. Service cars provided privacy and convenience. They picked people up and dropped them off. There was no long, tiresome chat listening to the political opinions of a cab driver or detours to increase the fare. Just you and your service car. They were all hovercraft, and everyone called them 'floaters.'

She rides to the station to see what the trains are doing. They're at a dead stop, the operative word "dead." A few people on the street try to wave her down. She can't take on their terror; she has a load of her own. Various piles of clothes lie in puddles of sand on the sidewalk. It turns her stomach with its strangeness.

She heads to the hospital thinking, "There must have been patients in there who had the vaccine, along with some medical staff." She wonders if the medical staff would stick around to care for the patients. Who knows? Nothing is moving around the exterior of the hospital, no ambulances screaming in with emergencies, not a soul. Inside, a woman in pink scrubs is talking to a male, plus two women in wheelchairs. They are circled in the main lobby. She approaches them and asks if they know what's going on. They've come to the same realization she has. They had the Libertas1 shot and were spared. The hospital beds are probably filled with backless hospital nighties and sand. It would have been too early for any surgeries to start, but there will be patients still alive upstairs in the beds. That's a problem Alex can't solve. Her morals shift quickly in this new game of death. Conscience is a negotiable commodity.

She wishes them good luck and leaves. Good luck? They'll eventually starve. She rides silently back home. So, it's at least the entire city that got hit. She wonders again how widespread this is. Why isn't her mother responding in Victoria?

Reality is settling into the pores of her body. Her body wants to eject it. She starts crying, then uncontrollably sobbing. It's like projectile vomiting, coughing up phlegm, eyes swollen shut, spewing her grief. Her body can't contain it or get rid of it. She does this for days. She does not answer the door when Cora knocks. After a while, Cora stops knocking. She may think Alex is dead. Alex is good with that. She has to do this alone. She brings Sam in his pillowcase up to bed with her. It's amazing what little volume the human body reduces to without liquid. She does not believe in an afterlife but talks to him anyway, asking him what she should do. He doesn't have much to say. He was her beating heart, the blood that ran through her veins, her life. She needs him here with her to get through this, damn it.

She's already unbearably lonely.

Outside, the grass needs mowing, crops keep growing, and fruit ripens. That part of the world seems untouched. No bees are buzzing. The little pollinators are no more. They're bee sand. The sun rises and sets again, but their little zoo next door is closed for business.

Chapter 2

THE GETAWAY

Someone's banging on Alex's door and ringing her doorbell. He looks like a kid, maybe one of her neighbor Bill Kracker's students. He disappears as quickly as he came. Right after that, she hears screaming outside on the street, but it's an adult male voice. That also stops quickly. It didn't sound good. Then a spray of bullets hits her house. They bounce off, but someone is pissed at her or just pissed at everybody. She can't see much from her window or cameras. After a few days of silence, she risks it and steps carefully outside. Cora's body lies on its side in the middle of the road, blood dried on her mouth, and a bullet wound in her chest. She's quickly turning into a dry carcass. Alex's skin surface contracts. There are people out here killing people. She goes back home and grabs a gun. She's a different woman than yesterday as she walks back into the street with her gun out in front of her, looking in every direction.

She uses her code at Cora's house. The door slides over, and she moves in carefully, gun first. She tries to mimic how police do it in movies, covering herself from any exposure. She checks all the rooms and finds no one there. The house looks undisturbed except for an enormous supply of government biscuits piled up in the pantry. When would Cora have gotten these, and why? Maybe they were always there. You don't know everything about your friends. Cora's corpse is light enough to carry now, and Alex lies her down on the couch with Fred's game box. She feebly says to her, "I'm so sorry, old friend, this is a sad ending." She wonders what Cora was doing in the street and why she was shot. She also wonders what happened to the kid banging on her door. Did he have anything to do with this? Was he the one who shot Cora and shot at the house? Who was the guy yelling?

Alex returns home, still with her gun extended, looking all around her. The situation is now perilous, and she knows she's not safe and must leave, or she'll be trapped in her house forever. She has to suck up her grief and survive. It's time to hit the road.

Her name is Alex Smith, Alexandra, but no one called her that. She and her now dead husband Sam lived close to Lake Ontario in a small Southern Ontario city. She's almost thirty-six years old, the backside of her thirties, as they say, heading fast for forty. Yesterday, she was a contract researcher providing consumer and political research for several clients. She no longer knows who she is now, other than a widow. She loved her work. It took her down rabbit holes she couldn't have imagined. Her husband, Sam, was an accountant and investment advisor. That makes him sound boring as hell, but his humor was dry and accurate and his observations of people and the world, often cruel, made her laugh so hard her belly hurt. He wasn't perfect, but she liked him. He was smart, kind, and loving. She's cocky, mouthy, and opinionated. She had a few close friends who got her, most of all, Sam. They were happy.

She's from Victoria, British Columbia, and her mother still lives there. At least, Alex hopes she does. She still can't get her on the SAT. Her mother is a therapist for adults with autism. She and Alex are very close, and screen chat most days. They both had a brush with cancer and had the Libertas1 cancer shot. The cancer cells stopped dividing, and they were fine. Alex heard this vaccine was no longer available. There were multiple news items posted about this, speculating the manufacturer was holding out for something from the government or had been influenced or even bought by another government, possibly not one of the good ones. India is a world problem now and certainly not an ally. Alex wonders if this could have had anything to do with the current disaster. She can't worry about that now. What's done is done. She has to survive.

When she was twelve, Alex's dad died of a stroke, devastating both her and her mother, but they had each other. Sam's parents died early as well. They were both only children. Like most people, they worked at home, with Sam's office on the lower floor walkout and Alex's on the top floor. He did the cooking, not her interest. They had no children, just a well-loved sixteen-year-old dog, Princie. Gone too. They lived in a protected Smart Home because they could afford to. They each had a gun, but other than at the shooting range, had never shot them.

Her clients were mainly legitimate businesses, sometimes governments, researching the competition and the market. Some potential clients seemed a bit nefarious, out to get the goods on someone. Alex was very discerning and did nothing illegal. She refused some contracts if she mistrusted the client. She didn't need the business and wasn't interested in being part of someone's blackmail. She's researched the movement of guns and drugs between countries, as well as big pharma and the money behind it. She's looked at health care, hospital systems, daycare, politicians, political parties, banks, lawyers, and charities, to name a few. She didn't publish; she was the backgrounder. She researched many product fields, with the client wanting all the competitive information available. There are lots of stories out there behind the tick-tock of our lives.

One of the more intriguing areas she investigated was the survivalist product industry and the people who bought that stuff. They weren't all crazy rednecks dressed in plaid wool shirts with suspenders and outsized beards. They were often your ordinary neighbor next door. She looked at food and shelter and camping gear and weapons. She checked out tools to clean water, good camouflage, gadgets for this and that, and ways to disappear and stay alive.

There were always media rumblings about nuclear threats overseas, not to mention North America's probable devastating response. Sourcing a lifetime supply of food and access to clean water just seemed smart. If it was even possible to survive a nuclear storm. There were many suppliers and options. She was optimistic then and assumed they would live until they were at least 100 years old, so they needed about 70 years of food. That's a lot. It had to be portable, not boxes and cans. She found just the thing and ordered ten years' worth to check it out.

The delivery arrived in a small plain brown box. You would have thought she was ordering sex toys. However, you don't advertise you have food if no one else does. The package was so compact she thought the supplier got the order wrong and only sent a few. When she opened it, there were 11,000 thinnest of thin wafers. She didn't count them. You're instructed to eat three a day, 400 calories each, 1,200 calories a day. It's supposedly a sustainable diet. They resemble communion wafers of old. Bread of my life, as they used to say in the catholic church. You add water, heat them, or eat them cold. They turn into large thick biscuits, quite chewy and oddly satisfying. The package lists sixty flavors, with the flavor lightly imprinted on the wafer. You can eat something that tastes like chocolate cake for supper, roast beef for breakfast, and fruit for lunch. She guessed you would get to know what comes after chili con carne after a few rounds. They're light as tissue and would be easy to pack up seven of these sleeves if you had to move quickly. The water filter cleans regular water and desalinates seawater. It's also feather light and has a lifetime guarantee. She wonders to whom you would return it after the nuclear blast if you found it wanting.

She lived a week on these flavored wafers. She's a snacker, so only having three meals daily was tough. On the first day, the 400-calorie breakfast tasted like beef stew and carried her to lunch. Lunch tasted like oranges. Supper tasted like chicken. After a week, she lost 5 1/2 pounds and knew she could do this if she had to.

She ordered a lifetime of supplies for her, Sam, and her mom. It was her mom's surprise birthday present. This stuff wasn't cheap. She told her mother to lock it in the safe and tell no one she had it. Her mother thought she was being ridiculous but agreed. Alex now has food for two lifetimes, having Sam's share as well. Most other people will run out shortly.

Her mother may still be alive with communication cut off because of this catastrophe. She's Alex's only link to sanity. She's worried about her safety and has to get to her, somehow. That means solar biking across the country and boating across the Georgia Strait between Vancouver and Victoria, without being seen. She grew up on Vancouver Island, but the ocean terrifies her. She respects its ability to kill you with one enormous wave. After a storm, when she felt brave, she would stand on the docks at the bottom of Dallas Road in Victoria and watch the heaving tide come in. Even there, the ocean looked bottomless, great rolling green waves lapping by her. A rogue lick of its tongue can sweep you away; no time to gasp for air. Only you and your "I don't want to die" mind knowing you're never coming up again. The ocean is dangerous.

Alex is smallish, 5'5", 120 pounds now, and she'll be out there for all the hungry people to see as she crosses the country. She needs some good camouflage and decides to only travel at night without lights. She needs night vision glasses, dark clothes, camping gear, and rain gear. She at least has portable food and a water distiller.

She takes both guns and wonders if she could shoot someone dead. She may have to, and she's not ready to look at that idea directly. The ammunition is minuscule and stores in the gun. She could shoot it a thousand times. Alex hopes she won't have to shoot anybody a thousand times, or even once. She realizes she can also be shot and she needs a bulletproof vest. She rides out to the police station late, dressed in black clothes, with a black scarf around her face. The doors are open, but there's no one around. The main lobby has two piles of sand under uniforms behind the greeting counter. She passes through to the inner chambers of their crew room. There, stacked on shelves, are dozens of bulletproof vests. She guesses they'd need easy access to grab them and run. She tries on a few, remembering it may have to go over heavier clothes later. She finds one that fits.

She leaves the silent police building wearing her vest, thinking, "There's no one protecting us while we sleep."

She rides past a few other bikers, but they're not interested in her yet. Some even lift a hand in greeting. She knows it's early days. She then rides to the local outdoor store and sources a load of road supplies. She finds a lightweight pop-up tent and inflatable thermal sleeping bag. No more sleeping on cold, hard ground. Camping has come a long way since she last tried it. She never understood its appeal. Mosquitoes, peeing on your shoes, no place to poop, cookstoves. She hopes mosquitoes didn't survive this catastrophe. Goodbye, you little vampires. She thinks, *give me a nice hotel with clean sheets, a bathroom, and room service,* and then thinks, *I'll have to get over that.*

Even though it's warming up outside, she picks up a balaclava. She needs to take her whole appearance down to black for as much invisibility on the road as she can get. She'll travel light and packs the magic number of three for clothes; two changes and the one she's wearing. She finds wash and dry socks, bras, panties, shirts, and pants and figures she'll wash them wherever she can and hang them in the tent when she's sleeping. She finds a pee funnel for peeing in the woods like a guy. She's always envied guys who can pee anywhere. Now she can.

She moves on to a drugstore for painkiller patches, bandages, and wound cleaners. "Be prepared," the boy scouts used to say. All the heavy-duty painkillers are cleaned out. She has a decent supply of her own but wants some backup. She guesses some drug addicts survived. They'll be clean now.

Finally, she needs a fast highway solar bike. The back door to the nearest bike outlet is smashed in, but there's still inventory on the floor. She spots a powerful bike with generous storage that'll serve her well. It's blue and chrome and gleaming. She'll have to spray it flat black. She starts it up and it's as silent as cotton. There's spray paint in the store, she grabs several cans and sprays it down when she gets home. Pity. It was such a pretty bike. She disables the lights. She's ready to go.

A few years back, one of Alex's contracts had her looking into camouflage gear. Government and military sites were often blocked, but she could hack her way past a lot of their security. She researched who was doing what with camouflage in the military and the global hunting world. They closely guarded these secrets. Some small game farms were still available for hunters for a steep fee, shooting mostly deer and fowl. Creepy. She never understood hunting and killing animals who were minding their own business, not bothering anyone. Some people eat and sell game they've raised and shot, but secretly. Even the Indians don't brag about it anymore.

There's a security wall with all the military sites. Alex can't find much more than the usual stuff you think of armies or hunters wearing. Uniforms and tents color coordinated to the terrain. Vehicles are the same. Various aircraft and weapons were flying 'under the radar.' Not much new that wasn't already out in the public domain. *There must be more I can't get at,* she thinks.

Years ago, she read a news article about a Southern Ontario manufacturing company working with a fabric prototype that could make something the size of an apple disappear. There was never anything written about this later she could find. It had been quickly blacked out by someone, some organization, or...some government? She had tucked this away, thinking it might be useful someday.

The manufacturer's name was not mentioned. The article hinted at potential military use if they ever figured out how to make bigger pieces. It could have been a government lab. It was impossible to track down to see if they had made any headway. She had dug into military suppliers and bases, and old and current military airports that could handle cargo planes. She wonders what they might bring in to make this fabric. Or were they making it on-site? She had looked for anything indicating its location and came up with nothing.

She thinks they'd probably want to be near a quiet airport where they could ship goods out and receive supplies, under the radar, and probably near a U.S. border. There are many small airports in Ontario, but none are as quiet as she's looking for. The Trenton Air Force base is an hour from Kingston. Kingston has an old, retired military base, CFB Kingston, that still exists but is unoccupied, as far as she knows. Kingston could be a possibility. It's close to the border, not too far from a military base, and it has a small pilot training airport with a runway big enough to take cargo planes and small commercial jets.

She scopes the entire area using a GPS visual map. Nothing is going on at the old base she can discern. She zeroes in on a large fenced 30-acre site with no visible buildings. It's heavily forested, with no apparent signage and no identification. It looks like it has a high-security fence. When she expands the topical photograph, there seem to be a lot of cameras. Something is going on there. She has the site coordinates, so she should be able to find it. Her GPS is still thankfully working, logging into its little satellite that continues to spin around the earth. No human intervention required.

It's been weeks since the disaster. Alex imagines her mother alone and scared, unable to reach her. She's in danger, given she has food and others don't. Her mother has a kind heart, and Alex envisions her trying to feed everyone and running out herself. She needs to decide whether to head straight out west and take her chances camping or, take a risk and explore the slim possibility she can source better camouflage gear here. It could increase her chances of safety and getting there alive. If only she can find this manufacturing plant.

It could be a wasted trip, a shot in the dark, but Alex believes it's worth a look, even if it's dangerous. Camping across the country won't be a breeze. She figures it should take her about five hours to bike to Kingston at night. She'd spotted a lot of fencing, probably electrified. She takes one last local foray to a hardware store and picks up some electric wire cutters and protective supplies. She thinks, *shopping's easy these days. No lineups.*

When she and Sam envisioned their mutual deaths of old age, they always said, "No sad funeral." The survivor will have one big dinner party inviting their closest friends. They forgot there might not be anybody left for a dinner party by the time they died. Everybody else would be dead or feeble. It always sounded kind of fun in a macabre sort of way. One of their favorite places in Victoria was Anderson Hill. They decided to marry while sitting there watching the sun go down. There's an expansive view of the Straight of Juan de Fuca, the Trial Islands, and across the channel to the Olympic mountains and the golf course. It's a stunning array of the southern Victoria coast. The rocky expanse is covered with wildflowers and yellow broom in the spring. Princie loved to wander the hill, sniffing out wild things. She never found any. They said they would spread each other's ashes there when they died. Little did Alex know this would come true so soon. She finds a small pill container and fills it with some of Sam's and Princie's sand. *They'll travel with me,* she thinks, and *I'll scatter their sand around sunset.* She says to Sam, *I'm keeping my promise, but there'll be no dinner party.* Sam doesn't answer.

She still has him in the pillowcase on their bed and sleeps with him close to her belly for the last time. She thinks, *I can't cry anymore. The well is dry. I have a lifetime to remember him.*

She takes one last walk through the house and the garden they loved. Who knows what will happen to all the houses? Will the grass, weeds, and trees grow up and cover everything like the Mexican jungle? She buries the rest of Sam and Princie in the back garden under the forsythia bush. Sam loved that bush in the spring, yellow and promising, and Princie often napped under it in the cool earth on hot summer days. Alex packs the wafers, camping equipment, and clothes into the new solar bike. She has thousands of images of her life with Sam on her device. *Farewell, sweet husband of mine. Thank you for our time together.*

It's midnight, and she rides silently away from that life without looking back.

Chapter 3

CASING THE JOINT

She doesn't want to go down into the states because they shoot people on sight there, even in normal times. She'll ride around the top of the lake, connect to the 401 past Toronto, and then head to Kingston. She's dressed entirely in black, including the uncomfortable and hot balaclava, her night goggles, and bulletproof vest. She rides slowly and cautiously with no bike light to illuminate her path. A few bikes fly past her. They're riders aren't hungry yet.

She passes Hamilton, the dead steel town. No more smokestacks burning day and night. It's still ugly, never redeemed. Further on, some waterside lands have been redeveloped, but the core industrial land is too toxic to build on. All the nasty smoke-covered buildings sit, decade after decade, rusty dinosaurs and dragons with no more fire in their throats, slowly caving into themselves. Not even a death groan when they fall. An eternal public outcry goes on, but nobody wanted the expense of taking it on.

She leaves the highway just past the Burlington Skyway and takes Lakeshore Blvd. through Burlington and Oakville. This was always a pretty drive along the edge of the lake. Now the grand mansions sit silently in the dark. Alex and Sam always wondered who lived there and where they made their money. If they saw a For Sale sign, they'd wonder where they could be going. What had happened in their perfect lives to decide to leave this beautiful house?

No gardeners are working the vast lawns and gardens now. On the streets, there are a few random piles of sand with clothes on top, but the attack hit early. There may have been a few light sleepers and early starters out for a coffee. Runners. Nothing left but their sneakers, socks, and running shorts, if they haven't blown away. Rarely any street people here, so not them. The rest are asleep forever in their beds. They might have left a pile of pajamas and sand on their way to the bathroom for that early morning pee. They were maybe watching a screen that had gone blank, with no more news.

She reaches Toronto in an hour. Unheard of in the old days, last month. Has it only been a month since this happened? Even using a car service, you would still be on the road for at least two hours. Lots of people still commute into the city in convoys of service cars. It's fully lit up as always, ready for business. Poor Toronto. The floaters and trains are lined up, ready to be called. Nobody's calling.

Alex doesn't ride into the city. She envisions the early starters who survived. They would have come into the office to get some work done with no one around to disturb them. Then, no one came, their screens went dead, and nobody from security was responding. When they looked out their 31st-floor window, the streets would look strangely quiet, nothing moving. If they took an elevator down to the ground floor to look around, they would find their first piles of sand. She sees them running through the streets, trying to find someone. They would find only a few terrified survivors like themselves, panicked people wandering around trying to get information from someone, anyone. No one would know what happened. There would be more piles of sand and clothes on the streets. Soon, probably the same day, people would begin vandalizing shops. The food search would have begun. There might be food in drawers or desks, even if it's a clothing store or a computer store. The survivors would start ransacking the city. There aren't many grocery stores downtown, but they'd be quickly emptied. The government High Energy biscuit depots would be depleted. The survivors would understand there's no food…anywhere. Within weeks, those few survivors living in the apartment towers would start running out of food supplies. Many would begin examining their 'kill pill' boxes, reading, and rereading the instructions, wondering if they can go through starvation or end it quickly. It doesn't look like the cavalry is coming to save them.

The Cancer Society fundraisers were even more successful now that they had a cure, and they ran multiple lotteries for those that couldn't afford it. Still, too many were missed.

Survivors living in the suburbs and surrounding areas would all be going through the same panic and growing awareness that they alone survived. However, they're still going to die of starvation. The lottery winners now think they're not so lucky after all.

Alex rides on by Toronto and continues through the night, slipping silently by all the small cities along the lake and on to Kingston. In many of those cities, she knew people once. Everybody moves on. Now they're all dead.

Her new solar bike is comfortable and much faster than her little town bike. It will allow for fast getaways if she needs to get away. Her imagination conjures every likely kind of confrontation and trouble she could encounter as she rides. There's nothing to do but think. The sun's just coming up.

It's been a long night, and she's drained. She needs to lie down for a while and starts scouting for a place to pitch her tent. She rides up a well-treed country road and finds a heavily forested spot, not visible from the road. She finds some level dry ground, pops her little super tent and inflatable sleeping bag, and funnels her pee at a tree. She's getting good at that. She drinks some water, and settles in, with the morning sun breaking through the branches. In the quiet green breast of the woods, her tense body uncoils, and she's deep into a dreamless, healing sleep. She's out for ten hours. She hadn't slept that soundly since this all started. Her body just said, *that's enough*.

At four o'clock, she lifts her head, forgetting then remembering where she is and why she's here. Fear rises again in her belly when she considers her situation. She shakes off the sleep, heats some water, and adds a wafer. It tastes like pasta with a mushroom sauce. Not bad. Belly full, it's time for her to get to work. She decamps and rides down to the old military base to confirm her sense that it's closed, defunct, and nothing's going on there. There's still a sad old billboard sign swinging beside the entrance. There's so much graffiti on it that the name is barely recognizable. She rides the inner roads. Most buildings were demolished long ago, although some remain, and the road system still exists. There's grass growing up through the sidewalks. Windows are broken on any remaining structures. She's surprised the site wasn't razed and redeveloped. The Feds don't like giving up their property though. No one's coming here again, let alone manufacturing anything. This is not the spot.

Alex worries she's got this completely wrong and there's no manufacturing plant of material that can make apples disappear. Maybe she's out of her mind. She carries on, beginning to doubt her decision to come here at all.

She checks her GPS coordinates for the next site on her list. The route takes her east along the Great Lakes Waterfront Trail to an almost indiscernible private road, except for the barn-burning sign that reads, "PRIVATE ROAD. DANGER. ARMED SECURITY IN PLACE. YOU ARE ON CAMERA. TRESPASSERS WILL BE ARRESTED AND DETAINED. She thinks, *Christ!*

Someone wants to get their point across. She wonders if there's anyone alive behind the camera. This sign is too noisy to mean nothing.

The road is fenced, gated, locked, and surrounded by dense woods. She rides the fence line about a half mile back and is amazed to find a slight break. She squeezes her bike and herself through, thinking, *so much for the scary signage.* It looked like there had been a minor explosion there, tearing the fence. She also thinks, *I've nothing to lose but my life, hah, and I'm wearing my bulletproof vest.* Somehow, that doesn't comfort her. She notices there are cameras on her. Is someone watching her? If there is, they'd quickly know she's not a security risk using FaceREC. All her bona fides would be revealed. She takes the road north and is not intercepted. Alex thinks again, *so much for the sign.* She wonders again if maybe there's no one left alive in here to respond to her trespassing. Riding several miles deep into the woods, she comes upon a gated, electric-fenced area, barbed rolled wire on top, the works. Same 'overkill' sign, "Keep Out, or You'll Be Shot."

Cameras and speakers abound. This fence seems to stretch out and around with no end. Someone sure doesn't want people in here, or didn't, if they're alive. She wonders, *what the hell is going on in here?* The road continues into the woods, but she sees no buildings or signs of life. Hiding her bike in the forest, she walks the fence line and sees how big an area it surrounds. Probably for security reasons, a ten-foot cleared area runs next to it, so it's easy to walk. She covers almost 12 miles before she's back at the start, with no new knowledge. There were cameras on her the entire hike. It's nearly nine o'clock, and the sun is going down. There are no lights out here. Alex can't see a building anywhere on the GPS satellite map. She needs to get in with her wire cutters, insulated gloves, rubber-soled shoe covers, and electrical tape. She wishes she felt confident about doing that without frying her brains. There's a distinct, dangerous buzz when she throws a stick at the fence. She returns to last night's campsite. She'll tackle this early tomorrow. She's hungry, thirsty, and tired from the walk through the brush. Small mercies, no biting insects.

The sky's overcast and the air's cool for June. It looks like rain. *Better get used to bad weather,* Alex thinks. She finds last night's site just before the sun heads over the horizon and pops her tent. She loves this insta-tent and sets up for a late dinner. The rain is now thundering on the tent, but the deluge doesn't last long. She has her thermal sleeping bag on warm, and she's toasty and dry inside. She heats another wafer. Chocolate something. *What the hell, it's good*, she thinks. After hiking through the woods for hours, she needs a shower, but it'll have to wait. She thinks of the Robert Frost poem, *"The woods are lovely, dark and deep, but I have promises to keep and miles to go before I sleep."* She sleeps, though, and is up at sunrise.

Chapter 4

DO NOT TRESPASS

It's already hot at dawn, and Alex sweats under her bulletproof vest. She packs up, gets to the second gate again, and talks to the speakers she saw there. You never know. There might be someone alive in there who'll talk to her. She'll suck it up and try the wire cutters if that doesn't work. She'll have to cut a big enough hole to get the bike and her through. Alex has no experience with electrical wire cutters.

She's standing in front of the gate, possibly talking to no one. She launches into her story. "Hi, I'm Alex Smith, but I think you know that already. If you're in there, you know the world has gone nuts, and there aren't many survivors. It appears those of us who had the Libertas1 shot were spared. My mother in Victoria also had the shot and should have survived, but I can't contact her. I have no one left here alive, and I want to return to Victoria to find her. That means I need to ride across the country and somehow get across the Georgia Strait to get to Victoria. I have food and will be a mark the longer I'm visibly alive and out on the road. I know someone was working on some special camouflage several years ago. Given your high-security measures, I thought it might be you. I thought you might have something I could use better than the tents I got in the sports supply store. Are you the ones? Is there anybody in there?" Silence. She then does the ridiculous and yells, "Hello!" Nothing. She thinks, *crap, now I have to cut through the damn fence.*

She puts on the insulated gear and pulls out the clippers. The instructions had said to only cut one small part of the fence at a time and wrap off the ends with electrical tape to protect herself, so this will take some time. She taps the fence with the clippers and feels the vibration of the electricity coursing up her arms. She no longer thinks this is a good idea, but she'll know soon enough. Just as she goes for the first cut, a sexless electronic voice says sharply, "Stop, or you will be shot." She thinks, *okay, I'm listening.* She hears the faint sound of something moving in the woods toward her. Branches breaking? What is that? She thinks it's inside the fence. She can't define what the sound is. Pretty subtle. Is there someone coming up behind her? She can't see anyone. She lays her bike down under some brush and retreats into the woods, stooping down to watch. Coming up the road inside the fence, slowly floating along, is a dark green driverless hovercraft, about the size of a golf cart, but much sleeker.

No beer cup or cheery advertising logo here. No cutesy dog head sock on the one wood. This would almost be comical in any other situation. The cart floats strategically ten feet back from the gate. There's some clever camouflage at work here. The cart is covered with a material that reflects its surroundings, making it almost disappear. If it were twenty feet back in the woods, you wouldn't be able to pick it off. She's getting excited and now thinks, *I may have come to the right place.* The gate slowly slides sideways, about two feet. If she ducked in and tried to make a run around it, she's sure there'd be a weapon on her, taking her down. The camera's eye on the bot cart aims at her, obviously not hiding that well in the forest, and an electronic voice says, "Get in." Alex says curtly, "Not likely. What's going on? Who's operating you?" The bot says, "You will be advised accordingly." She wonders, "What the hell does that mean?" Her research instincts kick in. She wants to investigate but doesn't want to leave her bike and gear behind. She says as much to the bot. The bot says, "We will bring it to you later." Alex thinks, *we? So, there are at least two people behind all this subterfuge."* Leaving everything behind is too big a gamble, and she doesn't want to take that risk. She says, "No, I need all this stuff to survive. That's why I'm here. Can I ride behind or ahead of you?" Silence. The bot golf cart sits quietly. Alex is still outside the fence looking in. It's a Mexican stand-off. That she finds herself waiting for a floating golf cart bot to talk to her in the middle of a forest, strangely, no longer seems insane.

It suddenly burps alive, and the voice says, "Ride ahead." She thinks, okay, a small victory. Maybe. If only I knew where I was going and if I'll ever come out again. Is this some Guantanamo Bay of the North? She asks the bot, "What if I want to turn around and go back out?" Again, silence. Finally, the voice says, "You can decide." That gives her some relief, even though she's talking to a golf cart with whom she has not built a feeling of trust and friendship. They haven't known each other long.

She moves her bike through the gate and rides off slowly up the road, ahead of the bot into the woods. The gate quickly and silently closes behind her. The bot floats silently along behind her. The Teddy Bears' picnic song is in her mind "*If you go into the woods today, you're in for a big surprise...*" She always thought that nursery song sounded ominous.

Having walked around it yesterday, she has a pretty good idea of the size of this treed compound. Still, she rides for about 5 miles when the bot cart says, "Stop here." There's nothing around, and Alex gets nervous. Will they murder her out here in the middle of the forest, whoever they are? The road seems to continue past where they are and veers off to the left. There's a grassy clearing off to the right. Suddenly, a 20-foot-high lift-up door rises quickly and silently, still with the grass on top. The bot cart says, "Ride in and wait at the door at the end." A long, well-lit ramp runs deep underground. It could be a mile or more but the slope is gradual and she can't tell. The walls are perfectly finished and lit, as is the ramp. This isn't just a hole in the ground.

She says to herself, *holy crap*! Her heart is beating hard, and, as if in response, the bot says, "Don't worry, you will not be harmed." She's now thinking, *aliens? Are they aliens?* She suffers from repetitive nightmares with myriad versions. They all relate to her being stuck in a hot, crowded tunnel with no way back. She's living the nightmare. Can she get back out? She doesn't know. She could die right here. She considers her options. They know why she's here. They, whoever they are, may help her with her trip. Finally, it's Canada, for Christ's sake. How dangerous could it be? She decides to go for it. Hell, this new life is one big adventure into the weird. She enters, and the door quickly and silently drops behind her. The bot does not follow her down.

She rides slowly down to the end and encounters a large metal armored door. If someone gets this far, they aren't shooting or even bombing their way through this door. A fresh voice, a real one, a female with a slight island accent, says, "Hello Alex, welcome. I'm sure you're nervous, but don't worry, we'll explain all." Alex responds, "Yeah, you and your bot keep saying that." The voice ignores her sarcasm and goes on. "However, to protect us, you'll need to be quarantined for a few days so that you bring nothing in with you that could affect us. This will allow your body and lungs to expel and exchange every air molecule. There's a room ahead where you'll stay for this period. We require you to shower immediately using the soap and shampoo supplied. There are clippers and a mirror as we want you to cut your hair very short, along with your fingernails and toenails. Your bike and gear will be returned to you later. You'll be supplied with food and clothes. There'll be a camera on you at all times. We'll introduce a live mouse in a small cage several times daily. If the mouse dies, you could still be harmful to us. When the mouse lives for a day, we'll meet. Do you have any questions?" Alex thinks, *hell yes, I have questions*, and asks, "What is this place? Who are you? What are you planning to do with me? Can I get my clothes back? Can I get my bike back? There's food in my kit; I'll need to get it back. What if the mice all die?"

Silence. The voice is good at silence. The voice says, "If the mice all die, we'll release you back outside, and everything will be returned to you. We'll know we can't work with you, but we'll still be able to help you. I just ask you to trust me right now. We think you'll find the rewards in your future safety well worth it. I'll answer the rest of your questions if you pass quarantine. Are you ready to dismount and come in, or do you want to go back outside? All options are off then, and you'll be shot if you try to cut the fence." These are pretty clear options. Stay, find out what's going on here, maybe lose my life or save my life, or go, learn nothing, possibly risk my life." Alex decides to take a big bite of danger and says, "Yes, let's do this."

Chapter 5

VIEW FROM THE BOTTOM - 2092

The classroom carries the musky smell of teenage boys who didn't shower after gym and teenage girls who just got their period. They've yet to figure out how to disguise their odors of burgeoning youth and hormones.

The desks are a utilitarian prefab mystery with uncomfortable plastic chairs and aluminum legs. School furniture hasn't changed a lot over the decades. The chairs screech on the tile floors, but you can safely rock back on them, as kids have done down through the ages. The screen up front has a series of equations written across it. Jacob lowers himself into his seat, aiming at invisibility. He's in the back left corner of the classroom, with easy access to the exit, when the bell rings. *Please don't call on me, please don't call on me*, he pleads in his head. It's not to be. His trig teacher calls him out, "Jacob, would you like to come up and add to this formula?" Half the class turns and looks at him. The other half know what to expect and don't even bother. He wants to die. It's not the first time that escape has enticed him with its piped snake dance. Jacob looks at his teacher with pleading eyes and shakes his head, no. His teacher gives him a long stare and moves on to another kid. Escaped for another day. Jacob's body relaxes.

He won a scholarship to this tech school through a simple lottery draw, and his mother has high hopes for him. He's never taken to math or science and the complexities of the technology world. It's like a maze in his mind, and when he tries to think it through, he gets stopped at the first choice of paths. He won't make it through his first year.

He's thirteen and hasn't hit puberty yet. He's still small and showing no signs of early manhood. He's only 5' 2" and 100 pounds. He still has the blonde baby hair he started out with, teddy bear's ears that sit out on the sides of his head, and a gap-toothed smile he doesn't let loose often. When he does, women fight off the urge to hug him. He looks so sweet. His voice hasn't changed yet, and he could still sing in the choir if such a thing existed. He does know all the lyrics to every popular song and hums them in his head. He's teetering on the edge of a little boy and a young man, still leaning toward the latter.

He likes the next class, particularly the teacher, Mr. Kracker. His first name is Bill, but he'll forever be Mr. Kracker to Jacob. Mr. Kracker is a short, rotund, balding redhead with a ready smile for every kid in his class. No one feels threatened here. They're studying the history of the global climate this year. All the lost coastal cities fascinate Jacob. They might as well be Atlantis to him. When his teacher talks about the meat eaters, he's appalled. They used to eat cows, pigs, sheep, deer, and sometimes, horses and dogs. He can't envision someone sitting down to eat a cow. He pictures blood dripping from their mouths. No one eats meat; that would be disgusting.

Bill Kracker and his wife Helen don't have kids, but the teenagers who cycle through Bill's classroom give them joy. He particularly likes little Jacob. He's small for his age and an easy target for the crueler kids that always exist. Jacob doesn't often get bullied, he's not worth their time, but it happens.

He isn't going to be a tech whiz, he's in the wrong school, but Mr. Kracker hopes to guide this sad little boy into a better future some other way. He knows he's captured his attention with his class lectures. Jacob's essays and homework are well-researched and show promise. Mr. Kracker needs to get him into an education stream more suited to his interests and aptitude. He hates these lotteries, setting too many kids up for failure and possibly losing them forever. They quit school, stay unemployed and desperate, and join the generations behind them of misery. He hasn't discussed this with Jacob's mother yet, and she may not understand. He wants to catch him before he falls.

Decades ago, governments around the world came to their senses about housing. Economically challenged people needed free or very cheap rental apartments, not more houses they could never afford. Small cities of high rises were built to fill this need. As ever, governments never seemed to set aside enough money for ongoing management and maintenance. Anyone can get an apartment, almost for free, and Jacob and his mom and dad moved in a year ago. Jacob's mom thought it would be better for Jacob to have hard walls around him as he entered high school. They were only allotted a one bedroom, and Jacob sleeps on the couch. There's no place to do homework but the kitchen counter. It doesn't matter, since he rarely does homework anyway. Everyone hates living there. Twenty stories of beige recycled bricks, housing those that have been disenfranchised from this new world. The halls are tiled and bricked, and the sounds and smells of life, anger, desperation, and madness boomerang through the building. No one cleans those tiles or the graffiti-covered walls. If you can't manage the stairs, you've got a long elevator wait, when it's working. Those who can't manage stairs depend on neighbors to bring them food and supplies. The apartments are filled with people with their own torment, sadness, and lifetimes of failure. There are no jobs for the unskilled. The world has moved on and left so many behind. There are better buildings downtown. They're considered the gold rental prize, and are much more civilized. They're of course almost impossible to get into, with ten-year occupancy waits. Still, Jacob's mom put their name in. They could still hope.

A man across the hall from them suffers from a hallucinatory mental disease. He often mistakes their door for his and bangs on it for hours, screaming. No one comes to help him or them. He's a big guy and can be physically aggressive when he's in a state. Jacob and his parents hunker down and pray for the shrieking to stop. There's housing for all, but it's not a refuge or ever quiet.

Jacob misses the Camps. Before the apartment building, they lived in a large green canvas tent for most of his living memory, with an assembly of other families like theirs living around them. Like everything else in the world, the tent was powered by solar, made of an insulated fabric, so there was no problem with heat and A/C. His dad had built a wooden platform, they weren't right on the ground. Jacob had a partition between his cot and the rest of the tent, so he and his parents had a bit of privacy. He remembers the musty smell of the canvas, particularly after a hard rain. Rain on the tent made him feel safe somehow. His dad dug trenches around the tent so the water could run off. After some of the more brutal blizzards, when they were stuck inside, the men dug out pathways to the latrines and the water pumps, laughing and calling out to each other while they shoveled. There was a camaraderie then. It could be muddy in the off seasons, but that was alright; it was just mud and wouldn't hurt you. They were deep in the forest in a valley, protected from the bigger windstorms.

Jacob and his friends spent a lot of time hiking in the woods, playing on the creek and along the lake bank. The boys would walk to the ice's edge in the winter when the lake froze out for a mile. They'd hunch their shoulders against the freezing wind, feeling its bite cut their cheeks. Lying on their bellies, they'd hang precariously over the edge, inhaling the danger and watching the cold grey waves roll into the ice tunnels underneath, with their hollow slap and spooky boom. When winter broke into spring, it would serve up that first lime-green day of new leaves and sun-speckled tree canopies, the forest dripping with green. Then, exotic dead things washed up on the beach; thick, long fat eels from the deeper parts of the lake and big unrecognizable fish with their glassy dead fish eyes, rotting stink, and circling flies. On the hottest days in the summer, you could cool your feet in the water while walking up the beach for miles until you came across a fallen tree obstructing your path. The decision then was whether you stripped down and get wet again, waving your trunks above your head, climb up the embankment, not always easy, or turn around. It was a boy's heaven. He and his friends were all the same, without judgment, competition, or pressure. He was a contented kid there.

Everybody had a solar bike, some more powerful than others. Small and light, they were very cheap. People needed transportation to get around the city when they didn't want to or couldn't afford to call up a service car, a floater. Jacob's mom had a hooded version and rode hers out to work year-round. She had to call in some very snowy days, but these bikes were pretty good on snow and ice. His dad would ride with her every morning to the main road to keep her safe and, at the end of the day, meet her again and escort her home. His mom had friends there that made her laugh, and his dad was much more content in his own domain, even if it was a tent. Even with their thermal heaters, it could be damned cold in the winter, but they dressed warm, and it was theirs. It was quiet. Those were happier times for them all.

Grade school was all online, and he did reasonably well. However, he was never interested in math or science, programming, coding, computer games, or anything technical. He hadn't found his talent yet. Winning that tech scholarship brought nothing but the feeling he was drowning and going to disappoint his mom. He wasn't keeping up. He doesn't even want to. Jacob wishes he could go back to last year in the Camps.

At least they always had food, even if it was the government's high-energy Nutri biscuits. They had different flavors, breaking up the monotony. These were invented decades ago to feed people during famines and emergencies. The rise of the world's oceans and resulting decimation of cities and some coastal countries triggered multimillions of homeless, hungry refugees, often in their own countries and certainly in North America. Governments and mostly private enterprise found the money to distribute the biscuits free worldwide, virtually ending hunger in one stroke. No more news broadcasts of starving children. Everybody had access to these free biscuits. They're a running joke with those who can afford other food, but no one starves to death anymore. Jacob's mother shops the discount food markets to supplement their diet, picking up 'beyond their best date' fruit and vegetables and, now and then, a treat.

Jacob's dad doesn't work, hasn't ever that Jacob remembers. He watches sports every waking hour, slouched on the couch, scratching his beard and balls. He lives in sweats and beat-off sneakers, no socks. Showering has become a rarer option. Jacob's parents don't do a lot of talking anymore. They seem to have come to a truce of silence. They've nothing to share, just a couple of hamsters turning the wheel. They were young not very long ago but living in this apartment building has drilled them down.

Viruses have surged through the decades, killing the usual suspects, the unvaccinated. Governments gave up on lockdowns and mask rules decades ago after the riots. Huge virus field hospitals were set up in most cities to deal with the deluge of sick and dying people. This kept these viruses out of the main hospitals. Each bed had its own isolation chamber, and specialized virus staff worked there. It's an entirely separate medical system.

His mother is a disinfectant worker at the big field hospital out in the east end. She wears a hazmat suit all day, rebreathing her own air inside masks and face screens. She comes home with a swollen pink face, her hair and underclothes soaking from the plastic. She lives in her hospital scrubs. She must have other clothes, but Jacob never sees her in them. She keeps her dark hair short and rarely wears makeup. She used to be pretty. Now she's too tired to care.

It exhausts and depresses her, but she's the only breadwinner in this family, and they have to pay a little rent here, plus service fees for their devices. She's seen so much death she's almost immune to it. She doesn't want to bring anything home to Jacob. She's no longer sure she cares about her husband and is too tired to examine that thought. Jacob lost all of his grandparents to viruses and constantly worries about his mother. When she's home, she sleeps. Her sleep is dreamless, but she can hide in the dark, and her bleak life goes away, for a while.

When Jacob was ten, he developed a cancerous lump on his neck. His mother thought she might lose him. She had never felt such dread. Because she's a healthcare worker, she could get him the new Libertas1 cancer vaccine. It was expensive but accessible to healthcare workers and their families if they needed it. It stopped his cancer cells from dividing and saved his life. There are too many times Jacob wishes otherwise.

Sometimes his dad disappears for days. He'll get a call, mumble something into his wrist SAT, and he's gone. He always comes back with food, booze, supplies, and treats they can't usually afford. Sometimes he comes home with an injury. One time he came home with a bullet wound in his shoulder. He goes armed, and he's made it clear to Jacob he's not to ask where these supplies come from. He brings things for Jacob's mother they would never get; wine and perfumed lotions, a warm sweater she'll never wear, and chocolate. He tries to make her smile when he can. He's rarely successful these days. She thinks, *if he gets killed or jailed or, worst case, comes home disabled, he's no use to her and Jacob. Not that he is now.*

Jacob knows exactly what his father's doing. He belongs to a gang of men who break into unprotected houses. He overhears his dad's murmured conversations with his buddies. They try to avoid violence, but residents fight back. Everybody's armed; not all neighborhoods have security guards, and only those that can afford them live in Smart Homes. Jacob knows his dad's cronies from the years at the Camps. They thought they were rebels when they were teenagers; now, they're just bored, out-of-shape middle-aged men looking for some action. His mother takes his 'gifts' from him and says nothing. Jacob wonders if someday his father just won't come back.

Chapter 6

THEN AND NOW

Jacob's teacher, Bill Kracker, and his wife, Helen, live in a secure zone in a Smart House and often invite the class over for movie nights. Not all the kids come. The techie kids only take his class because they have to. They're not interested in the past, only the future. They think the kids who go to Mr. Kracker's are out-of-touch geeks. Still, the invitation is open, so 10 or 12 teenagers regularly come. Mr. Kracker arranges a solar bus to transport them safely there and back home. Helen helps the kids make up pizzas, and they get to make their own desserts and have great fun creating new concoctions, most of which are edible. None of these kids ever cook, so this is like a science project with results they can eat.

Jacob loves these escapes into this alien world. He's fascinated with the neighborhood and the house and asks lots of questions. He stares at the armed neighborhood security guards, and they stare back at him. He hopes he doesn't look like his father. A few of the kids, not all, live in Smart Homes, so this isn't a big deal for them. The rest live in lesser variations, whatever their parents can afford. None of these kids are wealthy. Those kids go to different schools.

Mr. Kracker always does the evening in three parts, food, followed by a short video on some segment of the history of the last 70 years with a brief discussion after. Then they get the 'shoot-'em-up' or 'blow em up' movie they really want to see. Jacob prefers the first videos.

When talking about the past, Mr. Kracker says, "It's all about the water. With warming oceans and rising sea levels, many states and countries had too much, and many didn't have enough. There are still catastrophic floods and droughts, year after year. The destruction of the world's rain forests, and Amazon jungle was almost irreversible, although there's some regrowth. There's a bit of hope there. Thousands of miles of forest burned to the ground, rivers and lakes ran dry, and millions of homes and farms were lost along with many more millions of lives.

Many survivors became refugees in their own countries or had to move elsewhere. They weren't welcomed and often found themselves homeless and starving. Mr. Kracker says, "I know you all hate the government biscuits, but many people would have starved without them." He then talks about the ingenious woman who was vital in sourcing the funding to get the biscuits distributed throughout the world for free, ending world hunger within a year. It was an astounding achievement. It's not perfect now, but at least people have food, shelter, and medical care.

He reminds them how the miniaturization of solar panels and batteries changed the world. In warmer climates, roofs and multiple flat surfaces were repainted with white barium sulfate paint to reflect the sun and cool the earth. These technologies and treatments significantly slowed down global warming.

He talks about Smart Homes, telling them they were built to keep people protected from the bad storms and the constant break-ins. They're fortresses with their own microclimate, power, water, and sewage systems. They're bullet, fire, wind, and earthquake resistant. "Not that we have many earthquakes around here," he says. Jacob remembers his father coming home with a bullet wound after one of his forays into someone else's neighborhood. He wonders if he's ever tried to break in here.

Mr. Kracker continues. "You know those medichips you all have in your forearms?" The kids all look at their arms and nod. He says, "The house will do a read on those anytime of the day or night. If there's a problem, your medical team will be immediately notified and respond with advice or an ambulance, if you need it. These houses are lifesavers." The kids who don't live in Smart Homes think about this. More than half of them have to contact their medical teams first, then a chip scan is done. They must be more proactive about their health than the lucky Mr. Kracker and his wife.

He says, "Some of you live in Smart Homes, so you know the house can do many things with a voice command." One of the kids asks, "Can it cook?" Mr. Kracker laughs and says, "The house can make coffee and cold drinks and operate a full bar if you like to drink. It can get parts of dinner started, and it'll tell you when your fruit is ready to be tossed and stuff like that. It'll play music, find anything you want to watch, and screen out anything you don't want. I find that handy; I get tired of the bad news." Jacob's family rarely had fruit in the apartment and would probably eat it, even if it were beginning to rot.

Mr. Kracker says, "One of the things I like about these houses is for services you guys are way too young to worry about. They can provide live-at-home health care for seniors like your grandparents, find them friends to talk to on their screens, and follow their health. Living alone can be fine, but many seniors can be very lonely and need help. These houses can provide companionship and watchful healthcare."

Jacob says, "My grandma fell and broke her hip." Mr. Kracker says, "I'm sorry to hear that, Jacob; was she hospitalized?" Jacob says, "Yeah, but she got a virus and died fast." At least three other kids pipe up and say, "My grandma and grandpa died of a virus too." Mr. Kracker gives this input a moment of silence and then says, "We've all lost people we love; it's hard." He knows he can't fix 'broken.' The virus waves continue to kill too many people.

He answers Jacob, "The house would know your grandma had fallen, and it would call for help." Jacob thinks, *if someone fell in our building, they could die where they fell.* Many of the kids have private thoughts about what they don't have compared to Mr. Kracker and his wife.

The kids watch old videos of kids their age serving food in restaurants, people working factory lines, cab drivers, bus drivers, and people servicing people instead of bots. In their young heads, it looks like the dark ages, slave labor before robotics were introduced. Jacob begins to understand what happened to his dad and grandparents before him. There was nothing left for them to do anymore.

Traffic jams and car accidents are a thing of the past. With self-drive solar cars, 'floaters' as they're called, most of these kids' parents work at home or commute once or twice a week. These driverless vehicles join long convoys to their destinations or take them to the commuter trains. There are still driveable solar vehicles, primarily trucks and vans, but not many. They can't imagine people driving themselves to work every day and putting themselves at such risk.

These kids have never eaten meat or fish of any kind. Protein plant products and chemical reproductions replaced these long ago. They all think eating meat and fish would be gross. Mr. Kracker tells them how that all changed in a short time. He shows them pictures of cattle herds grazing, chickens crammed into warehouses, and fishing trawlers out in surging waves. He says, "This all became unsustainable mostly due to the wild storms, but feed became too expensive, drug additives were banned, fish stocks diminished to almost nothing, and people started to move away from eating meat and fish. It just wasn't cool anymore." One of the kids asks, "Did they really eat animals with eyes and faces?" Mr. Kracker laughs and says, "They usually weren't eating animal faces, but eating meat was normal then. I know it sounds horrible, but many things people used to do that seem awful now were just a way of life."

He shows them a quick video of electronic mesh farming. He says, "Thousands of acres are covered with a thin mesh that reads, feeds, and waters vegetables, grain, and bean crops and then it rolls up by acre for harvesting and planting. The mesh keeps crops in place in the storms and wind. It's a wonderful invention. The farmers manage a central database. It's like a big computer game, in a way." A couple of kids digest this and say, "I want to do that!" He says, "We'll do a field trip this year, and you can see how it works."

He says to the kids, "In the end, people like you reversed the planet's warming, fixed the hunger, housing, and healthcare problems, and came up with solutions that worked. Some of you will be the next inventors who'll make the world even better. Imagine that?" Jacob doesn't think he'll be one of those. Mr. Kracker says, "We've got six working mines on the moon now, unheard of fifty years ago. They were just beginning to explore it with rockets. The world will change fast; catch it while you can.

He says, "There are still so many great jobs to be had, and I'll give you an example. We have two friends next door, Alex and Sam. Sam helps people make money." The kids all think that's great but don't know what questions to ask. It might involve math, and they don't want to get into that. He goes on and says, "His wife Alex researches products for companies. For example, if a company makes tents, she finds every other company that makes tents and finds out what they're doing, better or worse. Then her client can improve their product." Jacob takes this in. *I could do that,* he thinks. *I wouldn't need to be able to do math or tech stuff to do that.*

Helen says quietly, "That's not all she does." Her husband winks at her and says, "Another time." They have a brief moment where she reminds him that Alex and Sam are coming over tomorrow night. He asks, "Are they bringing the dog?" The kids pick up on that. "A dog! They have a dog? What kind of dog? What's its name?" Hardly anybody has a dog anymore, so they might as well have a giraffe for the rarity to them. Mr. Kracker says, "She's a furry mutt of indeterminate breed, very old and very sweet, and her name is Princess." Several of them say, "Can we see her?" and he says, "Sorry guys, it's late; I wouldn't want to bother them tonight."

There's a resounding "aww" from the kids. He says, "Maybe the next time you're over, I'll borrow her for the evening." They all think that'd be great.

When it's time to take the kids home, Mr. Kracker rides with them on the Solarbus, seeing each to their doors. It's too dangerous to do otherwise. A few parents come out for a chat. They like this guy; he's good with their kids, and they learn so much. Mr. Kracker sits with Jacob on the bus and tells him he wants to talk to his mother about getting him tested and transferred. "Tested?" Jacob asks in a panic. Mr. Kracker says, "Yeah, there are hundreds of jobs you'd be good at, but we need to find out which ones you'd like the most so we can train you. It's kind of like a game." Jacob says, "I'm not good at games." Mr. Kracker says, "We're going to find a better education solution for you, kiddo, don't worry. You'll like it." As they pull up in front of Jacob's building, he can feel the other kids' eyes on his back, and once again, he wants to disappear. Mr. Kracker says, "Are the elevators working today?" Jason says, "Maybe; how did you know about that?" Mr. Kracker says, "I grew up in one of those buildings." Jacob looks at him in amazement, and Mr. Kracker pats him on the back. "Good questions tonight. Let's talk tomorrow."

Jacob's mind is buzzing, and he thinks, *a chance to get out of tech class and do something I like? That would be a real lottery win.* His world is opening, and he's happy for the first time in a long time. He heads into the building, and of course, the elevator isn't working. It doesn't matter. He flies up the stairs, skipping steps.

Helen hugs her husband when he returns and says, "You're such a good man." He says, "Thanks, honey. Most of them will be fine, but I worry about a few of them. Little Jacob, in particular. He's a bright little light." Helen says, "You can't save them all."

She says, "Don't forget, Alex and Sam are coming for dinner tomorrow night.

Chapter 7

TERROR AND GRIEF

Jacob wakes up to get ready for school. He finds it odd his parents are both still in bed. Typically, his mother would be up and gone by 7:00. He decides not to bother them, but by 8:00, he looks in on them. From the hallway, he sees the bedcovers are flat, and then thinks he was mistaken. They both must have left earlier, although he can't think where his dad would be off to so early. Jacob is looking forward to talking to Mr. Kracker about the tests they spoke of last night. He grabs a couple of biscuits, takes the stairs, and runs into no one. He only vaguely registers that this is strange.

On a few landings, there seem to be piles of clothes with a lot of sand around. He can't figure that out, but he's running late. He bikes to school. All's quiet in the parking lot; no service cars, solar buses, bikes, kids, teachers, nobody. He wonders if he somehow missed it was a holiday today. He doesn't think so. He enters the classroom where his first class is held. There again is a pile of clothes in front of the screen, with sand spread all around it. He walks up to the pile, and it still doesn't register. He goes down the hall to Mr. Kracker's classroom; he's always in early and should be able to tell him what's going on. His familiar green sweater, checkered shirt, brown pants, socks, and loafers are on the floor. Underneath it is a pile of sand. A nervous tick of dread begins to fill Jacob's body core. He calls his mother; she should be at work by now. She doesn't answer. Even though he knows Mr. Kracker is lying at his feet, he begs the universe and calls him on his wrist SAT. No response.

He rides back home. There's no one on the roads, and there's an eerie silence everywhere. The elevator is magically working again. He thinks the government just turns it off at a whim to save money or servicing costs or something. He rides it back up to his apartment. He turns on the screens and discovers he can't pull up any information. Something is very wrong.

He doesn't want to go into his parent's bedroom but does. He sees a sleeve of the sweatshirt his mother sleeps in lying over the covers. At the end of that sleeve, where her hand would be, is a small pile of sand. Same with his dad. He sleeps in a t-shirt and underwear. He pulls back the comforter and discovers their bodies are now sand inside their bedclothes. Jacob feels ill. The room spins, and he falls to the floor in a faint.

When he comes to, he checks again that what he saw was not a bad dream. There's no mistaking it; his parents are clearly piles of sand. They're dead. He moves to the living room and plops on the couch. His mouth hangs loosely open, his heart is beating fast, and his eyes are glassy with shock. His brain is churning over the morning and the situation. He doesn't recognize the adrenaline charging through his body; it's like a drug. The apartment is so silent. His parents have retreated through a hole that closed in behind them. Aside from the sand, the evidence of their life force is no longer in this space. They're gone. The world has slipped into a deafening hush. He's too numb to cry.

A busy road runs by their building, but no service cars or bikes are running down on the street. He tries the screens again, but they're still just white static. His wrist SAT still works, but when he calls someone, no one answers. He can't pull anything up on the Newnet. He checks his other apps, and the only thing that still works is the GPS. He calls 911 and gets an out-of-service message.

He rides out around the city to see if he can find someone to talk to. He takes his father's gun. Jacob has never held this gun in his hands before, let alone shot at anything. He's watched his dad clean it and load a cartridge of ammunition. Everybody had guns at the camp, and they always scared him. In their world, there was only one use for a gun; nobody was taking potshots at squirrels. Probably everybody had guns in their building. He hadn't ever really thought about that. The men were more obvious with them at the Camps. He's terrified now, scared enough to carry his father's gun.

Downtown, he finds three men standing at a corner and pulls up beside one of them. The man looks this small little biker up and down and decides he's safe. Jacob says to him, "What happened?" The man seems ancient to Jacob, but he's too young to assess age. The man is probably in his early 70s, with a full head of white hair but he's standing straight. They all look worried. The man looks down at him and says, "Well, little man, it looks like we have a disaster on our hands. Most people in town have turned into strange piles of sand, and the only survivors are those who had the cancer shot. I'm guessing you had it?" Jacob nods.

He doesn't even know how to frame the next question. Does he ask, "What can we do? What are we going to do? (He's not part of their group, so he's not part of their 'we'). Or does he ask, "What can I do? None of these questions seem right. The old guy asks him, "Where do you live? Jacob's sixth sense tells him not to share this information. He answers with a generality, "On the other side of town." The old guy asks him, "Do you have food? Are you safe there?" Again, Jacob's antenna rises. He realizes many people will be looking for food soon, and he's in danger. His survival instincts have clicked in. He decides not to trust anyone. The men turn their backs on him and continue talking. He's just a kid, not worth including in their life-and-death conversation, someone decides. Jacob jumps back on his bike and rides away without saying goodbye. These people can't help him. The older guy turns as he rides away and calls out, "Hey, what are you going to do?" Jacob doesn't answer and turns the corner. He wishes he knew.

He returns to the apartment and tries to gather his wits. He'll need food, which will quickly be gone from the stores and the government biscuit supply station if he doesn't move fast. He loads up with two large backpacks and rides to the supply station. He figures the grocery stores will be emptied before the supply station. A dozen people are there filling up wagons and bike storage and sacks. He digs in and does the same. These people are in a panic and have no problem pushing him aside. The mood is frantic, and tempers are short. He keeps his head down and still manages to fill up, returns home, and heads right back to get some more. He spends the next two days biking back and forth to the warehouse, while supplies last. When he rides in for the last time, the warehouse is empty. There are latecomers here now, crying. There's nothing left. He has about six months' supply of Nutri wafers, if he's careful. He's not a big eater, so he could maybe stretch it. After that, he doesn't know what he'll do. Starve to death, likely. But not today. He no longer wants to die.

He lies low for a couple of weeks, afraid to be seen in the building halls. He doesn't want anyone to know he's here, let alone has food. The apartment doors are not secure and could easily be broken down. He has to find somewhere else safer to live. He decides to take a chance and check out Mr. Kracker's house; maybe his wife had the vaccine and is still alive, and she could take him in. He waits until dark, closes his door quietly, and takes the stairs, always listening for footsteps and slamming doors.

It's a half-hour ride, and he takes a deep breath before ringing the doorbell. No response. He bangs on the door and calls out. No response. He's getting desperate. "I need help," he screams. This was his last hope, and terror's creeping into his young body. Mrs. Kracker, Helen, doesn't hear him. She lies in a pile at the foot of the kitchen table. Her tea has gone cold, just like her pile of sand. She was at least spared ever knowing about Bill's death, and he hers. He had kissed her goodbye this morning as he breezed out the door. "See you later, honey," he said. She smiled at him, squeezed his arm, and said, "Yep, love you."

Alex hears all this noise next door, but she can't see who's making it.

Jacob then thinks *I'll try the neighbor with the dog*, goes to Alex's house and does the same thing, ringing the doorbell, banging, and calling out. Alex doesn't answer. As soon as he appears, he's gone. All is silent again. Alex decides to stay inside.

Cora's been taking strong sleeping pills for days. She wakes up feeling foggy, forgetting briefly where she is and what's happened. She then sees the game box containing Fred and falls apart again. Alex is no longer answering her door, and Cora thinks, *she may be dead*. That means she might be, too, soon. It's too large an idea to grasp, and she doesn't want to try. She checks to ensure her 'kill pill' is in her bedside table drawer. Those pills come in a special little green box with the name of the drug imprinted on it. No marketing logos, no skull and crossbones images, no "Danger, this could be lethal" warning. There is no "could be." It will kill you. She remembers being amazed at how casually her doctor gave her the prescription. "Sure," he said. "Everybody should have a choice." She wasn't interested in his political views at the time, but she did want the choice if she ever needed it. That time may be soon, but not yet.

She hears Jacob yelling outside. She's anxious to talk to another human being and stumbles into the street to see what's going on, her judgment long gone. She sloppily leaves her front door ajar. Jacob sees her. She calls out to him, "What are you doing here?" "Looking for help," answers Jacob. They're both out in the middle of the street, moving toward each other. They do not see the biker rounding the corner and coming at them fast. The biker's arm is straight out with a gun. Jacob watches with horror as Cora drops to the road, a gunshot in her chest. Her mouth is spurting blood, and she's gurgling.

Jacob runs between the houses to Cora's backyard. The shooter rides back and screams at Cora, who's now lying still on the road. "I'm going to starve to death because of you bastards who live here in your high-security houses. My son and wife are dead because of you." Jacob deduces this guy mistakenly thinks people living here have been spared and have probably caused this. Once again, the 'have-nots' get screwed. In a rage, the shooter kicks Cora's body, and she flops over on her side, mouth open, eyes glassily staring ahead. Cora no longer cares. The biker lets out an anguished sob and starts looking around for Jacob. Jacob has found a small hiding spot behind some old siding leaning against a shed. He's in a crouch in there. The shooter looks around the houses but doesn't think anyone could be hiding there. Jacob stays as still as he can. He sees the shadow of the shooter's feet pass by, then stand in front of his hiding place for too long. Jacob holds his breath. All is silent. The feet move on. It's almost midnight before he dares to come out. He can barely move, having been in a crouch for hours. He stretches and gets some feeling back into his knees and back. He creeps out and peeks around the corner of the house. The shooter's gone. The woman's body is still lying in the middle of the street. She has a gunshot in her chest, and dried blood is stuck to her face. He walks over to her and knows she's dead. Her body is already changing but not turning into sand.

It occurs to Jacob he has a gun and could be accused of this. Who knows who was watching from a window? He notices Cora's door is slightly ajar. He doesn't think twice and slips in, closing the door securely behind him. He holds his back against the locked door, trying to control his breathing. He's safe here but quickly realizes he's also trapped without a door code to come and go. He checks the door panel log, but it doesn't reveal anything other than who has codes. He sees the neighbors Alex and Sam did, as did Bill Kracker and his wife. As far as he knows, they're all dead. A device sits on a desk, and he searches it to see if he can find the codes. After several tries using different guesses, a list pops up with numbers and figures. One has the initials BKC beside it. Another has the initials ASC. One simply says 'us'. These should be Bill Kracker's, Alex Smith's and Cora's codes. He tests the 'us' code. It works.. He's relieved her filing system was so simple. He guesses she never thought anybody would be looking. Now he can come and go.

He spends the next few nights riding back to the apartment to bring over the biscuits he took from the warehouse. He keeps his bike lights off and goes carefully, stopping when he sees any movement on the roads and pulling off, out of sight. The apartment building terrifies him now, and he doesn't want to run into anyone. There must be someone alive in there. He takes the stairs and listens for doors opening and footsteps. He has slipped back inside off the staircase more than once while someone goes by on the stairs. His heart goes crazy.

He discovers quite a lot of food in Cora's cooler and the freezer. These two were big eaters. He should be good for almost a year. He's safe in his very own Smart Home. What a price to pay for security.

A few days later, the entry alarm light flashes and Jacob quickly moves to the rear bedroom and the master closet. There's someone in the house. The people who lived here seemed to have kept every piece of clothing and footwear they had ever owned, and it's all stuffed into this closet. The space spells musty, with the overbearing stink of old shoes put away wet years ago, stale perfume, and dried body odor. He moves an overstuffed laundry hamper aside and crouches behind it in the dark. Someone opens the closet door, and the light automatically comes on. Jacob hears a woman say, "Gawd, they were slobs." She closes the closet door.

Jacob hears this and smiles to himself. *Try being the one hiding in this stinky place.* He doesn't know who's in the house, but he deduces it's either Mrs. Kracker or their neighbor Alex. He'll check the entry codes after she leaves.

Chapter 8

THE CAMPS

Jacob hears no further movement in the house, risks it, and emerges from the closet. Breathing fresh air again is a relief. He checks the entry panel record and confirms it was Alex, the Kracker's neighbor with the dog. The dead dog now. He thinks, *at least Alex is alive, and maybe I can talk to her.* He remembers the Krackers mentioning Alex and Sam. They were supposed to come to their house the night of the disaster. Alex was the researcher with the cool job, and Sam helped people make money. Jacob idly wonders now how he did that. Money was always a mystery to him, other than his family never seemed to have any.

He's horrified to discover Cora's body is now on the living room couch. She resembles pictures of mummies he's seen. Barely a skeleton, but still dressed. On a table beside her is a game box. He lifts the lid and finds a plastic bag filled with sand inside. It must be her husband. He knows he can't sleep here tonight. Way too creepy. He waits until dark, crosses the street to the Kracker's house, and codes himself in. In the kitchen, he finds Mrs. Kracker's pile on the floor. He finds a small broom under the sink and a garbage bag and sweeps her up. He puts her in the bed in the master bedroom and wishes he had Mr. Kracker's sand to lay beside her. However, that's on the other side of town, and Jacob doesn't want to be seen on the road. In the next couple of hours, he moves his biscuits over to the Kracker's from Cora's house. He's always loved the Kracker's house. He feels safer here.

He checks out what would have been a guest bedroom. He's so tired, and a bed with a thick duvet calls to him. He crawls in and sleeps immediately. He dreams of his mother laughing at something. She reaches out to him, and he remembers her smell and how tight she used to hug him. It's a good dream for a lost, scared little boy.

Jacob putters around the Kracker's house for weeks, afraid to go out. There's lots of food in the cooler and the freezer, so he doesn't have to touch the biscuits just yet. He hears people outside on the streets, and the external trespasser lights flash on from time to time. He assumes they've come here to break into houses and find food. Several houses here aren't entirely protected, and the sound of glass shattering and doors being battered down echoes back through his house's exterior speakers. Mr. Kracker had said that this house was a fortress, and it proves to be, as various survivors try to break in, unsuccessfully. Still, each onslaught scares the hell out of him. He hopes the neighbor he now knows as Alex is safe. He finally pulls his courage together and goes over there one night, using the code he found, only to discover she's no longer there. This is a kick in the gut; he'd been counting on finding a comrade-in-arms. He wonders where she would have gone.

He's been thinking about the Camps and if anyone would still be there. He can't remember knowing anyone with cancer there, not that it mattered; no one had the money for the vaccine. There was always the vaccine lottery, but he thought that would have been well-telegraphed news if someone there won that. He has a longing to go there anyway. It was his happy place. He never rides out during the day and waits for the sun to go down before heading off. He always turns his bike lights off, gets off the road, and lays down with his bike if he sees someone coming. He's filled with unease when he turns off the main road to the old dirt road. Will he find a bunch of tents filled with sand and clothes?

He finds his family's old tent abandoned, with no piles of sand in there. The family that took it over must have moved on before the disaster. He walks around inside. It now seems so raw and rudimentary compared to the Kracker's house. He wonders how he could have ever felt safe there. But that was a different time.

Foot and bike traffic running between the tents in the encampment carved out a rough bunch of paths. The tents still stand, all empty but for the sand piles. He wanders through these and comes across the best surprise. Old Junie Compton sits just outside her tent, cooking up some food in a skillet. He doesn't know how old she is. Everybody just called her Old Junie. Junie is wearing a large turquoise cotton man's shirt over a pair of loose black pants. Her sleeves are rolled up. Her black hair, always a bit wild, is braided tight and tied back with a red scarf. She's only 56, not old at all, and has one of those ageless faces, with eyes slightly yellowed where the whites should be. These are eyes that read and judge people in a second. You can't get away with anything with Junie. She has a brilliant wide smile when she likes and trusts you, but that mouth goes firm and hard when she doesn't. Her smooth dark skin remains unlined. She's strong with farmer's hands and arms. She could hold her own in a physical fight if it ever came to that. Before he and his parents left for the apartment, Jacob had overheard his mother and her friends gossiping that Junie had breast cancer. She didn't get sick, and they thought no more about it. They would never know that Junie had won a vaccine lottery and was cured. Junie didn't feel it necessary to share her good fortune with many who had none.

She looks up and spots Jacob, and a wide grin spreads across her dark face. She says, "Well, aren't you a welcome sight, young Jacob? Come here, come here." He had always liked her. She and his dad had a great friendship, always teasing each other. Ever since he was a little guy, she had always welcomed him to her fire and found something sweet for him to eat or drink. She would tell him stories of farming tobacco in Jamaica before she came up to Niagara to work in the vineyards and orchards. The picture she painted of Jamaica was mystical to Jacob. Summer all year round and turquoise water and white sand. She was like a grandmother to everyone. She kept a small farm in a clearing at the back of the campsite and grew every vegetable imaginable. These she shared with everyone. She was also a bit of a medicine woman. She had herbs and potions for everything. As Jacob drew nearer, she said, "You're too skinny, honey. Come and share some supper with me." Jacob pulled up a lawn chair, and she served him a heaping spicy stir-fry. He barely remembers his manners and mumbles, "Thanks," while he wolfs down the food like a starving dog. He'd forgotten what a wonderful cook she is.

She sees a terrified young teenager trying to be brave and keep it together. He sees a safe harbor. She says, "Tell me everything, honey, start from the day you left. I was so sad to see you go, and it's been so long." Jacob looks at her, his body finally relaxing enough to bring tears to his eyes. Having someone he knows and feels safe with offer him some kindness and human contact breaks his stoicism. He falls apart and can't stop crying. She moves over beside him, puts her arm around him, and holds him until he quiets. They spend the night in front of the fire, and he spills his life to her. It feels cleansing to tell someone.

He described the horrible apartment, the classes he hated, his unhappy parents, Mr. Kracker's classes and kindness, and finally, the ray of hope before the disaster. He told her about finding his parents and Mr. Kracker's pile of sand and where he was living now. It was almost midnight when he finished talking. She just sat and listened, exclaiming softly but mostly listening. He finished with, "Now I don't know what to do next. I'm so scared, Junie." She looks at him and says, "Me too, honey, but we'll get through this. We'll figure something out, don't you worry." She smiles at him and says, "I'm so glad you made your way back here." He said, "Me too." She said, "Why don't you stay the night? It's fairly safe here, and I have a gun. Nobody thinks any of us in the Camps would have any food, and if they saw my vegetables, they wouldn't know what to do with them." They'll want to grab and run, not soak beans for a day. She says, "You keep your biscuits under lock and key for now; you might need them. As long as I can grow and cook, we should be okay. Mind you, I won't be making any casseroles ahead of time. No sir, one day at a time." She says, "I've only got one bed, but you're welcome to share it with me. I won't bite." She sees how tired he is. She says, "Why don't you go on in and get under the covers? I'll tidy up out here." By the time she climbs into her side of the bed, he's deeply asleep, and when she wakes up in the night, he's cocooned with his back against her belly.

Chapter 9

DEAD MOUSE IN THE HOUSE

Alex stands at the armored door at the bottom of the tunnel, wondering what awaits her on the other side. The woman's voice with the island accent says, "There's a small ante-chamber beyond this door. You'll find a hazmat suit there. Please strip and put it on and put all your clothes in the bin. Just lean your bike against the wall. We'll take care of it and your gear. The hazmat suit will protect us from you in your transfer from the outside to the decontamination space. You can move into the decontamination room after that." The door slides open into the wall. As advertised, Alex finds herself in a small space with doors on both sides. She enters and takes off her clothes, but not her underwear. The voice says, "Sorry, everything off." Alex thinks, *okay, it's been 15 minutes since I left the gate. I'm now standing in a small room, stark naked, talking to a disembodied voice, and I'm about to be entombed for an indeterminate time. I must be out of my mind.* She wonders how many people are looking at her and does not wonder if they find her nakedness sexually attractive. She is rock-solid scared." Alex puts on the hazmat suit. The voice says, "Thank you." Alex thinks, *she's at least a polite alien with a rich, pleasant, calming voice.*

The inner chamber door opens to a long hallway with a door just to the right and several other identical doors down the hall. *How many people do they have down here*? She wonders. *Is this some big human experiment? If there are others, how did they get in here? They can't have all breached the fence like she did and talked to the silent gate (and the golf cart, for that matter).* So many questions. The voice says, "Place your wrist chip against the panel beside the door and put your finger in the slot for a blood test. We need a medical read." Alex does this. The voice says, "Thank you. You'll be asked to do this twice daily while you're here. There is another panel and blood test slot in your room." The door slides open. "This is where you'll stay for the next few days," she says. Alex enters, and the door slides closed behind her. There's no handle. She won't be getting out of here without assistance. She's in a full claustrophobic panic now. Hot, sweaty, heart racing, mind going crazy. She thinks, *I've got to get out of here*. She tries deep breathing to calm herself.

The room is uninteresting. It has no soft surfaces, ice white with a relentless white overhead light, but the space isn't cold, and the floor tiles are heated. There's a single bed with tight white bedding, two pillows with no pillowcases, and a thin thermal blanket rolled up at the bottom. Alex thinks, *at least I'll have heat. I'm always cold*. There's a desk and a chair, but no keyboard and no one to write to. The bathroom is also decorated in early sterile white. The space is windowless of course. She's a mile underground. Still, a large window facsimile shows what appears to be a live shot of a lush garden outside, with sunshine, birds, and insects buzzing about, a running creek, and sounds of a forest glen. She wonders if the sun goes down in this fake window. It's fine quarters for a monk, student, or a prisoner. Alex thinks, *a place for contemplation, as in, what the hell am I doing here?*

She asks the voice, "What am I supposed to do while I'm here besides scrub down and watch mice die?" The voice says, "There's a remote in the desk drawer. The wall across from the bed is your screen. You can view anything from our library of films, TV shows, documentaries, music, theatre, and books. It's all there." Alex thinks, *great, binge-watching. Hope the room service is good*.

The soap and shampoo provided smell antiseptic and feel like they suck every drop of moisture out of her skin. Still, she scrubs down and wraps a towel around her wet body. Her hair is longish, straight, and she was going to cut it anyway for the trip, easier to manage. *Here we go*. She thinks. She takes the shears and snips her hair back very short. She stands in front of the mirror and thinks, *no makeup, pale as a ghost, no hair, and very thin. The bare me. No one to impress. Except for whoever is behind the voice and the camera. Whoever or whatever she is*. Knowing someone is watching her all the time makes her want to look over her shoulder. She can't detect where the cameras might be. The bathroom seems to breathe and inhale every molecule out of her. It's a strange sensation. This happens following every shower. She puts on the loose pajamas and pull-on socks provided. The pajamas are silky and warm and pale pink. She wonders if the male prisoners get blue pajamas. She's going crazy, feeling like she's in a petri dish. She's still frightened enough to be trembling. In her mind, she says, *Sam, what have I done here?* He never answers.

The voice says, "We're going to do a baseline test, and we're sending in a mouse. Don't be alarmed if it dies. It probably will. It's early." A slot opens in the wall near the door, and a small cage comes in on a tray. The little white mouse is over and down before the cage is even halfway in. Its body disintegrates into mouse sand almost immediately. Not good news so far. *Poor wee thing,* she thinks.. The cage is removed. "Well, that went well," Alex comments. The voice says, "You've only been here an hour. Why don't you relax and see if you can find something to watch or listen to?" There's a clock imprinted on the wall. It's Tuesday, 11:47 AM, June.

Alex checks out the entertainment library. She wasn't much of a movie watcher, but they have everything ever filmed since movies began, up to the last awards shows. The documentaries are heavier than she wants to get into, in this place. Reality is now, an obvious statement, but what she's living is stranger and more interesting than anything that could be filmed. Alex thinks, *I could write a hell of a documentary about this experience.* She says to herself, *I'll start it while I'm on the road, if I ever get out of here. It might keep me sane.* She has no idea who might be left to watch this documentary.

She reviews the movie selection. How about the ancient classics? She's read about some of these, but they are from so many decades ago. Alex wonders what the filming could have been like. She's accustomed to immersive watching now, giving one the feeling you're in the film, not just watching it. This will be a new experience. She opts for "Casablanca." A familiar title but one she's never seen. The screen pops into a full screen the size of the wall. Bogie comes into the bar. She needs popcorn.

Lunch comes in a tray through the slot at noon. It's better than anything she's eaten in the last month. A light garlic pasta, caesar salad, a fresh warm roll with some butter-like substance, a fruit bowl, and an urn of coffee. Not bad. She eats, settles in on the bed, turns on the thermal blanket, and watches the movie. She calms down. In fact, she's feeling almost too relaxed. It strikes her they've spiked her food with something to settle her nerves. It seems to be some kind of anti-anxiety drug. She feels like she's in a warm cocoon, and the world looks rosy.

The movie is sad but somehow comforting. The woman's voice checks in now and then. "How're you doing?" Alex answers, "Fine. Did you drug my food?" The voice says, "Your blood pressure and heart rate were too high. We needed to bring that down, that's all. Are you feeling less nervous?" Alex says, "Actually, I'm a bit stoned," The voice doesn't respond. Alex asks, "What's your name?" Silence. Then, "Francis." Alex says, "Nice to meet you, Francis. I feel like you're my space mother." Francis says, "Space mother?" Alex says, "Yeah, you might be an alien for all I know, or just an electronic bot. You're checking in on me, feeding, clothing, and apparently drugging me, so you're my space mother." Silence again. Francis says, "I'm a real person." Emphasis on the 'real.' Oddly, this gives Alex some comfort and an unearned feeling of safety. Francis never stays long or says much. Hours go by before she checks in again. Out of the blue, her voice asks, "Are you comfortable?" Alex responds, "As much as I can be, under the circumstances. I'm fed, I'm warm, I'm sheltered, I'm entertained, I'm drugged. I'm just not free." Francis says, "That will come." Alex spools through the movie selections and chooses Citizen Kane next. That's meaty. Good old Orson Welles.

At three o'clock, Francis asks, "Ready to do another mouse test?" "As I'll ever be," Alex responds. In comes the mouse. She doesn't even see it scuttle around. It's dead before the cage is in. Again. She thinks, *hope tomorrow is a better day for the lab mice...and me.*

At six, supper arrives, another tasty offering. There must be a great kitchen nearby. Alex starts watching "On the Waterfront." Marlon Brando when he was built. Then she watches a few television episodes of mysteries. She and Sam loved mysteries, an escape from reality. She thinks, *I'm living a bloody mystery.*

At nine, another mouse is introduced. It twitches, just for a second, but it twitched. It didn't die immediately. Things are looking up. Maybe not for the mice.

Alex has her movie selections lined up for the next day. Having absolutely nothing to do is getting old fast. She's always been a workaholic. She's now forced into a new activity mode she's uncomfortable with. At least in the past weeks, her days and nights were filled with planning her trip across the country and stocking her travel kit. She could concentrate on something other than dead Sam and missing her mother. She does some pushups and jogs around the room to get some exercise. In her semi-drugged state, she does it in slo-mo. Alex no longer cares she's on camera. She has nothing to hide. She gets under the covers, says goodnight to Sam, and immediately falls asleep.

On day two, she's awake at five, her eyes slam open, and her head is straight again. Facing another day of watching movies doesn't appeal, but she doesn't have many choices. There's no point in getting into a book because she hopes to be out of here tomorrow, if the damn mice stop keeling over. She circuits the room in a jog again, then does more pushups. She wants to keep her arms strong. She might have to lift something heavy on this journey. You never know.

She longs for the news. She was a news junkie, reading five or six news threads daily. There are always lots of little factos you can pick up on as a researcher and tuck away. She's not weaned yet and hungers for news of all of this. What's happening? Is there even anyone out there reporting? Interesting that all politicians, lawyers, thieves, liars, rapists, and murderers have been silenced.

Breakfast arrives, and Francis' voice greets her. "How did you sleep?" Alex says, "Fine, quite well, all things considered." She asks Francis, "And how did you sleep?" No answer. Alex thinks, *can't get personal with this chick, apparently*. She's surprised Francis even gave her name, if that is her real name. Francis says, "Please shower, and then we're going to do another mouse test." Alex complies, and the bathroom sucks her dry again in a whoosh. She puts on fresh pajamas and socks and watches the slot. In comes the mouse. She thinks, *come on, Mickey, live, live*. There's some movement as the cage slides in, but then, over he goes. Another pile of mouse sand.

Alex says, "Well, he lasted 20 seconds." Francis says, "Yes, that's progress." We'll do another test at noon. Enjoy your morning." Alex works her way through "The Grapes of Wrath," "The Treasure of the Sierra Madre," and "Metropolis" (which she particularly enjoys being a 1927 futuristic movie, a long time ago).

Lunch comes sharply at noon. Alex knows this may be the last time she'll enjoy real food. She'll be eating flavored wafers after this. Francis' voice asks, "Everything okay?" Alex says, "If I said I'm going out of my mind and have to get out of here now, or I'll explode, would you release me?" Francis answers calmly and quietly, "Of course. You're free to go anytime you request it. Do you want to leave?" Alex says, "No, just feeling out how trapped I am in here." Francis says, "However it may feel, you're not trapped. Now, let's do another mouse test." In comes the cage. Alex sees the little white mouse scuttling about. It's going to make it this time. She roots for him, "C'mon, c'mon." Then…it trips….and falls….and dies. She is sad about this little guy. She's killing rodents, everybody's dream, not hers. She asks, "How long did he live?" Francis says, "80 seconds". Must have a mouse death stopwatch somewhere. But…it lived… 80 seconds. Alex is slightly less lethal than she was yesterday.

Francis says, "We'll do two more tests today, one at six and the other at nine."

Alex spends the afternoon watching "Lolita," sexy for its time. She skips "It's a Wonderful Life," never a Jimmy Stewart fan. She jogs between movies and does pushups. Supper comes at six.

A fresh voice, not Francis, speaks. Alex wonders where the speakers are; she can't see any. This is a male with a slight Spanish accent. She thinks, *quite the international staff, if there are more than these two.* The male voice asks, "Ready to do another mouse test?" Alex says, "Let's do it." In comes the cage. She holds her breath. This little mouse is gray and is checking out all the edges of his cage for escape. She doesn't blame him. He's a Christian mouse before the lions. She's the lion. He survives.

Spanish accent guy says, "We're getting there. This is new to us as well." Alex thinks, *so, the guy wants to talk*, and asks, "What's your name?" He says, "Miguel." She says, "Nice to meet you, Miguel. Do you know what happened?" He says, "We'll share what we know if you pass quarantine." Alex thinks, *good, they know something*. This is more than she's been able to get out of Francis. She asks him if this is, in fact, a camouflage manufacturing plant. No answer. These two aren't giving out any information. Presumably, they want to keep their secrets, whatever they are, if she fails the decontamination test. Miguel says, "We'll leave the mouse with you for the evening and see how he does. The mouse scuttles about the cage. At nine, Francis speaks. "You made some headway with the mouse today, I see. We'll replace him with another mouse for the night and check him out to see if he's healthy." In comes another mouse, white this time.

The mouse lives on. Alex checks him throughout the night and is comforted by his cage scrambling. He comes over to her fingers and smells them but then moves away, probably too antiseptic. She's named him Captain Marvel. She's ready to do mouth-to-mouse resuscitation if she has to.

On day three, she wakes at five and checks her mouse. Still alive. Could this be the day? There are clean pajamas, socks, and bed linens on the tray. That doesn't bode well. Seems like she might be staying longer. Maybe yesterday's mouse wasn't as fit as he looked. Breakfast arrives at eight. She doesn't want to stay here another day or kill someone just because they're in her presence. At nine, Francis speaks, "Yesterday's mouse is well and healthy, and it looks like last night's mouse is doing well. We'll check him over, and if he's okay, I'll meet with you later today, and we can talk." Alex thinks, *hallelujah! Freedom and information.* The mouse cage is retrieved. Alex says to the mouse, "Hang in there, little mousy; please be healthy." Francis says, "Some clothes will be provided later this morning."

Chapter 10

THE GRAND TOUR

Lunch comes, and Alex thinks it's maybe her last decent meal. It's a spinach quiche with a salad on the side and a lemon tart for dessert. She's unsure how they make fake eggs and dairy these days. She doesn't want to look at it too closely. All the chemicals are yummy, though.

Francis says, "The last mouse is healthy and was completely unaffected by you. Congratulations. We're going to bring you in. Here are your new clothes." The wall slot opens, and in comes a small stack of clothes. The fabric is light as air, all black. Tights with built-in feet for socks, a hooded long-sleeved top that fits tightly and holds her breasts up and close. No bra required. She likes that. A tiny pair of underwear, barely bikinis, but not a thong. They're simply crotch covers. *Thank you, Francis.* Alex thinks. The shoes are also weightless. They look like a pair of beach shoes she had at home, sleek and pull-on. She's dressed and amazed at how thin she is now in the mirror.

The wall screen flashes on. Alex is looking at an office of sorts, desks, chairs, cabinets, bookcases, multiple screens, keyboards, paperwork, files, a fern, and tropical beach pictures. A real workspace. The Francis voice says, "Watch." Alex sees a caramel chin appear and, just as quickly, a face and then an entire head. It's a woman's head. This woman is stunning. She has high cheekbones and full lips. Her nose is prominent, with a bit of a roman rise at the bridge, but in a strong and handsome way. Her skin is flawless. She has loose dark curly hair cropped short to her head. She looks like Michelangelo's David. She's probably early 40s. As Alex stares at this bodyless apparition, she thinks it must be a special effect or a hologram. It's hard to absorb because she feels she could reach out and touch her face. Francis laughs at her and says, "I know. It's a bit strange to take in. I'm wearing one of our invisi-suits. I'm all here. You just can't see the rest of me." Alex's mind is going crazy. They did it! They created the fabric. This is the place and the reason for all the secrecy. She's beside herself with excitement. The risk was worth it. She's found gold at the end of the rainbow.

Francis says, "Two live mice are a good sign but not a guarantee of our safety, so I'll need you to wear a hazmat suit while you're with us. You'll have your own air supply, which is recirculated and cleaned within the suit. I'll explain later, but we don't want to alarm our people with someone walking through in a hazmat suit, so this one is made from our invisi-fabric. They won't be able to see you."

"Our people? They?" Alex can't wait to hear who "they" are. The slot opens that brought the mice, food, and clothes but Alex sees nothing but a pair of pink rimmed glasses. Francis says, "Put the glasses on so you can see the suit. The suit has built-in glasses, so you won't need them when it's on. Alex does this and looks back at Francis on the screen. She now sees Francis' full body in a faint pink outline under her head. She's sitting down, so Alex can't get a read on her physically. She thinks, *okay, I'm getting this now.* She puts on the hazmat suit, seals herself in, and looks in the bathroom mirror and sees nothing. She's disappeared. Unnerving.

Francis says, "When your door opens, turn right and go to the end of the hall and wait." Alex does this, looking over her shoulder and saying goodbye to her antiseptic cell. That was an experience. The door at the end of the hall slides open into another antechamber. She enters, the door closes behind her, and she feels the room inhale. That's the best way she can describe it. Every fiber of her body is pulled away from her body. Francis says, "It's an extractor. It removes any remaining harmful cells on the suit. Please come in." The opposite door slides open silently.

Coming from a sterile white room, Alex is blown away. In front of her is a jungle of lush greenery, ferns, tropical plants, flowers of all kinds, and live birds flying around. Although she has her own air supply, she imagines the air to be fresh, warm, moist, and almost humid. The fake sun seems to leave spots of gold everywhere. This massive park does not seem to have borders, and it's impossible to judge its size. Several people walk and run the trails, sit on benches, and lie on the lawn. She sees the edge of a tennis court through the greenery. Two gardeners work the beds. Francis says, "You like?" Alex says, "You've created Eden in your basement. Wow."

Francis is tall, maybe 5'11". She moves easily and confidently, like someone who feels good in her body. She has a lovely, deep chuckle. People walk and jog by but obviously don't see them. She and Francis keep out of their way. Alex finds it a bizarre sensation. She follows Francis through the park to a vine-covered stone wall. Of course, what would a stone wall be without vines? They have thought of everything in this park design. There's no obvious door, but one slides open. They enter the office she saw on the screen.

Francis flips back her hood, and she's a floating head again. She says, "We designed and built that park years ago to give our staff a more natural experience, even though they live underground. It's very well used. The sun even goes down around nine PM, and a few stars can be seen. We have low lamps along the paths and in the gardens at night. It's made a big difference to morale."

She says, "I know you have a million questions, but let me tell you about what we do here and a little about myself first. Save your questions, I may answer them. I'm the general manager here, and I report, well, reported, to a president. He was located in Germany, where we have another manufacturing cell. He was off site when this all happened. Therefore, didn't survive. I manage this site with Miguel. We're responsible for 118 people living down here, not including ourselves."

Francis continues, "None of the people here are local; they're all internationals. We have medical staff and all the equipment needed for most tests, scans, and surgeries. The contractors are exceptionally well paid, with excellent benefits. They sign a confidentiality agreement tied to a very sizable bonus, even if they're let go. They're advised that should we discover they've broken this agreement; we can garnishee their future wages anywhere they work. We've never had to do this, a testament to our screening. A small percentage do less than two years and want out. It's working underground that gets to them more than anything. They work for six months, then are off for three. We fly them in and out. Well, we did before all this happened. It allowed for a personal life, although it was a struggle for some, primarily due to families. As I said, we screen people thoroughly before hiring and try to screen out those with heavy personal obligations. They all pass high-security clearance. Only a select few with the highest security clearance know about and work in the invisi-fabric department. We keep it segregated. Bots do most of the labor, of course.

Alex says, "I understand that working underground, even with this fabulous park, would get to you. Don't think I could do it." Francis says, "We screen people psychologically before we bring them down here." She says, "Compare these people to miners in the old days; they have a much better gig." Alex says, "Yes, but at least the miners got to go home at the end of the day." Francis says, "I think the mining camps on the moon would be the worst, and I understand they were having lots of problems, fights, breakdowns, and suicides. They get rotated back home every six months, but the thought you could get stuck up there forever would always sit with you. Now they are. Who knows what's going on up there now? No contact with earth. No supply rockets. They must be desperate. There are over 1,000 miners up there. Our people are stuck here underground right now, and they might as well be on the moon, except we have a lifetime of supplies. They're still stuck. I want to find them a way out before they start to break down."

She continues, "Only a very few in the upper echelons of defense in Canada and the U.S. are aware this operation exists. Our sister site in Germany is located under an old, decommissioned U.S. military base and is also kept completely covert. However, with so many people involved, information does get out. Human nature is what it is. People talk. We worked hard at dispelling any releases. There have been some, but not many. The article you read a few years ago about our fabric hiding an apple was one. As your research revealed, we managed to quiet that down quickly. There aren't many secrets in the world, and we're always trying to keep a lid on ours." We've had a few internal breaches, one of which has become problematic. I'll tell you about that later.

Alex says, "I knew there was more to that hidden apple story. I'm so glad I chased you down." Francis laughs at her. "Yes, watching you in action outside the fence was hilarious. We were so impressed."

She says, "When staff returned from leave, they were quarantined, as you were. We couldn't take any chances on anyone bringing disease down here." Alex says, "Aaah, that explains what was behind all those other doors in my corridor."

Francis continues, "Although the invisible fabric was a valuable part of our business and top secret, it was a tiny part of our business. There's no advantage in having all armed forces invisible. We were extremely selective with our clients. Lots of people want to disappear. We didn't sell to most of them. It was also very expensive. We have invisi-paints and various items that supplemented that business as well. We can now make many things disappear. The Israelis came up with a kind of sheet many decades ago that essentially made their soldiers look like rocks in the desert. The Chinese have been trying to get at our technology for a long time. Probably have it in some lab somewhere, but it hadn't surfaced in product availability. If they had it, they weren't putting it out to market. Same with the East Indians."

She gets up and stretches and bends down and touches her toes. She grins at Alex and says, "Gotta stay loose." She goes on, "The greater part of our business was the design and manufacture of very high-end technologically superior uniforms and camouflage and technical gear for organizations worldwide. Not all military. We also sold food and all the paraphernalia you researched a while back; plus, many things you don't even know exist. You bought your survival food from us. Alex says incredulously, "You're Livlong Inc.?" Francis grins and says, "Among other brand names." We have a record of everyone in North America who bought survival food through our supply and government channels. It's unlikely many survivors will match up to those with the food. Most of those with food will now be dead.

Alex can't wait any longer and asks the burning question, "Do you know what happened?" Francis says, "Our satellite cameras reflected a worldwide rolling collapse of everything with a heartbeat, other than those few who had the Libertas1 vaccine and us of course. Our German cell reported the same thing. We have extensive labs in both cells, but our techs have not yet nailed down what killed everyone. It's not a substance we were aware of or familiar with. Most of the earth seemed to be hit by a satellite bomb. We don't know who it was or why it was up there. The protective factor in your vaccine needs to be identified. We hope to duplicate it and inoculate our cell and our sister cell in Europe. We know it's not supposed to have any impact on healthy people and only goes right to any cancer cells. Still, it's a stab at protection if we can isolate the secret ingredient that protected you and the other survivors from this gas, virus, or whatever hit the world. None of us have had the vaccine. We screen out potential medical problems before bringing anybody down here."

Francis takes a deep breath and continues. "As you probably read in the news, the manufacturer of Libertas1 supposedly ran out a few months back, so we can't even find a sample. I think they were planning to hold the world governments to ransom to pay for it. Maybe one thing had something to do with the other? I've been in this business too long and see a conspiracy around every corner."

Francis puts her hand on Alex's arm. "You're probably wondering why we allowed you in. As charming and beautiful as you are, we needed your blood for our labs. We hope to isolate the vaccine's protective factor in your blood genome and DNA and copy it. I know, unsettling, but we haven't had many vaccinated survivors come knocking at our door. We couldn't believe our good fortune when you showed up." Alex says, " I almost electrocuted myself." Francis laughs and says, "We wouldn't have allowed that. You would have been tased before your cutters hit the fence." Alex says, "How could you be so sure I wouldn't just ride away?" Francis says, "I've seen your work. You're like a dog after a bone. I knew your curiosity would overcome your common sense. I knew you'd want to get to the bottom of our mystery site. We had an invisible drone follow you back to your camp the first night. We knew where you were. If you decided to leave, we would have tased you and brought you in. We couldn't risk letting you go. We needed your blood samples. They could be essential to our survival. I did try to reassure you of your safety; however doubtful that might have sounded to you at the time. Besides which, you had the wire clippers poised to snip. You were coming in, invited or not." Alex says, "Well, I'm glad now it rolled out the way it did. If I had woken up in a locked sterile underground decontamination cell, I would have gone out of my mind." Francis laughs again, "Don't worry, we would have given you an anti-anxiety shot before you woke up. Just like the drug we gave you on the first day. You would have been fine." Alex says facetiously, "Good to know you were thinking of my sanity and not just my blood." Francis says, "Don't kid yourself. It was all about your blood."

She goes on. "None of us can leave until the air is safe or we're vaccinated. We'll probably never know whether this gas or virus was released intentionally or accidentally. The perpetrators are likely all dead or locked down somewhere as we are, so it doesn't matter anymore."

She says, "Of course, we now have a huge problem. We used to say if you work here, you're set for life. But none of the staff can go home again. Many are grieving, terrified, and in a bad psychological state. We're stuck, and we don't know if we'll ever be able to leave and live. There's little for them to do, and idle hands are dangerous. We have no clients to supply and likely won't ever again. Well, you, of course." She smiles and patronizingly pats Alex's arm and goes on. "The plant is already irrelevant. We have food and water for everyone for their lifetimes. Our air systems self-clean. We have medics and all the technology you could want. However, they no longer have their loved ones; if some are still alive, they can't get to them or communicate with them."

She touches Alex's arm again and looks at her. "You know how that feels." This woman exudes warmth and kindness. Alex hasn't cried in a while, but Francis' sympathy makes her eyes fill. She chokes it back and tries to shift the focus back to Francis. Alex says, "I do; thank you for remembering that." She then asks, "What about you? Are you married? Do you have children? Where are you from, and who might be left back there?" Francis says, "Saint Lucia. I've long been divorced, no children." She pauses for a moment after saying that. She continues,

"My stepfather was still alive when I was last home, but he would be gone now. Many aunties, uncles and cousins, and friends...all gone now. I'll never see Saint Lucia again." In this saddest of times, her saying this is particularly poignant. Alex envisions Francis' small hot tropical island, empty but for a few survivors who won't know what happened, with no one to ask. The palm trees would go on bending and blowing in the warm wind. The sugary sand dunes would continue to roll over into the turquoise ocean. Fishing boats would bob at their docks. There wouldn't even be a steel band to play a lament in the background. A tropical nightmare.

Francis says, "Moaning won't help us. Good science will, or time. If I can get them out of here, we also have to help them set up new lives. I'll get teams working on this. It'll be a worthwhile project and keep them busy for a while." Alex thinks, *she sure is a pragmatic woman. I'm worried enough about my own survival, let alone 118 struggling people.*

Francis stands, stretches again, and says to Alex, "We need to get you safely across the country with the right gear, and we'll get to that shortly. In turn, we're asking a few things of you. Besides your blood, which we now have copious amounts of, thank you, we want you to be our eyes on the world, sharing what you see as you travel across the country. We need you to test soil, water, and vegetation. It seems unaffected, but we don't know if it's consumable and if things will continue to grow and regenerate. We'll be testing the regrowth of seeds in our labs, but what's going on in the world in seasons forward will tell the tale. We want you to report on the state of the people you find, large agriculture, if it still exists, and food supplies.

We're providing you with a new powerful invisible solar bike. The trays on the bike can transmit information about your tests back to our labs. You can put your research and journalism skills to use. Who knows, we might be able to figure out a way forward together." Alex responds, "I'll do whatever I can."

Francis then puts her hands on Alex's shoulders, looking into her eyes. She pauses, then says, "We also may need you to assassinate someone."

Alex freezes, "What? I've never killed anything but houseflies and mosquitoes. I'm not sure I could kill a person." Alex then asks, "Who and why? What's going on?" Suddenly, her future, as she had imagined it, has flipped on a dangerous edge, much more perilous than she had envisioned. This is a big ask. She wonders, "If I don't do it, will they not provide me with the equipment I need?" That question hangs between them.

Francis says, "I mentioned earlier there was a breach. A few years back, we contracted an Indian IT operator, Diya. She was from New Delhi. Her credentials were impeccable, and our security surveys passed her with flying colors. We detected her hacking into our secure systems very early into her contract. We discovered she actually worked for RAW India, the Research and Analysis Wing of their foreign intelligence agency. She was a spy. We arrested her and removed all of her communication chips but one. She had a follower chip embedded in her spine by RAW, and we would have risked physically disabling her if we removed it. She spent two years in isolation in a high-security prison in the States and then was extradited to India. Her life would have been entirely dispensable there. She was no longer of use to them, and she would likely have been quietly and quickly assassinated. Any information she had garnered from us would have already been transmitted, so that ship had sailed. As it was, RAW India already knew what we did here, so she didn't really learn much new. She did, however, learn where one of our spies lived, and he had an invisi-suit, bike, and all the gear.

She wants me and everyone here dead. She managed to get back out of India, probably wearing a metal jacket so that her spinal follower chip could not be detected. We think she came back by boat. According to our information, she hid out in a house across the street from where our guy lived in Connecticut, killing the man who lived there. She waited for our guy (his name was Richard Jackson) to come home. He lived in a Smart Home, but she managed to get to him before he went in. He was in his invisi-suit but had just pulled his hood back as he entered the door. She shot him in the head. She's one cold blooded woman. She got his suit, bike, invisi gear, and of course his bike screen. She was then able to crack into our communication system. The day before the attack, she showed up with body bombs. She was the one who blew up that small opening in the fence you found. We didn't have time to repair it after the attack. There was no way she could have ever gained access down here, but she's an enormous threat to our future when and if we can come up top. We need her gone.

Alex thinks to herself, *you have a big dangerous problem, but so do I. This woman Diya will obviously kill anyone to destroy Francis. That means me.* Alex asks, "Where is she now, and why didn't you kill her while you could?" Francis says, "She had on the invisi-suit, so shooting her would have done nothing. Even we don't have a magic bullet to get through our own material. It's impervious to weapons. She's up top nearby, keeping watch. Our I.T. team is working to block her from reading our communications, but they haven't found out how she managed to hack in yet. She had cancer and was near death and had the vaccine. However, her organs were so severely damaged before she got the vaccine, her health is still severely compromised. We can read her body in the suit, and we think she's dying. There are no guarantees, of course. She could live long enough to harm us. She wants to eliminate all of us. We have to take her out first."

Alex says, "I don't even know what assistance you'll be able to offer me yet, but this is a big ask. I need to digest this." Francis says, "I completely understand, and be assured the protective gear we're providing you with will save your life and is not predicated on your killing this woman." Alex says, "If she doesn't kill me first." Francis does not respond.

Francis changes the subject and says, "Would you like to have a look around?" Alex says, "Can't wait." In the back of her mind is a murderous woman waiting for her up top. Alex tries to put her out of her mind for now and pay attention to the tour. They leave the office, enter a door on the far side, and go down another long hallway. This place is a rabbit warren of corridors with secret doors. They come up to another armored door that Francis operates with her iris, and it quietly slips open. She says, "Before we go in, flip up your suit glasses." Alex does this. They enter another vast space, empty this time, an extensive silent warehouse with all kinds of equipment she doesn't recognize. Nothing is currently operating, and a large open space is in the middle. Francis says, "Now drop your glasses." Alex is astounded; the empty floor is now stacked with huge rolls of light pink, invisible fabric. This is such a military advantage; it's hard to consider the breadth of its uses. She swears a lot but resists with this polite stranger. Inside, she's thinking, *holy fuck!*"

Francis says, "The invisi material is made of myriad microscopic mirrors and a thread that mimics spider webs, stronger than steel. The mirrors trick the eye, reflecting the surroundings and the brain immediately adjusts, thinking it's not seeing anything." She adds, "I'm not a scientist and am doing a poor job of explaining this, but as you can see, it works."

They do a tour of the entire plant. It's immense, and they walk for miles. Alex asks, "How was this all blasted out without it hitting the media? There would have to have been an enormous amount of dirt and rock taken out to create this vast underground space, let alone the sound of the blasting." Francis says, "That was before my time here, but from what I understand, a new blasting treatment was used that was largely silent, with considerably less impact on the surrounding environment. The soil and rocks were all stacked in the forest under the trees, so none of the forest was affected. They did not want the work detected by any satellites. Large, covered trucks moved it out at night. No one knew what was in those trucks. We have several entrances, so these were varied. The construction took about three years."

They continue through the uniform plant, where a group of people sit at a table. Their heads are down, no lunchtime break laughter here. No work, but a camaraderie of misery. In the food processing plant, a few people wander disconsolately through. No more work for them. The hospital ward staff at least have jobs and have a few patients they're treating. There's a sizeable gym. Two fitness instructors are working with a couple of women, and several people are running on treadmills and working the equipment.

In the lab, the techs are working away. Heavy weight on them. They're expected to find and create the vaccine and save everyone's life. No pressure.

A few people swim laps in the Olympic-sized pool. The kitchen staff is busy making lunch in a full industrial kitchen. This would be the source of the delicious meals Alex was served. The dining room is laid out formerly, with tablecloths, flowers, and small lights for the evening. At least it doesn't look like a cafeteria. There are a couple of small coffee kiosks available around the park. The laundry is also busy, so some work is being done servicing this group. Alex guesses not everybody chooses or gets the self-clean clothes she's wearing. There's a hair salon. A good haircut goes a long way to feeling good. They even have a pub. Francis says, "We have a lot of fun there, good danceable music, and it's a place to go, other than your apartment."

She shows Alex the sleeping quarters and says, "We provide each person with a bachelor apartment." These are homey and comfortable, unlike Alex's decontamination room. They also have the same fake window Alex had in her room. It's raining out, according to the fake window.

There are completely equipped workshops, hobby areas for woodworking and sewing, and art and technology labs where people can create and play. There are computer games rooms and immersive movie rooms, and libraries. There are small and large meeting rooms. There's the park she first encountered and a large indoor vertical garden for their fruit and vegetables. Francis says, "We wanted to make this anything but an underground worksite where you never see the light of day. Natural light is used throughout."

Francis reminds Alex of the obvious. "I know you're aware of your personal position living in this new world. You'll have food and protective supplies, and most people won't. Millions of the survivors will starve to death, and you'll need to look away and walk away. You can't save everybody." Alex says, 'I think about that a lot, and I know there'll be life and death decisions I'll have to make. I'm particularly not at ease leaving a child behind. Hopefully, I won't see any, even though I'll know there'll be survivors somewhere. I'm not even vaguely comfortable with it, but I want to live and find my mother. I figure I'll take each day as it comes. You don't think about what it could mean to buy a lifetime food supply. It has to mean in the worst case, others won't have food and will die."

Francis says, "Obviously, we all want to get out of here, but it has to be safe. Not much of a world to return to. We'll be sending mice up top regularly to get a read on the air, and our bots can gather vegetation and water up top and bring it back for testing. We also want to hear about how people are surviving, or not, over the longer term. We don't know whether Diya will follow you or stay on here waiting for us to surface. If she follows you, you'll have to make your own decision about how to respond."

She continues, "The bubonic plague killed as many as 40% of the world's population, and the survivors still built new lives." Less than 2% of the world had cancer which doesn't sound like a lot, but still, there are a lot of survivors. There were over 10 billion people alive when this hit. If even 1% survived, that's still 10 million people. That's if they got the shot. If they could even afford the shot. A big if. But there are still a lot of people left. The earth has not been completely erased of people.

Francis has an almost insurmountable challenge ahead with her people. They all know they're buried alive.

Chapter 11

TOOLS OF THE TRADE

Francis says, "Let's talk about your gear. Everything is almost weightless, including your bike, food, and tent. We want you to travel light and be fast on your feet if you ever need to make a run for it."

She says, "There are several key pieces. Your invisi-suit is a loose jumpsuit with feet, gloves, and a complete hood that pulls down over your face. It's so light you won't feel the hood on your face. The suit glows a pale pink when you view it with the glasses and is entirely invisible to anyone else's eyes. Even though your suit will last a lifetime, circumstances could cause you to lose it. It's invisible, after all. Therefore, we're providing three backup suits and an extendable waterproof bag to carry your gear when you're off the bike. The suit is like armor. No bullet, knife, or projectile can penetrate it. The material is completely waterproof but breathes. Night-vision goggles can't detect it because it doesn't reflect heat. It keeps your body temperature steady in all climates. It's self-cleaning. We know where all our suits are all the time, so we won't lose you, not that we can get to you if you get into trouble.

All the camping gear is also invisible. We're providing medication patches, an enhanced medi-chip, an additional reader chip, and a SAT phone, currently not in operation, and enough flavored wafers for two lifetimes. If you lose those, we can tell you where to get more. We'll also want to insert a lens in one of your eyes so you can always see your invisi-gear."

Alex says, "Wow, this stuff is amazing." Francis says, "I used to wish I could live for hundreds of years to see what inventors come up with next. Being alive to witness these inventions has been a gift. Future inventions will have to wait a while now, sadly."

She continues, "We've also given you three sets of clothes to be worn under the suit, just like you're wearing now, along with winter wear. You won't always want to be invisible. These clothes are self-cleaning, wash up easily and dry immediately. You'll have replacements if you lose a piece."

She says with a grin, "Now for the practical. You are vulnerable when squatting for a poop or a pee. The pants unzip along the seam at the back and under the crotch to accommodate your urine spreader. You won't have to drop your pants." Francis goes over these toilet basics quickly, like a sales pitch. Alex responds, "Well, that's handy."

Francis says, "You'll want to shower, but we don't recommend it unless you're in a Smart Home. You'd be too vulnerable. Birdbaths are better in the interim, or just go dirty." Alex says, "I'd envisioned dipping into a lake at night." Francis says, "There you would be, naked, unarmed, and visible. Even at night. Don't do it."

She continues, "We're also providing enough invisi-fabric to hide a piece of very large equipment. You never know. When squeezed, the fabric adheres to itself if you need to seal the edges. A special cutter is included in your gear for this material if you need it. We suggest you try to keep it intact. It folds down to nothing."

She says, "As I mentioned, we're giving you a new powerful invisible solar bike. Everything on the bike folds down to the wheel size and fits into your carry bag. The tires are made of a special fabric and can't blow. You can pick your bike up with your baby finger. We've provided you with invisi-paint if you ever have to get another bike and disguise it. All your food and supplies fit on the bike. We have it down to an art form. It also has a fold-down bubble hood." Alex will learn later how handy that hood can be.

Francis continues, "The bike has a small portable communication and scanning panel. If you're in earshot of anyone, communicate with us from within your helmet and transmit oral and visual reports from there. You don't want to be heard. Because Diya is tuning in, only talk to us from the inside of a Smart Home. She won't be able to hear or see anything on the panel when you're within those walls. The bike has built-in lab trays to test your soil, plant, and water samples. It reads these and sends the data back to our labs. You won't need much for a sample."

She continues, "Your bike helmet fits closer to your head than the one you've been wearing but provides much more protection should you fall. It nests into itself for easy packing. Even though you'll have a built-in eye lens to see your invisi equipment, your helmet has built-in high-powered night vision glasses and can be adjusted to zoom in or out. You'll also have a camera built into the fabric of your suit hood, which you can turn on or off, and one permanently installed on your bike. We'll also provide you with three pairs of loose glasses to see the suit when you're not in it. There may come a day when you have to share these with someone."

She pauses and asks Alex, "Still with me?" Alex laughs and says, "Taking it all in."

Francis says, "Your tent and camping supplies all fold into one-inch squares. The tent pegs self-drill in and out. The one downside to the suit and tent is you are still a solid object inside it, and your outline can be seen in rain and snow. You'll need to be particularly careful in Victoria during the rainy seasons. If you make it there." Alex says, "Yeah, the big if. Haven't thought about that trek in a few days. Had my mind on dead mice."

Francis continues, "We'll enhance your medi chip, so we'll always have a full read on your health. We hope you'll stay healthy, but things will happen, and you'll age, and we may be able to give you some medical advice. We can also scan your entire body, or anybody, for that matter. Our medical staff can then share any problems and advice with you. There'll be times when they can't fix the problem, nor will you be able to. It's a hard truth about all of our futures. We may die of something simple, like a heart attack or a simple infection, because no one will be able to operate. You'll probably need painkillers, antibiotics, bandaids, and tourniquets at some point in your life. We're giving you a lifetime supply of those. We can guide you as to what else you might need medically. Hospital pharmacies will have been locked, and you might be able to access some things others can't get at."

Today, we'll insert a communication chip into your forearm that has many functions. You'll need to access many locked spaces, Smart Homes, and regular locked houses. If you must risk it, you might need to get into hotels and certainly the boat for your crossing. You'll need to get into computers and various things that need an iris read, code, or physical reader. You position your communication chip in front of the camera eye or on the device or the key slot if it's old tech, and it'll open. It will open a safe or even an old hasp lock. It's all done with minuscule magnets."

She continues, "The chip is also a life reader. This means you can tell if anyone is alive within an approximate 10,000 sq foot space. It will show red if someone's alive in the space and blue if there isn't. You can control it and direct it into any space. Alex says, "I like that chip option. I had visions of some old coot sitting in a kitchen chair in front of their door with an ancient, cocked rifle aimed at whoever came through it...like me."

Francis says, "With that chip, you can reach us if you aren't near your bike or have lost the bike for some reason. It will alert you when we need to speak to you with a vibration. As I said, put on your helmet to talk to us. You can send us a quick beep if you can't communicate at that time."

She adds, "We've given you a new lighter SAT phone, which currently isn't working. Our tech staff are trying to hack into all the communication satellites to get these operating again. They say that nothing should have shut down but there must have been a big burp in the system when most of humanity disappeared. They're trying to solve the puzzle. That's why you haven't been able to contact your mother." She looks at me and says, "I'm sure you've considered your mother may not be alive to answer." Alex nods. She thinks about that outcome constantly.

Francis shares, "They're also hacking into communication satellites so that we can reach out through HAM radio technology, get the Newnet up and running again and at least some version of television. They're optimistic they can figure this out.

She goes on, "Every piece of your gear has a finder tag embedded in it. You'll always know where it is through the finder technology in your helmet and bike. If you lose both, we can't help you. If you lose anything or it's taken from you, you can track it through the finder tech. You might not be able to retrieve it, but at least you'll know who has it and how dangerous that might be. You may have to take steps you'll be uncomfortable with to retrieve a missing piece." Alex says, "You mean kill someone to get it back?" Francis says, "Yes, you have to face that. The suit and bike in the wrong hands would be very dangerous." Alex thinks again, *I don't know if I can kill someone.*

Francis goes on, "It'll be dangerous out there, Alex. Starving, frantic people can do crazy things. Survivors will be ransacking everything. Try not to take shelter in a non-Smart Home or a place with one door, like a motel, hotel, or even an apartment. You always need to leave yourself a way out. Even your tent has a back flap. If you find shelter in a house, it should be a Smart Home. Otherwise, sleep rough and keep your escape options open."

She says, "We went through your bike gear and replaced and upgraded a few things. We've provided you with a water cleaner/desalinator that pulls moisture from the air and cleans it, so you'll always have drinking water. We've also provided a very efficient little food warmer for your wafers."

Francis continues, "You can't be heard outside the tent, so you can talk to us, cough, snore, or fart. No one will hear you. Remember, the tent can be seen in the rain, so camp under trees or some protection, so you don't stand out in a storm."

Francis says, "You'll like your all-in-one stun gun and shooter. The stun knocks the person out for about six hours. They wake up with no memory of what happened the previous day or so. This allows you the choice of just disabling whoever is a problem without having to kill them." Alex says, "I like that option a lot." Francis goes on, "As you can see, it's the size of a pen with a red end, the killing end, and a blue end, the stun end. You aim and press the center button. It's finger-activated and will know your thumbprint. No one else will be able to use it. Simple. It's a heat seeker, so it'll be hard to miss your target. It has enough minute ammunition to last you a lifetime or take out half of an army. It can be attached to your suit or your street clothes and is undetectable. We'll provide you with three of these just in case you get separated from your gear. Always have one with you, even when you're sleeping."

Francis then takes Alex to a small shooting test range to practice. She introduces her to her bike and shows her how to scan and send lab samples, communicate, and break the bike down, so it's hand portable. " The bike is so light Alex wonders how it'll support her. Francis deftly makes a minor cut in Alex's forearm and slips the new chips in. It's bloodless, and she seals it with surgical tape. She skilfully pops the new see-all lens in her left eye. Alex says, "You've done that before." Francis smiles.

Francis dead-eyes Alex again. "Last but not least, we're providing you with a small atomizer of poison. You may not get the opening to shoot Diya, but if you get some of this on her suit without her knowing, she'll eventually touch it. It will kill her immediately. Be assured she's also carrying some of her own." Alex says, "Christ Francis, I'm as good as dead before I leave." Francis says, "If you get sprayed, do not take the suit off, do not touch anything, go directly to a Smart Home and shower in the suit. You'll know where she sprayed. We have supplied you with an extra pair of protective gloves, put those on, take the suit off after you've showered, and leave it where it drops. Put on one of the other suits we provided. Maybe lie low for a few weeks, so she'll think you're dead."

She puts her hands on Alex's shoulders and looks her in the eyes. "We hope you have a long life and come through this safely. We are giving you a tremendous advantage with this gear. Use it safely and wisely and guard it closely." Alex looks back at her and says, "I'll be honest. I feel like I'm in more danger than before we met. I thought I had a challenge getting across the country before." Francis says, "There were already people out there who would kill you for your food. None of us will ever feel safe again. It's our new reality."

Francis says, "Diya may not follow you and will choose to stay here and wait us out. We'll know that when you leave. However, she's driven. She'll know you're connected to me and will think she can hurt me by killing you. She's right. I'm sorry to ask you to put your life in danger, not to mention commit murder. Think of this: if our little group gets to the top, we'll start a new little village of life and maybe a future for the planet. She could end all that with one well-placed bomb. She needs to be killed if you get the opportunity."

Alex says with humor, "Sure, place the world's future in my hands. No pressure. Thanks." Francis responds with her huge laugh and hugs her. She says, "I think you'll survive."

Chapter 12

FRANCIS

As they finish up, Francis says, "It's getting late, and it's raining hard up top. Do you want to stay over and leave in the morning? Because of your hazmat suit, you would have to eat back in the decontamination room with me on the screen rather than in person and sleep there tonight. We could spend the evening together in my suite after supper and get to know each other." Alex had thought she'd left that cell forever, but the idea of spending an evening getting to know Francis was very appealing. She's the first calming human contact she's had since the disaster day, and Alex wants more of that. She's only known her briefly, but Francis' confidence is bracing. Alex will be talking to her or someone from here for a very long time, but she'll probably never see Francis again when she leaves. She says enthusiastically, "Yes, I'd love that." Francis says, "I'll walk you back there. You can take the suit off to eat and relax, and I'll join you on the screen. I think we're having pseudo steak with potatoes tonight." Francis laughs out loud again. Alex thinks, *I love the sound of her laughing, anyone laughing*. Not many survivors are still laughing.

Things are the same back in her decontamination cell, except the fake window now shows a rainy evening. Alex wonders if it might be a camera up top. She always loved a rainy night when she was dry and warm inside, listening to the rain on the roof. Alex remembers she's a mile underground, not quite as cozy. She has an hour until Francis checks in again, and she flicks through the entertainment options and finds some old music concerts. She plugs into her favorite band but doesn't feel much like dancing. She knows a lonely, treacherous trip awaits her tomorrow.

At six, the slot opens, and in comes what looks like an authentic steak dinner, roast potatoes, and asparagus in a butter like substance. There's a bonus, a bottle of Merlot from a local winery. The screen brightens, and it's Francis in a grey tracksuit and back in her suite. Alex can now see how fit she is. Her dinner plate is in front of her, and she raises her wine glass and says, "Bon appétit and good luck to both of us." Alex returns the toast.

Alex says, "I had a food industry research contract on my desk when all this happened, but I never got to it. I would have loved to know more about the chemicals we eat and their effects on our bodies. I know the old real meats and dairy were just a compilation of chemicals. We just didn't call a carrot's components by their real scientific names. There was always more to the new food than that. It would have been a 'meaty' project." She grins at her bad joke. Francis says with a smile, "Shut up and eat your chemicals."

They finish their meals, and Francis holds up the wine bottle and says, "There's more of this back here. You'll have to drink it with a straw through your hazmat suit. Put it on, and I'll come and get you." She shows up in her invisi-suit again, and they walk what seems like a mile through the complex to her living quarters. Her suite is sizeable, no bachelor apartment here. She has an open-concept main room, a bedroom, a full kitchen, a den/library, and a large, elegant bathroom. The decor is modern and bright, with lots of colors, and very comfortable. It's a home.

Alex takes in the room. There are pictures of many places and people on the walls. Family and friends, laughing together. Dinner parties, people smiling and toasting the camera. Beachy looking patio parties overlooking the ocean, with sunburnt people sitting around with half-full glasses of drinks, looking a little drunk and windblown. Their cotton and linen shirts are open to bathing suits. Everybody's feeling good about where they are. An older couple sits close together on a swing. Are they Francis' parents? There's a graduation picture of a younger Francis with longer hair, framed degrees, diplomas and awards, and some sports trophies. She had a full, happy life. Her library is crammed with books Alex hasn't read but always meant to.

They settle on Francis' comfy cream couches, and Francis stretches out full length. She's one long girl. Alex is restricted in her hazmat suit, but she settles in. She says to Francis, "Tell me about how you got here. It must have been an interesting path." Francis says, "Okay, but I hope I don't put you to sleep." She takes a sip of her wine. "You already know where I'm from. I'm 46 years old, and these days feel a lot older. I was an only child. My mother was young when she had me, barely 15, and she didn't see my father much after their first few dates. He was only about 16. My mother said he was part of a ship's crew in port from Majorca and that he had great hair and could dance. I guess he had enough charm to steal a fifteen-year-old girl's heart and break it. He doesn't know I exist, and I didn't have any desire to disrupt his life later through a DNA search." She goes on, "My mother and grandmother raised me. It was a happy household, with lots of love. My mother continued her education and eventually became a CPA. It was a considerable feat given her circumstances, but she worked hard and did it. She met my stepfather in her 30s. He worked in the same office as her, managing the sales department."

"The company they were with sold all kinds of island souvenirs, trinkets, and trash, as they call it, but it was very successful. There's no end to the junk tourists will pick up and bring home with them." Alex says, "Yes, I probably own some of it. Can't resist a tropical plastic thingy when I travel." Francis says, "Try growing up with both parents in that business. A lot of tropical plastic thingies migrated home." She goes on, "They had such a happy marriage, always laughing, lots of hugs and long looks at each other. He was wonderful to me. Listened to all my teenage gripes and gave them credence, cheered me on. I adored him."

She continues, "When I was in my young teens, I ran track and won a few races. I considered pursuing a sports career for a year or two. I still run on our track here and could run for miles when I was home. She shakes her head sadly. "I suspect my beach running days are over." Alex says, "You never know. There are still lots of beaches left." Francis says, "True, won't ever be like home, though." Alex says, "I also did a bit of running, just little five-mile runs, but I enjoyed it. Sam and I used to run together at the end of the day." Francis says, "I think that showed up in one of your bios, and I noticed you jogging in your room. Not sure when you'll be able to run free again, maybe when your gear is stashed safely at your mother's."

She goes on. "At fourteen, I met a boy, Joseph, and fell madly in love, as you do at that age. He had the most beautiful eyes. However, I got pregnant, and that was the end of my running career and my life, I thought at the time. There was no judgment from my mother or grandmother. My mother had me as a teenager and was cruelly treated by the ladies of her time. Joseph's family did not live on the island, and as soon as they learned of my situation, they quickly left with their boy. No pregnant island girl for their son. I didn't even have the chance to say goodbye to him. He found a way to contact me without his father finding out, and we stayed in touch throughout my pregnancy. He promised he would come for us when he had finished high school and university and had a job and some money. Even at that age, I knew that would never happen."

Francis says, "We all wanted this baby; me, my mom and stepdad, and my grandmother. We welcomed her into our lives." She smiles and looks back at a picture in the bookcase. "I had a gorgeous little girl with Joseph's eyes, long fingers, and the chubbiest little legs. I called her Matilda after her grandmother; she was to be Matty. Seven days after her coming into my world, her little heart stopped. A fatal deformity that the hospital did not pick up. Just like that, she was gone. My milk had just barely come in. I was devastated."

Alex says, "I can't imagine how awful that would have been." Francis responds, "Joseph sobbed on the screen with me. He continued to check in, but his calls got more infrequent and eventually stopped. I had a rough time with it for a while. I quit school, stayed home, hated myself and my life." She walks Alex over to the bookshelf and shows her a picture of a newborn snuggled up in a pink blanket. Baby Matty stares straight out at the world. She did have gorgeous eyes. She would have been a pistol like her mom if she'd lived." Francis continues, "After some time, my lovely parents and grandmother gently nudged me back into life. I returned to school with a new drive. I wanted to do something important, didn't know what."

She takes a drink of her wine, stands up, and stretches. "I didn't run today, and I feel like a lump." Alex says, "Sorry. I took up most of your day." Francis shrugs that off. "I run early in the morning usually. I didn't feel like it this morning." Alex sucks in her wine through the straw in her hazmat suit and tries not to make a noise.

Francis sits down again and continues. "I was interested in the human mind and psychology as it related to how the world worked. As a teenager, I vainly thought I could fix the world. I went to school in the states and earned my master's in business psychology. I briefly considered going for a doctorate. I didn't want to teach or do research, though. I wanted to run a business that helped improve the world. I wanted to jump into life. Like many grads, my first jobs had nothing to do with saving the world. I did what I could to gain experience and add to my resume. I was always looking for the right job fit and scoured international job postings for something that looked right. I did lots of volunteer work in those years, working with job creation organizations and urban housing. Nothing came up that made me want to jump on board."

Alex says, "You were much more dedicated to being a good person than I was at that age. I did want to get on with life after university but was pretty unfocused for a while." Francis smiles at her and says, "You figured it out. You're focused now."

You were ready to break in here to find out what was happening. Not many young women would do that or even get that far. I loved watching you trek around the fence on that hot day. That's my girl, I thought." She looks at Alex affectionately and laughs.

She continues, "When I was in my twenties, I was working at one of my volunteer jobs, sourcing housing for tough family cases. I met a guy, Paolo. Nice enough guy, cute, and we seemed to have the same interests. We got married. In retrospect, I don't know why. He did not have my drive and was looking for someone to have a few kids with and have a pleasant life in the suburbs. I wanted more than that. We split amicably after a few years. Last I heard, he was married with two kids and was living happily ever after in Connecticut." She looks away. "They're probably all dead now."

Alex says, "I had a few romances before meeting Sam, but when I met him, that was it. We worked well together because we gave each other complete freedom to be ourselves. Humor, but no real judgment. He was the coolest guy." Francis says, "You were both fortunate to have your time together. I hope that memory sustains you." She says, "In my case, my marriage was a small, forgettable chapter of my life. No harm, no foul, as they say."

Francis continues. "Meanwhile, I started to explore government postings all over the world. I was too inexperienced to even be considered for any ambassador positions, but it sure intrigued me. I had high ambitions for myself. Eventually, I joined the U.S. Government in a large job creation department. I worked my way up to Director by the time I was 35. I launched some successful national training and work placement campaigns and felt I had found my niche."

Francis looks at Alex and asks, "Are you bored blind yet?" Alex says, "God no, keep sharing; this is great." Francis says, "I can rattle on, but back to the story."

She continues, "I was working in Florida then. One memorable day, my assistant came into my office and said, "You won't believe this, but the vice president's office is on the screen for you." I asked, "Who? What vice president?" I couldn't think of anyone I knew in a vice president's role who might be calling me." My exasperated assistant then said, "Francis, it's the Vice President of the United States." All I could think was, "Damn, what did I screw up? I quickly checked my hair and makeup and told her to put him through. There he was, on the screen, with a big smile. I couldn't believe it. He spoke robustly as if he needed to impress me. Hell, I was impressed."

Francis shares the conversation with Alex. He says, 'Good morning, Francis,' and I just said, 'Good morning, sir.' I was so nervous. He said, 'It must seem strange to hear from us, but we've been watching your career for a while and hearing good things about your work.' I said, 'Thank you, sir.' He then said, 'I have an interesting opportunity I would like to discuss with you. Would you be willing to fly up to Washington to meet with my aides and me to discuss it?' I said, 'I'd love to meet with you. I don't suppose you could tell me more now?' He's a very relaxed guy and just laughed and said, 'All will be revealed.'

They flew me up to Washington the next day, and I went into his office, nervous as hell, getting passed through a lot of security on the way. There was a male and a female with him I did not know and don't know to this day. A couple of aides or whatever they call them. They invited me to sit, and we went through the niceties. 'How are you? We've had nice weather, but your weather is always nice in Florida.' Francis says, I'm thinking, w*hy are we discussing the weather? Why the hell am I here? Let's cut to the chase.* And he did. He said, 'We have a highly secure military supply arm that few people are aware of. This arm manufactures leading-edge military equipment, not just for the U.S. but for the world. The plant is a very unusual operation in an unusual location that requires someone with psychological business training to be part of the management team. We have been watching your career and think you may be a fit.'

Francis says to Alex, "I was thinking, *unusual location?* I know we've established a few bases on the moon, but as far as I knew, they were largely mining operations.?" She says, "I desperately wanted to say, "If it's on the moon, I'm not interested." I decided to keep my mouth shut and asked politely, "I guess it depends on where it is and what the specifics and needs of the job are. What would be your expectations of me?" She looks at Alex and says, "How mealy mouthed did that sound?" Alex laughs and says, "Well, he was the Vice President; you had to remember your manners." Francis says, "He then said, "It's good to be cautious; you'll need that in this job." Francis says, "Long story short, it was this job, not on Mars. He was right about being cautious, but it has been the most rewarding thing I've ever done. I feel our tools helped to keep some parts of humanity safe. I couldn't stop wars, but I could help save lives."

Alex says, "That's one hell of a career trajectory. You make me feel humble with my little research company." Francis says, "Don't underestimate your humble research company. You had an excellent reputation in your field. You were well known in the right circles. You did very well." Alex thinks, *high praise from someone tapped by the Vice President for her job.* She soaks it up.

Francis says, "Enough about jobs. What about your cancer treatment? How did you feel about the hysterectomy? Had you wanted kids?" Alex says, "Sam and I both grew up without much contact with kids and no burning desire to be parents. Neither of us had even had to change a diaper, and the idea didn't appeal. We had a comfortable life and didn't want it disrupted with babies." She shares, "I admit to a side of me wanting to experience pregnancy just to be part of that club. However, the idea of handling a toddler having a meltdown, a teenager smart-mouthing me, or a child with mental or physical problems didn't have any curb appeal. The hysterectomy resolved all that forever, plus it removed the cancer. I would have never been sure if I hadn't had the vaccine."

Alex asks Francis, "What about your mother and stepfather?" Francis says, "Yes, it was a very tough time in my life. My mother got an infection from an insect bite. It traveled rapidly through her system, went septic, and took her in two days. My stepdad was never the same. He had a heart attack a few years later, but I think it was simply a broken heart. My grandmother outlived my mother and just died a couple of years ago. At least this disaster will have ended my stepfather's loneliness."

Alex asks, "Who's Miguel, the guy who delivered the mice to my room?" Francis tells her he's her co-manager. She describes him as her mainstay and fills in for her when she's away. She says the team loves and respects him and that he's a very talented leader and a trusted and dear friend. She says, "He can see the humorous side of every situation and keeps her sane." Alex says, "He sounds like Sam." Francis touches Alex's arm and says, "Yes, a true friend is hard to find. I am so sorry for your loss of Sam." She goes on about Miguel. "He's from Sao Paulo, Brazil." Alex says, "A long flight home." Francis says, "Yes, and he'll probably never get back there again, like all of us down here." Alex asks, "Hmmm, probably wanted your job?" Francis says, "He much prefers I carry the lead on the responsibility of this cell and is always happy to pass the reins back to me when I'm back. He'll be an excellent leader when I leave if I ever can. He doesn't want my job. I trust him implicitly."

The two women suspend the terrifying world outside for one night and try not to think about what's ahead of them. They share life stories, kill a few bottles of wine between them and laugh a lot, despite the world that waits above them. Alex discovers Francis isn't as noble as she appears, sharing her flaws and mistakes with hilarious stories. She tells a great story. This allows Alex to talk about her failures, some of them quite spectacular. They seem irrelevant now. They talk about their craziest and scariest clients. Alex shares she was often confused with a private detective who can 'get the dirt on anyone.' She says, "That was true, but it was not my business model. I've had some very insistent and domineering men and women demanding I work for them to follow up on their various paramours."

They talk about their avatars. Alex's is a magnifying glass with legs and arms. Francis' is a cartoon fox. Alex thinks this is an insightful choice for her. Francis says, "I never showed my face to my clients or potential clients and always used my avatar. People who got through to me were mostly, but not always, vetted by the Department of Defence. Some disturbing characters occasionally found me. Nothing's completely secret anymore, as we all know." She says, "I never disclosed what I did, where I was, and definitely not what we had to sell." She says, "I would ask them what they were looking for and the intended use. They always lied." They'd say, "I hear you have a cape that makes you invisible?" Frances says her standard answer was, "That's a rumor that's been going around for years. It's not true. I wish it were. It would be very exciting." She says, "Then I'd end the conversation and block any further communication."

Alex and Francis are like two doves in a storm, nestled together, bending with the wind in their underground tree. Without words, they become friends for life. When Francis' eyes rest on Alex, it's with warm affection. Alex thinks, *she should have had kids; she's a natural mother. I've had no one sane to talk to in the past six weeks. Not Sam, not my mother, not my friends. Not even the silent acceptance and wet nose nuzzle of my dog Princie. Francis has become my anchor in one evening. I haven't left, and I miss her already.*

Francis says, "I have a meeting with all my people tomorrow." I'll tell them about you and our hopes for using your blood to develop a vaccine. I'll break up the remaining work and schedule job shares to keep them busy. I'll set up project teams to develop plans for life back on top. They'll need to think about agriculture, food, water, and their continuing health. They need to have something to look forward to. I'm also going to introduce the idea of babies. If we survive, we'll need to think about the future. I'll leave that with them to digest. If we create the vaccine or the air clears, the elephant in the room will be who will be the first person to go up top. Humans aren't mice. Lots to talk about. There'll be inner squabbles and breakdowns and perhaps a few people making a run for it. I anticipate all that. I'm hoping we can overcome our human flaws. Miguel and

I can't fall apart. They need leaders, even a guiding parent figure, if you will, but we must find a way to go forward.

Alex says, "I wish I could be there for that speech." Francis says, "You have your own work to do, and it's time for you to get moving on your trip."

She puts on her invisi-suit and walks Alex back to her old room. They are both quite drunk and a bit weepy.

Francis says, "I admire brave people. You're one. I'll be watching for your reports and looking forward to seeing your smiling face on my screen. You can do this. You're not alone."

Alex says, "Your people are so lucky to have you." Francis says, "Only lucky if we can get out of here safely." She's a realist to the last. Alex says, "I can't thank you enough for everything you've done for me." Francis says, "We can't thank you enough for your blood samples." Alex looks at her one last time and says, "Bonne chance, mon ami." Francis says, "Yes, bonne chance."

Alex's door opens, and she's back in her room. She knows she'll be hungover tomorrow. She falls into bed in a deep, wine-filled sleep. Back to the future, as that old movie title said.

She still hasn't committed to killing anyone.

Chapter 13

DIYA

Before she was eleven years old, Diya was identified as a top student by RAW, the foreign intelligence agency of India. They scouted all students country-wide, watching their grades. Diya stood out early. She was an only child and, being a girl, was not highly valued by her father, other than as a future commodity to sell. They lived in a small rural village in deep poverty. Her father had no work. Her mother sold cheap saris on the street and was beaten regularly by her father if she didn't bring in enough money. They were living a miserable existence. Diya's father looked forward to the time he could get a dowry for her and sell her off to the highest bidder. She was a pretty little thing, and a few rich old men in the village had their eyes on her. Much has stayed the same over the decades in rural parts of India. RAW knows they'll have to make their offer early. Girls are sold off as young as nine or ten in the remote villages.

Just after her eleventh birthday, Diya climbed into a floating service car and turned her back on her parents and that life. Her father gleefully counted the high bounty he received for her, and her mother just turned away, no tears, silently thankful her daughter will have a better life than her. She was an odd child. Diya looked straight ahead, self-composed, feeling nothing. She seemed to be missing the emotion gene and hadn't ever felt love, happiness, or sadness. She'd never cried, laughed, or even smiled. Some might have said she was on the spectrum, if that were even recognized where she came from. It had been a loveless childhood, and she had been a child hard to love. Diya hadn't noticed.

After several hours, the service car floated up to a large, low building. There was no signage out front. She had very little with her, just the clothes on her back. The door to the building slid quietly open. A voice directed her to go in and said she'd be safe. She had no reason not to believe this voice and entered, looking around. There were no exterior windows, and the interior entrance hall opened into a large, tiled space with a few stiff looking sofas, chairs scattered about and some side tables. It's a 'wait until the next thing' space. After about ten minutes, a woman entered, dressed in what Diya thought of as western dress. She was in close fitting dark pants with a loose cream sweater over a cream blouse. No one's wearing saris here. She said, "Welcome, my name is Jane. This is your new school. I'll take you to your quarters."

Diya thinks, *Jane? That not your real name. You're as Indian as I am.* Jane takes her up a flight of stairs to a long hallway and stops at an open door. The room is split in half with two beds, desks, bookcases, closets, and screens on either side. An Indian girl about Diya's age turns around with a big smile and says, "Hi, I'm Mary. Welcome to our room." Diya thinks again, *Mary's not your real name.* Mary's also dressed in casual clothes that look more American than anything. Jane said, "Mary will be your roommate, probably for many years, unless the two of you decide that's not working. I've asked her to pick a few clothes for you, and they're in your closet. If you don't like them, you can choose something else. You won't be wearing your sari here." Diya hasn't had many choices in her life, so the idea she can decide if she doesn't like her new roommate and what to wear is entirely foreign to her. Her mind is buzzing as she takes all this in. Jane says, "I'll leave you with Mary, and she can fill you in. Tomorrow morning we'll do an orientation, and you'll begin to understand why we brought you here. You're very special to us." No one has ever said anything like that to her before.

The following day, Diya learns she'll be trained to work for the government, her ultimate role to be decided in the future. She still has high school and university to get through. She didn't realize then she had entered spy school. Over the next decade, the students learn many skills, including multiple languages, with specific training on speaking without an Indian accent. Their studies include advanced maths, sciences, and technology. They know their way around computer systems intimately and can hack into anything. They're also well indoctrinated in India's world views about specific countries, particularly the States. Diya eats it all up and quickly learns to despise all Americans, British, French, Germans, and Chinese for their various real and perceived affronts and threats to India. They give her a new name, Diane. She'll need to blend anywhere. She insists that Mary, her roommate, still call her Diya. She thinks no one would believe her name was Diane anyway. Not many Indians named Diane.

Mary gets accustomed to Diya's seeming lack of emotion. She's not mean, sarcastic, or unkind, just very quiet. She keeps her side tidy and responds when spoken to. She just isn't a normal, happy teenage girl. They study quietly together and live together peacefully. Mary has other friends in the school she can have a laugh with.

Many years later, Francis' recruiting team hires Diya, and it isn't long after that Francis begins to feel uneasy about her. She has a coldness in her eyes and is unresponsive to humor or small talk. She was much more animated in her interviews, and Francis now believes that was a well-trained act. She does her work but doesn't mix with the rest of the team and retreats to her apartment at the end of her shift. Francis keeps a close eye on her and spots her too many times in places she shouldn't be. She's an expert technician, but dangerous because of that. When they detect her hacking into their own systems, Francis has her arrested, sent back to the states, and put in solitary confinement for almost two years until the extradition back to India is organized.

Francis was surgical with Diya's removal. She was escorted up and out to a waiting service car, which took her back over the border to prison. They didn't want her talking to anyone. They had no worries. Diya knew her knowledge was worth money, and she planned to hang on to it until she found the right time and buyer. She never got the chance.

She knew going back to India was a death sentence. They'll want her silenced fast. She has a finder disk in her spine that they follow her with. She sources a metal vest that allows her to move around undetected while she plans her return to North America. It's hot and uncomfortable in the summer heat, but it saves her life. She buys her way onto a small freighter, stays low, and sails back to the States within months.

While working underground in Kingston, Diya uncovered an American spy in Francis' sales records. He'd been supplied with an invisi-suit and all the gear. He lived alone in a Smart Home in a Connecticut suburb when he wasn't traveling worldwide. Diya doesn't have access to Smart Homes, but she thinks she can attack him before he enters his house, if she's very patient. She desperately wants that gear to easily cross borders and ultimately take out Francis. That black bitch was so cool and superior. Miguel would be a bonus.

After landing in New York, Diya steals a solar bike, rides to Connecticut, and moves into the house across from her target spy. She shoots the owner of the house and moves his body out back, so it won't stink. She's a practical murderer. Then she waits. Her spy hasn't been home for a while and she hopes he's not on a long assignment or worse, comes home when she's not watching.

A month into this surveillance, she experiences stomach pains. She takes the chance of missing her spy returning, goes to a medical center, and is diagnosed with cancer. They highly recommend the Libertas1 vaccine. Not being a citizen, she's not eligible for it, but she has lots of stolen money and sources the vaccine on the black market. That still costs her a fortune. Soon after receiving it, the vaccine vanished overnight from all medical offices and the dark web. She hadn't been following the news or the rumors. It didn't matter. She had the vaccine. However, she wasn't entirely lucky. The cancer had already damaged her organs before it was stopped, and she's still sick and dying. She's also bitterly angry. She hadn't ever felt much emotion in the past, but her ordered world is now nonexistent. Her own country has turned against her. It's as bad as all the rest. She has no purpose and no refuge. This new emotion coils, slithers, and hisses in her brain. It's an actual feeling, unknown to her, and she almost embraces it. Francis and Miguel will pay for this. That's her new life's purpose. Destroy them.

She's living on pain patches but surviving. One night, around ten, her target spy's service door slides to the side. He's home. She can't see him because he has on his invisi-suit, but he must be tired. He lets down his guard and slips back his hood in the dark. There's his floating head. He's across the street, but she's an excellent markswoman. She shoots him in the back of the head and watches it explode. Quickly crossing the road, she closes the service door and checks his pulse. He's dead, if not brainless. Diya strips him of his suit, puts it on, and with the hood up, can now see his bike and gear bag. She searches through that, tossing anything she doesn't need. The bike's communication panel is the prize. Now she can hack into Francis' unit. She heads north to Canada and Kingston.

Before crossing into Canada, she sources some portable explosives with a plan to toss these into the various entry tunnels to the Kingston underground site. She's sure that will draw someone out. She's forgotten about the surface guard bots. It's her inane plan that someone would come to the surface, she'd kidnap them and hold them for ransom. The ransom would be Francis coming up. She works over in her mind ways to torture Francis before killing her. Her fantasies of vengeance have gone over the deep edge. Because of the heavy-duty pain patches she's using, her thinking is sloppy, bordering on maniacal.

Diya knows they'll identify her at the gate but doesn't realize they knew she was coming. Francis and her team have been following the stolen invisi-suit. Her plan was to work fast before the armed bots showed up to neutralize her. As far as she knew, they couldn't hurt her in this invisi-suit. She walked a mile down the electrified fence, exploded her way through, and started running to the nearest hidden tunnel. She thought she knew where the entrance tunnels all were but it's late spring; the foliage has grown up, and now she isn't so sure. Francis and her team watch her hike around, looking for tunnel entrances. They have some choices. Walk her off the property, have the Bot knock her down, strip the suit off her and send her on her way, or kill her outright once the suit is off. They don't like killing people, even Diya. They have no intention of bringing her down below. The invisi-suit also reads her health and she's very sick. She has body bombs strapped to her torso. At least when she has the invisi-suit on, they know where she is.

After hiking up the road further than she wants to, she nears a tunnel entrance in the back of the property. Francis' team send out a small bot tank. Its mechanical voice tells Diya she's being escorted off the premises and that if she tosses an explosive, she'll be captured and killed. In a moment of sanity, she realizes they could knock her out and remove her suit. She needs the suit. She walks out quickly with the bot tank close on her heels. That she thought she would get closer indicates the level of her recklessness. She's not thinking straight.

Francis and Miguel will regret not killing her then and there.

Diya had commandeered a house in Kingston, having shot the occupants. The mounting body numbers do not concern her. She needs to think. The hike through the site exhausted her, she slaps on some pain patches and sleeps.

The satellite bomb attack steals into Kingston overnight, killing most residents, as it did the rest of the world. Diya observes the quietness of the town the following day. She rides out and sees the piles of sand and clothes in the street. It takes her a while, but she figures out something big has happened. She has no one to talk to, and her usual screens are dead, as are the screens in the house she's parked in. Reading the bike screen, she picks up conversations between the German site and Kingston and learns what happened. Diya thinks they don't know she's hacking in. They do.

Diya doesn't care that it might be the end of civilization. She's dying anyway. However, the Kingston crew are not inoculated and they're all stuck underground. They won't be surfacing any time soon. She might never get to kill Francis before she dies. She has to figure out what to do next.

Chapter 14

MY HOME AND NATIVE LAND

It's almost ten AM, and Alex feels like she slept with her mouth open all night, probably snoring. She smacks her lips to get them working again. As expected, she's hungover. She rouses herself, has a shower, and gets into her sleek black clothes. A tray slides in with steaming hot porridge, maple syrup, buttery toast, peanut butter, and two pills labeled' headache pills' in a small envelope. Just the thing for a hangover. Someone has a sense of humor. She downs all this and feels much better. She puts on her invisi-suit and checks the bathroom mirror. Still invisible. Still, unnerving. Alex thinks, *at least no one will be looking at me naked anymore.* Miguel comes on the screen, the first time he's shown himself. He's in his early 40s, a good-looking Latino guy, nice even features, some remains of old acne scars from his youth, brilliant white teeth, and a big broad smile.

"Good morning. How are you feeling?" He asks brightly. Alex says, "Better after the breakfast and convenient drugs, thanks." He laughs and says, "Good, we wanted you in the best shape for your day's ride. Your bike is packed, ready, and sitting on the ramp outside the antechamber. Are you ready to go?" Alex says, "I better be." She says, "Francis speaks so highly of you. Thank you for being her friend and supporter." Miguel says, "It is my honor and pleasure. I love Francis." There is a hint there that he might really 'love' her. He says," Thank you for contributing to the vaccine development." Alex says, "My pleasure. I hope you can do something with my contribution."

Miguel says, "Alex, Diya is just outside the gate, across the road. It's Francis she wants, not you. She shouldn't bother you. If she does, remember she's a cold assassin, and you'll need to respond quickly. There'll be no time for niceties." Alex says, "I still don't know if I can kill someone." Miguel says, "You may have no choice. It'll be you or her."

Alex looks at the screen, inhales deeply, and says, "I guess I can't delay this anymore." He says, "Goodbye and safe travels. We'll be listening for you."

Her door slides open, and she looks down the hall to the door to the right that took her to the big green park. However, her exit door's on the left. She goes into the antechamber, and the door slides closed behind her. Parked there is her invisible bike in a faint pink outline, packed and ready to go. She hops on and rides slowly up the ramp. The lift door rises, and she's back in the forest alone. Her life before her. The door silently descends, and once again, all she can see is the meadow. No door, no safe underworld. The knowledge of its existence weighs heavily on her heart. She rides to the first gate, and it slides open. Everything is wet from last night's rain. The temperature gauge on her bike already reads 75 F. It'll be hot today, but she's perfectly comfortable inside her invisi-suit. Francis told her they could provide broad weather warnings, but not much more. She reaches the last gate to the road. She knows Francis is watching her leave. She turns around, gives the camera a last wave, and blows her a kiss. Underground, tears run down Francis' face. She says, "Be safe, my friend. We'll talk soon." That warm rich voice with the island accent will keep Alex sane for the rest of her life, however long that is.

Diya's been watching the exit. Alex picks her up in her bike mirrors immediately. Diya's invisi-suit and bike give off that now familiar faint pink glow. Alex's heart speeds up. She had a day of feeling safe with Francis underground. That's over. She knows it's Diya or her, and she must be cautious. She just might have to kill her.

Diya thinks, this woman, Alex, seems special to Francis. If she cares about this woman, she needs to die. I can at least hurt Francis that way. Like the bile in her gut, the hate roils, and she decides to follow this new woman. She doesn't know where she's going, but it shouldn't take long to get to her.

She ponders how to kill her, given she's protected in that suit. She has a small vial of poison with her, enough to do the job. She thinks, *I just need to get her close enough to wipe it on her suit without her knowing.*

As Alex rides off, she sees Diya tailing her. She's still not comfortable murdering anybody in cold blood. However, the thought of doing this entire trip with Diya riding behind her would also be intolerable. She needs to deal with her early and fast. She thinks, *I could ram her with my bike, get her on the ground, rip off her hood and shoot her.* She also thinks, *Diya could kill me first and certainly spray me with that lethal poison.* Alex decides that option is too dangerous. Still, she keeps her small atomizer of poison out and ready. "Get it on a glove or her bike handles," Frances had instructed.

Alex is still innocent in this perilous new world and naively thinks, *I'm just going to ride back and face her. Who knows, maybe we can resolve this.* Diya can't believe her eyes. Alex is riding straight toward her. She asks herself, *what's she up to?* She wonders if Alex has some extra killing gadget supplied by Francis that Diya is unaware of. She stops her bike and waits for Alex to ride up, all of her nerves on edge. Alex nears her but stays well back. Alex says, "I know you have poison and weapons and, for some reason, want to kill me. I want to know why. I don't even know you?" Diya says coldly, "Any friend of Francis' is an enemy of mine." Alex says incredulously, "So, you're just going to follow me wherever I go until you kill me?" Alex does not tell Diya where she's going, suspecting she doesn't know.

Diya coldly says, "That's the plan." Alex is near enough and Diya takes her chance and rushes her bike at her, with her poison atomizer extended. Alex quickly moves to the side, and Diya misses. Alex sees an opportunity and kicks Diya's bike hard as she passes. Diya's surprised by this and goes down, falling awkwardly and hard on her face. She feels an immediate sharp pain up through the middle of her forehead, and almost faints. She can feel hot blood inside her hood on her face. She's sure her nose is broken. Diya screams at Alex, with tears of pain running down her face, "You'll pay for this!"

Alex wasn't ready to kill her, but she knows if Diya wasn't an enemy before, she sure is now. She takes off fast and heads up the road. Diya's in too much pain to follow, but she will.

Two women with poison on their minds.

Now that Alex has this special gear, she can access Smart Homes along the way and stay there. She'll have to now, with Diya riding behind her, it's too dangerous to camp. Francis told her Diya can't get into Smart Homes, nor can she see their communications when Alex is in one, so she keeps her screen quiet. Most of these Smart Homes will have piles of people sand in them, but she'll have to get over that. She might have better access to food in freezers and coolers and not have to rely on the flavored wafers. She had wanted to ride through a few smaller towns in each province to provide more information for her soil, water, and vegetation sample reports. With Diya in her shadow, she needs to keep moving.

She plans to make Thunder Bay tonight, but it'll be a long day on the bike, with a few stops to pee and eat along the way.

Highway 400 was always slow in the summer. The large volume of cottage goers in the northbound armada of service cars was yet to begin; it's still only May. Today the car trains are at a standstill. There are very few bikes on the road. Her mirrors give her a quick vibration when someone's in view so she can easily stay out of their way. The last thing she needs is a bike collision. Diya's nowhere to be seen.

Alex has lots of time to think while she rides. Her mind goes to survivors on cruise ships. They would have come down for the breakfast buffet feed. There would be piles of shorts, t-shirts, sandals, and sand everywhere, but no other passengers or crew. Someone would head to the bridge, looking for a person in authority. They'd all be dead. Alex thinks but isn't certain that if no pilot is detected, ships, planes, and trains are programmed to dock, land, whatever, at the next available port, airport, or station. No worry about running out of fuel because they all run on solar. There would likely be many seniors on a cruise ship, many with money, so a more significant percentage of cancer survivors would have had the vaccine. Some of the crew might be alive but too junior and inexperienced to respond to a disaster like this. Maybe someone would take the lead, get to the sound system, and address the passengers to meet somewhere. There would be chaos.

Meanwhile, the ship would cruise along to the next port, and the survivors would have to figure out how to get into the lifeboats to get off. Only to land possibly on a tourist island now deserted, with dwindling food. If they're a little luckier, the ship might dock back in the states or whatever continent it sailed from, giving them more options. There would be more food reserves on the ship for a while. This would be a lot to handle for anyone, let alone someone with diminished physical capacity and stamina.

The few people left on planes would probably not find any pilots alive in the cockpit or one terrified one who can't contact the nearest tower. However, planes can land themselves, weather permitting. Bad weather usually needs an expert pilot, and that could be tricky. If the plane did successfully land, the few surviving passengers would have to figure out how to get off through the escape doors or slide down the rubber ramps, if they could figure out how to get those working. No ramp rats would be wheeling up sets of stairs. Then there would be the big empty airports, full of piles of clothes, sand, and luggage. She wonders if the gas or virus or whatever it was would have reached the elevations of the planes or the ships out in mid-ocean. Envisioning everything coming to a stop in the world is enormous. It's hard to stop thinking about the different scenarios of things people thought were important and now aren't.

Alex thinks about starvation a lot. She has had to fast a few times and hated it. She needs to eat. She felt like crap, nauseous, weak, and shaky, and her stomach hurt. It'd be a horrible way to die. Millions of survivors will certainly starve once all the food is gone. That will already be happening.

She wonders, *can this all blow off the earth into space and disappear? Can the world fix itself?* It's an unanswerable question.

Alex thinks of her last conversation with her mother. Her mother is a good-looking, active woman, lots of fun, lots of friends, and never short of a companion for dinner or a concert or whatever. They had a bit of a stiff conversation about the food supplies Alex had sent her for her birthday. She said, "Mom, I hate to envision you sitting around laughing with your friends about the present I gave you for your birthday, dismissing me as a worrywart who thinks the world will end. That food supply needs to be kept between you and me. It could save your life someday." Her mother was very silent at the other end of the call. Alex said, "Christ, mom, you've already told somebody, haven't you?" Her mother says, "I may have let it drop with a few friends, but you're a worrier, and I'll never need this food. Besides which, it's horrible." I would have preferred a spa day or something." Alex asked her where she'd put it and asked her to put it in their family vault. Again, silence. Alex asked again, "Where did you put it?" Her mother said, "It's under the sink right now, just to get it out of the way." Alex wanted to wring her neck. She said, "Mom, please, this is serious. Please put it in the vault right now. I'll wait." Her mother said, "Oh, alright, just to settle your mind."

When Alex's dad turned their house into a Smart Home, he built a secret storage area into the kitchen floor. It could only be accessed if you knew the right tile to press. It's a sizeable space for storing valuables. Alex always thought it was ingenious.

Her mother came back to the screen. "Okay, it's in there. Can we not talk about this anymore?" Her mother hates confrontation, particularly with Alex. Alex says, "Thank you. The topic is closed." Her mother went on to chat about a new guy who was a friend of a friend, somebody named Robert. Not Bob, not Rob...

Robert. *Sounds full of himself*, Alex thinks. Her mother had been seeing a bit of him and quite liked him. She said he was funny and a bit younger than her. Alex asks, "How much?" Her mother says, "Oh, ten or twelve years, or thereabouts." Alex thinks, *or fifteen, maybe?* She also thinks, *it's her business, and she's happy, so that's all that matters.*

Now Alex wonders if Robert knew about the food and if he has anything to do with her mother not responding to her calls. Her mother didn't tell her she and her friends had a tasting party for the wafers, with wine and lots of laughs. So much for that secret. She also didn't tell her that she shares her house security code with a few friends, so they don't have to wait to be identified when they visit her. So much for security. But Alex doesn't know this yet. Hopefully, there'll be some answers when she gets there. If she gets there. She mostly thinks, *I don't want to die.*

Diya returns to the house she's been camped out in, removes her hood, and surveys the damage on her face. Her nose sits slightly sideways, and her face is already swelling across her cheekbones and eyes and turning purple. She puts ice on her nose to stop the bleeding, applies a pain patch, and knocks her nose back into place with a firm push. She then vomits up breakfast and last night's dinner. She has to get back on the road, or she'll lose Alex's trail, and she so wants to kill her now. She washes her face, pulls down her hood, and heads out again. She's now several hours behind Alex, but she'll catch her.

As Diya rides, her thoughts run over her youth, and she briefly wonders about her mother's life after she left home. She thinks, *she's at least better off dead.* She doesn't think this out of any real concern, it's just a fact. Diya excelled in spy school and then moved quickly through the ranks to become a trusted international spy with assignments in various countries. She's now multi-lingual, although that skill won't do her much good anymore. Her country was pleased with her, and she enjoyed a large apartment in Delhi when she was home, which wasn't often. Her government wants her to disappear now. She knows too much. She doesn't know if anyone is left on this side of the world who would still be able to find her. She wonders why they would bother, given the state of the world now. She feels relatively free of Mother India. She does not think fondly of her parents or old acquaintances. She never had any real friends and didn't need them. She does not know that she's not the only one on the road following someone. She has her own shadow. She wonders where this Alex woman is going and what she's feeling and thinking. Fear, she hopes. Fear and stress can make you drop your guard and make mistakes.

Alex rides by Barrie but doesn't ride in. It was a stopover for groceries before you hit the cottage in its earlier days. It had become a bedroom community for Toronto. Few people commuted anymore.

Northern Ontario is primarily rocks, trees, small ponds, and lakes. The ponds are mossy and were probably alive with mosquitoes, flying things, and frogs. Not now. She's never enjoyed this portion of a road trip across Canada. It was always long and boring.

The roadside forests are dense and dark, with a lot of scrub brush and a few open meadows. There are no creatures scuttling in the underbrush. No deer, bears, foxes, coyotes, or wolves. No squirrels flying through the trees. No birds. It's been said that trees and plants communicate somehow. That makes sense. We're all in this together. She's happy the growing things weren't decimated by the gas bomb. At least so far. There must be quite a conversation going on between them now.

No one's on the road, not even parked service cars. Just her, Diya and a diligent silent stranger following Diya. Alex's bike flies, but so does Diya's. Alex has yet to see her in her rear mirrors, though.

She stops in Sudbury for lunch and a bathroom stop. She's never been there before, and it surprises her. It has way more greenery than she expected. She had anticipated a desolate industrial desert.

Alex always loved the sounds of a warm summer afternoon. The buzz of a distant lawnmower, kids squealing in someone's backyard pool. It's dead quiet now. Dead for sure. Lawns are already long overgrown; the gardens need weeding. City boulevards are knee high with grass and weeds. Dandelions are just floating seed pods in the air. She thinks again of all the old INCA sites in Mexico where the jungle had just moved in. It will happen here and everywhere. Except Canada does have winter to knock it back for six months.

She spots a Smart Home, does a wrist read on it with her chip, and gets back a blue read. Nobody's alive in there. She makes sure and walks around the house. Nope. All dead. It's her first 'break-in,' and it feels strange. She checks around to see if anyone is watching the door. It doesn't seem so, and Diya isn't visible. Her wrist chip slides the side door open, and in she goes, bike and all. She feels some relief as she drives into the house, and the door slides shut. Diya's nowhere to be seen, but Alex knows she's out there. Mr. dead guy is in the living room on the couch, watching the now black monitor. He had yet to dress because there was only a pair of pajama bottoms, a t-shirt, and slippers piled up over the now recognizable pile of sand. She finds the missus still in bed. Her very long sleep-in. Alex finds it unsettling walking around inside someone else's house, judging their décor, tidiness, and life. She checks their cooler and finds frozen bread and, in their cupboard, peanut butter. Pay dirt. She toasts herself a peanut butter sandwich and sees what else is still edible in there and finds an orange. Not a lot else, but lots in the freezer that will never be dethawed. These folks had a vegetable garden, but not much was up yet. Alex connects with Francis, giving her an update. Francis tells Alex that Diya's back on the road and on her trail. They have Diya's invisi-suit in their sights. She reminds Alex not to let Diya get close because of the risk of tossed poison. Like Alex can forget that.

She's not sure of the status of Smart Homes in Thunder Bay. She expects there wasn't much money up there to afford that kind of refurbishment. It should take her a couple of hours. She has to find a Smart Home tonight.

Chapter 15

A NEW LIFE

Jacob wakes to the smell of something cooking and remembers where he is. Junie sits with her back to him, stirring food in a pan on her fire, humming to herself. He wonders how she can sound so content in these scary times. He feels safer just being with her, though. She turns, sees he's awake and says, "Well, good morning. Are you hungry?" Jacob's always hungry. Like all teenagers, he's a burning furnace of calories. Junie says, "I expect you need to pee first, and just to be safe, I'm going to walk over to the latrines with you." She winks at him. "I have your back." They stroll over together, and she waits outside while he takes care of business. Junie is wise enough not to entirely trust their safety there and is always armed. They walk back to Junie's tent, and she serves him a steaming plate of food. He has no idea what it is, but it's filling, and he downs it quickly. Junie says, "Let's talk about what we'll do next." Jacob is hopeful Junie has a plan because he sure doesn't.

For many of his young years, Jacob had been watching how other people lived. He visited neighborhoods without security guards, where the houses were either semi-protected or not. It was where what you might call the rest of the people lived. He wanted more for himself but needed to figure out how to get there from here. He wasn't good in school, not that that mattered anymore, and he has no real skills. He knew he didn't want to end up like his dad, robbing houses and dealing in stolen goods.

There was an extensive park in the middle of one neighborhood he frequented. Nobody bothered him there. He was just an unarmed kid, not considered dangerous. The neighborhood was unguarded, and he could sit on a bench and watch without being bothered. One family had two young kids under six. If he got there early enough, he could catch the father getting picked up by a service car on Mondays and Fridays. He imagined him being taken to a train where he commuted into the city. He pictured the man in an office in a highrise with a desk job, doing whatever people did there to earn a salary. Enough to pay for the house they lived in. He couldn't imagine what one would do to earn that money.

The woman met other mothers at the park. She never came alone. Safety in numbers. Kids did all their pre-high school education online now. Parents without money had to consciously plan get-togethers for their kids to teach them socialization skills. They held big gatherings at least once a week. Some safe halls and parks specialized in that kind of thing with lots of free activities, workshops, sports camps for the kids, and free coffee and soft drinks for their parents. They could buy cheap lunches for everybody, and families made a day of it. It worked.

He didn't know the woman also worked, but at home. Their house was, of course, fully solar, and mostly fortified. Still, they had experienced several break-ins, and they both worried about their security all the time. Most of the people doing the breaking in came armed, like his dad, and the couple had learned to give them whatever they wanted rather than risk their lives. They were saving up to make their house a truly protected Smart Home, but they already had a heavy mortgage, and money was tight.

Jacob thought they were rich and envied them. He didn't realize they lived pay to pay and worried all the time, particularly about their kids' futures. They're relieved there's now a vaccine for cancer, even if they'd have to take out a second mortgage should they ever need it. They feel insecure in their home and their lives, and there's the constant threat of nuclear war. The employment landscape changes constantly, and it'll be hard for their kids to choose an education stream to match the needs of an economy that's so mercurial. You can train for something, and the work will be replaced by something different or better before you've finished your degree.

Then the attack came, and this young family's worries were reduced to four piles of sand in their beds. Jacob never returned to that park.

Junie starts talking with Jacob about what they need to continue living. Junie asks Jacob what he thinks. She doesn't want to dictate to him. She wants him to be part of this. These are life and death decisions. Jacob says, "I want to live in a Smart House in a good neighborhood." Junie asks, "What would you eat for the next ninety-odd years of your life?" Jacob says, "Most of the unprotected houses still have food. I would eat that." Junie says, "The food in those coolers will be unusable about now, except for maybe the bread, which won't last long. The food in the freezers will be unusable in less than a year." She says, "Do you have any other ideas?" Jacob hadn't thought that far down the road. He says, "Okay then, what would you do?"

Junie says, "You're right. We need a safe place to live, particularly in the winter months. Smart homes will be almost impossible for us to break into, so we need a house we can get into and then maybe fortify once we're in. As for food, the Camps have been living off of my little mini farm out back for years. If we could find a larger farm with an intermediate Smart House we can get into, and possibly a vertical farm for fruit and vegetables in the winter, that'd be perfect. It would require a lot of hands-on work from both of us. We also might be able to help other survivors. What do you think about becoming a farmer?"

Jacob had never thought about farming in any way, let alone him being a farmer. He also hadn't thought of other survivors, people needing help. He was a one-man show in his head. Junie watches Jacob's face as he digests these ideas. She wonders if he can grow up quickly enough to meet the challenges ahead. She needn't have worried. In his mind, Jacob has already joined Junie's army. He thinks she's the greatest and wants to get started. He says, "I don't know anything about farming, but you could teach me."

Junie says, "I've been thinking about all the farms in Niagara on the Lake. We could take over one of them and work it out. I know for sure many have vertical farms. Why don't we do some scouting?"

The next day they ride off to Niagara on the Lake. It's not far up the road. Junie knows most of the farms pretty well. She's worked on many of them. House access is a crucial ingredient. They ride up the lanes and try house doors, some of which are open. They find piles of sand under clothes in these houses. The people who lived here felt secure enough to leave their doors unlocked. Many of these farms are a mixture of orchards and vineyards and would be hard to convert. They find several with vertical farms. Junie has watched how computerized farming works but has never had her hands on the keyboard. She has complete confidence she can figure it out. She's technologically savvy for a farm girl. Even though he's not a techie, Jacob knows a thing or two about that stuff. He's thirteen, and all teenagers know more than her. Jacob races around, looking at everything. He envisions Junie and him running a farm, maybe feeding other people. His new potential life unfolds in his imagination.

When they return to Junie's tent, they sit down and discuss their choices. Junie says, "There's still lots of food to harvest, and wherever we choose, we'll need to do that by hand while we figure out the bot system." She asks Jacob, "Was there anywhere you could see yourself living? You were excited about every farm we went to today. Did you have a favorite?" Jacob definitely had a favorite. It was a big modern farmhouse they could get into, with lots of room. He remembers it was called the Argyle. He has never lived anywhere with lots of space. It has many acres of vineyards out back, an orchard, and a vertical farm. He can see them living happily there. He tells Junie which one. She says, "That one was my first choice too."

Junie says, "It's decided then, the Argyle farm it is. Let's make one more visit before we make the move." She eyes Jacob sharply and says, "We also need to get you into some fresh clothes. Have you even changed since the attack?" Jacob looks at her sheepishly and, with a grin, says, "No, do I stink?" Junie says with a kind smile, "Yes, son, you do."

Chapter 16

BABES IN THE WOODS

Alex is enjoying the speed and lightness of her bike. She's not looking forward to the brutal windstorms on the prairies and doubts she'll get through unscathed. Her bike is so light the wind could easily pick it up. Francis warned her to find shelter rather than try to rough it out in a prairie windstorm. Her life is on this bike. She can't risk losing either.

It's late afternoon, the shadows are getting longer, and she's nearing Thunder Bay. Thunder Bay's claim to fame was it was the homicide capital of Canada, not a destination of choice. Between poverty, homelessness, mental health, and addiction issues, nothing ever got fixed. Bombardier was the principal employer here. It was a prominent manufacturer of mass transit vehicles, mainly floater service cars, but that was big business. Thunder Bay's other claim to fame was the Fort William Historical Park. It's a reconstruction of the North West Company's Fort William fur trade post, as it was in the early 1800s. A memorial of the beginning of the Indians' troubles. Alex wonders if they hated that place.

Diya knows Francis gave Alex an access tool to Smart Homes that she wishes she also had. There wasn't anything in the Connecticut spy's kit that could do that. She doesn't know it's an arm chip. She hasn't picked up any communication between Francis and Alex and wonders if she's been blocked.

Alex sees Diya in her bike mirrors. She's caught up. Not good. It's been a very long day, and Alex is body tired and stressed when she pulls off the highway toward town. She thinks, *Diya's going to follow me to a Smart Home and we're going to have another murderous altercation. I'm still not ready to kill anybody, even her.* She watches for her, but Diya is strangely no longer behind her. She doesn't realize Diya, tired and dozy from her painkillers, missed Alex making the turn. When Diya realized she'd lost her, she cursed herself, turned back, and tried to find Alex on the road. She'd disappeared into the bowels of Thunder Bay.

Diya's pain has sharpened on this ride, and she needs to apply more pain patches and lie down. She decides to camp out on the highway and wait Alex out. She doubts Alex will ride on tonight. She'll be looking for a place to sleep too, but she'll find a Smart Home. Diya's sure Alex will ride by her campsite tomorrow, and she'll be waiting for her. For now, she needs to sleep. Diya thinks it's only a short matter of time before she takes Alex out. Then she'll ride back to Kingston and wait for Francis and her entourage to surface. She has plans for them. If she doesn't die first.

Alex scouts the higher-end houses along the river, sees a good prospect and slows. She then says to herself, *oh crap*. A kid is standing outside of it. It's the last thing she wanted to see on this trip. It's a small girl, very young, about six. She's thin and her dark, straight, thick hair looks dirty and uncombed. She could be First Nations; Alex isn't sure. She's in shorts and a matching top of blue stripes with sneakers and no socks. She's crying and just standing there with her little shoulders heaving. Alex thinks again, *Crap*. She turns around and rides back to her, checking her bike mirror for Diya. There's no sign of her but this is dangerous. She could ride up anytime.

Alex wonders how she can introduce her invisible self to this terrified little girl without scaring the hell out of her. She dismounts, takes out a pair of pink glasses, and says, "Hi, don't be scared. My name is Alex, and you can't see me because I'm in a special invisible suit. Maybe you saw that in the movies?" Alex can't think of a movie, but she throws that out there, anyway. The little girl is now wildly looking around, trying to find the source of Alex's voice. Alex says, "There'll be some glasses that'll appear in front of you. Don't be scared. Put them on, and then you can see me." The girl stops crying, and Alex gives her the glasses, which will look like they're floating in the air toward her. Probably the weirdest thing this little girl has ever experienced in her short life. Alex is counting on the young girl's lack of experience to not turn this into something too scary. She tells the girl, "Just put them on, and this will all make sense." The girl backs away from the floating glasses, but then, brave little thing that she is, she grabs them, puts them on, and stares at Alex.

Alex says again, "Hi. See, not so scary. I'm just a girl in an invisible suit on an invisible bike." She thinks, *right, like you'd see every day in Thunder Bay*. She asks her, "What's your name?" The girl says, still staring wildly at Alex's pink outline, "Mommy told me to never talk to strangers, and you're a stranger." Alex says, "And a little strange too," but the girl doesn't get the joke. Alex says, "Your mommy is very smart, and you should always be careful, but I'm not going to hurt you, honest. I just wanted to find out why you were crying." She thinks, *like, I don't know.* The girl says, "I woke up a long time ago, and my mommy was gone, just her nighty in the bed, and daddy didn't come home from work, and I don't know where they are. They don't answer my calls, and neither do my abuela y abuelo or my Toronto grandma and grandpa." Alex thinks, *okay, that answers one thing. She's part Spanish, probably Mexican.* The girl starts crying again, saying, "My brother is inside and won't wake up." Alex thinks, *oh Christ, there's two of them, and this little girl doesn't realize her mother is still in that bed, dead.*

Alex asks, "Is this your house?" The girl nods while she sobs, shoulders still heaving. Alex says, "Can we go in and check on your brother? Maybe I can help." She thinks, *What the hell do I know about unconscious little kids?* She asks the girl, "How old is he?" She says, "He just turned three." Alex thinks, *great, two babies. What the hell am I doing?* Alex's mind is racing. The little weeping girl is sticking to her guns and not moving.

The problem has just compounded because Alex sees a biker approaching. It's not Diya, but she needs to hide the girl quickly. She says, "We need to hide you from that biker coming down the street to stay safe. I'll stand in front of you, and you can hide behind me, so he won't see you. Do you understand?" The girl nods. Alex shields her somewhat from the biker's view as he passes by. He slows down and looks. He's sure he saw a kid as he approached, and he's sure he saw a hand and a leg all on their own as he rode by, but now he thinks he may be losing his mind. He rides on, looking back over his shoulder. Alex thinks, *poor bugger, he's going to start believing in ghosts after that.*

Alex says, "I'm going in to check on your brother. You can come in with me or not. I promise I'm not going to hurt him or you. I just want to help." She wheels her bike over to the door and applies her wrist to the entry reader. The door opens. The girl asks, "How did you do that?" Alex decides it will be best to be straight up with this kid. She rolls back her sleeve, shows her the wrist chip bump under her skin, and tells her what it can do. She also tells her she's looking for her mom, too. Alex figures there'll be a better time to tell this little girl her mother is dead. Now's not the time. She moves her bike inside and looks at the girl and asks, "Are you coming?" The girl follows Alex in.

Alex strips off her invisi-suit, and the girl is all big staring brown eyes. Alex says, "See, just a normal person. The girl can't take her eyes off her, trying to figure out this weird woman dressed in black in her house.

Alex asks, "Where is he? What's his name?" The girl leads her to her brother's room and tells Alex, "Tom." The room smells like fever, urine, and shit. This little guy is unconscious, hot as hell, face flushed, soaking wet, and a mess in his pajamas. She has to do something to bring his fever down fast. She contacts the medics in Kingston. Kingston is her new Houston. She says, "Hi guys. I have a bit of a problem here. This little boy is sick, and I don't know where to start other than try to bring his fever down." She detaches the scanner from the bike, presses his wrist health chip against the commute button, and sends over the reading. "Can someone there tell me what's wrong with him and give me some advice?" She waits. Ten minutes pass, but it feels like an hour. She holds little Tom limp on her lap while she waits. She asks the girl again what her name is, and finally, she tells her, "Anna."

The screen lights up. It's Francis. She grins at Alex and says, "It didn't take you long to get into trouble. I won't even say anything about your situation. We'll figure that out later. We're pretty sure he has viral meningitis. He can survive it, but you need to run a cool bath and bring his temperature down fast. He's very sick." *No kidding*, Alex thinks as she holds this hot little fellow in her arms. Francis says, "Viral meningitis doesn't respond to antibiotics, but if you keep him cool and get some fluids into him, he'll come around. In your kit, you have some high-dose ibuprofen patches. Cut them into thirds and apply one to his chest. It will help to bring the fever down. Reapply a patch every four hours. He's very dehydrated, so see if the little girl can find a baby bottle or funnel to get some liquid into him. Report back when you can. Don't worry; we're here." Alex thinks wryly, *yeah, don't worry*. Francis says, "Diya's parked outside town on the edge of the highway, probably waiting for you to come by." Alex thinks, *at least she's not across the street*.

Alex runs a cool bath, removes Tom's soaking wet pajamas and smelly diaper, and steps out of her own pants. She gently and slowly drops him in. She soaps him up and washes his hair. He needs a haircut. His eyes roll back in his head, and he doesn't wake up. She has to be very careful holding on to his now soapy, slippery little bare bummed unconscious self. Anna sits on the toilet and watches her quietly. Alex asks her if there might be a baby bottle around as that might be easier to get some liquid into him. She thinks it isn't long since he would have had a bottle. Anna scurries off and brings one to her. Alex fills it with warm water and gives him a small drink while he's still in the tub. It washes out of his mouth. She keeps trying, and finally, his mouth begins to suckle.

A recent memory, she hopes. Little Tom takes in a tiny bit of water. Alex asks Anna if they have a thermometer, and again, she goes off and brings one back to her. She puts it under his arm for now. No point sticking it into orifices that might be problematic. He's still very hot but doesn't seem as bad as before the bath. Alex tells Anna what a great job she's doing helping. She asks if she can find some clean pajamas for him and a clean diaper or pull-up. Anna goes and gets them. Tom has not opened his eyes. Alex is terrified. *Don't die on me, little guy,* she thinks. Thankfully, there's an ample supply of pull-ons. He's still being potty trained. Lovely. He probably won't be getting up to the toilet for a while, and Alex will be changing diapers.

She continues to try to get some water into him. He responds a bit more, not opening his eyes but continuing to suckle on the nipple. He's still a baby. She gets him out of the bath, towels him off, and wraps him up in it. She asks Anna where the clean sheets are and suggests they change the bed and do the laundry. Anna says she knows how to do that, and they strip the messed bed together. She stuffs all the soiled sheets in the washing machine and gets that going. Alex gets Tom into some pull-on diapers and clean pajamas and lays him down on the couch while she and Anna remake the bed. The room already smells fresher. One day on the road, and she's already saddled with two little kids, one of them very sick. It could be a better start.

Alex realizes these kids must have both had cancer to have had the vaccine and survived. Yikes, what a nightmare for their parents. She asks Anna what they had. She says, "Leukemia." Saved from that for this. What a heartbreaker. She brings Tom back to bed and tucks him in. Anna says he likes it in mommy and daddy's bed. Alex still needs to find a way to tell Anna about her mother's pile of sand under the covers, but it's still too soon. She says, "Let's keep him close to us for now. The kitchen is just around the corner. Do you think that's a good idea?" She wants badly for this little girl to trust her. Anna nods. Alex then remembers it's way past suppertime. "I'm starving." She says, "Are you hungry? What have you and Tom been eating?" Anna says, "Cereal, bread, and juice, but the almond milk got yucky. Mommy told me not to use the stove or microwave." Alex asks her if there's powdered milk in the house or baby formula. Anna says, "Maybe powdered baby formula up in the top of the cupboard." Alex looks, and sure enough, there's an ample supply left over from Tom's recent babyhood. She mixes some up in a bottle for him, warms it up, and takes it in to him. He takes the bottle. Yahoo. She is so relieved to get something into him. He drinks nearly half of it, eyes never really opening, and then falls back to sleep.

Their mom had frozen at least a month's worth of casseroles. Each one is large, and they can spread it out over a few days. Sam did the cooking in Alex's former life, so she's glad she doesn't have to cook. *Thank you, mommy,* she says in her head to the pile of sand upstairs. She says to Anna, "We'll warm up one of the casseroles your mom made tonight and stay close to Tom." She goes back in to check on him. His face is still pink and sweaty. She goes into their parent's bedroom. Anna's mother is there, a pile of sand under the covers. Anna just never bothered to pull the covers off because they had gone flat, and she didn't think her mother was in there. She just assumed her mother was gone and didn't twig. Why should she? Alex tucks mom's sand under the covers.

They eat, but Anna is still very stone-faced and apprehensive. Alex says, "You've done a wonderful job taking care of Tom all this time. That must have been scary and hard work." Anna says, "I remembered how mommy did most things, but he never wanted to brush his teeth, and I didn't like changing his diapers. Stinko." Alex smiles at her and says, "Yes, one of the nasty things of life, poop." Alex scans Tom again and sends it over to the lab. They respond immediately. "Much improved, temperature coming down, but remember, you'll need to apply the ibuprofen every four hours." *Like I'd forget.* She thinks. It's now almost 9:30 PM, and she's running on adrenalin.

Alex suggests they both sleep with Tom tonight. He at least has a double bed. It will be a bit crowded, but she can reapply the ibuprofen without disturbing the two of them. She sets a timed alarm. She says, "Do you want to have a shower and brush your teeth before you go to bed? It'll make you feel better." Anna says okay and does. While Anna's in the shower, Alex quickly checks Anna and Tom's parents' medicine cabinet and drawers for drugs like ibuprofen strips. There's a locked cabinet with every imaginable kind of medication. One of her parents must have been a doctor or nurse. She'll go through everything later to see what she can use. The house is large and low-slung, with a partial upper floor for the parents' bedroom and office. It's modern, comfortable, open, and sunny, with tall windows, large spread-out sofas and screens, books everywhere, and interesting, unique art. They had taste and education and were doing well.

Anna comes out of the shower, a tiny little waif with wet straight dark hair, slightly tanned skin, and big dark eyes. Alex combs out her hair. It's thick and tangled. She helps her dry it and gets her into her pajamas. Alex is feeling uncomfortably domestic. She says again, "It'll be okay. We'll get through this." Anna starts to cry again and asks, "Where are mommy and daddy?" Alex lies and says, "I'm still figuring that out, but you're okay. You're safe." Anna says, "You won't leave us alone, will you?" Alex says, "Absolutely not. You're safe with me." She's not as sure of that as she'd like to be, but she wants this little lost girl to feel safe. They tuck into Tom's bed under his comforter with the blue ponies. Tom and Anna snuggle up together. Alex is on the outside, curled around them. It's only been a few hours since she met these kids, and she has a sick little boy against her belly and his terrified sister beside him. They all fall asleep deeply until the alarm vibrates four hours later. She checks Tom's diaper and reapplies his drug sticker. Anna doesn't even wake up.

Alex wakes with a start in the morning and looks at Tom. His face is much less feverish, he's no longer quite as hot, and his eyes are open. He immediately screams when he sees Alex, calling out for his mother. "Mum, Mum, Mum." He's sick and sobbing uncontrollably, terrified of this stranger so close to him. Alex thinks, *trust me, Tom, I wish she were here too*. Not to be. The med people back in Kingston told her he would probably have a headache and be nauseous. She needs to keep him cool, pain-free, and hydrated and wait it out. She gives him another bottle, and he vomits up the little bit of liquid she got into him. He looks at Anna and whimpers in his soft little boy voice, "Where's mommy?" Aaah, the big question. Her wise, six-year-old self says, "We're looking for her, don't worry." Anna calms him down, but he still stares at Alex in fear and uncertainty. She says, "Tom, I'm Alex, and I'm here to help you feel better." He's still groggy, and she doubts he understands much of her little speech. She asks him if he needs to pee, and he nods with big raindrop tears running down his face. He allows her to carry him in and set him down on his little potty. He's very modest and says in his little boy voice, "Don't look." She looks away and hears the tinkle. At least some things are normal.

Alex asks him if he's hungry, and he nods. She suggests they have some breakfast together. She's hoping to get something solid into him. The little guy is still very weak, so she carries him to a highchair at the kitchen bar and checks the pantry for possible breakfast options. There are juice packages in the cooler, and she pulls these out for both kids to get them started. She asks herself again, "What the hell am I doing in Thunder Bay making breakfast for two little kids with a woman who wants to kill me trolling the streets outside? I haven't even made it out of Ontario. I don't like kids particularly and sure don't know what to say to them. This is screwing up my plans." They had eaten through the cereal in the past six weeks, but there's lots of bread in the freezer, so that's a start. She wants to get something healthy into them both. There are packaged pseudo-omelets, so she makes these up with some toast. She wonders how her flavored wafers will go down with them if she has to resort to them. She hopes they're not picky eaters.

Tom has his juice and a couple of mouthfuls of omelet and eats some of his toast. He's falling asleep in his chair. He's getting warm again, so she carries him back to bed, checks his pull-on, still dry, applies a cold cloth to his face and chest, and stays with him until he's back to sleep. She'll give him another cool bath when he needs it. His temperature is high, but no longer dangerously so. He's still fighting it. At least he kept breakfast down. *We're going to be here for a while*, she thinks.

She checks in with Kingston and asks how long it might take him to recover. They tell her about a week to 10 days. That gives her some time to come up with a new plan.

Days go by, and she's exhausted and weepy when she's awake enough to feel sorry for herself. Tom wavers between being sick and feverish and a typical chatty, active three-year-old, like she knows what that is. Then his temperature flips up, and they start all over again. Anna relaxes a bit. She continues asking Alex whether she knows where her mom and dad are and where her grandparents are. Alex always says, "I'm still trying to figure that out." She thinks, *what a liar I am*. Anna becomes more talkative and shows Alex pictures of a Spanish-looking older couple taken with her and Tom. It looks like they're at a restaurant table. She says, "These are my daddy's mom and dad. They're from Mexico. We call them abuela y abuelo. Daddy speaks Spanish at home, so we can talk with them. They can speak English but like to speak Spanish with us. They have a restaurant here. We go there lots." She then shows me a picture of another happy couple with the kids and says, "These are my mommy's mom and dad, my grandma and grandpa. They live in Toronto and come to see us as much as possible, but mommy says it's a long way. They sleep in my bedroom when they come, and I sleep with Tom. I've called them a lot, but they don't answer either."

Alex knows she has to take these kids with her or stay here. That's not an option. She has to figure out how to safely get the three of them out of here, with Diya following them. Diya doesn't seem to have any problem killing people.

Anna chats about what she learned in grade one, and Alex finds grades two to eight on her tablet and her mom's. She's such a clever little thing, and Alex will have to figure out homeschooling when she gets them to Victoria, if she gets them that far. She'll be getting a hell of an education in the coming days and years.

Chapter 17

TRUTH AND CONSEQUENCES

It's time to have a serious talk with Anna about her parents and her grandparents. Francis advises honesty is the best. She says to Alex, "Tell her everything, including the part about her mother in the bed. She'll see a lot more piles of sand in her lifetime, so you may as well start with her mother. If you can find their father, all the better."

Alex sits Anna down and says, "I have something to talk to you about." Anna stares at her with her big eyes. Alex starts with the big picture, what may have happened, the satellite bomb theory, and the survival connection to the vaccine. She keeps it simple. She then moves on to when she first found Princie, hoping to introduce her to the idea impersonally. A dog sand pile isn't too scary, unless it's your dog. She's trying to keep it not too gruesome. She then tells her about finding Sam and his weird disintegration into sand. Anna stares at her, her little brain making the horrible quick connection.

She asks solemnly, "Are my mom and dad dead?" She pauses, then asks, "Are they sand?" Alex thinks, *here we go*, and says as gently as she can, "If they didn't get the vaccine, that's what happened to them. It's what happened to everybody on earth, I think." There, it's out.

Anna looks at Alex in horror and yells accusingly, "You're lying!" She races up to her parent's bedroom, and Alex follows her. Anna pulls back the covers. There is her mother's nighty, the sand, and a tiny glitter of gold. Anna starts to panic, looks up at Alex with wide, pleading eyes, and asks, "Is that really mommy?" Alex says, "I'm sorry, honey, but yes, it's her." The tears start. Anna's mouth opens wide and seems to lock before a sound comes out. She's inconsolable. Alex doesn't know how to comfort her. She's not much of a hugger, and Anna doesn't want to be touched right now, anyway. Alex sits with her and acknowledges how sad it all is. She says to her, "Cry your heart out, honey. I did when I saw Sam and my dog. It's the only way to get through this. Feel as sad as you need to." Anna is pacing around the room, fists clenched. She doesn't know what to do with her horrible sorrow and fear. Alex tells her, "I'll try to find your dad and bring his sand back here to be with your mommy." Anna looks at her, the reality sinking in; her parents aren't coming back, ever.

Not really knowing what to do next, Alex thinks, *be practical*. She says, "Let's get your mom's sand into a bag, so we don't lose any of her." Between sobs, Anna says softly, "Okay." Anna touches her mother's nighty and puts her fingers in the sand. So much for her to take in. The gold turns out to be a very delicate necklace with four intertwining hearts. Alex asks Anna, "Did your daddy give this to your mom?" Anna is hiccupping air in her tearful response, "Yes, for Mother's Day." Alex says, "I bet your mom would want you to have it." She retrieves it from the pile and clips it on her. Anna looks at herself in the mirror and touches the hearts, barely controlling her trembling lower jaw. She says, "Where's daddy's sand?" Alex tells her she'll go to his office and try to find him. She says, "I can't promise I'll find him, but I'll try." She thinks she might have to lie about this, given Diya is waiting outside for her somewhere. Her scruples are no longer an asset. They shake out the nighty, pour Anna's mother into a pillowcase, and place her back on the bed. It's an awful thing for a six-year-old to have to watch.

Alex suggests they go downstairs and get Tom and make up some hot chocolate, and then Anna can tell her all about her mom and dad. They leave the bedroom with Anna looking back over her shoulder at the bed and her mother's pillowcase of sand.

Alex sits down with Tom in her lap and asks Anna, "What are their names?" Anna says, "Dierdre and Tomas, but everybody called my dad Tom. Tom is named after him, but his name is just Tom." Alex asks, "And what's your last name? Anna says, "Castaneda." She takes Alex on a tour of the family pictures scattered throughout the house. A happy foursome, a laughing little red-headed mom, and a short and swarthy good-looking dark-haired dad, a Mexican lad, both in their late twenties. Tom is on his shoulders; Anna is leaning against her mother, holding her hand. The good old days, just a few weeks ago.

Anna says, "My mom had short, red, curly hair. Tom and I didn't get it. We got our dad's hair." "And eyes," Alex says, "You both have gorgeous dark eyes." Anna says, "Mommy's were blue. She used to say we had chocolate eyes." Alex likes that description of their eyes; they are dark chocolate brown. She continues to prod. "And how about your dad? What was he like?" Anna says, "He's really strong; he can lift mommy and Tom at the same time." Alex says, "Wow, that's really strong."

She asks, "Did he make you laugh?" Anna says, "My mom says daddy thinks he's SOOO funny." She's obviously imitating how her mother teased her father with this comment.

Feeling like the grand inquisitor, Alex continues. "Did your mom work?" Anna says, "She was a nurse on the phone." Alex says, "So she worked at home?" She thinks she must have had a challenging caseload here in Thunder Bay. That explains the fully stocked medicine cabinet." Anna says, "Yes, Tom and me weren't supposed to go into her office except when she opened the door. Tom didn't always listen, but mommy never really got mad." She smiles at him and pats him in a big sister patronizing kind of way. He's just listening and watching them both. He knows something is making his sister cry but doesn't know what. He says, "Don't cry, Anna," in his little boy voice and reaches out to hug her. Sweet little guy, already kind. Alex continues, "and your dad, what did he do?" She says, "He built houses." Alex thinks, *aaah. A real estate developer. She may never be able to find his pile of sand.* She asks, "Do you remember what company he worked for?" Anna says, "Castaneda Developments." Alex deduces, *so, he owned the company. They live in a very nice house, so they must have been doing well.*

That was the hard part, and at least now Anna knows her parents and grandparents aren't coming back. She can start the very beginning of healing. Alex knows what a long road that is. She's still on it.

Alex thinks, if I can get these kids to sleep tonight, I'll take one of their parents' bikes, just wear black, and I'll go out to find dad. She thinks, *Diya won't be expecting a woman to be riding around in the dark.* They eat, and she gets the kids ready for bed and sticks another patch on Tom's tummy. Alex tells Anna, "If you wake up in the middle of the night and notice I'm not here, I'm only out looking for your dad's sand. I'll be back, I promise." Anna's eyes fill. Alex says again, "I promise." She asks Anna, "Can you sleep with Tom again tonight? I'm going to sleep on the couch." Anna nods, and Alex asks if they would like her to read to them. Anna says, "My mom and dad read to us every night." They select a book together, and she spoons around them and reads them to sleep. Anna is exhausted from crying, and Alex is just exhausted.

"*The best laid schemes o'mice an' men gang aft agley.*" Thank you, Robert Burns. There was no search for dad that night. Alex fell dead asleep on the couch and slept through the night. She forgot to turn on the alarm for Tom's patch. At first light, she wakes with a jolt and thinks. *Some mommy I am.* She changes Tom's diaper and applies another pain patch. He's still running a temperature, but not too bad. He whimpers a bit but goes back to sleep. He's quite clingy and often falls asleep in her lap, sucking his thumb.

Alex thinks, so, this is single parenting. Terrifying and completely exhausting, and heart-stealing in one big messy package.

She decides to wait to leave the house at night to search for dad's sand when Tom feels better.

Chapter 18

SHE'S GOT A TICKET TO RIDE

Alex and Francis discuss the challenges of Alex taking the kids with her on the road, particularly with Diya hovering. Alex knows Diya would kill all of them, but she sure doesn't want to stay in Thunder Bay. They decide to hide in plain sight, going without the invisibility suits, and riding a regular solar bike with a sidecar for the kids. Diya doesn't know what Alex looks like, nor would she be expecting her to be traveling with two kids without the protection of the invisi-suit and bike. Alex will pack the kids' invisi-suits, her tamped down invisi-bike, and her gear in a saddlebag. It's a dangerous option but it just might shake Diya off their tail. Alex can always zap anybody who tries to attack them, other than Diya. She knows now she has to kill her.

Francis says, "You do realize it won't even be as simple as that, and that's not very simple. These two are babies. You need to get them and you safely across the country while being followed by a murderous, angry, mentally unsound woman, then across part of the Pacific Ocean, and then be their mother for the rest of your life. In a world with no food, you'll be the only one with food. You'll have to hide out for the rest of your life. You've bitten off a huge chunk of life, dear friend." Alex laughs miserably because she has no choice other than to leave them to die. That's not happening. She says to Francis, "Yes, remember that conversation we had that night? No kids for me. That didn't last long."

Alex is resigned to her new fate and knows she has to get on with it. She says, "First, I need to find a suitable roadworthy sidecar with a bubble top." Francis says, "According to my records, there's only one bike store in Thunder Bay, and I doubt they're big enough to have sidecars, let alone hooded ones. You may have to go back to Sudbury." Alex says, "Too dangerous. Tom's still sick. I can't leave him alone just yet and go to Sudbury, let alone risk getting killed and never returning to them at all."

After about ten days, Tom's temperature is back to normal. He's sleeping through the night, and she cuts back on his drug patches. It's time for her to check out the bike store. She's thankful her GPS still works. She searches the area and finds the bike store and the kids' dad's office. Thunder Bay isn't very big. Francis confirms Diya is still outside the city, and Alex takes her chance. She waits until the kids are asleep. It's dark, and she rides out on one of their parents' bikes, lights off, hoping she won't be picked up by Diya or anyone else. The bike store is still locked but brightly lit, with all its inventory still on the sales floor. She guesses not many survivors needed solar bikes. They're not edible.

She turns off all the store lights as she enters, but there are no sidecars on the sales floor. There's a small warehouse in the back. *Please*, she says to herself, *let there be a sidecar back here*. The warehouse is crammed with boxes of accessories on shelves and the floor. It's a disorganized mess. Back in the corner, under a pile of loose boxes, she sees a gleam of metal. Lifting the cardboard, she sees a sidecar, a sturdy aluminum little green vehicle with a pullover rain hood. There are three different styles jammed in back here. She reads the bumpf about each one. She chooses the most expensive one with the heat and air conditioning option. She'll need that if the kids aren't going to be in their invisi-suits. She then chooses the most powerful bike on the sales floor. She also picks up three audio helmets so she can communicate with the kids while they're riding. She thinks, *I hope this will be safe for the kids, but I don't have any choice. I have to get to my mother and we're not staying here for the rest of our lives. I have to risk it.*

She hooks up the sidecar to the new bike and exits through the double door at the back of the shop. One task done.

Now she's off to find dad. It was early when the attack happened. He'd already left for work, so maybe he was in his office when it hit. Alex thinks, *I hope he wasn't in a service car en route when it hit. I'll never be able to find him then*. She finds his office on a side street. It's well-signed and looks flourishing. She can't imagine real estate development in Thunder Bay being too lucrative. Still, his business probably encompassed the entire region and included commercial sites. The front door is still locked, but there are lights on inside. She goes in, passing by the empty cubicles of desks to find the boss's office.

The door's closed. Alex opens it and finds his sand pile drifting off his office chair and onto the floor. Pictures of the family abound on his back credenza. A loving daddy. She's now getting too used to shaking sand out of clothes and sweeping it up. A bag in his garbage pail hasn't been used, and she drops his remains into that. It's an ignominious end for a guy who seemed like a wonderful dad, husband, son, and provider. She'll bring him back to the house and thinks she and Anna can then decide what to do with him and her mother. The backyard garden is an option. Overgrown, but maybe they can clean it up together and place their piles of sand there. Anna likes projects. It's a possibility.

Alex rides back to the house in the dark, terrified about the future for the three of them. Can she do this?

She's well into the third week with the Castaneda kids. She's put dad in a matching pillowcase with mom, and the two of them are upstairs on the bed, side by side. Anna goes there often and sits beside the bed. Alex lets her be. Tom seems to have warmed to Alex and will sit in her lap and come for a hug, and they play with his cars, trucks, and puzzles and draw and color together. She's never been a video game player, but he has simple ones they can play. He chats away about everything with lots of questions. "Why do cats meow and not bark?" "Why do flowers grow?" "Why do birds fly so fast?" Alex thinks, *all good questions, Tom*. She makes up silly answers, and he loves this game.

Anna is still deeply mourning her parents and alternates between quiet weeping and just being quiet. She's very depressed, and Alex has no idea what to do for her. Francis says, "Let her process it. She'll be okay." Now and then, Tom asks, "Where's mommy?" or "Where's daddy?" but seems to be satisfied with the "We're looking for them" answer, and the question seems to have subsided.

Anna does like a plan. "What are we doing today?" Alex remembers kids are programmed for activities; dance, sports, music, play dates, and school. She can't offer any of that to either of them right now, if ever. There'll be no kids to play with, just a few scared and worried adults like her. Anna will have to adjust to her new reality, but they'll all be busy just surviving. That will be the new activity.

Alex tries to sketch out the day for her. The blind leading the blind, for sure. They live as though there's no danger outside, the world hasn't ended, and life is normal. They pretend there are endless meals in the freezer and no dangerous trip ahead of them. It's an insane bubble. They plan the meals for the day and if they need to do laundry. They vacuum and dust like two little homemakers, and Anna has started on her grade two work. She loves to read, so Alex assigns her books from her parents' library she thinks she'll be able to handle and asks her to provide a report at the end of each day.

She tells her they need to make up little invisi-suits for the two of them, like hers. Anna takes to this project and looks at the patterns on the screen Francis has supplied. With the special pink glasses on, they figure out what needs to be done with the fabric. It's kind of fun and much easier than she thought it would be, given the fabric adheres to itself. No sewing required.

She'd like to take them for a test drive in the sidecar, but that's not safe. She hopes Tom doesn't get motion sickness or scared.

For Tom, Alex follows the toilet training instructions she found in a book in their mother's library. She creates a schedule, sets a timer, and sits him on the potty every hour with rewards for production. She's not supposed to hurry him. Alex thinks, *well, there's a bit of a hurry, Mrs. author of toilet training. We've got to get moving.* She's been working the routine; they have good and poopy days. This is her new life, thrilled if Tom poops in his potty and eats all his supper and if Anna smiles.

Alex tells Anna she has a bit of Sam and Princie's sand with her and asks if she would like to have some of her parents with her. Anna thinks about this for a while and says, "I don't want to leave them. Can't we take them all?" Alex gently reminds her they have limited space, but if she could find a small container, she could take part of them with her and have them forever. She introduces the idea of putting Anna's parents' remains in the back garden. Alex says, "We'd need to clean up the garden and get it ready for them. What do you think?" Anna says incredulously, "You mean bury them out there like we did with my turtle?" Alex thinks, *maybe not the best suggestion after all. There's probably a goldfish or two out there too.* She says to Anna, "Where would you like them to be?" *Besides alive and here with you instead of me,* she privately thinks. She says to Anna, "We'll do whatever you want." They do nothing.

Chapter 19
KINGSTON - A MAP OF THE FUTURE

Francis wants her team to develop tactical plans and options for their lives, start thinking about the future, and move on from what's happened. She's not an authoritarian leader. She likes to build teams of engaged people who feel they're doing something worthwhile while enjoying their work and lives. She decides to give a 'state of the union' talk and ask for input on her ideas. Once these are received, they'll develop project teams, determine who'll work on what, and get things done.

She has psyche workups on every one of her contractors and knows all their strengths and weaknesses. The leaders and potential leaders, the strategists, the rule followers, the troublemakers, and those likely to fall apart and/or bolt have all been identified. These contractors were pre-screened thoroughly, and applicants with problems or who might create problems were eliminated early. They didn't catch them all. They missed Diya and that's turned deadly.

She's prepared well and gathers them together. Her heart goes out to the searching faces in the room. They hope she has a solution. *Please fix this for us*, their eyes and faces say.

She looks warmly out at them all and begins, "As you know, the attack on our world brought an irreversible change to our lives. We've lost family and friends. Our hearts are broken. We don't yet know what caused it. Our labs have isolated the substance, but it wasn't identifiable, obviously lethal, and moved fast. There's no known antidote. The only survivors were those who had the Libertas1 vaccine for cancer."

She continues, "Given our grapevine here, I'm certain you all heard we had a guest over the past week. Her name is Alex, and she's a professional researcher. She came looking for some more advanced camouflage for a road trip she's taking across Canada to Victoria to find her mother. She's very resourceful and tracked us down. That was fortunate because she had the vaccine, and we could take many blood samples. Hopefully, we can isolate the magic ingredient in the vaccine that protected her and the other survivors from the substance that killed everybody else."

She says, "A few months before the attack, the vaccine manufacturers cut off supply, so it's impossible to find any remaining doses anywhere. I think it was a move to increase monetary value and to force political change, probably not for good. With Alex's blood samples, our talented lab techs are working long hours to develop a vaccine that will protect us all and allow us to go to the top again. They're sharing their knowledge with the German site lab staff, so a larger team is working on this. This isn't a simple task, and you must understand we may never get there. Until then, we don't know when or if the air will clear enough for us to go up top again, if food and water sources will be affected, and what the long-term effects of this substance will have on earth. There are many unknowns. Our bots are testing daily above ground. Alex will send us test samples of water, soil, and vegetation from across the country as she travels. So far, things are still growing and don't seem to be affected, but we don't know whether they're edible or will reseed. The pollinators are all dead."

She says, "We're lucky to have our own sizeable garden and, as you know, food and clean water for life. We won't starve or die if we have to stay here, except from old age and boredom." A murmur of laughter passes through the group. "None of us want to spend the rest of our lives here, but we'll need patience while our labs work on this enormous project. We'll keep you posted on their progress. I'm sorry to say, waiting for this and/or waiting for the air to clear could take a few years, or longer. The ultimate solution may be we have to live out our lives here. We'll need to make plans for all of those scenarios. I need your help with that." She sees many heads drop. They were hoping for more promising news, a way out. They're thinking, *this doesn't sound good*.

She continues, "I recognize that if we get up top again, not everyone will want to stay together. Some of you may want to search for loved ones, alive or dead. Some of you may just want to return home, even though it'll be unsafe and probably unsustainable. That's your choice, of course, and we'll do everything possible to make your trip safe." Francis does not mention the invisi-suits she gave to Alex. She doesn't want 118 invisible people out in the country traveling around. She takes her stewardship of this valuable and dangerous inventory seriously. The two people in the audience with higher security clearance who know about the invisi fabric exchange looks.

Francis continues, "I've developed some projects we'll need in all scenarios. You're much smarter than me, and I've surely missed something obvious, so please share your ideas. We'll post these project ideas on the Uni-site. You can add your own projects and ideas. You have a month to think about this and contribute where you can. Project teams are also being set up in Germany, and I encourage you to bring in their ideas and bring yours to them. Fortunately, our mutual satellite still allows us to communicate. When the projects are agreed on, we'll develop teams, task lists, and rules of operation to which we can all agree. You can work on as many project teams as you wish. Once we have your sign-up for the projects, team co-leaders will be identified."

Francis says, "I've put a few ideas together to get you started, not necessarily in any order of importance. They're all critical and mesh with each other. This is mainly if some or all of us want to stay together, but if you move on, you could probably take these ideas to whatever society you find yourself in. We'll all have to start over."

She says, "Let's start with vaccination survivors. Many people who had cancer got the vaccination, not all, unfortunately. There might be 500 survivors right above our heads in Kingston. How do we reach them? They'll be unable to access food or medication soon, if not already. How do we integrate with them, help them, or do we? We certainly have enough food for any of the survivors, although they may not like our tasty, flavored wafers." A chuckle passes through her audience. "There'll be a cross-section of humanity, kids and old people, people with mental and medical challenges, people with gripes and anger and fear and PTSD from the shock of all of this. They may not want to deal with us, and we may not want to deal with them. Not everybody will be grateful. It's an enormous challenge and one I hope we rise to."

"Location: If we get back to the top, either by vaccine or the earth righting itself, we'll all need to think about where we want to live. I believe locations with the ability to grow things should be a big consideration in our choice. Weather and availability of water are also key, of course. So, agriculture and its potential should give us ideas of where we should be. There are lots of choices in North America. Kingston would not be my first choice. They have real winter here." This also brings a few laughs. She lets that die down but adds, "Canada has many areas with very arable land, successful farms, and pleasant climates. The Niagara area is gorgeous, with mild winters and hot summers. Let's not overlook it and decide to head south. I'm not crazy about living in the states again, even after this disaster. Not sure we could start over cleanly with that very divided group. That'll be your choice."

"Housing: We'll have our choice of houses that aren't occupied by survivors. How do we avoid disputes over a preferred house? Lotteries? I hope you can come up with some ideas. Given that gangs will no longer be roaming the streets, all unoccupied housing would be available and probably safe. You don't have to stick to Smart Homes, although you may still prefer those. I would. The severe storms probably will continue for years."

"Agriculture/food: In addition to our own internal supply, we'll need to grow our own food. We'll have to learn how to farm. With no insects, we'll need to figure out how to pollinate plants quickly. The outside surviving people will need to be fed wherever we choose to live. It will become dangerous if survivors can't find food. Right now, there'll be less than a year's food supply out there in the freezers of the world. Once that's gone, people will need something else to eat. It's a big deal and requires big ideas."

"Governance: Since we're starting with a clean slate and can hopefully get it right this time, if some, all, or any of us stay together as a community, we'll need to look at how we plan to govern. New laws would have to be developed, negotiated, and agreed on. We'll need these to keep each other safe and, frankly, civilized. We'll need new forms of policing and enforcement to deal with crimes and misdemeanors. We're all still human. This is a very broad topic, but an important one if we start a new society. I look forward to hearing what you all think of that. Let's not start another world war over some minor disagreement."

"Healthcare: We and the other survivors will all still get sick at some time or break an arm or a leg. We'll age and die. There are still a lot of diseases out there, and the viruses were still running rampant when this happened. There will still be mental illness. How do we prepare for all of that? There are hospitals and pharmacies full of medications, many of which will have already been purged by survivors. I believe it would still be possible to amass a large drug supply from all those resources, set it up as a super pharmacy and dispense as needed. Yes, many things will expire eventually, but our lab techs here and in Germany may be able to recreate some of these. Not all, but we'll need drugs and someone who knows about them. We'll also need medical practitioners of every type. We have some very talented doctors here today, and there will be some out in the group of survivors. It won't be perfect, but we're starting with a huge knowledge base. These aren't the dark ages regarding medical care. We know so much now."

"Finance and money: None of us have money anymore. It's all gone. Nothing to measure our worth or level of success. We're all in the same category. We're not poor, we have a wealth of resources to sustain us, but we don't have investments or bank accounts that mean anything. We'll need to consider how goods will be traded and fair practice. Bartering is as old as Methuselah, but it might be something we'll need to consider. Or we move to a centralized system of providing for all. There's no need for money because everybody has at least the basics to sustain their lives. I know. Sounds like a socialist kibbutz. These are just some ideas to get you thinking about how you would like your new world to approach this."

"Security, access to locked things: How do we access the Smart Homes we might want to live in or hospital drug lockers or other things that might be important to our survival?" Francis does not share that the technology to open most things, including Smart Homes, old locks, and computer programs, is available. It could be dangerous in the wrong hands. She wants to see what they come back with on this one.

"Communication: We'll need the clever I.T. folks to get our equipment up and communicating again. Thankfully, we can communicate with each other and our German cell because we have our own satellite. We should be able to hack into other communication satellites. We'll need to find a way to reach the rest of the world. There are a lot of satellites up there, many owned by one entity, and these should be reachable. There'll still be surviving people around the world working on this. I have great faith that we'll be able to reconnect with the rest of the world."

"Education: This is very important. You're all very skilled, some in very specific specialties. Most of you went to school for years to gain your skill or experience. Still, your knowledge will need to be shared and taught. There are too few of us left to only rely on the last person standing who knows how to pull a tooth. Yes, dentists, we'll need you to teach others how to do that. The same goes for the I.T. people, the medical staff, the lab techs, the engineers, and all people with special skills. We'll need to actively establish cross-training programs and maintain them. Now I know there'll be doctors here saying, "I can't teach someone how to operate on a heart." However, if you die and I need my appendix out, I want someone to have at least a good idea of going about that, or I die. Most of us will need medical help sometime in the future. Developing these training programs will require a lot of thought. I'm counting on you all to recognize your talents and figure out how to share this knowledge."

"Services and Infrastructure: Roads will disintegrate, vegetation will invade, buildings will fall down, and mechanical and electrical things will break down. These things will need to be fixed, rebuilt, or abandoned. Who's going to do that? Who's going to prioritize what needs to be done? You'll be the mayor of your own world, and you won't have to worry about who votes for you. We'll need to fix what needs fixing. Many of you have those skills and might enjoy being part of that solution."

"Transportation: We'll all have solar bikes if we get to the top. We don't have enough here to supply all of you, but we could get them from bike shops, empty houses, and many places. We'll have to find some solar cars and trucks that can be driven because we can't just call up a service car anymore. There are still a few out in rural areas. We'll need to amass a fleet as we have to do some scouting that requires bringing back more things than we can carry on a solar bike and a sidecar."

"Entertainment and Sports: It's not all bad news. You can still play tennis or soccer or whatever is your pleasure. You might want to think about setting up some simple teams. You artsy types can start your own theatre groups. Musicians can make new music and hold concerts. This 'happening' sure should spawn interesting movies from aspiring film producers and directors. Your options for entertaining yourselves are limitless."

"Clothing: We have our own factory for making clothes, although probably not your fashion choice unless you're into the military look. We could repurpose some of that manufacturing equipment or rebuild it elsewhere. The shops and houses will be filled with clothes. You might be stuck in a fashion rut for a while, but I've seen your clothes and am confident you'll find your way out of a fashion time warp." This brings some laughs from some of the audience in the back, who are, in fact, dressed in edgy outfits.

"Weapons: We make weapons of all kinds here, and I won't suggest you be unarmed. However, this is the perfect time to look at that and how we can better manage guns. Too many people have fallen to shootings over the years. That needs to change. I know it's a different world; hopefully, the survivors won't be so trigger-happy. You can't discount the big world of survivors who'll come at this with an entirely different outlook."

"Death: Eventually, we'll all die. I hope if we're successful with the vaccine and/or the air clears, there isn't something more lethal waiting for survivors in years to come. We don't know. Unless we want to set up burning funeral biers, bodies will have to be buried. Not a pleasant thought, but how do we want our bodies treated if we die down here? Does a bot carry out carcasses up top into the woods?"

"Last of my thoughts but not least, babies: We can't be the last people on the planet and need to consider adding to the population. Many of you will think bringing a baby into this world is dangerous, even here. What kind of life will they have? If we want to save this planet, those who can might want to think about having children. You can do it the old-fashioned way, or we can offer In Vitro Fertilization. We would need a sperm donor or donors for that and some wombs. I know this will give you some pause, but if we continue to be on this planet, someone has to have babies.

I look forward to all of your thoughts on that." Some of her audience smiles, some look down at their hands or laps, and some stare at her with blank faces. She knows this will have stirred them into profound decisions about how they want to live out their future, wherever it is.

She silently walks back and forth across the stage, thinking. She then lifts her head and looks at them, spanning the audience. "My project ideas are just a start. I know you'll bring more well-thought-through ideas on how we go forward. If we have to stay here, you're free to choose how you want to participate, or not. Not everybody is a joiner. I know that. No judgment. If we get above ground, you can choose where you want to live and how. We'll help you in every way we can. We need to build a plan that can be taken anywhere and implemented. It won't be perfect. Nothing is, and we can adjust as we go."

I know you'll have a million questions, and I ask that you send them to me through our Uni-site. If you're okay with having those questions shared, I'll share them and my answers with all of you or preserve your privacy, if that's what you want. Your concerns are my concerns. We all want to live long, happy and healthy lives."

"You have a month to think about all of this. Add your ideas, meet with your colleagues, and talk to the German cell folks so that we can build these project teams successfully. I very much look forward to your input. Once we have that, we'll meet again to discuss how best to take this forward, amalgamate the suitable projects, and start looking for team sign-up."

"You know I'm always available one on one. I don't want to discount the seriousness of all of this, and I know it sounds very sci-fi, but have some fun planning your new world and life."

Francis finishes with a simple, "Thank you, we'll get through this."

Francis and Miguel leave the room. The audience stands up and is immediately buzzing with conversation. There's a roar of voices. A few are angry. They hoped she would deliver a solution to get them out of this. They don't know where to place this anger because they know she can't fix it. Some teams are already forming. Some people are quiet and deeply sad, with reality truly setting in regarding the severity of the situation. Some stand back and watch the group with amusement. Leaders, loudmouths, and opinions emerge quickly. She's right about one thing: people are people.

Chapter 20

MOVING ON UP THE ROAD

It's early, and Alex and the kids plan to leave Thunder Bay this morning. Alex wakes up to an alarm in the house and a light flashing. The front door is wide open. With her heart racing, she quickly closes it and goes and checks on the kids. Her mind immediately goes to Diya. Is she in the house? She discovers Tom is not in his bed. She wakes Anna in an absolute panic, saying, "Tom's gone. Have you seen him?" Anna flies out of bed and says, "No," and they race through the house, calling his name. He's nowhere. Alex realizes he has to be outside through that open door. She can't see any evidence of Diya.

A woman stands partially hidden in the back corner of the kitchen, quietly watching them. She holds a gun. It's not Diya. Alex and Anna enter the main room, look to the kitchen, and see her simultaneously. Anna screams. The woman says to Alex, "Shut her up."

Alex puts an arm around Anna and says, "Where's the boy?" The woman answers cagily, "I don't know, I didn't see no boy." Alex's blood runs cold. This woman is late 40s and has seen better days. She's dressed in a t-shirt with an unknown band logo, The Unicorns. Alex has never heard of The Unicorns. She's wearing well-worn black dirty tights, baggy at the knees, and beat-up sneakers. Her hair is part blonde, red, and gray with a streak of green. She has many tattoos on her body, including her face. It looks like she had large piercings in her ears once, but there's nothing in them now but the gaping holes in her lobes. She looks worn out, not edgy. Maybe she was a rebel once as a teenager, but years of hardship have done her in. She says, "I need food. Get me some." Alex says, "First, I have to find the boy." Alex has her stun gun in her pocket but doesn't want to zap this woman if she knows where Tom is. The woman says again, "I didn't see no boy." She's not so sly this time, and Alex thinks she may be telling the truth. Alex says, "I need to look outside, then I'll get you some food. Are you okay with that? The woman aims her gun at Alex and then Anna and says, "Food first."

Alex frantically thinks, *where's Tom?* She's trying to remember what's left in the cooler and ready to go; all she can think of is bread. She says, "There's bread in the cooler, that will get you started until I can fix you something better. Is that okay?" The woman backs to the cooler with her gun aimed at them, moving it back and forth between Alex and Anna. She opens the cooler door with one hand, grabs and opens the bread bag, and begins stuffing slices in her mouth. She's obviously starving. Alex asks again, "Can we look outside for the boy? He's only three. He's a baby." The woman says through a wad of half-chewed bread, "Yeah, go ahead, but don't go beyond the doorstep. I've got a gun on you. You promised me more food." Alex keeps her arm around Anna, and they go out the front door and call for Tom. Nothing. He's nowhere to be seen. Alex turns on the woman and says, "If you've done anything to him, I will kill you." Alex doesn't think about this at all. A switch has turned on in her psyche. She would kill her if she harmed Tom.

The woman says icily, "I think I'm the one with the gun."

Alex has a flash. She needs to check her bike storage to see if the glasses are there with Tom's invisi-suit. He's an imp and may have put on the suit and gone out for an adventure. The trouble is all of that is in her invisible bike parked across the room. She says to the woman, "I need to check something across the room. Will you let me do that?" The woman says, "Don't bother getting your gun. I'll shoot you first. I really don't care." Alex believes her. She says, "No, my gun is upstairs. It's some medication this little girl needs. She has to take it first thing in the morning, or she'll have a seizure." Anna looks at her with surprise but gets it, clever girl that she is. The woman continues to stuff bread slices in her mouth and says, "Get it, but I have my gun on you." Alex takes Anna with her, keeping her arm around her. She crosses the room and opens a drawer, pretending to look for the fictional seizure drugs. This creates a bit of subterfuge while Anna stands in front of the bike. Alex immediately sees that the flap on the bike's saddlebag that held Tom's suit is open, and a pair of glasses is gone. She knows he's outside somewhere in his invisi-suit. She says quietly to Anna, "Don't be scared." She turns back to the woman and zaps her. The woman drops to the kitchen floor. Anna screams. Alex says, "Don't worry honey, she's not dead, just asleep for a long time."

She says to Anna, "I think Tom's outside in his invisi-suit. She checks the saddlebag, and sure enough, the suit is missing. Alex thinks with horror, *if Diya is anywhere around, she could see Tom's invisi-suit and grab him.* They don't have time to check in with Kingston for Diya's position. She says to Anna, "Let's go look for him. Stay close to me." Anna looks over her shoulder at the woman's body on the kitchen floor as they leave the house. Alex says, "I'll move her after we've found Tom." She asks Anna, "Any idea where he might have gone?"

Anna says, "Maybe the park down the street? There are swings there, and he really liked to swing." They run to the park. She hears the swing squeak in the wind before they turn into the park. For a moment, she's hopeful. The swings drift back and forth in the breeze, but there's no sign of Tom. Alex looks at Anna. "Where else do you think he might have gone?" Anna says, "There's a pool down the street. We used to go there with mommy and daddy." They take off running. The pool is fenced, but the gate hangs open. Alex's heart is in her mouth. The pool hasn't been skimmed for almost two months since the attack and is covered with leaves and garbage. She takes a skimmer, brushes the surface to see to the bottom, and does a complete walk around the pool, half expecting to see Tom's little body down there. He's not there. Alex turns to Anna. "Anywhere else?" Anna says, "There's a trail over there where we used to go for walks. It goes into the woods." Alex thinks, *great, a bloody forest. We'll never find him.*

Maxine Buttersby lives in a Smart Home on the park's edge. She has been holing up since the attack, afraid to go out. Her husband and two teenagers are sandy piles, still in their beds. She's been sleeping on the couch. The morning after the attack, she biked into the neighborhood to get information. She saw no one. She continued downtown and found two people talking on the street. She stopped and, through the conversation, figured out why she had survived, and others hadn't. The cancer vaccine. It didn't take her long to realize she was in danger because she had a good store of food, at least a year's worth. There hadn't been many intruders banging at her door and windows, but there had been some. She sleeps with her gun. On this day, she looked out the back window at the park. In the distance, what seemed like a small boy's head wearing odd pink glasses bobbed down to the entrance to the trail. He didn't seem to have a body. She thought she was going mad. Tom had taken his invisi-hood off.

Alex worries that Tom might return to the house before they do, and he won't be able to get in. She doesn't want to leave Anna alone, particularly with a body in the kitchen. She has to take the risk that Tom headed down the trail. The trail drops at the entrance, curves, and bends every 30 feet. They can't get a long view. They keep on calling for him. Alex wonders, *at what point do I give up and turn back?* She's frantic. Anna is getting tired; this has been a lot of running for a little six-year-old. Alex asks Anna, "Do you know how far this trail goes?" Anna says, "We always turned back after a while. We never went to the end." Alex pulls out her GPS and takes a read. The trail goes on for miles. A little three-year-old guy will be tired by now. She hopes he hasn't gone off the path. He might not even be in here. He could be anywhere.

Anna is crying, and Alex sits her down on a bench. Alex continues calling out for Tom. Anna sobs out, "We'll never find him. What if he's lost forever?" Alex thinks to herself, *Yeah, what if?* She doesn't know what to do. She needs to continue searching the trail by herself and brings Anna back to the house. Anna says, "That woman is here. I don't want to be alone with her." Alex knows it's time for a tough conversation. She says, "That woman will be asleep until tomorrow. I zapped her with a special gun. She will not bother you. You'll be safe. I promise you that. We need you here if Tom comes home while I'm looking for him. You need to be very brave and do this for him." Alex goes on, "I know this is hard, honey, but we have to find him." She looks down at Anna, "You'll be fine, I promise." Anna sniffs and says, "Okay." Alex drags the woman's body to the garage, so Anna doesn't have to look at her. Alex says, "Just stay by the window and watch for Tom." Alex rides all around the neighborhood, calling out for Tom. Maxine hears a woman's voice calling out "Tom" outside her house. She sees no one when she looks out the window. *Strange things are happening out there*, she thinks.

Alex rides slowly back down the trail, calling out Tom's name. She gets to the end, and it winds up at a small lake. Alex thinks, *he couldn't have gotten this far*. She dismounts and does a walk around the edges, looking into the sludge of the water. She thinks, *if he got this far and has fallen in, he's already dead*. She sees no sign of a body. Heartsick, she turns the bike around and rides slowly back. About a mile from the entrance, she sees a flash of white in the woods, and her senses quicken. She calls out, "Tom, is that you?" A great wail comes from a lost little boy. He's got his hood pulled back, and his floating head is swaying back and forth. Alex makes her way through the thick brush, pulls him out, and then hugs him. She says, "We thought we'd lost you. You scared us to death. Where have you been?" Tom clings to her and says, "I was looking for mommy and daddy, but I couldn't find them." Alex's heart is breaking for this little boy who has quickly become her baby. She avoids the lost parent subject and says, "Come on, let's go home. Anna is waiting for you. Promise me you won't ever run off again without us. Do you promise?" Tom looks at her with his big chocolate eyes. "Are you mad at me, Alex?" Alex hugs him tightly and says, "I could never be mad at you."

Before heading back, Alex removes his invisi-suit. She doesn't want to take any risk that Diya might see it if she's around. Tom is still in his pajamas. Alex pops him into the sidecar, and they ride back to the house. Anna comes running out when she sees them ride up. She's sobbing with relief, and Tom calls out to her, "I sorry, Anna, I sorry."

Alex's heart rate steadies, but that was more danger than she was prepared for. She doesn't know how traumatized Anna is by all this and will talk to her about it once she gets them out of here. She'll have to keep a closer eye on Tom. They were so close to a real disaster.

She asks Anna if she's okay. Anna seems to be calm. She's a hard kid to read. She nods at Alex and says, "Yeah, but that woman was scary. Are you sure she's not dead?" Alex says, "I'm sure. She'll be fine."

The woman in the garage in the faded Unicorn t-shirt will wake up and will have what's left of the food in the house. She won't quite remember how she got there, let alone Alex and Anna. She'll decide to stay in the house. It'll seem safe. Unfortunately, she'll eventually starve to death in that house. She won't be fine.

Alex packs up the bike and the kids, and they're ready to go. She can drop into stores along the way and pick up any kids' clothes, videos, books, and pull-ups she'll need. She found a collapsible potty chair for Tom, and he's doing better with that. He's not perfect, but he's getting there. His pull-ups take up room but are necessary cargo. Just in case, Alex found their birth certificates and passports. She and Anna negotiate the things she wants to bring with her, given the limited space.

Anna finally agrees to take only a bit of each of her parents in a small container. They find a small tin box, and she goes upstairs to spoon them in. Alex thought this would be difficult for Anna and watched her from the doorway. Anna is more interested in measuring precisely the same amount of spoonfuls. This kid is an A-type, for sure.

Thunder Bay to Winnipeg would have been approximately eight hours had Alex done this without the kids. Now they'll need to stop for bathroom breaks and snacks and a stretch and lunch, so she sets her sights on Kenora. That should be about five hours. Add three hours for stops. *Doable*, she thinks. The first day will be the true road test for the kids. Alex and Anna do not discuss leaving the remains of Anna's parents upstairs. Mr. and Mrs. Castaneda are together, asleep forever. She guesses that's good enough.

Taking a deep breath, Alex pushes off toward the highway, wondering if they'll encounter Diya. It's been well over three weeks since she turned off to Thunder Bay. Her new bike is as fast as her invisi-bike, although it has weight, and her invisi-bike does not. The kids seem to adapt to this new adventure, and she can talk to them through their bike helmets.

Diya initially camped out just at the edge of Shabaqua Corners, thinking Alex would have to pass that way and choose either Highway 17, the high road, or Highway 11, the low road, if she continued on. She's listened in to gossip between the Kingston and German sites and they seem to know about Alex. She's traveling across the country to find her mother and is supposed to be sending back soil, water and vegetation samples to Kingston along the way. However, Alex has disappeared somewhere in Thunder Bay. Weeks go by and there is no sign of her. Diya doesn't have many choices. Return to Kingston and wait for them to surface. This might never happen and she knows she's dying. She can stay on the road and continue to look for Alex. Killing her would give her some satisfaction. She thinks, *she can't have been just going to Thunder Bay. There's nothing there. Francis wouldn't have outfitted her with all that gear and access just to get to Thunder Bay.* She wonders if Alex got scared and turned back to Kingston but there's been no gossip about her returning to the underground site. She wonders if she missed her altogether. Diya wasn't awake every hour. She's been feeling quite sick over the past week and wonders if she'll survive long enough to kill any of them. Her head aches and the pain patches don't help her nausea. She has to make some decisions. Going with her gut, she decides to stick with the 'follow Alex' plan and continue on. Alex is traveling across the country and probably reporting what she sees to Francis. If so, Winnipeg would be her next stop, if she hasn't passed it already. Highways 17 and 11 change numbers and converge at Ste Anne just before Winnipeg. Diya rides there to see if she can pick up her trail. She doesn't have many choices left.

Alex and the kids have a smooth day, with no sign of Diya ahead or in her rear mirrors. Good weather and one-hour breaks for the kids work. Alex stops for lunch in Dryden, finds a Smart Home, reads it, and it's okay to enter. She says to Anna, "There'll be sand piles in here. Are you okay with that?" Anna nods and says, "I know what they are." No one was here when the disaster hit, so it's sand-free. So far, she's avoided camping and flavored wafers other than the first two nights in Kingston. There isn't much food in the house, but she can make up a decent lunch, and they're on their way again. Tom dozes off into his afternoon nap shortly after they're on the road. He had a busy morning. Anna rides quietly, watching the road, lost in her thoughts. She and Alex chat quietly back and forth about this new world, what to expect on the road, and their lives until now. Alex is constantly impressed with Anna's stoicism and hopes she's not irrevocably damaged under that façade. The rest of the day passes safely and pleasantly. A few people ride by but don't seem interested in her little party of three. They have their heads down, racing somewhere.

    They get to Kenora around 5:00 PM and find a beautiful Smart Home on the water. Alex reads it, gets nothing, and reminds Anna again there might be piles of sand in there. Anna says, "I'm okay." Alex only finds one pile of sand in what looks like a guest bedroom. The sand is under a sweatshirt and shorts, no underwear, so Alex can't tell what sex this person was. The rest of the house is immaculate and very expensive. She thinks the person may have been the caretaker. There's very little food in this cooler. She thinks it's a vacation home for someone. She heats some wafers for the kids to see how they go down. Amazingly, they both munch them down without comment. Alex doesn't ask them how they like them. If they hate them, they have a problem. They may be what they're living on later in this trip and when they get to Victoria. They watch a movie together, and she puts them to bed in a double room. Before he drops off to sleep, she reminds Tom, "Promise me you'll never go out again without me." Tom says, "I promise." Alex doesn't like sleeping in strangers' beds, so she takes the couch. She sleeps in her invisi-suit and could be on her feet quickly if someone returned to the house. One day down. She's aiming for Winnipeg tomorrow and is plotting her route as she goes. She plans to hop across the provinces, Kenora to Winnipeg, Winnipeg to Regina, Regina to Medicine Hat, etc. They'll eventually get to the coast. The mountains may be a challenge, but her new bike is a beast of burden.

    As they approach Winnipeg, Alex's heart stops. There's Diya in her telltale invisi-suit sitting on a tree at the edge of the road. Alex says to herself, *please don't notice us*. She doesn't speed up, slow down or look at her. She carries on as if she doesn't see her. Diya sees a woman ride by with two kids in a sidecar. She thinks it's unusual that a mother and two kids all survived the disaster and wonders vaguely where they're headed. They may have a Smart Home in Winnipeg or know where one is. It doesn't matter. They're not her target. She looks down the road behind them to see if she can see Alex's invisi-suit and bike, but there's nothing. Alex breathes a sigh of relief. She has fooled Diya, for now. They ride on. Diya waits, not knowing Alex has already passed her.

    In Alex's memory, Winnipeg was the land of mosquitos and lakes in the middle of the country. No more mosquitos. Nobody is buying the 'I survived mosquito season in Winnipeg' t-shirts. They have another quiet day. Tom likes to run off some energy when they stop for their one-hour breaks. So much vitality in a little boy package. He's a force, but she never takes her eyes off him now. They stop at a couple of Smart Homes for lunch and overnight and get through another day. Alex sends some water samples back east and asks them if they see any differences, changes, or improvements. "Still reading the samples" is the answer. Once inside a Smart Home, she also tells Francis they've passed Diya and seem to have gotten away with their ruse for now. Francis says, "We think she's feeling very sick; with a little luck, she might just die."

Chapter 21

STORMY WEATHER

Saskatchewan is one long stretch of prairie and wheat farms with a huge snow globe sky. There's always been a running joke about it being the only province in Canada where you can sit in your living room and watch your dog run away for three days. Alex remembers a friend from Regina saying he could hear his ears crackle with frost while crossing the street on freezing winter days. It has its own stark beauty for all of that. The rolling fields of golden grain, now mesh farmed to keep them safe from storms, have a particular end of the earth's edges feel. Electrical storms spray lightning across the sky like a garden hose's first uncontrolled erratic spurts. Explosions of Fourth of July firecrackers without the audience. Thunder cracks and the clouds scuttle fast toward you, rolling and changing. Summer storms are almost tornadoes here. They come up quick and can roll most things not tied down.

Just past Regina, outside Moose Jaw, Alex senses a weather change. The big sky is cloudy and roiling, black clouds pitching toward them, lightning flashing on the horizon. She can feel the wind buffeting the bike. Her wrist chip vibrates a warning. There isn't much shelter out where they are. It's all agricultural. All the old pretty farmhouses are long gone, demolished by the wind. They've been replaced with in-ground homes with low-sloping roofs. They're hard to see from the road. A side lane comes up, and Alex takes it. The few remaining trees along the road are almost blown over sideways. She has a tough time keeping the bike on the road. The sky has turned dark green now, and she's thinking tornado. She fights the wind. The sky lights up with shards of lightning, looking as if the glass ceiling of the sky might crack and fall. Anna and Tom look up at her wide-eyed. She assures them they'll be alright. She's not so sure. She sees the thin line of a roof ahead, rolls up to the door, and reads the house to find it all clear. No one's alive in there. She quickly moves the kids and the bike, and the sidecar in. She'll deal with the sand piles once they're safe inside. She searches the house and finds the sand of a woman, under her flowered cotton nightie, still in bed.

A kitchen monitor shows the outside utility building's door slightly ajar. There's a light on. Alex thinks, *crap, someone might be alive and coming back to the house*. She moves the camera around, looking for life. Nothing. She can't see any piles of sand out there either, but the door is open, and the wind would probably have blown anything up against the far wall of the building. She thinks she should go check, but the storm is roaring over their heads right now. It would be suicidal to go out in it. The rain is thundering on the roof, the sky has gone smoky black, and she once again assures the kids they're safe. She tells them this house has been here for years and is built just for this kind of storm. Neither of them is crying, which amazes her. Little buggers are brave.

Suddenly, Alex spots a biker rolling into the utility building. It's a female, and when she takes her helmet off, Alex sees she's in her early 20s. The girl is soaked through, her hair skinned back from her forehead. Alex figures she didn't have time to put her rain gear on, if she even had any. The girl sits on the floor, shakes out her hair, and is obviously going to wait it out. Alex thinks, *at least she's safe inside*. Alex turns on the speaker and says, "Close the door." The girl looks around the space to see who said that, and Alex tells her she's on a monitor at the house watching, but she should stay put until the storm passes. As the girl gets up to close the door, another biker arrives. *Bloody central storm station here*, Alex thinks. It's a guy. A big guy who looks like the old-fashioned bikers of yore. He muscles his big bike through the door and sees the girl. Alex is not liking this.

He takes off his helmet and has one of those small, low bald heads that disappears into his shoulders, turtle-like. He has almost no neck. Lots of tats on his skull. Alex thinks derisively, *such an attractive look*. He looks like a gym rat, overbuilt upper body and skinny legs. In Alex's mind, too much testosterone, no brain.

He doesn't waste time and asks the girl if she has any food. She tells him she doesn't have much, and it has to last her another couple of days. He says, "Give it to me." The girl says, "Piss off." He moves toward her, pushes her aside, and starts searching her bike storage. She isn't going down without a fight. She jumps on his back, whacking away at him. He swats her to the floor with one powerful arm. Her face is bleeding. He looks her up and down, and says, "You've got something else I haven't tasted in a while," and moves toward her. This guy doesn't waste any time. Alex thinks, *how horny can you be coming in out of a bloody tornado off the road*? He pushes her down with one strong hand, pulls out a knife, and holds it to her throat. He has his knee on her chest. The girl has stopped kicking and lies there wide-eyed and terrified.

Anna stands beside Alex watching this play out, all big dark eyes. Alex turns off the screen and says, "I'm going out to help her. Watch Tom." Anna nods and says, "Be careful." *Wise words from a six-year-old.* Alex thinks, *yup, jumping into a hurricane to go fight a guy with a knife attacking a girl, I'll try.* The building is about 200 yards away. Alex slips outside and is immediately flattened against the door by the wind. She thinks, *there's no way I can walk across the yard in this gale. I need to get down low and crawl over. I hope I'm not too late.* She crawls as fast as she can. The wind, now roaring, is the only thing she can hear. It picks her up in one big gust and slams her 50 yards away, up hard against a fence. She feels a burning pain in her shoulder and her arm is completely useless, except for the screaming pain. Alex is sure it's broken. She tries to move it, but it shrieks at her. Still, she's got to get to this girl. She gets back down on the soaking muddy ground and continues to crawl with one arm, using her good elbow to propel her along, wincing all the way. She hits the door, which still stands open, and the guy is on the girl, his pants already down. Thanks to the girl's tight pants, he hasn't made any headway with her. Alex zaps him, and he falls back. His penis is waving around like a flagpole without a flag. In any other circumstance, it would be comical. His knife rattles to the side.

The girl looks horrified and asks, "Is he dead?" Alex says, "No, just zapped. He'll be out for about six hours and won't remember anything when he comes to, but we've got to get you to the house. I've got two little kids back there. I'll come back and get your bike when the wind dies down. He'll still be out." She's crying and saying, "Thank you, thank you." They leave buddy on the floor, waving his flag of surrender. Alex tells the girl, "I've hurt my arm, so one side of me is out of commission. We'll need to crab crawl back and stay as low as possible in this wind. They move slowly, clinging to each other, giving them extra weight and ballast, and they make it to the house. It's a long, wet, muddy, painful crawl. Alex's arm and shoulder send knife jabs with every move. Alex is thinking as they crawl, *if my arm and shoulder are broken, I'll have to set it somehow. I won't be able to pick up Tom. Getting the bike and the sidecar in and out of houses and, ultimately, the boat will be tough.*" She lightly curses, *crap, crap, crap*.

Alex and the girl fall through the house door to two little faces staring at them. They're both soaking wet, filthy, and gasping. The girl still has blood on her face, where she was thrown to the floor by the guy. Tom starts to cry. Alex says, "It's okay honey, we're okay, don't worry." He turns into Anna, and she puts her arm around him. Alex and the girl look at each other and inexplicably start laughing. The girl says, "Oh my god, I'm so glad you were here." Alex says with a grin,

"Yeah, me too." She asks the girl how her face is. She says, "Just some road burn, I think. Nothing serious." Alex gives the girl her good hand and says, "Hi, I'm Alex Smith." The girl says, "Krista Bronikowski, nice to meet you." When Tom sees them laughing, he laughs too.

"You're all dirty," he blurts out. He finds this funny. Alex introduces Krista to the kids with a brief story of why they are with her. Krista says to the kids, "This is a fine way to meet, ay you guys, falling through the door soaking wet?" Anna gives her a begrudging smile. Tom is still all eyes, holding onto Anna. Alex says, "I've really buggered my arm. The wind threw me up against a fence. I hope it's not broken." Krista looks at her with a frown and says, "Let's dry off and clean up, and then I'll look at your arm. I actually know a little about broken bones." Alex says, "Are you a doctor?" She's thinking, *way too young*. Krista says, "No, hardly. I'm a farmer. I just graduated from agricultural college in Guelph. You take some courses in animal husbandry even though few farmers keep animals anymore, but some do. You learn how to determine a break and how to set a cow's leg, if you don't have to put them down." They both go into the bathroom and clean off the mud. Krista cleans up her face, and they towel off. Alex says, "There might be some dry clothes that fit you here. Check the bedroom closet upstairs. Just ignore sleeping beauty." Krista gives Alex a look over the kids' heads and climbs the stairs to the bedroom. She comes down in a pair of jeans that are a bit large on her and a sweatshirt. Alex's clothes dry almost immediately. Krista pulls at the fabric of Alex's now dry shirt, looks at her with a question on her face, and says, "Interesting?" Alex says, "I'll fill you in later."

Krista says, "Let's look at your arm and shoulder." She gently takes Alex's arm, and moves it around, testing for mobility, squeezing the shoulder and elbow joints, and feeling all around the arm. Alex yelps with every move. Krista finally says, "Good news. We don't have to put you down. You're not going to the knackers. It could be broken, maybe a fracture, or you could just be bruised and pulled a few tendons. You probably hit the fence at a bad angle." Alex says, "Is there a good angle to fly into a fence midair?" Keeping up her levity, Alex says, "Anyway, I'm too young to die." Krista says, "If you have some painkillers, take them, stick with them, and have a hot soak in the tub tonight. You'll probably be stiff and sore tomorrow but improving. You'll need to force yourself to keep it moving for quite a long time, even though it hurts, or it will freeze up on you." "Thanks, doc," Alex says. This girl is comfortable to be around. Anna asks, "What's a knackers?" Alex looks at Krista with a grin. "Over to you."

Alex sends a scan of her arm and shoulder over to Kingston. A medic comes on and says, "Good news and bad news." You have a humerus fracture in your upper arm, but we don't see any bone fragments. You'll need to immobilize the arm with no shoulder movement for about two weeks and then increase the shoulder's range of motion. That's the good news. The bad news is it could take several weeks to months for the arm to heal completely. It's going to be painful for a while.

Krista looks at Alex and says, "It's going to be hard dealing with the kids and the gear." Alex says, "Yeah, that's top of mind, but I'll figure something out." She has no idea what she'll figure out, but this isn't Krista's problem, it's hers. Alex says, "I'll give you my full story over supper." Krista says, "Me too."

Krista turns to Tom and Anna. "Tom, would you like a pony ride into the kitchen so we can find some grub?" She lifts him up on her back, and he doesn't complain. He asks, "What's grub? She says to him in mock disbelief, "Grub? You've never heard of grub? It's dinner, lunch, breakfast, something to eat." It's what we cowgirls call food." She looks at Alex and grins. Alex likes this girl. Krista says, "Let's look in the cooler and see what's there." All three of them bury their heads in the cooler. A photograph wouldn't do it justice. They are cute as hell, just their bums up. Tom is enjoying this new adventure. Alex hears her yell out, "Paydirt...pizza! We're going to have pizza." Tom screeches, "Pizza, pizza." Krista asks Anna, "Have you ever cooked a frozen pizza?" Anna shyly answers, "No. Mommy did all the cooking except for Fridays." Krista asks, "What happened then?" Anna says, "We went to abuela y abuelo's restaurant for dinner, and we could have whatever we wanted." Krista says, "Hablas Espanol?" Anna and Tom both yell simultaneously, "Si senorita!" They are incredibly excited that Krista can speak Spanish. Krista says in Spanish, "Que tipo de restaurant?" They both shout, "Mexican!". She says, "That sounds like fun. You could have anything you wanted, all the tostitos you can eat? I love Mexican food. What lucky kids." She goes on. "I don't think there'll be any restaurants open for a while, so it's a good time for you to learn how to cook a frozen pizza the right way. We don't want to wreck it, do we?" Anna shakes her head solemnly, no. Krista says, "First we dethaw it and then warm it up in the oven. That way, it's not soggy. Can you set the nuke mobile to dethaw?" Anna is enjoying this special attention and asks, "Nuke mobile, what's that?" Krista says, "Where have you kids been, hiding under a rock?" Anna finds this very funny. Krista shows her every step, carefully explaining what to do and why. How to set the microwave, take out the thawed pizza, preheat the oven and set the timer, and finally, how to get it out without burning her hands. A complete lesson for an eager-to-learn little girl who follows every instruction closely. Krista has won these kids and Alex over in half an hour.

She doesn't tiptoe around the kids like Alex does. She jumps in and invites them into life.

Krista's not a beauty. She's fair, freckled, and sunburned. She wears no makeup and has a face that has spent lots of time outdoors. Her hair is long, straight, reddish-blonde, and tied into a ponytail. She's tall and strong looking, with a solid farm girl's body. She has biceps. Alex has never had biceps and has always admired biceps on a woman. Krista has big even teeth, braced early probably, and an easy smile. Nothing fancy about her, no airs.

Alex tells Krista she admires her natural way with the kids. Alex says, "I've been afraid of them, of Anna's sadness, Tom's very young age and health, and my ability to see them into the future." Krista tosses that aside. "Kids are so resilient if they feel loved and safe. It's hard to wreck them if they have those two things." She goes on, "Frankly, I'm thrilled to meet these two. I didn't know if I'd ever see another kid again, let alone two of them. I ran a bunch of kids' farm programs over the years. They loved it. I loved it. Open minds, big sponges. Kids want to learn and do."

Over pizza, Alex fills Krista in on her adventures. She holds back the Diya story for now. She doesn't want to scare the kids. Krista has invited Alex and the kids to her farm so that Alex can rest up her arm, and Alex has accepted. She'll be traveling with her for a while, so she has to share some information about the gear. Krista doesn't believe the invisi-suit story until Alex puts it on and shows her. The kids insist on putting theirs on too. It's like Halloween for them. She gives her a pair of the special glasses so she can see their outlines. Tom dances around with glee in front of Krista. "Holy smokes, this is the coolest thing," she says. She's right. Alex tells her about her plans to get to Victoria, and Krista goes right to the first trouble spot. "How will you get the three of you and your gear across the strait?" Alex shares her plans to commandeer a boat she can manage. Krista frowns and looks at her with a question on her face. "I dunno," she says doubtfully. Alex doesn't respond because, honestly, she doesn't know either.

Krista tells Alex about her dad's farm in Taber, Alberta, and finishing her FARA master's degree in food, agriculture, and resource economics at the Ontario Agricultural College. She hoped to work with her dad and his assistant, Sal, to further develop the farm. She says her mom died young and knows her dad will be gone now too. He didn't have the vaccine. However, the assistant Sal had it and may still be alive. That's her hope; to reach him and work whatever is left of the farm. She tells Alex her dad hired Sal from Mexico when he was fourteen and he's like an older brother to her. He's been with them for twenty years, and they are very close. He's family. His fiancé Carly was her best friend, and they were looking forward to their wedding this fall. Sal will be shattered if he's even still alive.

Krista says, 'While I was away at school, Sal completed an engineering degree locally." She goes on, "He likes to build and fix things. He's good at everything he touches." She tells Alex she shared all her lectures with him, so he knows as much as she does about the advancing science of agriculture. Her father relied on him completely. They were a good team. Krista says, "We were already doing a lot of advanced farming and could grow just about anything." We installed a sizeable, inverted farm in the ground to grow food all winter. Alberta's weather has become so unreliable we needed to be sure of our food stocks. Time will tell if whatever fell on us has damaged the crops. Doesn't seem to have so far, but we're only in the first season. Alex tells her about the samples she's sending back to Kingston, and Krista wants to know if they have shared any results. "Not yet," Alex says. "Might just be too early." Krista says, "We could easily feed a lot of survivors off our farm. I hope we can make that happen." Alex tells her she'll put her and Francis together in a screen meeting. They can learn a lot from each other.

Alex asks, "What cancers did you and Sal have?" Krista says, "Both of us had melanoma. Too much Alberta sun when we were kids. We were vaccinated. It was caught early." Alex asks, "What if Sal is gone too?" Krista says, "I'll have to do it myself. There'll be somebody still alive in town who can probably help me." Between the intrepid Francis and Krista, Alex feels like a mewling weakling. Whatever grief Krista is feeling, she's moving past it. The kids, particularly Anna, soak all this up. Alex thinks Krista's forward attitude might help Anna's broken heart heal.

A couple of tablets are lying around, and Krista scrolls through them. "Great, they'll love this one," she says. She's found a family-friendly comedy and sends it to the larger screen. She says, "I wonder if they had any popcorn?" The three of them go look. Alex hears a triumphant yell, "Popcorn!" The kids laugh their way through the movie. Even she enjoys its silliness. These kids haven't had this much fun since their parents were alive. *No thanks to me*, Alex thinks.

Alex reminds Krista they need to retrieve her bike before the mastodon in the barn wakes up. The wind has died down, and this is a simple task. He's still out cold.

The kids are getting sleepy, and Krista asks, "Do you mind if I put them to bed?" Alex says, "Not at all." She tells her where the clean pull-ups are and their PJs. There are a couple of spare bedrooms, one with double beds, and she rides Tom in, with Anna in tow, and they go down like rocks.

Once the kids are asleep, Alex tells Krista about Diya. Krista asks, "What's your plan if she shows up?" Alex says, "Given she's in the protective invisi-suit, there aren't many options. Get some poison on her? She's smart enough to not touch her suit if I do that. I have a chance if I catch her with her hood off." She looks at Krista and says, "I've never killed anyone, and I didn't want to start. She'll kill me if I don't kill her. Now I have the kids to protect, and you. I can't let her get near any of us. Krista says, "Don't worry about me." Alex worries about them all.

Her painkillers are wearing off, so she takes the opportunity for a long hot bath and more drugs. She's been limited to quick sink baths since she met the kids. She wonders how single mothers with little kids do it. She stares at her naked image in the mirror. Looking back at her is a skinny pale woman with a bad short haircut. Her hair already needs a trim, so she finds some scissors and cleans it up with her one good hand. Her shoulder is bruising, and her arm looks a bit swollen. She thinks, *I used to be okay-looking with some makeup and a curling iron. I'm definitely a plain jane now. Oh well, no one to impress.* She slips painfully back into her black outfit. Hard to do with the damaged arm. She looks like an unmade-up cat woman.

Alex says to Krista, "I'll take the couch, and you can have the other spare room. The couch is long and wide. There's an oversized duvet and extra pillows. Alex is so tired. Krista heads off to bed. The house sleeps.

Alex wakes to a vibrating alarm in her arm chip and looks at her screen. Francis is there, and she says, "Diya's in your immediate vicinity. Better check the property cameras." Alex pulls up the utility building screen. There's Diya in her invisi-suit, taking shelter from the storm. Diya looks at the guy on the floor with his pants down and casually shoots him. This girl is one cold bitch. Alex watches her for a while and then sees her pull her hood back. Her visible head bobs around. Diya's face is very swollen, but she seems to be in more pain than just her face. Her face is contorted, reflecting a deep body grimace. She's suffering. Alex thinks, *now's my chance. She won't hear me coming with the wind still howling.*

She pulls on her invisi-suit, cringing with pain as she pulls it over her broken arm and draws up her hood. At least Diya can't kill her with a bullet in this suit.

The thought of shooting someone in cold blood is making her shake with nerves. She goes out to the utility building, quietly enters from the rear, and lifts her gun, aiming at the back of Diya's head. Diya senses someone is there, and says, without turning around, "I can kill you before you kill me." She doesn't yet know it's Alex behind her. Against all instincts, Alex stops long enough for Diya to turn around. With her hood off, Diya can't see Alex, but she knows there's someone there. It's Alex's invisibility that gives her away. Diya's holding up her poison atomizer. It looks like a water pistol. A deadly one. Alex knows Diya can reach her with it. They're only a few feet apart.

Diya says, "I know it's you." Alex says nothing. Diya says, "Did you know your beloved Francis is a master spy? She's been lying to you. She caused a lot of death in my country. She sold her services and information to the highest bidders and spread her knowledge of who was buying what around the world. She probably portrayed herself as a poor island girl. That's a load. She has big homes not only on the island she came from but in Florida, the South of France, the Algarve, and a huge apartment on the park in Manhattan. She's a whore." Alex is taken aback, not knowing whether to believe Diya. She only spent one day and night with Francis. She doesn't really know her. Her brain is computing several things in one split second. "Does this change anything? Not at this moment. Does she still need to kill Diya? Yes, she does. Can she press her gun kill button before Diya sprays the lethal poison? She's not sure."

Diya senses Alex's silence as hesitation and takes her chance. She shoots her poison indiscriminately around, hoping she'll hit Alex's suit, anything. Alex ducks but isn't fast enough, and the lethal liquid now drips down the front of her invisi-suit. Although she can't see Alex, Diya sees the clear liquid has hit something that's moving. *Success*, she thinks. *Just a matter of time now.* Alex watches a cruel smile reach Diya's swollen face. It doesn't warm it up.

A shot rings out from across the space, and the top of Diya's head blows off, spraying blood and brains all over Alex's masked face. Diya's body drops to the ground, the poison spray atomizer falling out of her hand to the floor. She isn't smiling anymore. Krista stands at the back of the space with a gun raised, arms straight out. Alex looks at her in astonishment. Krista says to Alex, "Now we're even."

Alex can barely stand with the shock. She says to Krista, "Where did you learn how to shoot like that?" Krista says, "I'm a prairie girl, remember? We all know how to hit a target." Alex says, "Thank Christ for target practice." She then says,

"I have to get out of this suit without getting any of the poison on my bare skin, or I'm a dead girl." In the corner of the room, left over from the days of chemical farming, is a safety shower. These used to be in every utility building. Alex remembers Francis' instructions, "Shower in the suit, then carefully remove it, wearing gloves. Touch nothing with your bare hands." She does this, warily stripping out of the suit. She drops it to the floor. She takes a shovel, carries the suit out back of the building where no one would need to go, and leaves it there. Alex is free of Diya.

Krista says, "I wonder if they had any booze in the house. I need a drink. You?" Alex thinks, *this girl is made of steel.*

Krista goes through the kitchen cupboards and asks, "How do you feel about scotch?" Alex says, "A double, please." Alex tells Krista what Diya told her about Francis. Krista says, "Well, you'll have to ask Francis, but I suggest you wait until you've calmed down. You probably should let her know Diya's dead, though." Alex does that, calling up Francis and telling her Krista took her out. Francis says to Krista, "I know you don't realize it, but you saved many people's lives tonight." Krista says, "I had a favor to return," and smiles at Alex. Francis says, "That service building seems to be a stopping-off point for many people today. You need to get Diya's body, her invisi-suit, and that poison out of there as soon as possible. Alex says, "Right after this stiff drink."

After an hour, the two of them look at each other, and Alex says, "We've got to do it. Let's get it over with." The wind has died down considerably, and they walk easily over to the building. They come to a full stop. There's no body, no invisi-suit, no bike, no gear, and no poison sprayer. Diya has evaporated into thin air.

Alex says in a low voice, "I know you killed her. Half her head was gone." The ever-practical Krista is looking at the floor. She says, "Something's been dragged to the door here, probably her body. Let's not panic. Let's search the property. There has to be an explanation." It's pitch dark, but they grab some lights and follow the drag marks. They go deep into the woods. Alex says, "No animals survived the attack, so this has to be human intervention." They lose the trail. Krista says, "Let's wait till first light and come back and search again."

Back in the house, Alex recontacts Francis and tells her what happened. Francis goes quiet. She says, "We're not picking up a reading on the suit, so if someone has it, it's in a secure 'no read' bag. They may have taken the bike screen, but we're not detecting the bike. The person who did this must know we can follow the invisi-suit. India's spy department would have been very disturbed that Diya got away and returned to the states. Before the world attack, someone may have been assigned to follow her and kill her. They have their own satellites, so they might still have access to the technology to read her spine disk. They may have been following her for months. She continues, "I'll bet you'll find her body deep in the woods tomorrow, with her spine torn out. They wouldn't want any of their technology to fall into the wrong hands. Alex says, "Christ, isn't all that spy stuff over now? The world has been destroyed. There's nothing left to control." Francis says, "Apparently not, for India."

At dawn, with the kids still asleep, Krista shakes Alex awake, and they go back out in search of Diya's body. As Francis guessed, they find her a half mile into the woods. Someone has cut a thin surgical line down her spine and obviously removed her spine disk. They find her bike tossed into the woods and some of her gear, but not the bike screen, her invisi-suit, or the poison atomizer. Her body was thrown without care into a pile of leaves. Sad end. At least one poison has been eradicated. A complete waste of a human life when so few humans are left.

Now someone has their technology and, most dangerous of all, the bike screen, but has yet to use it. Alex and Krista wonder if this person will want to follow them. Alex lets Francis know they found Diya's body cut open as she had predicted. Francis says, "Chances are, this person thinks they can get back to India and be a star. Maybe they don't grasp what has actually happened in the world. Keep your eyes peeled for unusual followers, and don't use the screen to communicate with us unless you're in a Smart House. Someone else has that bike screen now and can listen in. Alex thinks, *wonderful, I thought I was free of that threat.*

Chapter 22

HOME ON THE RANGE

Alex tossed and turned all night, thinking about Diya's demise and this new person out there, possibly following them still. She wonders if she'll ever feel safe again. Krista is unflappable. She murdered a woman last night and slept like a baby. In the morning, Krista makes up pancakes for the kids. They're excited about the trip, particularly with Krista added to the parade. Alex is relieved they don't have to worry about meeting the guy who attacked Krista on the road. Diya took care of him.

Krista has devised a firm sling to immobilize Alex's arm, and Alex takes more painkillers. She needs them. She thinks, *good thing I cleaned out Anna's mother's medicine cabinet before leaving. I've got enough drugs.*

They're only about six hours away from Krista's farm, so they should be able to make it today, even with the kids' stops. Krista helps Alex load the kids and their gear onto the bike and sidecar. Alex thinks, *I could have managed with one arm, but barely.*

The weather has improved, and they enjoy smooth sailing on the bikes, flying across the prairies. Alex is constantly looking behind her for oncoming bikes. She sees potential trouble everywhere. The kids love having Krista riding ahead of them. They're on her like glue when they stop, and she doesn't disappoint. She always says something to make them think and laugh. "Did you see that big rock? How old do you think it might be? Older than your grandpa?" What did you like? What didn't you like?" She invites them to be observers on this trek. Alex is now invisible to them. She asks herself, *am I jealous?* She thinks, *a little, but truthfully, I'm enjoying having some pressure taken off me to engage these little folks. I'm not good at it, and Krista is a rock star.*

Very few bikers pass them heading east. They ride on, ignoring Alex and Krista. A few more bikers are heading west, as they are. Alex thinks, *everybody has their own journey now, looking for food, safer shelter, other survivors, and a solution. Most will never work it out and will eventually die. They weren't killers before, and they aren't now.* She's wrong.

An hour in, a guy pulls up past them, waves at Krista and points to the side of the road to pull over. Krista does that, looking back at Alex. He parks his bike and walks back to her, taking off his helmet as he nears her. He's a nice-looking guy, about 5' 10", early 30s. In any other situation, Krista might stop and chat with a fellow traveler on the road. He's smiling, doesn't look too menacing, and may have just wanted to exchange information or say hello to a fellow survivor, particularly a girl. Still, Alex doesn't want to take the chance of him being able to grab Krista. As he nears her, she zaps him, and Krista reaches out to break his fall as he hits the dirt. They put him in a comfortable position. Alex thinks, *that's number three. This taser sure has come in handy.* She couldn't have done this so nonchalantly two months ago. She looks down at the guy and apologizes, although it doesn't bother her a bit. These are different times. Anna and Tom watch the show from their sidecar. Nothing surprises Anna anymore in this new, weird world. Tom doesn't understand what happened and looks over the side at the guy on the road as they drive by. Alex says to him. Don't worry, Tom, he's just taking a nap, he was tired, and we helped him lie down. They ride on.

So much for the nice day. The weather changes again, with the temperature dropping fast. Prairie weather is unstable, with incredible swings. Clouds are scudding across the sky, and a pulverizing wind is blowing them all around. Alex is not sure they'll make it to Taber tonight because Krista will be freezing. She doesn't have the right clothes for a winter blow in July. Alex pulls ahead of her and gets Krista to pull over. She suggests they aim for a Smart Home if they can find one and wait for the temperature to come back up. Alex knows Krista is disappointed, but she's also practical, and they agree to pull off at the next farm lane. It isn't long before a road comes up, and they turn off, but it's a long drive into the farm. The house is small, built into the ground, with a long sloping roof. She keeps Krista, and the kids out of the house camera sightline, approaches the house and takes a read. It shows red. Alex says to Krista, "There's someone still alive in there."

The service barn is small, not much more than a large shed, and they would need to get all of them and the two bikes and sidecar into shelter and out of the wind and the coming rain. It won't work. Even though she's standing off from the house, Krista might be visible to the house cameras, and Alex definitely is. You never know what weapons the occupant may have or what they might be thinking. Alex approaches and speaks to the door speakers. "Hi there, my name is Alex, and I'm traveling with two kids and another woman to our family farm in Taber. She's hoping this person might take pity on a fellow farmer. She says to the door and the camera, "You might know that it's turned frigid, and we're looking for shelter for the night. We have food. We don't want any of yours and don't mean any harm. Can you help us?" Silence. Alex wonders if the person is waiting them out, hoping they'll go away, or is disabled, half-dead, or asleep. She can't take on another responsibility. It's hard enough with the kids and maybe now Krista and, of course, her broken arm. They need shelter soon. The wind has picked up, and Krista is shivering. Alex suggests she go in on her own to check out the situation. Krista thinks that's too dangerous. Alex is willing to take the risk. They need to get out of this weather fast. She gives Krista the winter jacket Francis had supplied her with, which helps. They both have tents, but Krista's won't keep her warm, and Alex's is barely big enough for the kids and her, let alone the bike and sidecar. They really need to find a house to wait out this cold spell. She needs to go in and find out what's going on.

Alex uses her wrist chip and slowly opens the door, keeping to the side and out of gun range. She sees no one, but the lights are off. She switches her glasses to night vision, and in the back of the room, behind a couch, she glimpses the top of a man's head. She calls out, "I don't mean any harm. I'm in your living room now. Can we talk?" Silence. Alex says, "I can see you behind the couch. I know you're there." A male voice says pleadingly, "Please, go away, leave me alone." Alex wonders if this poor fellow has had other intruders trying to break in. She asks, "Has someone been bothering you?" He says, "Almost every day, someone's trying to break in. I want it to stop. How did you get in?" Alex says, "Don't worry, we won't hurt you, and no one else can get in. You're safe in your house." She restates what she said outside the house. "We have our own food; we don't want any of yours. Do you have a good stock?" He's silent again; he doesn't trust her. He says, "I have nothing to give you." She says again, "Seriously, we don't need your supplies, just shelter from the storm." He says, "I'm sorry, I want you to leave. I can't have you here. Find another place."

Alex realizes this won't work. This guy's too stressed. She says, "Okay, we're leaving. I hope you have food. We could have shared some if you didn't." He says, "I'm okay. Just leave." Alex does, shutting the door behind her. She finds Krista and the kids and says, "There's a guy in there, but he's being terrorized regularly by road people trying to break in, and he sure didn't want us there. We're going to have to continue on and try to find another spot."

They ride away, but this poor man's terror stays with Alex for a long time. She remembers Francis' words, "You can't help everyone, and you'll need to come to terms with that." Today's one of those days.

The guy's name is Ralph. Ralph watches them ride away. He goes to his lower floor and checks his food stocks. He's got enough to keep him for more than a year. He would have more if he could get out and tend to his farm. The survivors keep coming looking for food, banging on his door and windows. He doesn't think he can live like this much longer. He's looking at his gun as a solution for his desperation and loneliness. He has a kill pill but somehow finds the gun calling to him.

Alex and Krista continue another ten miles up the road and find another service road. This time they're luckier. The farmhouse at the end reads dead. They go in, Alex scouts the sand piles and cleans up three, one in the bathroom, one in bed, and one at the foot of the bed. Their dog likely. They find lots of food options in the freezer and spend the night there. By morning it's back to summer again, and they're off. Crazy weather. Krista says with a laugh, "Try farming in it."

At Highway 875, they turn off and drive south. The Bow River snakes under them, as does Old Man River. They pass by numerous farms. Large squares of farm real estate growing everything they once ate. All the crops seem to be thriving. Alex understands why agriculture is in Krista's blood. They reach Taber. It used to be the corn capital of Canada. Not any more. Corn oil was identified as a key contributor to obesity many years ago and it was replaced with healthier oils, and chemicals, of course. That killed that market. It's still a small flourishing farm town, or was. It had about 10,000 citizens. Krista signals them past it, east along Crowsnest Highway, and then down a long farm road. They reach an electrified fenced compound with lots of 'No Trespassing, Electrified Uncuttable Fence' signs. Alex doesn't know why this surprises her. Krista comes from an advanced farming family, and security would have been essential. Krista opens the gates from her bike with a voice command, and they ride along a long road to a large, low house and many outbuildings. This is a considerable farm holding, not a small family farm. Alex hopes Sal is still alive. Krista can't manage this all alone.

They dismount, and the kids are out of the sidecar. Tom is immediately in a race to everywhere with his helmet off. Krista says, "Give me a minute while I check the house, okay?" Alex says, "Of course." Her dad's pile of sand may be in there, as may be Sal's. This could be very tough for her. She comes out with a grin on her face. "He's not here, but he had toast and jam for breakfast, burned the toast, and left some jam on the counter. I can still smell the burned toast. He must be out on the farm." Alex says carefully, "And your dad?" Krista says, "Sal would have cleaned him up and put him somewhere, maybe buried him with my mom." She seems so practical and doesn't show any sadness about her dad's death.

Krista says, "Let's get the kids and you in and settled. They can share a bedroom for now, but we have lots of bedrooms if Anna wants one of her own." Alex thinks ahead. *Before I leave here, I'll have to get back into my invisi-suit and get the kids into theirs. I'll also have to spray my bike and the sidecar with the invisi-paint.* She also thinks, *right now, I need another pain patch.*

The house is a very sophisticated Spanish hacienda. It's built low into the ground with a curved roof. The rooms are large with cool tiled floors the color of clay and old dark wood, thick masonry walls coated in cream stucco, and wrought-iron railings on the stairs. The rounded archways between rooms cradle the doorways and invite you beyond. It's beautiful and another surprise. Alex asks, "Who designed the house?" Krista says, "My mom and Sal designed it together. My mother wanted Sal to feel at home. She liked Mediterranean architecture, so they hired an architect to build it. It's cool in the heat of an Alberta summer and warm in our freezing winters. The floors are heated and radiate warmth into your bones after a wintry day out on the farm. I love this space." Alex says, "I love this space! What a place to grow up."

Krista says to the kids, "Go on, have a look around." This is a great new game for Tom, racing from room to room. Anna follows him a little more shyly. "What do you think, Anna?" Krista asks. Anna says with almost whispered awe, "It's beautiful!"

Chapter 23

SALVATORE THE SAVIOR

It's almost 5:00 PM, and Krista looks out the window. She wanted to surprise Sal, so she parked the bikes in an outbuilding. She looks at Alex with a huge grin, lifts her shoulders with pleasure, and says, "He's coming." The door opens and a guy who looks more like a Spanish toreador than the short Mexican farmworker Alex had envisioned comes in. He's tall, slim, and drop-dead gorgeous. His hair is longish, black, combed straight back, and he's in a light cotton shirt and tight pants, with work boots. Alex thinks, *if this were a movie, Spanish trumpets would be playing, castanets would be snapping like rattlesnake tails, and for sure, there would be a snorting bull.*

Krista is across the room from the door. Sal sees her and says with a huge smile, "Bienvenida!" She rushes to him with her arms open, and they both hug tightly, crying and laughing. He stands her back, looks at her, and runs his hand over the mark on her face from a few days ago. She dismisses it, "I'm fine." He looks around at the kids and Alex. "And who is this?" Krista introduces them and tells him the kids are part Mexican and can speak Spanish. They're both already in awe of this guy, just looking at him. Sal begins speaking in rapid Spanish to them, and their faces light up, answering him easily. Alex has no idea what they're chattering about, but they're having a great time. He's making them laugh. Krista tells him she'll catch him up on everything that has happened to her since the disaster and wants to hear everything from him. He puts his hands on her shoulders and says to her, "Your dad didn't make it." She lowers her head, and her eyes fill. "I figured that. Where is he?" He says, "I put him with your mom. It's where he would have wanted to be." She says, "Thank you, Salvatore. They both loved you so much." She says, "and Carly?" He says, "She's gone with all of her family. They're all gone." His eyes also fill. He says, "There's so much sadness here, but we're alive, and we need to move on." He says, "After supper, we'll go to pay our respects." She says, "Yes, I have to face it sometime." This is the first time Alex has seen Krista show any signs of grieving. Krista and Sal are managing much better than she is, but time has passed for all of them.

Sal says quietly to both women, out of earshot from the kids, "I'll tell you what's happening in town later. We have a few problems." He says, "Do not go outside the compound without a gun. It's very dangerous now. People are hungry, angry and agitated."

Sal pours wine, and they sit down to talk before dinner. He gets the kids some soft drinks, and they tuck in on the couches, all ears around adults, as kids often are. Tom returns to Alex and cuddles into her lap, thumb in his mouth, getting sleepy. He's missing his naps. She snuggles him into her arms. She loves these kids.

Krista fills Sal in on her trip after leaving school, her meet up with Alex, and their adventures together since they met. He says, "You were in a lot of danger, hermanita. I am so thankful you came back to me safe." He looks at Alex. "Thank you for saving her." Alex says, "She saved me. What a shot this girl is!" I owe her my life. Besides, she's doctoring my broken arm and lifting toddlers in and out of sidecars for me. I wouldn't be here without her." She shares some of her adventures with him, keeping back some information about how much gear she has. She thinks, *you never know. I just met the guy.* He says with fascination, "Can you show me your invisi-suit?" Alex says, "Sure, I'll even put it on for you." She does this and comes out, and he's obviously unaware of her presence. She touches his arm, and he jumps. "Boo," she says and hands him a pair of glasses so he can see her outline. "Dios mio!" he says, "That's incredible." Alex thinks, *I'm sure keeping this a secret. Good thing the media is shut down. Hilarious.*

Sal tells his part of the story. "I got up for breakfast, and your dad wasn't there. He was always up at dawn, so I knew something was wrong. I couldn't pull up any news or anything on the screens. I went into his bedroom, and he was already that strange pile of sand on the pillow and under the covers. I didn't know what to do or what to make of it. I thought I was having a bad dream. It was like a horror movie, only real life. Like you two, I contacted our security people, the police, the fire department, Callie, and our neighbors. Nothing. I then knew something dire was going on in a broader area. I rode over to Callie's. She was gone. She never even got out of bed. I checked on her family, also gone, piles of sand. I was in complete panic mode and did a circuit of the town, finding a few people around to talk to. We all quickly figured out the only survivors were the ones who had the vaccine. I couldn't get hold of you, hermanita, although I was pretty sure you would have survived. I just hoped you could make your way back home. I knew you were on your way, so there was no point in my going there. I would have never found you, and you would have arrived here, and I would've been gone."

He looks at the ceiling and then at Krista, his eyes filling. We'll figure this out together, hermanita." Alex says, "hermanita?" Krista says, "It means 'little sister,' although it makes me sound like a little warthog. He's called me that forever." She punches him on the arm and says, "Yes, dear brother, we'll figure it all out."

He says, "I'm starving, I'll make dinner, and we can talk while I cook." Krista says, "Sal is a fabulous cook." She says to Anna, "Would you like to be Sal's sous chef?" Anna says, "What's that?" Sal says, "It's the second in command, lots of power without all the responsibility of the head chef, one of the best kitchen jobs you can have." Anna says, "Okay, what do I do?" Sal, like Krista, is completely at ease with kids. He finds several jobs she can do with his supervision: chopping vegetables, stirring pots, and watching the timer. He has Tom sitting on a cushion on a kitchen stool so he can watch. He includes him completely in all the conversation, asking for his opinion on onions or leeks, mashed or fried, spicy, or not. Tom loves word games like this. Every now and then, Sal says something to them in Spanish and then looks at Krista and Alex, making the kids laugh out loud. They have their secrets. The kids already love Salvatore.

Supper is a delicious vegetarian dish with a bit of spice and heat but not too much, along with warm homemade bread with vegan butter melting into its crevices. Apple pie to follow. Krista is right. This guy can cook. The kids eat their whole supper. A miracle.

After the kids are in bed, Sal tells Krista and Alex, "Before the attack, we were experiencing quite a bad outbreak of a new strain of the virus in the area. The latest anti-viral pills were being distributed, but there were the usual people who refused to take them. If we're going to help everybody, we need to first find a stock of the latest anti-viral drugs and, if needed, disguise them in something we feed them. Everybody left has to be inoculated, no matter what they think. We'll also need to protect ourselves and dress in hazmat suits. We can't risk getting sick or bringing it home to the kids. We're going to have to be very careful. I've had my drug dose, but neither of you nor the kids have. Let's start with the nearest pharmacies and look for the drug." He goes on. "Alex, you can protect us with your super-duper ray gun, so it's imperative you are one half of any excursion we take." Alex says, "Yeah, I love my super-duper ray gun." Krista says, "I'll take the first shift with you tomorrow morning, and we can hit all the drugstores and clinics. There are only four drugstores in town and six clinics, so it shouldn't take long. Is that okay with you Alex?" Alex says, "Yeah, as long as I have my pain patch adhered, I'm ready."

The pain in Alex's shoulder and arm has kicked in again, and she's ready for a hot shower and more drugs. Krista shows her a bedroom and suggests she have an early night, and they talk in the morning when they're doing the drugstore run. Krista says, "I think you should stay here for at least three weeks until we get your arm somewhat mobilized." Alex says, "I can't think about that now. My arm and shoulder hurt too much, and I'm too tired. The painkillers aren't addictive, but they are sure knocking me out." Krista says, "It'll get better in time. Sleep well."

Alex is torn. There's work to do with the surviving locals, and Krista and Sal need her help, but putting off her trip for another three weeks puts her into August for the crossing. She really wanted to be across by now. Her mother is alone and in danger if she's still alive. A big if. She's got to get back to Victoria. Alex also can't imagine managing the bike and the kids while her arm and shoulder are in this shape. This isn't working out as planned at all.

After Alex goes to bed, Krista and Sal head out to the family graveyard. Krista's ancestors are buried here, including her mother and now her father. Krista notices that her parents' headstone is now carved with her dad's name and birth and death date. Sal did this. She looks at him and says, "Thanks, buddy. That means so much to me." He puts his arm around her. "They did so much for me. They were my other parents. After my parents were killed back home, I had no one and would have certainly been sent back. Your mom and dad saved me and gave me a life."

Krista is not a girly girl. She never had time for giggling about who likes whom with girlfriends. The boys in town liked her anyway. No games, straight shooter, not afraid of anything. She wasn't coy or flirtatious. She had lots of male friends, farming being a mostly male environment, a few female friends, and not much romance. She really didn't care or even notice. Some people don't send out the signal, and she was one of those.

Since they were six, Carly, Sal's girlfriend, had been her friend. Carly was a high school teacher, tall and attractive, but she just missed being beautiful. Like Krista, she was a no-nonsense type, especially with her teenage students. Not much got by her. She talked like a machine gun, hard keeping up with her. She had a killer wit. She made both Krista and Sal laugh all the time, usually in inappropriate places. It had been her sarcastic humor that had bonded the two old friends. Sal was flat out in love with her. How he was coping, Krista couldn't imagine.

Krista turned to Sal, looked long at him, and said, "I need to tell you something. Many years ago, dad told me he had changed his will so that we would inherit the farm equally when he died. He said you were as much a son to him as I was his daughter. He had planned to tell you on your wedding day this fall." Sal says, "That's not right. It's your inheritance, not mine." She says, "It's the rightest thing I can think of, and I'm so proud of him for doing that. You have put as much work into bringing this farm forward as he has." He reaches down and runs his fingers over the name and date carved on the tombstone. "Thank you, papa. I will not let you down."

Krista hadn't allowed herself to think about her dad or Carly through all of this. She had just been focused on getting home. Now she's back, and Sal is alive. She's standing here at dusk with her parents' gravestone at her feet. It begins to sink in, and she starts to fall apart. "Sal squeezes her shoulders and says, "You must cry, hermanita. It is the only way out of this misery."

Alex sleeps in late, missing the drugstore/clinic run entirely. It must have been the painkillers. The pain has subsided slightly, but it still hurts to move the arm, so she applies another pain patch. The Kingston medics said, "Don't let it get ahead of you. Stay on top of it." She does. There's no one home. Krista left a note saying they were doing a farm tour on the hovercraft with the kids and will be gone for a few hours. They can do the drugstore run in the afternoon. Farm vehicles have all been replaced with hovercraft. These are enclosed, heated, and air-conditioned, so the farm can easily be accessed anytime. All the other farming is done by variations of bot farm equipment. No more tractors stuck in the mud, no more red-necked farmers' tans.

In the note, she tells Alex to help herself to whatever she can find in the kitchen. The coffee is still hot, and Alex pours herself a mug and searches around. There's cereal in the pantry, strawberries and some oat milk in the cooler. That'll do nicely. This is the first time she's been alone for weeks. It feels strange. She tells herself, *you'll never be alone again with these kids, or at least until they're grown.* There's a daunting thought, but she's okay with it. She pokes around the house. Lots of family pictures with the four of them. Sal really is Krista's brother. She can see there's no romantic chemistry between the two of them. Besides, he was engaged. Poor bugger. Loses his adopted father and his girlfriend. Alex does muse that he'd be a catch, and you never know what fate will serve up for them. The dating pool is a lot smaller now for both he and Krista.

Around noon, they all come back. Tom and Anna are wearing matching sun hats, and their faces are pink from the sun. They come rushing in, bursting with farm news and hovercraft rides, what crops Sal and Krista grow and how they'll help, and something about the underground water and fruit growing down there. This is a wonderland for them.

Sal suggests to Tom he might like a snooze and tells Anna he has a great video for her to watch. Tom, who would often fight Alex before going down for a nap, gets carried off by Sal and goes down without a fight. Guess they tired them out this morning. Anna is watching an old video about a mother elephant and her baby. She'll never see one of those alive again.

Krista says to Alex, 'We have four drugstores to cover and about six clinics. If there are anti-virus drugs left, that's where they'll be. We should get moving." They ride out, watching for people, and stop at the first drugstore. These are set up like Smart Homes, pretty much impenetrable, but Alex has her trusty wrist chip, and in they go. They're still determining how they'll identify the drug as compared to others, but they get a lucky break. One of the pharmacy meeting rooms was set up to distribute these, and the paperwork confirms this was the drug. They take the entire supply, check the locked cabinets for any backup, and grab that. They wind their way through town and grab what they can from each pharmacy and clinic.

It's eerie. They see no one. Krista says to Alex, "I'm getting worried that we're too late for even the survivors. We haven't seen a soul." Alex says, "Yes, it's strange." Krista says, "We'll start knocking on doors tomorrow after I make up a bunch of drug cookies. That will get the drug into them, at least. They ride home with both their bikes stuffed with pill bottles. Krista gets to work on her drug cookies: one cookie, one mashed-up pill. Both Alex and Krista eat a cookie to test it and get the drug into them. They both agree they cannot taste it. They give one to each of the kids. Now they're at least inoculated. This time. They can only hope that with fewer people, there will be fewer viruses circulating in the future. Hardly good news.

Krista says to Alex, "We have a few hours before supper, and Sal and I have to do some planning. Why don't you take a walk around the farm and stretch your legs? The dome over the underground orchard is just on the other side of the house. There are hats and sunscreen at the door." Alex thinks this is a fine idea. Sal says to Alex, "Don't go near the fences. It's not safe. You may see people out there, staring in. Stay in the center of the farm. There's a road down the middle." Krista says, "I would be relieved if she did see somebody. Then we would at least know they aren't all dead from the virus." Sal says, "We'll find out tomorrow."

Krista and Sal have the entire farm up on the main screen, and intricate screens work with the main screen, flashing up, changing, and dancing together. Hard to believe this software is managing a farm. Alex doesn't know a thing about farming, so this is new to her. She thinks, *that would have been a great research project*. She's still a researcher at heart. She misses that work.

Krista and Sal launch into complicated discussions about what will be ready and when and what food they can share with the survivors. They go over tillage, planting, spraying, fertilization, irrigation, harvesting, capturing of seeds, storage, replanting, and artificial pollination. They have a small mill on-site for personal use, and there are a few mills in town. They won't worry too much about making great volumes of bread and pasta. There are very few people left to feed.

Alex leaves them to it and takes her break, walking for miles around the farm. She stays far away from the fences, enjoying the fresh air, the hot feel of the sun on her face, and the freedom of exercise without security around every corner. She's drugged her arm and shoulder into submission, so she steps out freely. The last time she ran was the night before the incident. She's hoping to run again someday.

She doesn't recognize any crops, but the colors and foliage change as she walks. The light mesh protecting and feeding all of this sends shots of sunlight back at her. It really is big sky country, with no trees for miles, and she can see where a windstorm could wipe it all out in minutes without this technology. The mesh is rolled back in one of the fields, and a bot thresher works away. Farm labor has completely changed in the past many decades. She thinks about how hard early farmers worked, even with good equipment. They still had to do it all themselves, and many just quit as the new technology increased yields and profits for those who could afford it. It changed the world of food supply and who was doing it. Krista and Sal are still farmers at heart, but the technology works for them.

Alex finds the underground orchard dome and looks in. The dome is misty in the heat of the day. This is a veritable jungle of fruit trees and vines, all climbing many levels of walls, irrigated and artificially lit. It's all protected from Alberta's wind, blizzards, and blinding summer sun. She still thinks advancements like these are a miracle, even though they've been around for many decades. Alex and Sal have a good supply of underground water and fields of miniature solar panels drawing water out of the air.

After a few hours, she returns, feeling guilty about abandoning the kids to these two busy farmers for so long. She had no need to worry. Tom's playing quietly with some of the building blocks she brought. Anna's reading, and Krista and Sal are still hard at it, planning the future. All is right with the world here. It's a different story outside the fence.

Chapter 24

SEARCH AND RESCUE

The kids go out with Sal and Krista in the morning and sponge up farm information. Sal quizzes them at supper every night about what they're learning. It's farm school. Alex cleans up where she can, takes care of the laundry and dishes, dusting, and vacuuming. She also makes up the daily supply of bread, thanks to the bread-making equipment. Sal has taught her how to do a few other things she can still manage with one hand. Alex has become the housekeeper, and she doesn't like it. She thinks, *I used to be somebody*.

Sal has had a man-to-man chat with Tom about how clever it is to not pee and poop in your pants. Alex loved watching that. Tom was all enormous eyes, taking it in. He has done well since that chat. The kids are relaxed, and Anna's much happier. All the fresh air and sunshine are doing them both good. They hadn't been outside in a long time.

They decide to send Sal out with Alex for the first excursion into town and get a read on the survivors and what their needs are, besides food. This is a farm town, so there wouldn't have been a big supply of Nutri biscuits. The government would have expected the town to have enough food to feed itself. They pick up a supply of medical hazmat suits at the hospital and put them on.

The streets are empty. The remaining survivors seem to have retreated to their houses, probably for safety but possibly because they're also sick or dead with the virus.

Krista's family was a big financial supporter of many community efforts, small and large; the hospital, schools, sports teams, you name it. Everybody knew Krista and Sal. Sal coached little league and soccer, and Krista ran the summer farm camps for the kids. The town population was only about 10,000, and Krista and Sal knew almost everybody in town and all the farmers for 30 miles out. They think there might be 100-200 survivors.

Alex reads the houses, and when they find someone alive, Sal goes in and calls out, "Hello, anybody here?" He knows who lived where. When the person responds, Sal speaks to them by name. "Hi Jenny, it's Sal. How're you doing? Do you need food? I brought you a cookie to start." The Jennies, Hals, and Stuarts, who were the bankers, high school teachers, and plumbers, all need to talk. They're terrified and usually have a pile of sand or two in their house that was their partner, parent, children, or cat. Sal and Alex keep the visits brief. Sal gives them an overview of what happened, the plan to move forward, and a promise to return. They get in and out as fast as possible, or they'll never be done. They can't absorb everybody's grief and terror.

They check the freezers and coolers and note who has food and who doesn't. Frozen and dry food is brought back from houses with no survivors. They don't bring any people back but recirculate food to those who need it and offer what little medical help they can.

Alex adds a new basic entry code to each house so that Sal and Krista can return and have entry. Krista and Sal don't have the time to come out every day. Still, Alex tries to do 3-400 houses daily, so the whole town and outlying farms are visited and will be recoded before she leaves. The survivors might not be happy about that, but it's the only way Sal and Krista can reliably check on them. Alex sets up a database, and slowly fills it in with the dead and the living. Unfortunately, there are few survivors. Alex thinks, *this is my new job, besides housekeeper in residence, recorder of the dead and dying.*

Sal enters one house to find Jimmy Brixton the only survivor. Jimmy had an appliance store and repair shop in town. He's sitting on his couch, bent over in pain. He's mid-sixties, completely bald, and in a loose cotton shirt and pants. His face is shiny with sweat, and the grimace on his face tells them what kind of shape he's in. Jimmy says to Sal, "You're a welcome sight, son. I didn't think help would ever come. I thought I was done for." Sal asks him what's wrong, and Jimmy tells him he has an unbearable pain in his gut. They scan Jimmy and send it off to the medics in Kingston. They get back to them quickly with bad news. He has a twisted bowel. There's nothing Sal and Alex can do for him. He'll die soon and in a lot of pain. Sal looks at Alex and says, "I've got to tell him." He sits with Jimmy and quietly talks with him, with his arm around his back. Jimmie starts to weep, and Sal holds his hand and says, "I'm so sorry it has come to this. I wish I could do more for you." Jimmy says, "My wife and kids are gone; all my family and friends are gone, and now I'll die here too." Sal says, "Yes, my friend. It's too sad to contemplate. There's great loss all over the world." Sal asks him if he can get him some stronger pain drugs. Jimmie brushes that aside. "If the pain gets too bad, I'll take the little green pill." ' Sal says, "If that's your choice, Jimmie, it's there to give you relief in an impossible situation." Jimmie says, "This seems to be one." Sal says, "I'll check in on you regularly." Jimmie says, "Thanks, Sal. I hope you and Krista and Alex stay healthy." Sal thinks grimly, *I probably won't see him alive again.*

After Sal and Alex leave, Jimmy goes into the bedroom and looks at the pile of sand that was his wife, Helen, on her side of the bed. He gets a glass of water, opens the bedside table drawer, and retrieves the pill. He climbs into bed beside her, gets under the comforter, looks over at her remains, and receives another sharp twist of gut pain that makes him draw his knees up to his chin. He's not a religious man but says anyway, "I'm coming, Helen, I'm coming." He downs the pill.

The grave danger of having no doctors to help in these kinds of emergencies now rings loudly in both Alex's and Sal's minds. They must be so careful about sickness and accidents. No one can help them.

As they continue moving up and down the streets, they find a young woman, Sheri, at home when they call. She greets Sal at the door with tears streaming down her face. "Thank god you're here, Sal," she says. Sal introduces her to Alex as a friend of Krista and Carli's. They nod at each other. Sheri jumps in. "Is Krista still alive?" Sal says, "Yes, she's home and fine." She then asks, "What about Carli?" Sal says, "She's gone." Sheri looks at Sal and says, "I'm so sorry. You guys were great together. I was going to be a bridesmaid. I already have the dress." She starts to cry again. Sal says, "You have great loss too. Did anyone in your family make it?" She shakes her head, "No." She says, "My grandmother did but went with the virus last week. At least, I think that's what she died of. She couldn't breathe." Sal asks, "Did you take the last virus pill being offered?" Sheri says, "Yes." Sal says, "Good, we're distributing it to anyone left alive, just in case they didn't."

Sal asks, "What's going on with your face?" One side of Sheri's face is very swollen and red. She says, "I've got an awful toothache; the pain is there even with the pain patch. Is there anything I can do?" Alex scans Sheri's face, and the Kingston medics get back to them. "This one you can solve. Amateurs have been pulling teeth for thousands of years. It would be best if you took her to a dentist's office, where you'll find the right tools to pull the tooth and the right drugs to knock her out before you do. Sal, you're a mechanical engineer. You can do this." Sal has known Sheri for years and wants to bring her some relief. He says to her,

"There's a dentist's office a few blocks over. Let's move over there, and if you trust me, I'll take out the tooth." She says, "Do you know how to put in the freezing?" Sal says, "I don't need to freeze it. We'll just put you to sleep for half an hour." Sal gets Sheri to hop onto the back of his bike, and they move to a local dentist's office. The Kingston medics tell him which tools and drugs to use and how to use them. Sal looks at Sheri and asks, "Ready?" She says, "God, yes, get rid of this pain." He injects the drug, and she's asleep in a minute.

Sal follows their instructions, and after some intense plier work, out comes the tooth, gushing with blood and pus. They tell him what drugs to give her to fight the infection. Sheri wakes up without a molar but pain-free. Sal asks her worriedly, "How does it feel?" She says it's sore, but it's no longer throbbing. Alex thinks, *and now Sal is the town dentist.*

Sal says to Sheri, "We'll check on you tomorrow. Take the drugs as prescribed and get some sleep. Once you're back on your feet, we need to talk. We'll need your help getting the people who survived back into some kind of life. We can feed everybody, but there's more to life than that. Are you up for that?" Sheri says, "You can count on me and Sal, thanks. You may have just saved my life. I could have died of the infection." Sal says, "We've all got to work together. I'm so glad I could help." He takes her back to her house, and they say their goodbyes for now.

After she's gone, Alex looks at Sal and says, "What a day!" Sal says, "Hey, I've got one volunteer. That's progress."

For too many of the survivors, it's too late. They have either died of the virus, starvation, heart attacks from the shock, or something else. It's hard to tell what took them. They notice the survivors' bodies are not turning into sand but more of a mummified state. Alex thinks, *thankfully, we haven't found any more surviving kids, although that means they're all dead.* Krista and Sal say they knew two families with kids with cancer, but they obviously couldn't afford the vaccine.

Over the weeks, they work their way through the neighborhood grid and then out to the farms. When they have checked every house and know who's survived, they check on them regularly and bring food and fresh fruit from the farm or neighboring homes. Sal and Krista are planning a town meeting to discuss the future. They're hoping to teach those willing and able to become farmers, but there are so few people left alive that it will be an enormous challenge. When Alex goes, they won't have access to the Kingston medics anymore. They'll be on their own. The future's not rosy.

Meanwhile, their farm is humming. Several wheat and bean crops are ready, and the mesh has rolled back, preparing for harvesting. They'll have way more food than they need but can use other farmers' silos that won't be used this year to store this year's crops. Unless the farmer survived, and few of them did, most farms will go to seed without attention. Whether the seeds will re-germinate is the big question. Sal and Krista are developing a way to pollinate crops without insects.

Alex introduces them to Francis, and she brings her new agricultural project team into these meetings. Krista has transmitted all her class notes and agricultural college lectures back to them. Alex thinks, *this bike screen and scanner are handy little tools.* They all talk for hours, and of course, the big question is, "Will the crops reseed after a prairie winter?" Krista and Sal will test replanting this summer, but that might not be the definitive answer.

In a private conversation, Alex asks Francis how it's going with the team. Francis says, "It's challenging, and they're challenging. I didn't think it would be easy, and it's not." She continues, "I'll fill you in when they get back to me with their input, but I'll tell you, my office is a busy place. Everybody wants a shoulder to cry on. These people are on the edge of desperation and don't want to be stuck here underground for the rest of their lives. We're trying to keep the lid on chaos and dangerous decisions to run."

Chapter 25

CHOICES

It's been two weeks since Alex broke her arm. The Kingston medics rescan it and tell her the bone is healing and it's time for physiotherapy. They give her a variety of exercises to do several times a day, and she's diligent. She needs to get this fixed. It hurts like hell, but every day is better. After a week, she still can't lift anything of consequence. The medics tell her it could be months before it's back to normal.

Krista and Sal have embraced Alex and the kids and act as if they're staying forever. Well into the third week, after the kids are in bed, Krista, Sal and Alex enjoy a second glass of wine and talk about the future of the farm and the town. So many things have changed, and so many decisions must be made about how it will all roll out. Alex is always working through her arm exercises, and Krista and Sal watch her wince as she tries to push through the pain.

Krista jumps in. "How about staying? We'd like that. You're part of our family now." She goes on, "I know you want to find your mother, and given the losses we've all experienced, we get that." Alex can tell she doesn't want to offend her regarding her plan to take the kids with her, but she also knows what Krista thinks of that plan. Alex thinks, *I've been 'handled' before, and I know when someone's handling me.* Sal says, "If your mother's alive, she'll likely continue to live for a while. You said she has food. There's nothing for you in Victoria if she didn't make it, but you have us here. You could stay even for a year until your arm heals and the kids are a year older. You might decide to stay with us forever. We would love that." Alex is not fooled. She's not a farmer and can't help them much with or without a broken arm. They also want access to the Kingston medics. That goes when she goes. She knows this is really about the kids. These two love these kids already. They probably think they'll never have any of their own now. This is their chance for a family. The kids would be safer and happier here on the farm. Alex knows this. She's just not ready to face it.

She says, "I'm not an idiot. I know the kids would be better off here, but I'm very conflicted about how I feel about that. I've only had them for a short while, but I love them as my own. I guess it's my ego, and I can't let that get in the way of their safety. I started this trip to get to my mother and never thought I would be taking on two little kids, but I did. I'm not great at it, but I'm learning. I also don't want to give up on my mother. She may need me. The kids are an enormous responsibility; I'm signed on for it. I don't want to unload that on you two. You're great with them, but you already have so much to do with the town survivors. You don't have the time to care for and raise two little kids in the middle of a disaster like this." Krista says, "You misunderstand. We want the whole package, all three of you. We're busy, but so are many parents, or they were. It's good modeling for kids to see their caretakers busy and involved in life, and we need help to do everything we want to do. We need you." Alex thinks, *Yeah, you like having a housekeeper and a built-in babysitter.* But that would sound nasty, and she doesn't say it out loud.

Sal says, "It's a big decision, mi amigo. Please take all the time in the world, at least a year, to think about it." He winks at Alex. "We would love if you would stay." He gives her a big grin and offers to top up her glass. "More wine?" He's a rascal.

They don't talk about it again for days, just continue their daily routines. Alex thinks of nothing else. She knows they don't want her to take the kids across the water. It's too dangerous. She doesn't want to take the kids across the water, either. Krista and Sal wouldn't say it, but they probably don't trust her to take care of them in the future. She's also not sure she has what it takes. It scares the hell out of her. The kids love it here and have stabilized.

Alex rides out to get the kids some fresh clothes and returns to the compound yard. Sal is coming across the front patio with Tom on his shoulders. Tom is tanned, giggling like mad with his hat askew. He's a happy little boy. In the house, Anna and Krista have their heads together in front of the screen with the farm management software. Krista is showing her how it works and is getting her to call up information. Anna's enthralled.

Alex knows what she has to do.

That night, she tells them. "I've made a decision. I hope you're okay with it. I must find my mother, alive or dead; she may be my last living relative. I miss her terribly. The kids are so happy and relaxed with you. They were a mess when I found them. I can't think of a safer place for them, and I don't think they'd be happy leaving. It would upset them all over again. If I leave the kids with you and go and find her, what would you think about me bringing my mother back here? She'd probably love the idea of being a pseudo-grandmother. We wouldn't have to live here, but we could help in any way you could use us. She's still young and active. If she's gone, I could still get back in that boat and sail back. If I can do it once, I can do it twice." They look at each other, and Krista says, "I love it. What a great idea!" Sal says, "Thank you, mi amigo. You know we will care for them like our own and wait for your return."

Alex is not completely honest about the reality of ever coming back. There are mountains to ride through, an ocean to cross, and dismal, starving people running out of options. She still has a long road ahead of her. She thinks of her mother with two adopted grandchildren, and it warms her heart. But getting her manicured mother into a rubber boat to cross the strait back to Vancouver with Alex at the helm is another question altogether. Let alone on the back of a motorcycle all the way to Alberta. It makes her laugh to think of it.

Saying goodbye to the two little ones she has grown to love will be the hardest farewell. However, they'll be safe, and she needs to get to her mother.

Alex takes Anna for a walk in the compound. Full of her new knowledge of the farm, Anna tells Alex what each building is used for. She has a new confidence, and a happy little girl is emerging. She skips as they walk along. Alex tries to remember the last time she herself skipped.

Alex says, "You know, you're my hero. You were so scared when I met you. Even when you missed your mom and dad so much, you helped me get Tom better. Thank you, honey. I'll never forget that." Anna says softly, "You're welcome." Alex had hoped for a reciprocal acknowledgment of what she did. She doesn't get it. Alex reminds herself Anna is only six, without the social skills of an adult. She pushes on. "We're all going through an awful thing, losing so many people we love. You have been very brave, and I like how well you and Tom have become friends with Krista and Sal. They really love you both." Anna smiles but says nothing. *Enigmatic little rascal, this one*, Alex thinks.

Alex tells Anna she'll be leaving soon to find her mother, and she needs to talk to her about that. She tells her about the trip through the mountains and then in a boat over the ocean to Victoria. She says it will be very dangerous, and she worries about her and Tom. She asks Anna, "How would you feel about staying on the farm with Krista, Sal, and Tom?" Anna is very silent and then looks up at Alex and says quietly, "I would like that." Alex feels a stab in her heart that Anna hasn't chosen her. She isn't even making a fuss about Alex leaving. If she had, Alex would still have convinced her to stay. Still, she would have liked for Anna to have some regrets about Alex leaving. She squeezes Anna's shoulders and tells her that's an excellent decision and that Krista and Sal will be very happy to hear it. They love having them here. Anna does not respond to the squeeze. Not a touchy-feely kid. Alex says, "Who knows, if I find my mom, we might come back here again." Anna responds with a weak, "That would be nice." Alex thinks, *Yeah, I don't believe it either*. Saying goodbye to sweet little Tom will be much harder.

Chapter 26

ADIOS AMIGOS

It's the last night, and they're drinking wine on the cozy couch in that lovely Spanish room. *The last safe night,* Alex thinks. They talk about their plans, Alex's trip, and how they wish there were some way they could communicate. They all hope some nerd survivor somewhere will figure it all out and reconnect them again. Francis has said that her I.T. people are sure they can hack into other communication satellites. It's just a matter of time. They'll need to find out which satellite Taber's SAT phones and telecommunication were feeding from. Satellites were all controlled by one huge international network. Technology is not Alex's thing, but she sure hopes it's someone's.

Krista and Sal say again how grateful they are she has entrusted the kids to them. Alex says, "It's where they belong." They say, "You should be very proud. You saved their lives, and we will never let them forget you." Alex says, "Oh, I'll quickly become a distant memory in their young minds. I don't kid myself on that one. Tom won't even remember me." They say, "We'll make sure they remember you. We have pictures of you together. We'll remind them." Alex says, laughing. "I'll become that annoying story you two keep bringing up. I can see them rolling their teenage eyes."

Before she goes to bed, she goes in and pulls Tom's blanket over his shoulders and rests her hand on his warm little back, feeling him breathe. She sits with him, watching him sleep. He twitches, lost in some little boy's dream. Leaving him shatters all her thoughts she ever had about not wanting children. In this short time, he's become hers, and now she knows she has to let him go to keep him safe. It's one of the hardest decisions she's ever made.

The following day brings another hot sunny morning in early August in Alberta. Alex is packed up and re-suited in her invisi-suit, and they all gather in the courtyard to say goodbye. She has her hood back and is just a drifting head to them all right now. She hugs the kids and thanks them for their precious time together.

She takes a long look at their little faces. "Who will they become?" She wonders. Tom doesn't know what's going on, but it seems exciting. Krista has her hands on Anna's shoulders, and Anna says quietly, "Thanks, Alex." Alex is sure Krista prompted this, but she'll take it for what it is. These two are Krista and Sal's now. Alex takes Sal's hand with her invisible one. He still jumps and laughs and says a handshake is not good enough. A hug is needed, and they embrace. Krista and Alex look long and hard at each other. They've been through some life-changing times together.

Trying to keep it light, Alex says, "I'll have my people call your people." They're both crying. Krista hugs her tight. Alex swallows her sadness at saying goodbye to these dear people, probably forever. It's as if they're dying. She goes back and hugs Tom hard, looks long into his chocolate eyes, and inhales his smell for the last time. *My baby boy*, she thinks.

Alex forces herself to mount her bike and says, "Gotta go, my friends. Have a happy and long life. Thank you for everything." Krista says, "Thank you for everything you've done. You saved the kids. You saved me. You decoded the town's houses, and now you're leaving these wonderful kids with us. You're amazing." Alex flips that off with a smile, "All in a day's work, ma'am." Krista says, "Please, please be careful and try to come back to us. You're a part of us now, and we don't want to lose you."

Alex rides away, looking over her shoulder at them all standing there waving in the morning sun. They were her family for a short while. She turns at the curve in the road, and they're out of sight, gone, a dream. They turn back to their busy day. Alex thinks, *I don't know how many more times my heart can be broken. Maybe I'll make it back someday.*

She swallows her tears, heads back to the TransCanada, and turns west to Calgary. It should take her about three hours. She's still riding past massive farms with miles and miles of glittering mesh holding the field, grain, bean, oil, and seed crops in place. The wind still creates a wave of the green tops reaching out to the sun. It's like a large concert of fans at a rock concert swaying back and forth.

It's been three months since the attack. Survivors will be hungry, frantic and more dangerous. Alex knows she'll have to be steadier in her resolve to ride on past. She can't save everybody, and one leads to another. She knows these decisions could get more complicated.

There are fewer bikes on the road. Alex thinks people are hunkering into their safe places and perhaps only going out to forage for food, or they've already starved to death. No one's following her, so far, and she hopes whoever butchered Diya and took her gear went back the other way. They would hopefully have lost her trail while she was in Taber.

She's been through Calgary a few times and has a rough idea of the city's layout. It was always soulless to her, but it wasn't her town. She likes green spaces with lots of water. That's not Calgary. She drops down into the city off the highway from the north. Calgary used to be a big oil and cattle town with about 1.2 million people. The city had many active businesses and residential centers in its day. With the disappearance of the oil and meat industry, the city became a ghost town for many decades. There was lots of crime, and the remaining struggling people resorted to gangs and break-ins, with no security to stop them. Alberta's weather had become so extreme; unbearable heat waves, blizzards, big melts, tornado-like winds, and never in the seasons you would expect them to be. Not a place you'd want to live. Then, like a phoenix, it resurfaced as the tech capital of Canada. The old downtown high rises and business towers were refurbished and refortified.

The techies all lived and worked in these buildings, rarely coming out onto the street. Now dust zephyrs are blowing down the empty alleys of the streets, rolling and bouncing off buildings and fences. Before the attack, Calgary still held the Stampede every year to honor the city's heritage. A few farmers kept bulls and cows for the riding and wrangling of the rodeo. Fewer still kept horses, but the remainders were trotted out for the annual parade. It was a sad affair. Few people cared about the old cowboys and Indians. Last Alex heard; it was on its last legs. No one was coming out for an old-west show that was no longer relative to anyone's life or experiences.

She had been to one stampede when she was in her late teens. She drove in with a group of girlfriends from Victoria. They bought cowboy hats and went to all the pancake breakfasts and parties. They danced their tails off with strange new guys in tight jeans and once a year cowboy boots and never got around to going to any rodeo events. Bull riding and cow wrangling held little interest, but the boys did.

Alex rides over to the grounds where none of that will ever happen again. The animals are gone, along with the cowboys and cowgirls. No more animal smell, that sharp tang of cow dung, a smell she oddly always liked. There's no more rising dust and the smell of leather, saddles, and unhappy animals roped and ridden into submissiveness. She could never see the sport in all that. She envisions the skinny, rough-looking cowboys dressed in leather pants and cowboy boots, full of adrenaline, piss, and vinegar. They ride large angry, snorting bulls, one hand in the air, and not for long. They break their bones and then get right back on for what she always thought was an insignificant purse. She guessed it was a club they wanted to belong to. Riding around to the various rodeos in the States and Canada and competing, getting a name for themselves in that small circle. Everybody wants to be famous. She remembers a line from an old Judy Collins song, popular what seems like 1,000 years ago. "He loves that damned old rodeo as much as he loves me. Someday soon, goin' with him, someday soon." Alex hears that high clear voice in her head, particularly poignant now.

Alex doesn't think testing anything in Calgary will give Francis and her crew any new information, so she heads to the mountains. Maybe the mountain lake water is different. Banff is about two hours away. It doesn't take long to pass through the foothills, and the terrain changes fast. The mountains are still off in the distance, but she gains on them. Still very few bikes out here. She passes by Canmore and then on into the park where the town of Banff sits. Nobody's selling park passes today in the booth. It's a funny town, with wide streets that look kind of western, and alleyways of smaller houses running in the back of the main street. Colossal fir trees everywhere. It was always a tourist mecca. It offered the usual schlock, along with pricey cashmere sweaters from sheep still allowed to graze somewhere on a distant foreign slope. They're gone now. There were always expensive designer bags made from some chemical substance and tiny high-end clothes targeting the smaller Asian market who traveled here in busloads. They loved Canada's wealth of space. There must be a lot of sand now in those huge, crowded Chinese and Indian cities, a veritable beach.

The town always felt dark to Alex. The mountains seemed to crowd around like tall protective grandparents, shoulder to shoulder with their ancient white heads. She hadn't been around mountains for a while and had forgotten how they seemed to carry a feeling with them. They're old guards, still standing erect, shoulders back, watching the centuries go by, thrusting up from an ice age long ago. They're still speechless, silently witnessing man's frailty, foolishness, and comparatively quick demise. "It didn't have to be," they seem to say. "You had choices."

Tall cedars are everywhere, still dropping pinecones in the parks, casting long shadows. Alex feels like she's in a canyon. Any piles of sand on the street have long blown away. It was predawn when it hit, so few people would have been out. There's no evidence of the herds of elk that always hung around town, gone with the last windstorm that blew through town. Gone forever. She can't even think about all the creatures that no longer exist. It's too big a tragedy to embrace.

She takes some water samples from the Bow River and then rides to the Upper Hot Springs at the Shamrock Resort Hotel, thinking that spring water should be different. She had sent well samples from the farm back to Kingston, but the Kingston labs share no results, so she's in the dark. Even though the springs would constantly refresh the water, Alex still views large pools shared by lots of people as big toilets. It has been a while since anyone has peed here. Not a soul around. The surviving hotel guests are still in there or have decamped into town to find food. She checks the kitchen, and the coolers and freezers have been emptied. She guessed the rooms' mini bars would be the same. She sends samples off, then heads back up to the Fairmont Banff Springs Hotel, the grand old lady, now almost two centuries old. The hotel looks worn with its overgrown grounds and gardens. Alex stayed here before and was always struck by the ghost stories that went with the hotel. Tourists love ghost stories. Some jilted bride or drowning boy, always in wispy white garments, appropriately dressed like ghosts. They've got lots of company now. If only someone remained to share the new ghost stories with. Alex takes a sample of the spring water and sends it off.

She's hungry and would prefer real food if she can find it, rather than wafers, so she rides back to town looking for a Smart Home. She finds a few off Banff Avenue and reads them. One's still live. There's someone in there. She doesn't want to know. She chooses a dead house down the block. Whoever lived here is gone. No sign of anyone's remains here. Ski cottages always have a smell, hard to describe, dry heated cedar, sweaty ski boots, something. Their skis, boots, and poles are in a separate equipment room, along with their winter clothing, waiting for the next season. It looks like a couple and two kids lived here, or it was their winter ski house. Who knows? There are pictures of them around the house, lots of parties. They had fun here. That's something. They left a casserole in the freezer. She doesn't know how old it is, but she thaws it and eats some.

She wants to make Lake Louise her last stop before she heads into the heart of the Rockies and leaves Banff. Just her and the Bow River at her side. It's been with her for a while.

Lake Louise is a hamlet with about 1,000 people living there. Any survivors are lying low, probably protecting their remaining food stocks. No farms like Taber to draw on here. She rides up to the Fairmont hotel. Both the Banff Springs Hotel and this one always had the lushest carpets. There was always the hush of money and luxury and history and winter in the plush. You wanted to take off your shoes and run in your bare feet.

Someone broke into the bar but missed the stash of scotch bottles underneath the counter. She pours a double and sits in one of the oversized leather chairs, looking out at the lake. She savors the burn of the scotch. The lake is still mediterranean turquoise, flat as glass, and serene. No birds swooping down over the surface. It's on its own now for centuries to come. She should hike out to the glacier and take a sample, but that would take another day, and she doesn't have the right tools to get into the core. She has another scotch.

This hotel had its own spook stories. She can't remember any of them specifically, more white ghost clothing. She wonders, "Why don't ghosts ever wear navy or tan with a nice pair of stilettos? Always that boring white?"

Alex suddenly senses a subtle noise behind her. Standing too close is an older guy, with a big belly still, bald, late 70s, dressed in a matching navy sweatsuit, a look that doesn't look good on anyone. He must have been a guest when this happened. He's probably been eating his way through the coolers, freezers, and minibars. The master code for the rooms would have been somewhere at the front desk. He's staring at her scotch glass going up and down, unattached to anything he can see. This will be a specter story he has no one to share with, poor bastard. He looks terrified. She puts down the glass and moves away from the chair in case he gets brave and comes nearer. She wishes she could ask him to join her, but that's not to be. He remains, and she leaves, thinking, "Good luck, buddy. I can't help you."

The hotel would have been full when the attack happened. There would have been many surviving wealthy seniors with a cancer history and enough money for the vaccine. They have no way home now, no service cars or solar buses operating, and no way to communicate. Stuck here until they figure out a plan, or don't, and starve to death. She's not their savior.

Alex envisions these grand old buildings slowly degrading over the years, taken by the weather and lack of attention. They'll be gone forever in the years to come. That will apply to most structures around the world. Maybe 500 years from now, people will trip around the fallen bricks and mortar of places like this and talk about the old days. The old days are now. She thinks, *maybe my journals will survive, and they can tune into what happened.*

It's been a long day, and she wants to get into British Columbia today, so she heads to Golden, about an hour away. The last time she checked, around 4,000 people were living there. There might be a Smart Home or two. They may not have needed them in such a small community. As the Columbia River runs along its spine, there should be some good water and vegetation testing opportunities. In town, she chooses a house, reads it, and it's dead. She finds just two piles of sand in the bed. They never have to hit that alarm buzzer again. Alex has become very blasé about these disintegrated bodies. Amazing what you can get accustomed to.

Her arm and shoulder ache, and she applies a pain patch, prepares supper, and settles in for the night. It'll be a long haul through the mountains tomorrow. She grabs a duvet and a pillow and curls up on the couch. The kids would be tucked up in bed in Taber by now. She misses them. It pours outside. She falls into a deep sleep with the sound of the rain on the windows. She's never been lonelier.

Chapter 27

DESPERADO

Desperado
..."Oh, you ain't gettin' no younger. Your pain and your hunger, they're drivin' you home.
Freedom, oh freedom. Well, that's just some people talkin.
Your prison is walkin' through this world all alone."
Eagles, 1973

Junie and Jacob have lots to think about concerning their move to the farmhouse in Niagara on the Lake. She needs to bring the contents of her condiment cabinet and her remaining dry food. Jacob will need to move his Nutri Biscuits stored at the Kracker's house. Junie wants to keep her small farm. Many vegetables and beans need to be harvested, and they don't know what will be available at the new location over the winter. They think about how they might move everything without being too visible. They agree it has to be done over a few days at night. They sit in their lawn chairs in front of her tent and plan. He's only thirteen but has a logical way of thinking. He's come through a lot with the loss of his parents and favorite teacher, but he has backbone. Junie is looking forward to living and working with this young man.

It's midday, and they hear a bike coming toward them fast. Jacob sees him first. He says to Junie, "It's the same guy who came through the Kracker's neighborhood and killed that woman. I think he's crazy." Junie always has her gun in her pocket and puts her hand on it. The biker races up to them and does a spin in front of her tent, kicking up dirt, eying them both. His gun arm is stiff and high, swinging back and forth between them. He's alternately wild-eyed or staring straight at them. He's not in control. He gets right to it. "Do you have food?" Junie says, "I have nothing prepared, but I can make you something." The biker says, "I'm not interested in a family barbecue. Let's see what you have." He brushes past the two of them into her tent and opens her cooler. Junie looks at Jacob and waves her hand quietly behind her, signaling him to keep calm. Junie knows there isn't much in there he can grab and run with. He looks in her condiment cabinet and says, "What's all this?" Junie says, "Just spices." In one big gesture, the biker topples the condiment cabinet onto the floor and says in anguish, "I need food!" He turns to Junie, aims his gun at her, and says, "You're eating something. Where is it?"

In one quick movement, Junie shoots the gun out of the biker's hand, and it goes flying off into the woods. Jacob knows enough about marksmanship to know how difficult a shot that was. He has new admiration for Junie, the gunslinger. The biker stands there with his now empty hand, staring after his gun, his face dissolving like a toddler heading into a tantrum.

Junie doesn't take shit from anyone. With her gun still pointing at him, she says, "Now pick that cabinet up and put everything back. Who the hell do you think you are, coming here and messing with my stuff?" The biker looks at her with surprise and fear. Junie says, "Do it now. You know I will shoot you if you don't pick that cabinet up. I'm tired of punks like you." To Jacob's amazement, the shooter complies, rights the cabinet, and makes a half-ass attempt at putting everything back on the shelves. He at least gets everything off the floor. He's also crying. Once this is done, Junie says, "Now get back on your bike and ride away. If I ever see you here again, I'll shoot you dead." The biker looks at the forest where his gun skittered off and thinks, *I'll get another gun, and then I'm coming back to kill this bitch.* The kid looks vaguely familiar to him, but he can't place him. He remembers shooting at Cora in a foggy rage, but he doesn't clearly remember Jacob. That day is now hazy in his memory. He mounts his bike, giving Junie a filthy look, and peels away in a cloud of road dust.

After he's gone, Junie says to Jacob, "He'll be back, and soon. We need to get out of here fast. He'll want to kill us." She has a wagon she attaches to her bike. She used it to move her produce around the Camps. They quickly load that up with her herbs, unguents, and dried food. It's broad daylight and unsafe to be seen, but they have no choice. They ride back to the safety of the Kracker's house. Fortunately, no one's on the road, and they got there unharmed. Jacob codes them in, and Junie enters the great room. She says, "Wow, this is beautiful. I can see why you love this place." Jacob says, "We could just stay here for a while." Junie says, "I think we should stick with the farm, honey. That gives us a chance to grow food and feed ourselves. We can't do that here." She grins at him and says, "Besides, I hate those bloody Nutri biscuits."

The biker's name is Peter, and he wasn't always crazy. He's out of his mind with grief and anger and now hunger and fear of his own death. He also hasn't had his anxiety meds for months and doesn't know where to get a new supply. These calmed him, kept him stable, allowed him to live a normal life, and kept him sane. He has searched the back rooms of every pharmacy in town, hoping he might find some, with no success. He and his wife Janie had just had a baby boy. She was still nursing him at the time of the attack. Peter found them entwined together, a bundle of still sweet-smelling nighty, a tiny blue onesy, and those hideous piles of sand where his son's chubby little legs used to be. Peter had skin cancer years ago, and his benefit plan covered the vaccine. He survived the attack on the world, but he wishes he hadn't.

He was a talented gardener and a tree specialist and could bring green things back to life long after their owners had given up hope. He had worked for a large gardening contractor for many years. It was a good company with good benefits and decent pay. He had been better off than most. Still, he and his wife couldn't afford a Smart Home or even a house, and their apartment needed to be more secure. When the baby came, the threat of break-ins haunted them both. Unfortunately, he bought into every conspiracy theory that came his way. Without his medication, his rational brain no longer filters his thoughts. He now believes all the people who lived in Smart Homes had survived the attack and are living safely in their homes with many years of food supply. His landscaping work had been chiefly in Smart Home neighborhoods. He knew who lived there. He'd known Cora.

The day he murdered Cora followed an awful night. He hadn't moved his wife and baby boy's remains, and he sat by the bed, looking at them, filled with such pain and anger he couldn't contain it. He was robbed of every bit of joy and love he would ever experience. His mind was racing like the old days, before he got medical help for his mood swings. He thinks, *those bastards living in those Smart Homes have to pay. They must have had something to do with this disaster.* Finding Cora and that boy in the street just confirmed it. They had survived, but his family had not. Shooting her dead was reflexive. She was in the way of his gun. It gave him no relief.

He had long run out of food in his own house. They never had much backup in the apartment, and he didn't like the Nutri biscuits, so they didn't keep any on hand. He raided unguarded houses, rummaging through their coolers and freezers. Still, he wasn't the only survivor, and most of these houses had long been ransacked.

After his unsuccessful visit to the Camps and his encounter with Junie, he broke into a few houses and found a replacement gun. In a moment of sanity, he thinks he might go back, apologize, and ask her nicely to cook something for him. Something about the boy with her haunts him. He's sure he's seen him before. Peter waits a while and returns. He gets to Junie's tent. It's been stripped and he knows they're gone for good. He knocks the empty condiment cabinet over again and tears down the tent in a rage. He's so hungry his belly aches. He sits down in one of her lawn chairs and sobs as if his guts will turn inside out.

He finds a new neighborhood to raid but there's little left. All the surviving desperados got there before him. He begins to eye the 'kill pills' in the green boxes in people's drug cabinets but he's still not ready to die.

He heads to the Niagara on the Lake farms. There'll be fruit ripening. He wouldn't know what to do with any vegetables he might find. He starts with the fruit.

Chapter 28
OVER THE HILLS AND FAR AWAY

In Golden, B.C., Alex sleeps through the night, and it's still raining in the morning. She can only leave once the skies have cleared. She'll be too visible if she's still being followed. Staring out the misty window at the rain splattering down, she thinks, *I'm having a hell of a time getting across this country. It should have taken me seven to eight days. It's now well over two months, and I have a long way to go.* She reaches out to her mother in her mind. *I'm coming, mom. Please be alive.*

Francis checks in on the bike monitor. "I thought I'd give you a day to digest yesterday. How're you doing?" Alex says, "Mixed. Sad and lonely and feeling like a failure for abandoning the kids. I miss them, especially Tom. I'm so grateful to Krista and Sal for taking them on, and I'm ashamed to admit, feeling great relief they did. I adored little Tom, but Anna and I never really bonded. I was the bad news bear in her world. I don't know how my relationships with the kids would have developed if I'd gotten them safely to Victoria and raised them. Anna and I would have had problems as she got older. She was her own girl. Krista and Sal were so relaxed with them. Not me. I was a mess from the get-go." Francis says, "Stop feeling sorry for yourself. You didn't abandon them; you saved their lives. That's huge."

Francis goes on, "You made the best choice for their well-being. You were an excellent mother, as brief as that time was." "Seemed like an eternity to me," Alex says. Francis says, "You were expecting Anna to be a grateful adult and to respond accordingly. Six-year-olds don't know how to be gracious or grateful. They're still needy little nestlings with their beaks wide open, figuring out the world. Her world had been turned upside down." Alex says, "I know. I was terrified caring for those two, scared Tom would die, and I didn't know how to help Anna through her grief. I felt completely inadequate, not to mention exhausted. I don't know how single parents do it. Thankfully, they were both good kids, no tantrums, not brats. They'll thrive with Krista and Sal. They'll have a different life than they would have had if their parents were still alive. They'll be farm kids. It's all for the best. I can't dwell on it, but I'll never forget them."

Alex changes the subject. "Any updates on the samples I've been sending over? Is the lab seeing any changes?" Francis says, "More with the water than the soil and vegetation. The wind and rainstorms are affecting the air quality, improving it slowly, which is reflected in the water quality. We're hoping this all blows off into the upper atmosphere, but we don't know how long that might take. The changes are microscopic at this point. We certainly can't come up top and breathe the air yet. Our test mice continue to die." Alex says, "Yeah, I killed a few. How's the vax development coming?" Francis says, "A bit more promising. Our German cell has provided some excellent insight into its development and content. It's frustrating because this information would have been at our fingertips if everything hadn't been shut down. Our I.T. people are trying to hack into the lab satellites of the manufacturer who built the vaccine. It's been challenging isolating the thing in your blood samples that made you immune to the gas, virus, or whatever it was.

Our lab techs are very stressed. Too many people waiting for them to fix their lives. They're tired of being accosted by our people asking questions. Some people have been impatient and nasty. Keeping the lab techs happy and on task is a big focus of mine. We can't afford any of them having a breakdown." Alex says, "Quite the tightrope you're walking. How're you doing personally?" Francis says, "With Miguel's help, keeping it together. I have to."

Ever the pragmatist, Francis moves on. "What's your plan for today?" Alex says, "As soon as it stops raining, I'm heading for Kamloops. It's about four hours from here. Then I'll head south down the Coquihalla to Hope, another two hours, then over to Abbotsford, another hour, and on into Vancouver. I'm hoping to get to Vancouver tonight." Francis says, "Sounds like a big push. You may have to stop and camp out, actually get around to eating our delicious wafers." Alex says, "Yeah, I've been raiding a lot of coolers and freezers in the past few months. There are some campsites along the way. Not too many places to stop in the mountains if I get caught in the rain again. I've avoided your tasty wafers so far, but mighty glad I have them." Francis says, "Call if you need us, and don't risk riding in the rain. You've come too far to expose yourself unnecessarily." Alex says, "So far, I've shared my invisibility with two kids, Krista and Sal, and anybody else they decide to share that story with, and they will." Francis says, "I'm not worried about them. I'm worried about the murderous road warriors you might encounter. Be vigilant." "Yes, mom," Alex says. They sign off.

It finally stops raining, and Alex is back on the road. Her invisi-bike leaves a bit of a splash behind her in town, but no one's around watching the roads or her exit. The skies look like they're clearing. It's going to be steaming hot again today. Temperatures have been in the mid-80s for the past few days. She's comfortable in her invisi-suit, but anybody else out and about is frying. The Trans-Canada highway plays snakes and ladders through the mountains, curving around ancient rivers, lakes, and mountains. Back in the 1950s, civil engineers must have had the challenge of a lifetime designing this road. The cut blocks of stones at the highway's edge are still intact. Weeds and wildflowers grow out from the cracks. Glaciers cut some of the stone long ago. Men cut the rest. She notices more bikes with oversized baggage stowed on the back or pulling small, loaded trailers. They're the new emigrants heading west looking for food. Not much growing here. There's a polite non-combative camaraderie going on, even in this disaster. Bikers lift a hand in greeting as they pass each other, like the sports car drivers of old, she's read. Other than that, bikers are avoiding communication. Everybody's wary.

Alex gets to Glacier National Park and Rogers Pass quickly and carries on with the river keeping her company to the south. When the highway turns south, it doesn't pick up much civilization, other than hiking camps, until she hits Revelstoke. She doesn't bother going into town; she doesn't need to, and she pushes on, crossing the Columbia River. Sicamous is the next larger town, followed by Salmon Arm, but she also bypasses these. No time for sightseeing. By 2:30, she reaches Kamloops, and she's ready to eat. Her GPS identifies some wealthy-sounding street names south of the highway, and she cruises through those neighborhoods. A few people wandered around downtown, but no one was on these residential streets. There are more Smart Homes here, likely because there was more crime here. She picks a long bungalow, reads it, gets nothing, and goes in. She finds two adults and likely two teenagers in piles of sand. Lots of food, much of it beyond redemption, but the freezer holds a wealth of goodies. Mom liked to cook and freeze. Fed and watered, Alex heads back out on the last stretch down Hwy. 5, the Coquihalla.

She's still in the heart of the Rockies with mountains climbing to the sky in sharp edges, as if, hand over hand, they built themselves up with each peak above the other. It's said that ancient cultures and animals used the old trails and passes for centuries, as far back as 10,000 BCE. Is there food on this side of the mountain? You can hear that question down through the ages and again right now. When you live with mountains, they're a beacon, a go-to for your eyes, view, and location. *Ah, yes,* you think, *I'm looking south to the Cascades or northeast to Mount Baker. I know where I am.*

Chapter 29

A BAD SAD DAY

"We may lose, and we may win. Though we will never be here again. Don't let the sound of your own wheels make you crazy." The Eagles - 1972

Alex is thinking, *I really hope I don't have to kill anybody else; Diya was bad enough and I wasn't even the one who killed her, but she deserved it.* She comes around a bend and sees two men on the side of the road in a fight. One has the other on the ground kicking him, and the other is crying out, "Stop. Stop!" She hates violence and against her better judgment, she stops to see what's going on.

She hears a loud pop. The guy standing and doing the kicking jerks back, chokes out the word, "No," and falls back. He has a large red splotch of blood on his chest. The other guy is still on the ground, waving a gun. Alex is unsure whether the guy doing the kicking is now dead, but he isn't moving. She looks at the shooter. He's a big kid, about 17, carrying too much fat, a bit of a baby Huey and traveling light by the looks of things. He has one of those thin sparse beards that plague fair men with thin hair. His 'shaved all over but the top' haircut has grown in and just makes him look like an ass. Picked at acne on chipmunk cheeks round out the look of a kid closer to preteen than on the edge of becoming an adult. His belly bulges and strains at his waistband. He's over six feet tall, long past losing the baby fat. He's riding a town bike, not a highway bike. She's unsure how that will get him and his size through the high climbs ahead. He's in a hoodie and jeans and doesn't seem to have any other gear. He's not prepared for bad weather or anything. He gets up, looks at the man he just shot, and throws up. He then squats down on the road and sobs into his hands. Alex thinks, *this overgrown kid is not a natural-born killer, just scared out of his skull.* She comes in quietly and checks the other guy's pulse. He's in his early thirties, unshaved, dark curly hair needing a cut, like most surviving men these days. He was riding a highway bike. He was ready for the mountains. He's dead, for sure.

Thinking the kid needs help, Alex speaks to him. She thinks, *christ, maybe I should have been a mother. Here we go again.* She says, "Hello, don't be scared. This is kind of freaky, but my name is Alex, and I'm in a very cool camouflage suit that makes me invisible." He lifts his head and looks around wildly, waving the gun around. He's just killed a guy. Everybody he knows is dead. The world has gone mad, and now an invisible woman is talking to him on the highway. Alex is aware of the danger here. He's a big kid, and he's still holding his gun. He could easily start shooting wildly. She says, "I have a gun trained on you, and I need you to put your gun on the ground and kick it away from you." In her head, she's in movie cop mode. She yells, "Do it now!" He says, "Fuck off! Where are you?" He whirls around, trying to see her.

Alex thinks, *it always worked in the movies*. She stands back from him about 20 feet and rethinks this. She says, "I'm taking off my helmet and hood, and you'll see only my head. It'll look weird, but remember, I have a gun trained on you and can shoot you way faster than you can shoot me." She gives him a minute to digest this, then says, "Ready?" He doesn't answer and is still looking around for her. She removes her helmet and hood. He's now getting her floating head effect, unnerving certainly. She says, "You can't see the rest of me because I'm wearing camouflage." He says, "Holy fuck, are you for real?" A boy of few words. She says, "Yep. For real. Not a ghost, just in great camo." He says again, "Holy fuck!"

Alex pushes past this linguistic repartee and asks, "What happened here?" The kid hesitates and says, "I stopped for a piss and found this guy going through my bike storage when I got back. I pushed him off, but he came back at me like he was crazy. He knocked me down and wouldn't stop kicking me. I have my dad's gun, so I shot him to make him stop." Alex asks, "Are you hurt?" He says, "It hurts where he was kicking me, but I think I'm okay." She says, "I saw some of that. He was probably crazy with hunger, but you had a right to defend yourself."

The kid yells at her in a high-pitched squeal, "I just killed a guy!" He's sobbing. He's a big, terrified kid in the middle of a horror show. She checks the dead guy's bike storage. There's water and a bag of high-protein, high-calorie cereal. She used to eat this all the time for breakfast. The dead guy could have lived on this supply for more than a month. The kid says, "He only had rice or something on his bike." Alex thinks, *that doesn't jibe with the story you just gave me.*

She asks, "How do you know what he had on his bike?" The kid realizes she knows he's lying. Alex is wary of pissing off this unstable kid but asks, "What really went down here? Did he catch you going through his bike, not the other way around?" The kid yells, "Fuck off!" Quite the vocabulary. His voice cracks. He's stressed to the max, truculent and dangerous. Alex changes tack and asks him his name. "Sean," he says, with his head lowered. He sits on the side of the road, sunk into himself. She asks, "Where are you going? You're not really prepared for a mountain run." He says, "My parents, brothers, and sister are piles of sand at home. They're dead. The screens are dead, nobody answers my calls, and nobody's on the streets. I don't know what's happening. Last week, I ran out of food, and the stores were all empty. I'm riding to my grandmother's in Abbotsford to see if she has any food." Alex thinks, *and not see how your grandmother is or if she's even alive*. But she doesn't say it. She explains, "The only people that survived this attack on the world had the Libertas1 cancer vaccine. Did your grandmother have the shot?" He says, "I didn't know that. I haven't talked to anyone. I had it because I had lymphoma when I was twelve." He then says, "Yeah, I think she had some kind of cancer or something a while back, not sure." Alex says, "Then she may still be alive." She asks, "When did you last eat anything?" He says, "I found a stash of candy bars under my brother's bed yesterday and ate a bunch of those." She thinks, *Great, now he's on a glucose crash, and it's probably what he's been eating for years, not just yesterday*.

Alex considers giving him a couple of her wafers to tide him over, but he would be just as likely to grab the whole sleeve from her. She doesn't want to get that close to him and his gun. She's protected in this suit, but her head is unprotected with her hood back. It would also be too complicated to get the wafers out, add water and wait for them to expand. Because he's starving, she shows him how to eat the cereal mix in the dead guy's bike storage. She tells him to add water, which expands, and he wolfs down a bowl and then another. He could easily eat up this entire supply in a couple of weeks or less. She questions whether she should ride away, but he's still dangerous and could stop and attack more people looking for food en route. He still has that gun. The only way she can get that away from him is to zap him and knock him out. She doesn't want to do that. He's still a desperate kid. She decides to follow him to his grandmother's. It's on her way.

She thinks, *At least I can intercede if he pulls this again with someone else*. She tells him, "I'm going to ride behind you to your grandmother's. I can provide you with some protection." He says with a sneer, "You?" she says, "Yep, lil' ole me." She thinks, *you're welcome, you piece of crap*. She doesn't tell him she's riding behind him to protect other people on the road. She says, "Before we go, let's pull this guy off the road and be respectful. We don't know his circumstances." He says, "Whatever." He has no compassion for his victim. Alex is losing all sympathy for this kid.

She goes through the dead guy's bike storage and pulls up his communication device. It's dead, of course, but she guesses he was hopeful. His ID says he was John Morgan Pallister. There are pictures of him with a pretty, young blonde and two young blonde girls. The kids look like him, so it's probably his wife and kids. They're likely all dead now. He had some supplies: rain gear, camping gear, food, and water. It doesn't look like he needed to fight with Sean unless he was being robbed of his essential supplies. Alex is pretty sure that's what Sean was doing. John Morgan Pallister was a young father, a husband, and his parents' son. With no help from Sean, she pulls his body further off the road. Her still mending shoulder and arm scream at her. She eyes Sean's proximity to her. He still only sees her head and is wary enough to stay back.

Alex quietly tells John Morgan Pallister she's sorry this happened to him, but they have to leave him here. There are no options. She puts his pictures and device inside his jacket against his heart. In her mind, she says to him, *no more sadness, John Morgan Pallister, no more sadness.* Alex tells Sean to take John's bike, he'll need it, and it at least has some supplies. She puts her hood and helmet back on and tells Sean to ride off and that she'll be behind him. When he can no longer see her, he wonders if he's gone nuts and never saw the floating head woman at all.

Alex thinks, *he's so seventeen and will eventually starve to death if he doesn't grow up fast.* He hasn't asked her where she's going, or even where she got her invisi-suit. No curiosity. He didn't even thank her for stopping. He's unlikeable, and she now wonders why she bothered to stop.

They climb over the Coquihalla Summit and have just passed the Box Canyon Chain-Up Area, a reminder of how treacherous this road is in a snowstorm. There's a turn in the road ahead, and as they come around it, Alex sees a roadblock with two guys who've set up an ambush. Their guns are raised and aimed at Sean. It looks like they have automatic rifles. There are three people on the ground and lots of blood. They look dead. Her adrenaline kicks in. She has to move fast. She pulls in front of Sean, pulls up her hood, and screams at him to turn around fast, ride back about a mile, and warn other riders to stop. She needs him to move immediately and thinks, *now's not the time for you to question me.* He sees the two guys, veers around, and rides away at top speed, looking terrified. Alex rides her bike out of range of the guns. With Sean's u-turn, they drop their guns. She yells after him, "I'll take care of this." The shooters obviously don't know who screamed at Sean, let alone who will take care of what, but they're now on alert, looking around and talking to each other.

She's in danger. Even in this suit, she can't take a stream of machine-gun bullets. She rides quietly up to the three downed bikers and checks their pulse. They're all dead. One of them is a woman. She hasn't seen many women on the road. There's blood everywhere. Their bike storages are open and empty. These two murderers are after food, of course. Standing off to the side and out of gun range, Alex observes the men. One is older, in his fifties, and one's in his late twenties. They look alike. Father and son? The older one is thin but still has a belly, is completely bald, and has tattoos up his muscled arms. He wears a sleeveless t-shirt, jeans, and old beat-off work boots. No need for a disguise. No one's going to arrest him. The younger guy has a buzz cut, also tattoos. He's rake-thin with a vest over a bare chest. His belly is concave. He has no ass; his jeans barely hang on him. His sneakers are torn and shabby. These two were struggling long before all this happened. Because of the high expense of the vaccine, there was a push to provide free shots to select charity cases. These two must have lucked out or stolen it at gunpoint in some doctor's office. Maybe dad discovered he had cancer, and the son had it too? Alex is guessing why they both would have needed it and that they might even be father and son. Maybe they're just two sad and desperate, murderous men. They have nothing to lose but their hunger now, and they don't care anymore. She thinks, *"If I tase them and take away their weapons, they'll just get more and do this again."*

A biker is approaching. He must not have believed Sean, or Sean didn't warn him. Maybe Sean's story of an invisible woman taking care of the problem up the road didn't ring true. That would be it. The two shooters have their guns raised. Alex doesn't have a choice. She raises her gun, puts her index finger on the red button, and aims at the older guy. The gun is completely silent. He drops. The younger one sees the other guy hit the road and looks around wildly. She doesn't give him much time to wonder. She presses the button again. The bullet finds him. She thinks, *congratulations, Alex. You're a stone-cold murderer. You've just ended two lives.*

The approaching biker surveys the bodies and turns around fast. Alex is shaking and gasping for air. She can't believe what she's just done. She finds a large boulder, leans against it, tries to calm herself, and vomits up her guts. She checks to see if they're dead. They are. Her legs are like rubber and barely hold her up. She goes through their bags and retrieves all the food they've taken. Not much. So much death for so little reward. She hides their guns behind some rocks and moves the barricades over to the side of the road. She doesn't want anyone else getting this idea, and she doesn't need two automatic rifles. Automatic Rifles, Christ! They were ambushing simple solar bike riders trying to get somewhere to survive. She can't move the three downed bikers physically. They're going to have to stay where they are. Now she knows what it feels like to live in an active war zone. She used to detachedly watch all those terrified people on T.V. in other countries going through hell. *Not my life,* she would think. Now it is.

Alex pulls herself together enough to ride back and find Sean. He's white-faced, wide-eyed, and parked on the side of the road, looking like he's in shock. This has been a terrifying day for this screwed-up kid. Alex thinks, *hell, it's been a terrifying day for me.* Thankfully, no one else had driven up behind him, and the other biker must have ridden past him and gone back. Alex lifts her hood and tells Sean the shooters have been eliminated. It's safe for them to pass. She says, "Just ride on through quickly and don't look." He says, "Are you sure?" She says, "Believe me, I'm sure." He remounts, rides on, and slows as they come up on the slaughter. Alex yells, "Ride through fast, Sean, keep going." He speeds up and gets by the bodies. A few miles down the road, he looks around and asks, "Are you here?" She rides up beside him, lifts her hood, and says, "Right here." He says, "Can we stop? I need to piss." She says, "Sure, right here is good." He goes off, does his business, returns, and says, "Did you kill those guys?" Alex says, "I had to. They killed three bikers, and we don't know how many others, and were about to kill you. They had to be stopped." Sean looks at Alex's floating head and says again, "Holy fuck, you're something." She takes a moment, then says, "We don't have far to go. Are you ready to ride?" Alex doesn't plan to share her personal feelings with this young schmuck. She'll examine this later. She'll call Francis, her personal psychiatrist. She'll need to talk this one through with her. Alex rides behind Sean and watches his broad back, her mind racing. She's finding it impossible to calm down, slow down her heart and normalize her breathing.

The few other riders they pass lift one hand and wave at Sean. He doesn't wave back. It's laughable, but they're still polite Canadians, even in the middle of a world disaster. These riders are going to come across the massacre up the road. Alex wishes she could have moved the three dead riders off the road, but her arm hurts after moving the guy that Sean killed. Maybe someone else will move them. Maybe they'll just dry out there on the highway in the August sun. There won't be any flies, at least, no rotting bodies. Just slowly drying human hides who, not long ago, had everyday lives. Taber seems like an eternity ago.

They pick up the Trans-Canada highway again in Hope and drop down out of the mountains into the fertile plains of the Fraser Valley. On previous trips, this always felt to Alex like falling into the welcoming arms of B.C. They leave behind the last of the mountain peaks. Old and irrelevant and watching from on high. They had their moment in the sun. Her nerves settle.

Before today, Alex always liked this part of a road trip across Canada. The mountains are behind you, and you're almost home. However, all she can think now is, *we got through that*, and *let's get to grandma's so I can drop this pecker head off*. She wants this day over. She thinks, *I was such a nice person earlier in the day. Now I'm a murderer.*

Ahead to the north, she can see smoke, and ash is choking the air. It's B.C.'s wildfire season, it's scorching hot, and there's no cadre of firefighters to fight back the blaze. These fires will come south. They have before. They're wiping out entire towns. As if there isn't enough worry. The shrubbery along the road works its way deeper into the forests. It's an invitation for ash to lick into it and take the forest down.

At long last, they turn off into Abbotsford. Grandma lives in town, and they pull up in front of a decent Smart Home. At least she's protected. Alex lifts her hood and asks Sean to wait before he goes in. She gives him the food she absconded from the two dead ambushers and a one-year sleeve of wafers. She reminds him how to use them, not to gobble them all down, and how to share them with his grandmother. She tells him he must travel to every farm he can find and see if someone is there and needs help. That's his only chance of finding continuing food, not to mention learning something. She's not sure he grasps how important this is. He's not a listener and sure doesn't want to be lectured by Alex. She gives him the food because she thinks his chances of saving himself are slim.

She says, "Buzz your grandma." Alex thinks, *if she isn't alive or there, I'm not sure what I'll do with him. I'm not bringing him with me.* Sean presses the buzzer and waits. Alex hears a voice saying, "Sean? What are you doing here?" This grandma sounds suspicious rather than happy to see her grandson. She's not delighted her grandson has shown up on her doorstep in the middle of a disaster. "What do you want?" his grandmother asks cautiously. This isn't looking good for Sean. He jumps in. He doesn't say, "Are you okay? How are you? I'm so thankful to see you alive." Instead, he says, "Everybody's dead, gram. I need some food. Do you have any?" There's a pause. She says, "You need to go back home and look there, Sean. I don't have enough to share." There's history between these two. He's not her favorite grandson. He then bangs hard on his grandmother's door. "Come on, gram, let me in." 'Gram' doesn't answer. He kicks her door, goes into a tantrum of anger, takes out his gun, and shoots it at the door. *Wonderful. That will get her to open up.* Alex thinks.

Watching this, Alex knows he's young and traumatized, but so is everyone. She's fed up with this selfish brat and decides he needs a nap. She zaps him. He drops onto 'gram's' front step. She moves him into a recovery position and takes his gun and the wafer sleeve she just gave him. She says to 'gram' in her speaker, "Your delightful grandson is out cold on your front porch. He'll be asleep for about six hours. There's a year's worth of food beside him. They're small wafers; you add water, and they become a biscuit. Eat one for each meal. It would be best to retrieve these while he's unconscious and then decide what you want to do about him when he wakes up. He also has some other food in his kit to keep him going for a while. He won't remember how he got here when he wakes up. I have his gun, so he isn't armed." Inside, 'gram' can't see who's talking outside but can see Sean folded on her doorstep. She thinks he's tricking her into opening the door. She says, "Who are you? I can't see you." Alex says, "Your guardian angel. Trust me. He's down for the count." She rides away.

'Gram' waits for a couple of hours and sees that Sean has not moved. The mystery woman who spoke is nowhere around. She steps out and quickly retrieves the sleeve of wafers. Sean sleeps on. She knows he can be dangerous. Her son and his wife have had a lot of trouble with him. She had a lot of trouble with his father before him. She's done with both of them. *Big selfish, spoiled brat*, she thinks. She locks her door.

As Alex rides on, she thinks, *okay, I feel sorry for 'gram' and this problem on her doorstep. Still, I'm immensely relieved to leave this potential load of trouble behind. I can't help him.* She keeps his handgun even though she has three of her own. You never know. It's perilous out here.

She rides into the lower mainland of Vancouver and heads over to Tsawwassen's ferry docks. There are two ferries docked here now with their ramps down, waiting for the morning passengers. The attack hit too early for anyone to have boarded. There might have been security staff on board. No one's around now. There's a light wind, and the water's choppy today. She's hoping it'll be calmer tomorrow. She rides back up the road to the town of Tsawwassen, near the U.S. border. There's a marina down in Point Roberts in the States. She'll check it out tomorrow if nobody's watching the border. She'll cross from Point Roberts and try to island hop. Hopefully, there's a zodiac there she can take. If ocean liners and shore patrols use them at sea for rescues, she should be able to figure it out. She finds an empty Smart Home and settles in. After this traumatic day, she can finally exhale behind these secure doors.

Alex replays the day in her head. Lots of pluses and too many minuses. She doesn't know what will become of Sean, probably nothing good. She again recalls Francis's words, "You can't save everyone." Alex weeps uncontrollably as the shock of the day sets in. She thinks, *I don't want this life. Make it go away. Sam, I need you. Mom, where are you?* She feels very young, vulnerable, and alone.

Chapter 30

NOT THAT EASY

Frances has a serious job with a mitt full of problems. Alex doesn't want to add to them, so she doesn't bug her or presume any favoritism. Still, she sends in daily reports, and they talk often. Francis seems to have her antenna attuned to Alex and will check in just when Alex needs her. Francis has boosted Alex's sinking morale many times on this trip.

Francis gave her team the promised month to contribute to the plans. Most of them enjoyed their work here. It was an unusual contract gig. They could leave any time and still walk away with a nice sum of money. They were all financially set. "Were" being the operative word. Money doesn't matter anymore. They saw themselves as non-conformists, lone wolves who didn't need anyone. It's no surprise that few of them like the idea of a new society started by their small group. They just want to get above ground and away. Most want to go home. The idea of living with all these people for the rest of their lives doesn't appeal. They know it makes sense, but it's not what they want. Several of them have had hook-ups with each other, of course. They all think of themselves as rogues and loners, so commitment isn't on the table. People are people, which often causes unrealized expectations, jealousy, and hurt feelings. With a few couples, there are thoughts of a future together. Very few.

Francis has met with most individually to get their opinions and feelings. For all of their wanting to escape, most have contributed a wide variety of thoughts and ideas to her original list. They're bored. It's an intriguing game and has initiated long conversations between them all, long into the nights of the past month. In fact, their camaraderie has never been better. They don't want to live these new lives they're planning. Those lives are still fiction to them. It's fun to discuss creating a new government with new laws and argue the validity of current laws. Considering starting a 'dentistry 101 class' is intriguing. Would you take it beyond extractions and cleaning to filling teeth? That's much harder and needs a lot of practice. Every idea is turned over and added to, questioned, or discarded.

However, even among the most educated, there seems to be an unwillingness to believe the world has changed forever. She needs to get that fact home to them, to inform their future decisions, if nothing else.

In her meetings with individuals, most have talked about going home. "Maybe my mother is still alive or my little brother," they say. "I've got to get to them." When Francis reminds them of who has survived, they recall that these relatives or friends did not have the vaccine. She witnesses their realization that those they held dear really are all gone. Too many leave her office saddened with all hope gone. It's the opposite of what she's trying to achieve. She runs through the list of her ideas for planning for the future with each of them, getting their personal input. Most only have thoughts on their interest or skill areas. She asks each what they want to do if they have to stay underground for years. Most can't fathom staying, let alone how they would spend their time. They can't get their heads around it. A few of them honestly say, "I might just leave." When she says, "Even if that meant certain death?" They say, "Yes, I don't want to stay buried here forever."

A few of the women confide they like the idea of having a baby. None of the males say this. These people were pre-screened to ensure they didn't have responsibility for children or any desire to have them. The women who are now considering pregnancy still want to leave. Francis asks them, "Do you see yourself pregnant or with a child, riding a solar bike back to Nebraska, or wherever you're from? You would find no one alive back there and no support for you and your child for the rest of your lives?" They hadn't really thought about that.

Some are realistic. They understand the sanity and necessity of working together as a group to survive and thrive. An astounding number of them don't.

Francis and Miguel talk long into the night about the team and how best to support them while driving home reality. This emergency has drawn them even closer to each other. Miguel bolsters her with humor and praise when Francis feels overwhelmed with the responsibility. Unconditional love, in fact. Weeks have turned into months. It'll become more difficult managing this unhappy group if they have to stay underground. People are losing their tempers, petty quarrels are breaking out, and some are unhappy with Francis and Miguel's management of the crisis. None have any better solutions. They're just so angry at being trapped.

Although only Francis and Miguel know this, the two lab tech teams feel they're getting a little closer with a test vaccine. They don't want to build up anyone's hopes. Today, they sent up two test mice with the new serum, and they both survived about 15 seconds before turning into dust. This is very promising. The air is clearing but needs to be faster. The lab techs think it could be another year before the air is clear enough to breathe. All bets are on the vaccine. Francis and Miguel plan a team meeting to update everyone on the survival ideas and the plan forward. She'll share the air improvement news because at least it's a light at the end of the tunnel and a fact, even if it's a long way off and the air may never be completely clear.

They gather again in the Meeting Hall. The room is filled with a cacophony of voices. As Francis takes the podium, all eager hopeful eyes turn to her, and the crowd quiets. She says, "Thank you for your insightful input into the survival plans. You have brought many excellent ideas and plans we could implement. I have shared these with you on the Uni-site. I also have a tiny bit of good news. Many people sit forward in their chairs. Our lab has been testing the air, water, and foliage daily. Alex, our friend on the road, has also been taking samples as she crosses Canada. It's not big and certainly not sustainable at this point. Still, they're seeing a very minuscule improvement in the air samples. Of course, we hope that whatever hit the world eventually leaves the earth. It could take a year or more for the air to clear and allow us to breathe it without dying. Still, it's improving". The crowd breaks out in applause. She says, "No need to applaud; it isn't anything we're doing. It's just happening naturally." She says, "As for the vaccine, both labs continue to work on it. Unfortunately, there's nothing new to report." She would love to share they're more optimistic, but there's no point in getting their hopes up if the mice keep dying.

She says, "You were hired because of your talent, individuality, and ability to work independently. You're unique and adapted to our unusual work environment exceptionally well. When you signed on, the freedom that went with the contract was attractive. You could leave if you wanted to without repercussion. None of you expected or wanted to stay here forever, nor did you want to stay together anywhere else. It's not how you see yourselves. In my conversations with you over the past month, it's become abundantly clear most of you, not all, but most would like to move on once and if we get back on top again. I understand that. I wish I could go home again too. However, my home and your home are not what you remember. Most people we knew are dead, piles of sand. There's currently no way to communicate with each other. You'll have food, but the survivors won't, and if you go outside, everyone will know you're surviving because you have food. You'll be in constant danger. This is the reality of your new life if you choose to go on your own. Hiding out in your old house, apartment, or cabin for the rest of your life. Please think about that.

She pauses and looks around the room. Some heads have gone down, and some nod in agreement with her. Some wait for her to provide new information, encouraging news, anything.

She continues, "We're the inheritors of the future. We can choose to make that the best future possible together or walk away and live alone for the rest of our lives, contributing nothing to the remaining human race. That's the choice. That is reality.

We're not talking about a commune or a kibbutz. We're talking about rebuilding from the ground up, bringing your individuality, skills, and incredible intelligence. You won't be expected to live on top of each other any more than you did before. There'll need to be strategic thinking and planning about the challenges we'll face. That takes group thinking, all of your talents, intelligence, and togetherness. We really need all of you.

If you want to leave, so be it. We have excellent camouflage gear to help you ride a bit more safely to wherever you're going. I suggest you find a partner and ride with them. You'll each have each other's back then. You may prefer to travel alone, but it'll be dangerous. Lots of hungry survivors. Your karate skills ain't gonna cut it." This brings a murmur of laughter. She looks at them. "Seriously, you might have to kill someone to protect yourself. Think about that."

She lets that sink in and then continues, "Getting back to my original list, for those of us who decide to stay together, I believe there are key things we'll need to concentrate on before rewriting the constitution, as much fun as that would be." This brings some smiles. She continues, "This is what we'll need to concentrate on initially:

Location: We need a temperate climate, arable land, and limitless clean water with preferably established farms. Our exploratory drones are available for you for site searches. They have an approximate 1,000-mile reach.

Food: How will we sustain ourselves and the remaining survivors? We have food, but actual food would be much better. Many of us will have to become farmers, learn about agriculture, and take over farms.

Healthcare: This is essential. We have three doctors, six nurses, and two dentists on staff. There'll probably be some medical professionals who'll have survived wherever we end up. Some of our doctors, nurses, and dentists may want to leave. We'll all need as much medical training as we can absorb to live out the rest of our lives.

Communication: Our I.T. folks here and in Germany hope to hack into the main communication satellites to see if we can reach out into the world. SAT phones currently don't work but they're getting close. Meanwhile, we can communicate with each other using our satellite, but not with anyone else.

Babies: We need to continue our species. None of you identified as wanting to have children when you came on board. If you decide to stay with the group and want to have a child or children, there'll be support there for you. If you choose to leave, there'll be none. You do not need a partner for this, obviously. Give this more thought.

We'll establish four teams. Sign-up is voluntary. Obviously, we don't need a baby team. This brings a laugh.

She says, "The teams will be location, food, healthcare, and communication. These will be ongoing working teams creating a plan, adjusting it where needed, and establishing who wants to work in these areas. You can be on all four teams or none. Try for one. Sign-up will be on the Uni-site. You have ten days to form these teams and two weeks from today to book your first meeting. Select captains and co-captains to mediate and manage the group. Develop your parameters and goals. I expect the first meeting reports on my desk the day after your first meetings. That's two weeks from now and a day. No exceptions. I'll be watching the sign-ups."

Francis then looks at them all and says, "What do we do in the meantime? This is where I step in and push my weight around a bit. It's unfair that the food services, laundry, cleaning, medical, personal services, garden, tech, and lab personnel carry all the load while others do nothing. So those of you who no longer have assigned work will have new jobs. The lab staff should carry on without interference. They have a big enough load without having to babysit a trainee. Many of you may have some tech skills, and I'll meet with that department to discuss their needs and assign positions accordingly. All the other work will be spread out and assigned, lightening the load of those still active departments providing services to us. I don't want to hear that you didn't come here to cook food, do gardening work, or whatever. We're doing this.

I'll meet with the medical department to discuss a curriculum. We'll all attend those classes. You might have to set a broken arm someday or pull a tooth. You should know how to do it. This will be progressive, and you can learn as much as you want to. I don't expect you to get your medical degree, but I expect you to educate yourself in health care. As we roll this out, you'll all hear from me individually. I'd rather you be angry at me and active than angry at me and under-employed and bored. Also, please stop asking the lab staff how they're progressing. They're trying to save all our lives and don't need the stress of your anxiousness about the vaccine development.

That's it for today, folks. I'll start setting appointments with you as soon as we have new work schedules sorted."

Francis leaves the stage and she and Miguel leave the room. They all start talking at once. Immediately, the push backers are griping. "She has no control over me anymore. I'll do what I want to do." Others remind those gripers that Francis manages a group of very different people and is trying very hard to save their lives and give them a future. They should stop thinking about themselves. The gripers say they're leaving anyway as soon as they can get up top safely. Many who don't have work right now welcome the change and don't care where it is as long as they're doing something. They all feel more optimistic, knowing the air is starting to clear. They might get out of here, eventually. They won't be stuck here forever. Most now truly grasp how changed the world is up top. Some minds were changed, and it was a productive meeting.

Francis and Miguel go to work immediately, meeting with each department head about the work-sharing programs and the medical training. They let no one off the hook and ask for work schedules with training and open shifts to fill. They have a hectic couple of weeks and get it set up efficiently. There are fewer grumblers and non-participants than they expected. The non-participants have alienated themselves. They were once considered combative but engaging individuals, now just lazy and obstreperous. The first healthcare 101 class is held with a 100% turnout. Lots of questions, participation, videos, and break-out sessions. They're entertained and interested. The four teams have excellent sign-up and have set their first meeting dates. It's coming together.

The night of the meeting, Francis and Miguel have dinner together later in her suite, as they do most nights. She takes a sip of her wine and says, "Well, how did you think it went? What were you seeing on their faces?" He says, "At the mention of the air possibly clearing, enormous relief. They needed hope. Letting them know they would have work assigned to them was received better than I thought. A few guys at the back of the room won't do it. That's okay, they want to leave anyway, and any friendships they have here will soon dissolve if they decide to stand down from this program. Not giving anybody an out was wise. It'll make them look worse when they refuse to work. Overall, people like rules and knowing that somebody has a plan for them, no matter their level of education, skill, or experience. I think some of them might even have fun doing different work."

She looks at him, worried, and says, "How about you? How are you doing? Everyone looking for inside information must accost you all day and share their grief and stress." He says, "I'm fine. I know how worried and scared they are. I have every confidence we'll get out of here, eventually. I'm kind of looking forward to setting up a new life with all the problems and hurdles we'll encounter." I particularly look forward to doing it with you." Francis has completely missed Miguel's messaging before. She touches his arm and says, "What a friend you are. I do love you." She means this in the most benign sense, and he wishes it were different.

He goes silent, takes a sip of his wine, looks at her, and says, "I've been thinking a lot about something. Please don't faint." She looks at him, thinking, *oh, oh, what's coming*? He says, "Okay, here goes. I've never told you this, but I would very much like to be a father someday. It would make me the happiest man in the world if you agreed to have a baby with me." Francis' eyes widen. He says, "Don't freak. We can keep our professional relationship and do it artificially, of course. You have said yourself we'll need to have children. Why not us?" She stares at him, silent, her mouth open. After a very long time, she finally says, "You have just blown me away. How has this not come up before?" He laughs and says, "It was a different world before, and I viewed my place in it differently." She puts her hand back on his arm and says, "First, I would never forgive myself if we lost our friendship. Second, I'm forty-six, getting a little long in the tooth for having a baby." He says, "Jesus, girl, you're the healthiest woman here. You can probably pop them out well into your fifties." She falls off the couch laughing. "Not a future I'd envisioned." She has to admit, though, having a baby has crossed her mind. Is it possible? Another chance?" She says, "Wow, I don't know what to say or think. I need some time to chew on this. It would be a huge decision for both of us." He kicks her toe and says with a laugh, "Well, you are forty-six, the clock's ticking."

She reaches over, punches him on the shoulder, and says, "Shut up already." She pours them a top-up on their wine. She says, "Christ, nine months without wine, I dunno." He says, "Could be longer if you nurse." She says, "You're not doing yourself any favors here."

She has a sparkle in her mind she never thought was there. *A baby. No. I'm too old. It couldn't work. It's dangerous. The first baby I had died of a heart defect. What if that came from me? What kind of world are we bringing it into?* Then she returns to....*a baby*. She does not tell him her thoughts. He finally says, "Well, it's almost midnight, and we've got stressful meetings all day tomorrow and for weeks to come. I should go." She says, "Yes. Since you've dropped this bomb of a lifetime in my lap, and I now have to sleep on a life-changing decision, I need my bed. I'm exhausted and a little drunk."

He rises to leave, puts his hands on her shoulders at the door, and looks at her closely. She thinks, *oh, oh, here comes something deep. I like him better when he makes me laugh.* He says with a grin, "There wouldn't be diaper service, but there would be all the diapers you would ever need out there." She laughs and says, "Hardly convincing of a life-changing decision. Yikes, pregnancy risks at my age, colic and baby poop, and nights up with a crying baby and two-year-old tantrums and snarky teenagers. Are you up for all that? Not sure I am. We have 118 kids out there right now."

He says, "I think they would welcome a baby and it would encourage other women to consider it. There would be lots of babysitters. You would have my full support. You wouldn't be doing it alone. Give it your good old Francis positive and negative review. Then go with your gut." She says, "If I say no, will you find someone else to have a baby with? I wouldn't mind." *She's absolutely lying when she says this, and it surprises her.* He thinks to himself, *that's an edge I hadn't thought about. I wouldn't, but I'll let her think I might because I think it would bug her.* He chooses to not respond to that question and says, "Whatever you decide, I'm okay with it. It's your body, and yes, there are risks. All I'm saying is, think about it. When you're ready to talk, we'll talk." He gives her a quick squeeze, and he's gone. She knows he just played her. She definitely doesn't want him having a baby with one of the contractors. Francis is a very private woman and doesn't like the idea of having the medical staff clinically injecting her with Miguel's semen, either. There's always the good old-fashioned way, but that would change things between them. She walks over to Mattie's baby picture and picks it up. She says, *what do you think, little one?* This is huge, and she wants to let it settle in her mind before she decides, but...a baby.

Chapter 31

FOUND AND LOST

Junie and Jacob discuss getting more clothes for him. He's growing fast and needs everything. He doesn't want to return to the apartment and get his old ones. They probably wouldn't fit him anymore, anyway. Bill Kracker's clothes don't fit him. Going out to a clothing store is dangerous. More visibility than they want. However, Junie has a gun and knows how to use it. She tells Jacob, "You'll just have to trust me to choose clothes for you. Ain't nobody gonna be judging your fashion choices." Jacob doesn't care about what she chooses, but he doesn't like the idea of Junie going out alone.

One morning, Jacob wakes up to silence. Junie's gone. He doesn't immediately worry. He thinks she probably ignored his concerns and went out early while he slept, knowing he would have tried to talk her out of it. Hours go by, and no Junie. Jacob's now worried. Besides getting him clothes, he can't think why she would leave and not come home. She has the codes to the other two houses, and he slips across the street and checks those first, wondering if she might have just gone over to check their pantries and maybe fallen or something. He's grabbing at ideas. She's not there. It's unsafe to be seen riding in daylight, and if she came back to not find him there, even though he would be out looking for her, she'd be pissed. He doesn't want Junie pissed at him, ever.

He waits until dark, knowing in his gut that something's really wrong. Junie has either had an accident somewhere or been shot. She may be dead. Too many thoughts run through his head. He can't manage the Niagara on the Lake farm himself, let alone the little one at the Camps. He wouldn't know where to start. He doesn't even know how to cook. She's become his pillar of stability, security, and hope. Everything was going to be alright with Junie. He misses her acutely. He doesn't name it, but he loves this woman as much as he loved his own mother.

He sucks up his courage, packs his father's gun, puts on his night glasses, and rides to the big mall up the road. That's likely where she would have gone looking for clothes. The large echoey dark halls of retail are empty. Every store door is smashed in. There would be no cookie crumbs left in the back office drawers. He searches all the stores, their back rooms, and under the racks. There's no sign of Junie ever being there. He comes to the sports equipment store and instinctively thinks she might have gone there. It has everything a teenage boy could ever want or need. He checks the back room and under all the clothing racks. In the corner of his eye in the dark, he sees something on the floor, kicked under a rack. It's a bike saddle bag full of clothes. Junie had a small Jamaican flag imprinted on the side of her bag, and there was the familiar yellow cross over the green and black background. She was here and dropped the bag. It almost looks like she tried to hide it. She must have been intercepted. There's no blood on the floor or signs of a struggle. He says to himself, *Junie, where are you*? He takes the saddle bag with him. He at least knows she was here. He rides all the edges of the mall parking lot where the floating service cars would have waited. There are still a few there, but most returned to their stations. He's hoping to see her bike. Nothing. He checks the ditches and under on ramps accessing the mall. Nothing. She's disappeared into thin air.

To be sure, he goes to the Niagara on the Lake farm they picked out and searches the house and all the grounds. She's not there. It's now teaming rain, and he decides against riding to the Camps tonight. It'll be muddy and dark, and Junie would think it was too dangerous to go there with the mad biker riding around. He can't see her going there in the middle of the night. Jacob rides back to the Kracker's house, blindly hoping she'll be there waiting for him. She isn't. He's alone now and has to figure out what to do next. He can't think of anything. He's feeling desperate.

Junie knew Jacob would not want her to risk going out on her own, but she thought she could make one quick midnight trip to the sports store at the mall, load her bag, and get back home without him knowing. She'd be okay. Even hungry people have to sleep. She looked forward to surprising him in the morning with his new duds.

Still, she takes some precautions. The Krackers each had a gun, and she tucks one in her bra and one inside her thigh under her loose pants. She has her own gun in her pocket. She's taken a bunch of Nutri biscuits, thinking she might need some food as a bargaining chip if she gets into a tight spot. Throw something to the wolves. She hates thinking like this, but its survival. She'll be hyper-vigilant. She has to consider all possibilities.

After Jacob falls asleep, she rides out. There's a large, big box store a few miles away and a much smaller sports store in the same mall. The big box store's lights are all on, too much visibility. She avoids that. All the glass is broken in the windows and doors of the sports store, but at least the lights are off. Anyone scouting this store might think that any food hidden in drawers or back coolers would be gone by now. She hides her bike in a field out beyond the mall. She doesn't want to tip anybody off she's in here. Using her bike saddle bag, she fills up with teenagers' clothes, winter gear, shoes, and boots, all in generous sizes he can grow into in the next year. She wears her night glasses and works quickly in the dark. When the deep male voice says, "Stop and turn around," her blood runs cold. She feels a gun barrel at her temple.

From her sideways position, she takes him in. He's about 6'2" and probably weighs less than he used to, but more than her. She can't overtake him. He looks unkempt, and she can smell his body odor. He hasn't showered in a while, too concerned with finding something to eat. She guesses his age to be early 50s. His hair has grown out from a shorter cut, going grey and oily. He's unshaven, and his clothes are wrinkled and over-worn. His face is gaunt and strained. His lips are now tight with stress and hunger. He's sweating, and she can feel the hand on the gun held to her temple shaking. He's nervous and very dangerous because of that. She thinks, *stay calm. Go slow. You don't want him accidentally pressing that trigger.* Her saddle bag is on the floor, and she subtly kicks it under a rack. He doesn't notice. She wonders if Jacob might find it.

He says, "You don't look like you're starving. Where's your food?" She can hear the anxiety in his voice. She thinks, *he doesn't really want to kill me. He just wants food."* Junie says, "I have my last Nutri biscuits with me. They're yours if you'll take that gun off of me. It's just me. I can't hurt you." He says, "Put them on the counter." She does. He still has the gun at her temple. His eyes flash to the biscuits, and he grabs one with his free hand, devours it, and starts on the next. He pockets the other two with his left free hand. He says, "Where's the rest of your food? Junie thinks fast and says, "I live out at the Camps. Do you know where they are?" He says, "Yeah, I've heard of them, so what?" She says, "I have a tent and a small farm there, and I've been eating my produce." He says, "Is there anyone else there?" She says, "No, everyone's dead." He says, "We'll go there, and you can show me your farm, and I can eat." Junie says, "It requires cooking first unless you like to eat raw vegetables." The guy says, "Let's see what you have." He says, "How did you get here?" She thinks quickly. *If I say, 'on foot,' he'll have to ride with me on his bike to the Camps. It'll be hard for him to keep a gun on me. I might have a better chance of getting away or shooting him.* She then thinks, *if I say on my bike, he'll want to follow me with his gun on me. However, he'll never believe I walked all this way to the mall from the Camps. Or will he?* She takes a chance and says, "I walked here." He says, "Bullshit, you wouldn't walk all that way. Where's your bike?" She says, "Actually, I walk everywhere. It's safer if I need to duck and hide quickly from people like you. I needed some winter clothes. It's only about 7 miles from here. Not that far." He looks at her long and hard.

Junie needs to earn this guy's trust, but he doesn't take his gun off her. He tells her to empty her pockets. She takes her chance, slowly palms her gun while she draws her hand out of her pocket, and quickly shoots his gun hand. She didn't want to have to kill him. He lets out a brief yell, pulling his bleeding hand up to his chest. She wasn't counting on him having a backup gun, but he swiftly draws and now aims that directly at her head with his free hand. Now she's in real trouble. He says, "Drop your gun, or I'll kill you right now, you fucking cow." She believes him. He says, we're going to your Camps, and you're going to feed me. Try anything again, and I'll kill you. I don't care anymore." He walks her to his bike with his gun at her back, tells her to mount, climbs on behind her, and says, "Ride." She's on the front and he never takes his gun out of her back. She thinks, *I'll bide my time and get my chance*. It's raining and they both get soaked. She pulls up beside her old tent. She still had a hot plate and a frying pan there. It's three in the morning and pitch black.

She says, "I'll gather a few things, then cook. You'll have to follow me out to the farm. I don't have a light to see what I'm doing." His hand was just skimmed with the bullet and has stopped bleeding. He's using it again. He's underestimated her and hasn't had the forethought to search her for more guns. She still has her two backups.

There isn't much left to dig up, and the ground is wet and muddy. She and Jacob have been clearing the last of the crops over the past few weeks. There are late potatoes, beans, and apples. She had left some cooking oil behind but had no spices. She'll have to make do. He says, "Get cooking. If you wing that pan at me, I'll shoot you, so don't even think about it." She fries everything up, and he gags it down too fast. He says, "You're going to be my personal chef from now on." She says, "There's not much left out there to cook." He looks around the tent at Junie's old double cot and says, "We'll sleep here tonight." He has cord with him. He came prepared. He ties Junie's ankles and hands behind her and then anchors her to the bottom of the bed. She's trussed up on the cold floor. He doesn't care. Somewhere along the line, he lost his ability to care. She says, "You can turn on the heat, you know." He says, "I'm not cold." She needs to pee but thinks she can hold on until morning. She shivers through the night, thinking and planning. She can't reach either of her guns with her hands tied, but tomorrow, when she cooks again, her hands will be free. He falls asleep on the cot, mouth open, snoring, but his gun never leaves his hand. His reflexes are still sharp. Junie does not sleep.

Chapter 32

ROCKING THE BOAT

Alex has a restless night. Yesterday's events sit high in her mind, with the dead bodies lying back there on the road in the blistering sun. She's killed two men. She and Krista killed Diya weeks ago. She's become a multiple murderer. She chews over her decisions and is okay with them in the end. It's a different world now. She has to figure out how best to get across the Strait and back to her mother. That's her priority right now. *Keep your eye on the ball*, she thinks. *Don't look back.*

Alex knows nothing about choosing a boat or how the instrument panels work. She plans to try out a few boats and see if she can figure it out. She's hoping there's a boater or two back in Kingston who can talk her through it. All she wants to do is stay in sight of land or an island, something she can swim to if she has to. That she thinks she could swim to an island in the middle of the cold Pacific is ridiculous, but she holds on to that thought. She's always imagining the worst outcome for this part of the trip. She's crossed on the ferry between Vancouver Island and the mainland hundreds of times. There's a lot of open ocean out there with nothing in sight for miles.

Francis pops up on the screen. "I just read yesterday's report. What an awful day for you! How are you, my friend?" Alex says, "I was frankly a mess yesterday. In the end, I left Sean to his own resources. He'll never make it, or he'll turn into a road shooter like the two guys I killed. He would have run into those two guys with or without me and probably be dead. At least he has some food supplies and time to figure out what he'll do next. I bet his grandmother never lets him in. I was trying so hard not to have to kill anyone. Francis says, "You had no choice. Those two needed to be stopped." Alex says, "It's a reminder of what people will do to get food. It's probably a small mercy that few people are left looking for food. It would be chaos. Can I say thank you again for the camouflage you provided me? It saved my life yesterday." Alex asks, have you picked up a reading on Diya's invisibility suit anywhere? No one's following me so far." Francis says,

"No, we don't know where that person is, who they are, or what their plans are. I'm sticking with my theory that the person was an Indian spy operative sent to take Diya out and retrieve her spine disk. They grabbed our technology while they had the opportunity. I don't think they're interested in you and may not have known about you. They may not even know who killed her."

Alex asks Francis, "Have you ever killed anyone?" Francis is quiet, then says, "Let's remember the business I was in. We made weapons and military gear that allowed people to kill others. So, I've probably killed a lot of people by supplying this gear." Alex asks, "Ever questioned yourself about it?" Francis says, "Lots. We were extremely cautious about who we sold it to, with no guarantees. I know what war does to humanity. You can't pretend nasty stuff isn't happening, with you or without you. I wanted to provide the best equipment we could to the good guys. It's sometimes hard to separate the good from the sinister. They don't all wear white cowboy hats." Francis makes no apologies and does not continue.

Alex says, "Diya seemed to have a different impression of you." Francis laughs and says, "Let me guess, I was working for every country that would hire me, selling our state secrets to the highest bidder, and had houses all over the world." Alex says, "That was pretty much it." Francis says, "That was always a rumor out there about me. I knew it. Given my job, I could have been working for many countries. I wasn't. Years ago, someone blew up half a street in Delhi, and many innocent people died. No one ever knew who was behind it, but she thought I was." Francis says, "Alex, the U.S. government paid me very well. I still had my original apartment in Miami and my parents' very modest house on the island. I had everything I needed. You don't have to believe me, but nothing like that ever happened. Yes, I had many offers, all of which were reported up the line. I had no secrets."

Francis pauses and asks, "I hope this hasn't changed your perception of me or our friendship." Alex laughs and says, "I dunno, the thought of you being a multi-agent and spy with stately homes and apartments worldwide was intriguing." Francis also laughs and says, "Sorry to disappoint you. I'm an honest bore."

She changes the subject, "If you need to talk about anything, anytime, you know I'm here." Alex says, "Thanks, and I want to say you're doing everything you can to save many lives right now. You're my hero, and I'm so grateful I have you at the other end of the line." Francis pauses, then says, "We have so far to go to get out of this mess. One day at a time." Alex says, "Amen to that."

Alex asks, "How are things going at your end?" Francis shares what she said at the last meeting and how the rollout is going. She sounds optimistic. She says, "I'm particularly interested in their site selection. Once we agree, we can make better plans based on where and what we should work with. We can start really thinking about life after Kingston." Alex says, "Life after Kingston. Sounds like a book theme." Francis says, "Maybe you could write that book." Alex says, "I would have to be your ghostwriter. You'll be there living it, not me."

Francis remains silent. Alex asks, "Any progress on communication?" Francis says her staff are still working on it. They're stymied because communication with the satellites shouldn't have shut down. They think they're getting close to solving the puzzle though." Alex says, "When I get to Victoria, I'm going to check every doctor's office on the island just to see if one or two doses of the Libertas1 vaccine might still be around." Francis says, "I'm not hopeful. It was so expensive. I'm sure any doctor would have wanted to sell even their very last dose."

Alex says, "In the next few days, I have to conquer the Strait of Georgia." Francis says, "I'm so worried you won't find your mother alive. You've pinned this whole treacherous trip on finding her alive." Alex says, "I'm realistic. She might not be, but there's no reason she wouldn't be. I have to find her, dead or alive."

Alex changes the subject. "Do you have any boaters on staff? I'll need someone to talk me through how to use an instrument panel and drive whichever boat I eventually pick. I'm a complete boating novice." Francis says, "I'll put something up on the Uni-site. I'm sure there'll be someone. You'll have to be careful to not be in your invisi-suit if you're going to screen chat with anyone back here and detach the screen from your bike." Alex says, "I know. I was planning to wear the invisi-suit under a flotation suit for the trip in case I fell into the water. I thought I'd go down to the marina without it on to check out the boats. You never know. There might be someone there who can help me. Old sailors never die and all that." Francis laughs, "I think that was soldiers, but never mind." Alex says, "I'll wait to hear from you if you find a boating tutor for me." Francis says, "Righto, talk later." They sign off.

Alex heads to the border at Point Roberts and approaches it slowly. She's worried there might be automatic weapons aimed at vehicles or people trying to rush past guards. No one's around. She gives it an hour to see if any bikers pass through. Time passes, and it's apparent that no Canadians are riding into the states today, nor is anyone coming north. There's no one in the customs booths. She rides slowly through. Nothing. Nobody's guarding America or Canada today.

Alex heads down to the Point Roberts Marina Resort. There are tons of boats there. She first goes into the marina shop to get a flotation suit. She chooses the most expensive one. She thinks, *it's great to shop for the best when you don't have to pay for it.* It has feet, gloves, a hood, and a drop seat, presuming she needs to pee or poop out in the middle of the strait. Be prepared. She looks at the kid's suits, thinking about Anna and Tom. They're safe running around a sunny farm in Alberta, not getting into a boat with a very inexperienced pilot. A pang of missing them runs through her.

She's somewhat familiar with the islands between here and Vancouver Island and decides to cross from Bellingham through the San Juan Islands. There are innumerable map books in the store. She chooses one with precise mapping of the islands and nautical miles and sailing times spelled out between each one. Boating for dummies. It should take her a full day to cross if she starts very early, and the weather is calm. That won't be today. It looks so achievable on the maps, just a hop between islands. Still, it's a bloody deep, unforgiving ocean she's crossing, and 5 or 10 miles in a heavy sea won't be fun, even if the next island is in sight. She can always stop at an island if the sea gets rough. Dog paddle over. Whatever.

There are a few books on how to choose a boat. She takes some time and reads these. Nobody else is shopping for boat gear today. The San Juan current guide is a book she finds useful. She'll read it tonight. She finds a map book that provides addresses of several Search and Rescue SAR stations down the coast. She might find the best stable and maneuverable boat at one of these stations. There seems to be one near Bellingham. She's been considering a zodiac and has a general idea of the size she's looking for. Not too small. She doesn't want to make this trip in a rowboat. There are a few small zodiacs at this marina, but she could see getting bounced out with larger waves. She gets into one to check out the instruments. There's a GPS plotter, which she was counting on, but not a lot else, but what does she know? *I need some good advice,* she thinks.

It would take another day to sail down the coast, so she decides to ride her solar bike to Bellingham to choose a boat. She packs the flotation suit into her large waterproof bag and hangs it off the side of her bike. Now it's invisible, and she heads off south.

She reaches Bellingham in a few hours and looks for the SAR station. This turns out to be the U.S. Coast Guard. Their boats are too big for her needs, and lack of skills. They are serious 'take down drug smugglers' boats with lots of technical gadgets. Nothing here will work for her. There are two marinas close by, so she rides over to the largest.

One of the boat recommendations she read about was a 27' hard top Life Proof Boat, supposedly virtually unsinkable. She likes that description. It's the right size for her to handle, with a sheltered cabin over the steering and panel area in the middle of the boat. The image shows it being driven by a sole driver. There are about 1,000 boats docked between the two marinas, and she walks up and down the wooden boardwalks, searching for a boat like that.

After a couple of hours, she almost gives up, but she finally spots her boat and jumps on it. The instrument panels are all computer screens now, not the dials of the old days. Alex thinks, *I just want to start the thing up, drive it out like an old-fashioned car, and follow a GPS map route I would set. Is that too much to ask?* These boats have been quite simplified over the years. She's been worrying about getting bounced out of the boat with a wave and being unable to get back in. This boat has a handy ladder that hangs over the side. There are even paddles strapped to the insides. *Like I could row this thing,* she thinks. It gives her some comfort, though.

Alex says to herself, *now or never*. She puts on her flotation suit and starts the boat up. Easy. Just push a button. There are electric engines in the back. Can't seem to get away from the big engines off the end. It runs quietly, barely a murmur. She opens the screen; it lights up, and there are many options. She thinks, *I don't want to sail the seven bloody seas.* Still, there's a GPS plotter/sounder, a compass, a weather reader, a pump key she hopes she won't have to use, and a VHF radio that won't do her any good, but you never know. It turns out to be easier to figure out than she thought. Almost idiot-proof. Almost. Any idiot can drown. She doesn't want to be that idiot.

Alex decides to take it out for a quick test drive. There's no one around. This is a huge marina, and she thinks, I would have thought a survivor or two would have been down here, fiddling with their boat. I don't think any fish survived, so fishing's out. Not everyone will know that. Her entire world is now on this boat. She tethers her gear bag to her waist and tethers herself to the boat, just in case. Using the boat's GPS, she charts a short course down the shore to Samish Island, backs the boat out, and sets off. It's a straight run, and she makes it with ease. The sea is relatively calm today. It's like driving a wobbly bouncing car, but she gets used to it. She's feeling a little cocky. She turns the boat around and heads back north. She still has to dock it and tie it off. That turns out not to be so easy, but she finally gets it back into its berth, jumps off with the rope, and ties it off. She doesn't know any sailors' knots, so she ties a double knot and hopes it holds. She jumps back on, grabs her gear, pops her bike out again, gets back onto the dock, and strips out of her flotation suit. She looks the boat over and thinks, this is my sea chariot. The name 'Zephyr' is painted on the side. It means a breeze from the west. She likes that. She beseeches the boat, *please, Zephyr, get me across safely. Please.*

Alex decides it's too late to sail out today, so she'll find somewhere close to stay and leave early in the morning, weather permitting. She's heard you're supposed to sail out with high tide but thinks, *I'm not going off to discover America, just Victoria, so I don't think that applies.* She's not confident enough to hit the open ocean, so hopes she's guessed right in staying close to the islands. She still hasn't heard from any boat experts back in Kingston. Maybe there are none.

Heavy smoke is in the air from fires burning down the Oregon coast. Every summer, the world ignites. Towns and lives and millions of acres of forest are lost. That won't change soon. Alex heads back into Bellingham to have a look. It's a sizeable city. The population would have been around 100,000. The rail tracks run right along the coast. She wonders how often that came up with developers feeling robbed of waterside property. She's looking for a spot overlooking Bellingham Bay to check the water conditions in the morning. That won't tell her what the calmness of the water will be out in the strait. However, if it's choppy in the bay, it will be worse out in the strait, and she'll delay her trip. She rides down to the historical section. A few men are hanging around the streets, all visibly armed. These guys aren't going anywhere, just standing up against buildings in the late afternoon sun or sitting on benches, watching and watchful. Alex gets the eerie sense they're waiting for the shoot-out in the OK Corral. None look like they're starving, so they must have food. They all look ready to explode. She guesses the female survivors are lying low inside somewhere or another virus has taken them out. Americans weren't big on vaccinations, and lots died because of it.

She doesn't want to stay too long with armed men standing around, even if they can't see her. She heads back to the bay and finds a house. After a walk-through, she finds a pile of sand with a dog collar in the middle. 'Rexie' reads his tag. Poor Rexie died alone. Where would his owner have been at that early hour? Nobody's in bed or in the bathroom. Odd. Maybe the owners were away and had a dog walker coming in? There's dog food and water. She'll never know. There's pizza in the freezer and wine in the cupboard. She settles in for her last night on the mainland, reading her book on currents. Not exactly a relaxing bedtime story.

Chapter 33

THE CROSSING

Tomorrow arrives, and Alex checks the water in the predawn light. There are lines of corduroy rivulets in the bay, small crests of morning silver sliding over the gray ocean. That means there's a slight breeze, but overall, calm. In the distance, she sees a small boat making its way out of the harbor, fishing gear out over the side, ever hopeful. She calls out to him in her mind, *no fish survived, buddy. They had heartbeats*. His boat is much smaller than the one she's chosen, but it cuts effortlessly through the water. That bodes well. The weather reader on her boat should give her more information. She finds some oatmeal and a bean cake for breakfast and enjoys one last cup of coffee. She makes herself a couple of sandwiches to take with her. Alex thinks, *I'll be digging into my mother's freezer tonight, I hope. Please be home, mom*. She's very excited at the prospect of maybe seeing her today.

The sun's up, and it's time to get down to the marina and get moving. Alex sees a guy working on his boat, but he's the only one. He's at the other end of the marina and won't see her until she pulls out with her flotation suit on, so she has time to loosen the rope and hop on with her gear. He'll probably be surprised to see a woman sail past him out into the harbor and may want to communicate. She hopes not. She turns on the screen and the weather reader. It's going to be hot onshore, but the ocean temperatures and winds look manageable, as much as she can understand what she's reading. After her midnight reading, she now knows a little about these islands' currents. She'll have to figure that out if she runs into something wild and crazy. From what she read last night, the worst currents are in the narrower passes between the islands and increase in danger as tides go in and out. Alex knows nothing of tide tables. She's glad her invisi-suit controls her body temperature because her flotation suit would be unbearable in this heat without it. She'll take a sample of the ocean water later.

She sets her GPS for the nearest island, Portage, and she's off, sailing out of the harbor. The guy on the dock stops and watches her sail out. He yells at her, "Hey, that's my son's boat," and waves frantically. Alex doesn't wave back. He yells again, "That's Billy's boat, you bitch!" Alex feels Billy won't mind she's taking his boat, but his dad sure does. He's probably lost everything, including Billy, and now she's stealing that from him, too. She gets it. Portage is about eight miles as the crow flies, but Alex is not a crow, and that's quite a distance in open water. She had planned to follow the shore around Bellingham Bay, make her way through the pass between Portage Island and Lummi Island and travel down to the tip of that, again following its coast.

She heads out of the harbor and watches the guy on the dock. He's now running toward his boat. Alex thinks, *that's not good*. He gets in and starts after her fast. He has a small three-engine speed boat, *as fast as hers*, she thinks, and he's gaining on her. She speeds up and heads straight out into the channel. She didn't want to have to do that. No more hugging the coast now. She looks back at him and thinks, *Jesus, he's pulled out a gun,* and she hears the ping of bullets bouncing off the water, coming too close. She's thankful it's difficult for him to take aim in an unstable boat, and so far, he's missed her and her boat. Alex can see his eyes and angry, contorted face. Alex thinks, *losing his son's boat means the world has really ended for this guy. He's determined to kill me.* She thinks, *it's just past dawn, and I am being gunned down by a crazed sailor before I get out of the harbor.* She also thinks, *I sure don't want to kill anyone else, so I'll have to zap him before he comes up on me or shoots a hole in my boat.* As he nears, he raises his pistol and aims the gun and his boat at her. It appears he's going to ram her. He misses again. He's apparently lost all sense and is only intent on stopping her from stealing this boat. His son Billy is likely a pile of sand in his bed, but this guy is taking no hostages on his behalf. He's lost his boy. He's damn well not losing his boy's boat. He's about 30 feet off Alex's stern with his gun leveled right at her. She needs to zap him now and veers in a hard left to avoid the crash. She takes aim, and her little heat seeker takes him down before he can press his trigger again.

His boat misses Alex by inches but charges on. He's fallen forward onto his dash panel, and the boat doesn't read its pilot is no longer conscious. He'll ram right into Portage Island if Alex doesn't stop him. Then he'll die for sure. She doesn't know if her boat is fast enough to catch up, but she'll try. She chooses the over-speed option on her panel, and her boat kicks in. The sea now has a low roll, and she's bouncing slightly over the crests. She matches his boat speed and pulls up beside him with less than a half mile to go. Reaching him will be a challenge. Alex doesn't want to fall out of her boat, but she's tethered to it and her gear, so she won't lose either. She quickly throws the rope ladder over the side. You never know. She gets as close as possible and leans farther over the side than she's comfortable with. The waves lick her face. She can taste the saltwater. She has her toes locked to the side of her boat, makes contact, grabs a corner of his jacket, and pulls hard. It's enough to dislodge him off the panel. He falls back into his boat, and his boat immediately slows.

Alex loses her grip, and she's in the water, being dragged by her own boat, which is now speeding toward the island. It has yet to sense there's no pilot. The Pacific Ocean is freezing on Alex's bare face and hands. She's swallowing seawater, and her arm is screaming, making it difficult to hand over hand her way along the tether back to the boat. When it finally slows, she's exhausted. She inches her way back to the side of the boat, places a tentative foot and hand on the ladder, hauling herself up and back inside with one arm. She falls on the floor, gasping for breath and vomiting up seawater. She thinks, *that went well.*

She looks over into his boat. His body seems to be in an okay position. He's bleeding slightly on his face where he fell. Just a surface scratch, so he won't bleed out. He's not dead. It's a good day, after all.

Alex's understanding of boats these days is that if they no longer sense an operator, they return to the port where they were registered, like good little robots. She thinks this even applies to cruise ships and tankers, but she's not sure. His boat comes to a complete stop just offshore of the island, then slowly turns around and heads unhurriedly back toward Bellingham. This guy will wake up safe and alive in his boat in about six hours.

As she watches his boat slowly bob back to its marina in the distance, she takes some deep breaths. She doesn't know why she's surprised by the insanity she's running into on this trip. She'd been naïve and hadn't imagined it would happen to her.

Having made it the hard way to Portage Island, Alex continues south to the tip, hops over to Lummi Island, and follows its coast south to Reil Harbor.

The next open water jump is from there to Sinclair Island, about four miles. Not too bad. Land is still in sight. So far, so good. The sea has developed a bit of a roll. From Sinclair, she sails down to Cypress Island, only about a mile and a half, and then she has about a three mile jump over to Blakely Island. She resets her GPS as she goes, and so far, it works. However, this has taken her much longer than she thought it would. It's almost noon. Like Vancouver Island, these islands are basically rocky outcrops that rise sharply out of the ocean. The islands themselves are heavily forested. The larger ones have at least two harbors, but many smaller islands have no tie-ups. Personal docks sometimes, but they're not all inhabited. Summer homes, luxurious cottages, small cottages, and year-round houses are built well back from the water's edge now. Many people lost their waterside properties over the past decades as the oceans rose. People got wiser about choosing their water views.

The wind is now rising, and the ocean roll is getting bigger. Alex is headed to Friday Harbor, but she has to get through the pass up around Lopez Island, down around the bottom of Shaw Island, and over to San Juan Island. The currents she read about last night are now obvious. Her boat bucks the waves, now small whitecaps, and the ocean wants to take her a different way. The tide must be changing. Alex thinks, *if I were a true mariner, I could wet my finger, put it in the wind, and know all. At least that's the way the stories go.* The waves are disorganized, tipping, cresting, and falling, going no particular way. She guesses a tide is coming in or out. The swells never looked that big from the deck of a BC Ferry with stabilizers. She's very nervous, bouncing around like a cork. She thinks, *corny, but I'm out of my depth. I need to head to shore as soon as possible and get out of this wind and angry sea.*

She read that you should keep the bow into the waves on high seas, presumably so you don't get rolled over on your side. She tries to do this, but it's a fight between her and this big, deep, grey ocean. It's the deep part that sticks with her. There's a considerable splash over onto the boat, and she presses her pump button to remove the sloshing water. It's gone in minutes. She thinks, *man, I'm glad I have an internal pump on this girl. Wouldn't want to be bucketing extra water over the side like some comic strip character.* She's been able to keep all her destinations in sight, and she can now see San Juan Island and heads straight for the harbor. Suddenly the radio burps alive. It's an electronic All-Points Bulletin to all mariners about the lousy weather. It must have been triggered by the weather radar satellite. The automatic weather reporter on her screen gives her information about the height of the seas, the wind speed, and incoming rain. It's all bad news.

The swells are now three to four feet. Alex thinks, *I won't be making Victoria today.* She pulls into the marina and finds a spot to moor the boat. Because of the wind and waves, she has to wrestle the boat into the dock. She's not looking forward to the jump-off to tie her down, but it has to be done. She waits for her moment, leaps, slips on the wet dock and goes down. She thinks, *at least I'm on land with my gear.* A driving rain has blown in, and there's no one around. Alex realizes the rain will make it harder for her to bike away to a campsite without being seen."

Friday Harbor was a booming small island metropolis before the attack. A little boating vacation paradise. You could stay here for days with myriad choices of activities and restaurants, and bars. It would have been a great place to come to in different circumstances. Back when life was still fun. It's not fun today. Alex leans into the wind and the rain, makes her way to the marine shop, and gets her flotation suit off. She thinks, *I may have to stay here for the rest of the day and the night, but at least I can't be seen if someone comes in.* The rain beats against the windows, and the windows inhale and exhale with the wind. She pulls out her sandwiches and has lunch. There's a coffeepot, she risks it and makes up a pot. Caffeine, nectar of the gods. She's feeling smug. She's made it this far, murdering sailors aside.

Around five o'clock, the rain stops, but the winds don't die down. Alex thinks, *I'm definitely sleeping on this island tonight, but I feel vulnerable in this space.* The marina shop is small and tight, with no open spaces and no back door, just merchandise aisles and the cash counter. Someone could come in for some unknown reason and bump into her. She's not safe. Alex doubts there are Smart Houses here. She'll have to move and find a campsite back in the woods. The GPS topography map on her bike indicates thicker forests further into the island, past the town. She rides inland, aware she's leaving a splash behind her but keeps watchful of any other bikes. There's no one out in this weather. She has yet to be spotted. She finds the road she wants, hikes into the woods, and sets up camp. The winds have died down, but it continues to rain. West coast weather. *Welcome home*, Alex thinks, *almost.*

She's been on high alert since she left this morning. Her body's stiff from steering and maneuvering a boat in bumpy seas. Her left arm and shoulder ache because of the shove she had to give to the guy in the boat and hauling herself back into her own boat. She fishes out a pain patch, her water heater, coffee, and a flavored wafer for dinner and realizes she's starving. This one tastes like roast beef. It amuses her that even though meat in most forms is entirely out of fashion and unattainable, manufacturers still try to capture the flavor. Francis' plant did an excellent job with this one. It's tasty and filling. Alex hasn't had her speaker on for this voyage, so she recaps her daily report for the folks back east and sends it on. Alex takes a certain satisfaction in summarizing her eventful days in a report. It's her life diary these days. Francis sends her back a quick "A belated bon voyage.

Stay afloat and stay away from armed sailors." Yeah, good advice Francis. Nothing flowery about that girl.

Alex beds down for the night with the rain rattling against her tent. She's dry, warm, fed, and safe, for now.

She's up at dawn, having slept well, all things considered. Another wafer and coffee for breakfast. The rain and wind are gone. It's going to be steaming hot again today. Time to get back on the water.

She gets back to the dock and checks around for people. A guy is sitting at the end of the pier in a lawn chair, looking out into the strait. Alex thinks, *Strange*. He's in his sixties, with a slim, soft-looking body that hasn't exercised in a while. He's in shorts, a t-shirt, and sandals. His hair is white, slightly receding, and tied back in a tail. Alex quietly thinks, *I never liked that look*. He's still shaving, apparently. No beard. He was probably good looking when he was younger. He has even features. He turns his hands around each other nervously while he scans the harbor.

Alex hops onto her boat, gets into her flotation suit, and is now completely visible. He spots her and comes rushing toward her. Alex's hand is on her gun, and she thinks, *now what?* He comes up to her boat and says, "Please, will you help me?" Alex immediately lies. "I don't have any food." He says, "No, that's not what I want. Something's happened to my wife, Ada. She's been unconscious for days. Our dogs are dead. I've knocked on all the doors on the island, and no one seems to be alive. They're all strange piles of sand. I can't get anyone to respond to my calls. My kids aren't answering." He chokes out panicked sobs. Alex explains to him what has happened to the world. The explanation won't help him, his wife, his kids, or his dogs. He takes this in but doesn't seem to, really. She knows many survivors are still living in shock. He pushes on, "Could you come with me and look at her? Maybe you can see something I can't. Wake her up." Alex thinks to herself, *there's no way I'm going with you to see your wife. I can't fix her, and there might not even be a wife. It could be a ruse. Nope. Too dangerous*. She says, "Sorry, I have no medical experience. I can't help her or you."

He then asks, "Are you heading to Vancouver Island? Could you find a doctor for us and send someone over?" Alex shakes her head and says, "The chances of finding a doctor alive are pretty slim, and I wouldn't know where to start. If I found one, I don't think they'd want to come here. Their personal circumstances are also dire. It's not safe to be seen out and about." He says, "Don't they take an oath or something? She's dying!" Alex feels so bad for this poor guy who can't grasp reality, but she can't offer him any help. He says, "Please, will you try? That's all I ask." Alex lies and says, "Of course, but don't hold out any hope. You'll probably have to let her go. I'm so sorry." He kneels on the dock and says, "I'm begging you." Alex thinks, *rip my heart out*. She says, "if I could find someone and convince them to come here, where would they find you?" He's already thought of that and passes her a piece of paper with his address and the harbor directions. She asks him if he has food, and he says, "Plenty, we have a farm." Alex says, "That is one bit of good news. What's your name?" He says, "Frank Michelson. My wife is Ada." Alex says, "I'm promising you nothing, Frank. I suggest you make Ada as comfortable as possible. Help probably won't come. There isn't any. I'm going to leave now. I'm so sorry." As she casts off, he stands there sobbing. Alex thinks, *maybe someone else will make a better false promise to him*. As she sails past him, he pleads, "Please, whatever you can do." Alex waves to him, wishes him luck, and motors out of the harbor. She thinks, *I wish I could have left him with some faint hope, but I don't believe in miracles. Never did*. She's putting all these sad tragedies in compartments with closed doors. She doesn't want to open them again. It's too hard.

She has a long day ahead of her. The weather has settled, and the ocean is relatively calm. Alex sails up the coast of San Juan Island and around the northern tip, then hops across Haro Strait to Sidney Island, and she's back in Canada. She wishes that made her feel safer. She sails over to James Island, comes around the other side, and finally, Cordova Bay is in sight. A sight for sore eyes for this tired sailor. There's nowhere to anchor here anymore. The sea washes angrily against the steep cliffs, so she still needs to sail down the coast to the Oak Bay Marina in Victoria to tie up. She's been sailing for at least eleven hours. She's exhausted, hungry, and desperately needs to pee. She thinks, *never could pee in a portable toilet*. This last leg takes another hour and a half, but finally, she sees the familiar sight of the marina and pulls in. She's home.

Chapter 34

RETURN TO EDEN

The Oak Bay Marina is a half mile further in from the original shore. Rising ocean levels put much of lower old Oak Bay under water. New breakwaters were built decades ago along Willows Beach and outside the marina area. Beach Drive is now a drive along the Willows Beach corridor, running alongside the ocean. Millions and millions of dollars of homes have gone over the years, eaten by an ever-rising salty foe.

Alex finds a perch for her boat and sails in. She thinks, *I'm getting pretty good at this, a skill I probably won't ever need again.* There are a few men down fiddling with their boats. Alex thinks, *I guess they feel safe here among old comrades. They obviously have some food source.* They all look up when she sails in. She's an anomaly, a strange woman in a boat, not from their club. She can see the looks on their faces and an exchange of glances between them. They think, *who the hell's she and where'd she come from*? They also think, *bet she wants food*. Alex has to get her flotation suit off and become invisible as quickly as possible. She also has to figure out how to get past these men.

She jumps off her boat, ties it down, and hurries toward the marina shop with her gear bag. This means she has to walk right by one of them. She keeps up a pace as she walks by and says with a smile, "I'd love to talk, but I'm desperate to pee, and no, I don't need your food." He laughs and says, "There's a washroom in the back. Help yourself." He shrugs at the other guys. Alex finds the washroom, removes her flotation suit, and stows it in the bag. She also has a pee and a well-deserved poop. Perhaps too much information, but this is her life.

The guy she spoke to is now in the marina shop, waiting for her to come out. She's a fresh face and might have news. He wants to talk to someone new. Alex cracks the washroom door a bit to see out and waits for him to turn around. He finally does, and she slips out the door. The aisles are narrow in the shop, and he's blocking most of them, especially the exit. She's dressed in only her invisi-suit now, he can't see her, and she can outwait him. She's in the back of the store with the fishing gear. He's up front by the register. Twenty minutes go by, and he finally goes over to the washroom door, now ajar, knocks, and asks, "Everything okay?" He now has his back to her, and she takes her chance and scoots out the door of the shop. He hears the bell and turns around to see the door swing, but sees no one. Alex thinks, not for the first time, *poor bastard. This will really screw with his head.* She's up the road looking back at him, and he rushes out of the store looking every which way. He yells at the other guys, "She's gone!" They'll talk about that for a while. She snaps her bike out, gets the gear set up, and rides off. Her mother's house is in Fairfield, near here. Her anticipation is high. She thinks hopefully, *in twenty minutes, I'll see my mom. Please let her be there and alive.*

She rides past all the familiar landmarks of her hometown and neighborhood. There's magic in this place. It has a smell of moisture and ocean and growing things. She always loved coming home and felt lucky to be a native Victorian. It has history and huge mossy rocks and rolling hills running up from the Pacific. There's lots of crummy weather with stretches of sun, given like a gift with a string that gets pulled just when you settle into some sunshine and warmth. It's windy. It's an island in the Pacific Ocean. The lawns and boulevards are now all overgrown, dry, and brown. August always fried the lawns, anyway. Water is scarce here on the Island, and few people watered their lawns. Still, some gardens are blooming, despite their lack of attention all summer. Victoria's very leafy, and the trees provide some well-needed shade on this steaming hot day. Fall's coming though, and they're already dropping their flotsam of leaves everywhere. Alex sees no one on the streets, not even a bike. She has a sick feeling this will not turn out well.

She pulls into her mother's driveway and notices the always manicured front garden is overgrown and unattended. Alex holds on to diminishing hope and thinks, *maybe she's too afraid to come out.* She reads the house. It's dead. Her heart sinks. Her mother is dead inside, or not here. Alex had so wanted to see her mother come rushing out with her beautiful big smile. Not happening. She braces herself, opens the garage, and rides in. The garage is a mess, not like her mother. She's a neatnik. Holes hammered into the walls. Odd. Alex is sensing this might be dangerous. She slowly enters through the side door into the kitchen.

She finds utter chaos. The house had been completely tossed. Cupboards emptied onto the floor, dishes smashed, furniture overturned, appliances pulled out from the wall, holes hacked into the walls. Her mother's lovely art collection is all on the floor, frames and glass smashed. There's glass everywhere. Alex dreads finding her mother's body. She moves from room to room. Beds upended, mattresses ripped open, sofas ripped open and upside down. Her mother's bedroom had really been ransacked. Makeup thrown on the floor, and drawers emptied. Underwear is scattered everywhere. The bed is stripped, and the mattress sliced. Someone was looking for something desperately. Alex is screaming in her head, *where are you, mom?*

Besides being a neat freak, her mother had one quirk. She was a chronic grocery shopper and always had a year's worth of frozen food. She would date, label, and circulate it, but she couldn't pass up a bargain of pseudo meat or a casserole on sale. Like Alex, she wasn't a cook. The freezer and coolers have been pulled away from the wall but aren't unplugged. The cooler is stripped of food, but the freezer still has months of frozen food. Not as much as her mother usually would have had, though. Somebody's been helping themselves.

Alex remembers her mother told her she had stored the emergency wafers Alex sent her in her father's secret space. To be safe, Alex sets the interior locks on the doors and sweeps the glass away from the floor. She has a plan and will sweep it back later so as not to give away her presence. She presses her dad's ingenious secret button, and the top slides back silently. The wafers are still in there. Alex thinks, *I bet this is what the invader is after. My mother probably told everybody who would listen her funny story about what her daughter gave her for her birthday.* Alex thinks, *whoever it is, they may return, given there's still food in the freezer, and they obviously haven't found the emergency wafers.*

She checks the code log in the security panel. Long before last April and the attack, it's obvious her mother had a very lax security system. Alex sees there are about five codes other than hers used regularly. Her mother had at least recorded who had the codes; all her girlfriends and the mysterious Robert. Only two of them have been entering since the attack in April. Her mother's old friend Joanne has been back three times. They'd known each other since they were kids. Alex thinks, *I'm going to pay a visit to Joanne.* The other is Robert, who Alex presumes is the 'friend' her mother was seeing. Her mother hadn't bothered to enter his last name. She sees he was here two days ago and seems to have been coming in a few times a week. Probably to get food from the freezer and likely to find the motherlode, the wafers. Alex thinks, *that means he's coming back, or possibly Joanne is coming back, and one of them can tell me what's happened to my mother.* She leaves the house as she found it. A clean up would tip them off. She sleeps on her inflatable mattress in her invisi-suit and waits.

Two days go by, and nothing. No visitors. Alex is frantic to find out where her mother is and if she's dead or alive, but she has to wait in what she now considers her broken home.

Her mother's house is a sizable Smart House, a bungalow with a rooftop cistern and access to well water. She was completely independent. It was a comfortable house, and her dad had opened it up considerably when he did the upgrade. Her mother had a taste for art and collected. She liked lively colors and images. She also has lots of collages of Alex and Sam and her and her father and her friends. The ever-present fresh flowers are now dead in their vases, looking like hanged men. You can't see in but there's lots of light. She has a private back deck, but it was rarely used. Few people barbecued in Victoria. The winds blew in off the Pacific after six o'clock, and you put a sweater on in August, even after the hottest days.

Alex wanders around her old house, now so disheveled it breaks her heart. She thinks, *that's alright. I can fix that later.* On the third night, around 11:30 PM, she sees a bike pull up. It's showtime. Alex still has her invisi-suit on. The panel lights up, and the door slides open. A hand reaches over and turns on the lights. It's Joanne. Alex thinks, *I'll be damned.* To confront her, she needs to get out of her suit, but she's worried that Robert will also show up and that will blow her cover. She thinks, *maybe if he sees Joanne's bike outside, he'll think twice and not come in.*

She takes the chance and quickly slips out of her suit in a back bedroom. Alex finds Joanne with the freezer open, helping herself. She comes up behind her and says, "Enjoying the groceries, Joanne?" Joanne jumps back, eyes wide, and says, "Oh my god, Alex, when did you get home?" Joanne then says, "I know what this looks like." Alex looks at her. Joanne has the good grace to say, "It looks like exactly what it is. I'm stealing your mother's food. I'm so sorry." Alex cuts to the chase and says, "Never mind that. Where's my mother? Is she still alive?" Joanne says, "I don't know where she is. After this disaster started last April, she wasn't picking up, and I came over. She wasn't here. I've been coming back to look for her, and when I ran out of food, I'm so sorry, Alex, I started taking hers. I thought she was probably dead." Alex asks. "When was the house ransacked?" Joanne says, "About a month ago. I came in, and it was like this, and it has gotten steadily worse since then. None of our friends who had entry codes are alive anymore. I don't know who else has access." Alex asks, "Do you know this Robert guy? He's been coming here a few times a week, according to the log." Joanne says, "I didn't know him well. He was a friend of a friend and started coming to our afternoon wine parties. He paid a lot of attention to your mother, and she started seeing him. She was quite enamored. They were doing a lot of things together and having fun. I don't know his last name." Alex asks, "Do you know where he lives?" Joanne says, "I think he was over in Esquimalt somewhere, but I really don't know."

Joanne says again, "I'm so embarrassed and so sorry. Your mother gave me a sleeve of those wafers you sent her, but I don't like them, and I've got to eat." She tries to veer off her guilt and says, "My god Alex. You're so skinny. I wouldn't have recognized you on the street." Alex says, "A world disaster and no makeup will do that." Joanne then says, "Isn't it awful what's happened?" Alex says, "Yeah, awful." She's not in the mood for a newsy chit-chat with her mother's old friend tonight. She says, "Look, Joanne, I'm sorry for your circumstances, but I suggest you eat those wafers. They'll feed you for a year if you only eat three a day. You can always eat less and stretch them out. Maybe by then, a food solution will have been worked out. Don't come back here. I'll be blocking your entry code. I need to set a trap for this Robert guy the next time he comes in, and I can't have you dropping by and screwing it up. I'm sorry for being so direct, but I need to find out what's happened to my mother." Joanne is crying. "I don't want to believe she's dead, but it's been so long." Alex says, "I'll let you know what I find out. If I find anything out." Alex continues, "I'm sorry, but I need you to go now. He might come tonight." Joanne says, "Of course I understand, and again, I'm so sorry." Alex says, "It's alright, desperate acts in desperate times." Joanne leaves in tears and rides away, guilty, embarrassed, and scared for her future. Also empty-handed. She'll be okay for a year, anyway. Alex doesn't contact her.

Alex presumes he'll come at night, hide his comings and goings by darkness. He doesn't come that night or the next night. She doesn't even want to shower on the chance he shows up. She's been home five days. It's around one in the morning, and she's in the living room, sitting in the armchair, watching the door, and dozing off. Suddenly, the panel lights up. He's here. Alex is on full alert and on her feet. He switches on the light. He mustn't have a security system where he lives and doesn't know there's a log of entries. Or doesn't care. He's well put together, good-looking, about 6'2", with dark hair buzzed short and clean-shaven. He looks to be around 40. He's in good physical shape, very buff, obviously works out. He's in a dark grey, expensive-looking sports shirt and tight cream bermuda shorts that fit his body and are crisp and ironed. He must wax his legs, no hair. He's wearing expensive loafers with no socks. He looks like a model for a sports ad or like he's on his way to his high-end golf club. The real giveaway is he's carrying a heavy claw hammer and a flashlight. She watches him patrol the house and move a few things around, rechecking furniture and holes he's hammered into the wall before. He doesn't hammer any walls tonight. He stops at the freezer, takes out a few things, and bags them. He mutters, "Where the hell did you hide them, you bitch?" Alex wonders if he's addressing her live or dead mother. He's definitely after the wafers.

His visit is brief, and he leaves, turning off the light. Alex left her bike outside, so she's ready to go. He rides off, and she's close on his tail. He rides fast and recklessly, looking behind him as if he senses her. She stays on him. He makes his way up to Pandora and across the bridge to Esquimalt Road. They wend their way through the backstreets and end up in front of a three-floor apartment building. Its exterior is dull grey and stained stucco. The building wasn't being taken care of. It would have looked dumpy even last April, but now there's garbage lying around and lots of weeds on the grounds. Given his personal presentation, Alex is surprised. She thinks sarcastically, *impressive digs, Robert*. He locks up his bike, palms his entry pad, and goes in. She needs to be careful here. She can't lose him but can't let him detect her either. She waits for him to get ahead and watches him take the stairs. She quietly lets herself in and follows him. He stops at 2B, such an elegant address. His presentation and this address don't match. There's something out of whack here.

He lets himself in. Alex doesn't follow. It would be tight inside, and she can't risk him bumping into her, not to mention seeing his door open. There's no back door to escape. She could go in and zap him, but that won't lead her to her mother, dead or alive, and will just put him on alert. She won't learn anything. She's pretty sure he knows what happened to her mother. Alex thinks, *she may not be here, probably isn't, but where is she?* She now needs to wait him out until he goes out again. It's now past 2:00 AM. She's so tired, but she wants to go into his apartment when he goes out next. That could be a day away or more. He just took in more of her mother's food, so he doesn't have to go out. She looks around to see if there might be any Smart Homes nearby to observe his comings and goings. Many houses here have done some safety modifications, but not to the extent she'd like.

There's no point in her going back home. A small bungalow sits just across the street. She reads it, it's dead, and she moves in. It has yet to be broken into, which is surprising. There are piles of sand in all the beds. Seven people were living here in three small bedrooms. An adult in one, probably the single parent, four kids in bunks in one bedroom, and two people in the other. Grandparents? Doesn't matter anymore. She can view Robert's building from the living room window. She naps through the night, sitting up on the couch, waiting and watching.

Chapter 35

BROKEN

Alex has a long wait. Two days go by with no movement from Robert. She catnaps hoping she hasn't missed him. She rarely leaves this spot on the sofa except to race to the bathroom or the kitchen to grab something to eat. She stands up and jogs on the spot to keep her body moving and awake. It's past midnight, and she's dozing off. She detects a flash of movement outside his building. It's him. He's riding away. *Probably back to demolish more of my mother's house*, she thinks. Alex ensures he's well down the street and around the corner before she crosses over to his building. It's still hot for August, even at this hour. There's an elevator at the end of the hall, but she softly climbs the stairs to apartment 2B and lets herself in. She uses her night glasses, no lights. Her first impression is of an air conditioner whirring away somewhere.

His apartment is a compact two-bedroom space. Open concept, ultra-modern minimalist, very little color, sterile. Not a speck of dust. Expensive designer pieces with one very orange uncomfortable-looking angular chair. Not meant for sitting in. It's a piece of art. Two large modern art pieces on opposing walls. Alex has never liked modern art and always thought it was a big con. There are no personal pictures anywhere. The interior of this apartment is right out of a magazine ad. A place you could never curl up on the couch under a comforter and have a nap. His kitchen is sparkling clean and burnished. Everything understated. This guy is anal. His freezer is full of food, neatly labeled in her mother's hand. In his cooler and cupboards, he has usurped some bread and oat milk and cereal from somewhere. His spare bedroom is his workout room and office. He has a set of weights, a treadmill, and all the gym toys. His computer desk is clean, with nothing on it. Alex is wary of opening his computer screens. She could be detected and decides not to. Another time. She goes into his bedroom. His bed has been made tight, almost to military standards. You could bounce a sewing needle on the cover.

She checks his drawers. Socks and underwear neatly rolled, lined up like soldiers. His bedside table contains a small revolver, loaded. Odd, he didn't take it with him. His bathroom smells of soap, today's shower, but everything's been wiped down. Towels hung with precision. No shaving gear or toothbrush on the counter. All neatly stowed in the counter drawers. He's hung his shirts and pants precisely the same width apart in his clothes closet. His clothes are expensive. He has taste.

At the back of his closet on the floor are two large grey banker's boxes. The usual place for passports and private stuff. Alex pulls these out and discovers one filled with women's jewelry. She recognizes some of her mother's. She wasn't his only paramour. The other box is full of cash. Probably over a million bucks in here. She hasn't seen cash in a long time, and this much is mind-boggling. Wow! She wonders why he has this money. She hopes her mother never gave him any. It looks like this guy was a professional gigolo. There's nowhere else to search in this apartment. Her mother isn't here. Her heart is breaking.

Alex thinks, *if she's dead, it's anybody's guess where her body might be*. She could have died when she was with him for any reason. He only had his bike as transportation, so he would probably leave her body where it dropped. If she died in this apartment, he would have moved her body elsewhere. That could be in the dumpster. She begs the universe, *please don't let me find my mother's body in his dumpster*. She worries she'll never find her.

Alex has an uneasy sense about this guy, Robert. He's likely searching for the wafers in her mother's house. Her mother would have told him about them in better days, before the disaster, before they were needed. She thinks, *she may still be alive if she has something he wants*. Alex doesn't want to think he would murder her mother, but her freezer will eventually empty, he may give up on the wafers and then she's no longer of any use to him. Alex is thorough and continues searching for clues. She walks all around the building and looks in the dumpster. To her great relief, her mother's body isn't in there. She heads downstairs to look in his storage locker. An old-fashioned hasp lock hangs on the door. She thinks, *let's see if my magical wrist opener works on this old technology*. The lock pops. Alex opens the door, and the smell of shit and piss overpowers her. There's no working light in the locker, other than the hallway light, but she has her night glasses.

In the back corner, behind a stack of musty boxes, curled in a fetal position, is what looks and sounds like a whimpering, beaten, and abused dog. Alex can't believe a dog has survived and moves in closer. She's mistaken, it's not a dog. It's a human. It's her mother.

Alex throws back her hood so her mother can see her face, and her mother's swollen eyes squint half open in the half light from the hallway. Alex says, "It's okay, mom. It's Alex. I've got you. You're safe now." Her mother moves her mouth to say Alex's name, but her words won't form. Alex says, "I'm here. I'll get you out of here and home." Her mother sounds like she has a mouthful of cotton. She mumbles something that sounds like, "He'll kill you." Alex says, "It's okay. He can't hurt me, and he won't hurt you anymore. Can you move?" Her mother slowly shakes her head no. Alex thinks, *How the hell am I going to get her out of here and on my bike and home?* She's not sure if she can even pick her up. She probably only weighs about 80 pounds, but that's still a lot for Alex, with her healing arm. She looks around for a dolly, something with wheels that can at least get her upstairs to the main floor. She breaks into every storage unit and finally finds a kid's wagon. That may do. She gently maneuvers her mother's body onto the wagon and pulls her toward the elevator. She's in horrible shape, beaten and bloodied. She has teeth missing, and she's covered in shit. Her left arm hangs loosely. She doesn't seem to have control of it. Her face is an almost unrecognizable swollen mess.

Alex races upstairs and gets some of her invisi fabric off her bike to wrap her in. She wheels the wagon up to the lobby and out the door. Anybody watching this would see a kid's wagon come out of the building all by itself. She puts the bubble hood up on her bike. She hopes it will support her mother's body while they ride. Alex will need to hold on to her tight. She uses all her strength to haul her up to the bike seat and quickly jumps on behind her. Her mother cries out in pain as Alex pulls her up. Alex's left arm is also screaming at her. She says, "Sorry, mom. This will be over soon. I'll get you home."

They ride slowly away and crawl home. Alex is terrified she'll drop her mother, with her slumping to the floor of the bike bubble, hurting herself even further. After an hour of inching her way through the night streets of Victoria and with immense relief, she pulls into their garage. If Robert was here, he isn't now. She doesn't know how to get her mother inside or even back down from the bike seat. She slowly lowers the bike and her mother to the floor sideways. Her mother curls back up into a fetal position. She reeks. Alex quickly returns to the kitchen and sweeps away the broken glass and crockery to make a path. She rolls her mother onto the invisi fabric and drags her in. That's the only way she can move her.

Once she has her in the kitchen and the door secured behind her, she does one crucial thing. She blocks Robert's entry code. Alex goes into her mother's bedroom, flips her sliced mattress, and places it back onto the bed. At least her mother can lie on it now. Alex needs to get her cleaned up. Her mother calls out to her from the kitchen floor, but it's a mumble. She can't say Alex's name clearly. Alex returns to her and tells her she'll get her into a warm shower and then into bed. Mindful of the broken glass everywhere, she drags her toward the bathroom and the shower stall and sets the water temperature. She strips off all her mother's clothes. They're stuck with shit, blood, and piss. Alex has to open some wounds to peel her mother's shirt and bra off. She cuts her pants off. Her mother is skin and bone and so badly bruised everywhere it's hard to tell where she wouldn't hurt. Alex slides her mother onto the shower floor, leans her body against hers, and lets the warm water run over her mother's naked, beaten body.

She watches her mother unfold and relax a bit with the heat of the water. Alex washes her hair and removes all the accumulated blood and grime. She slides her out, dries her off, wraps her in a towel, and leaves her on the bathroom floor while she makes up the bed. She slides her into her bedroom and applies pain patches. She realizes her mother will probably need diapers, for a while at least. She had some old period pads in her bedroom. She pulls some panties onto her and puts the pads inside for now. Alex thinks, *I'll have to take the chance of a messed-up bed for now and leave her briefly tomorrow and race out and get some adult diapers.* With one last heave, Alex pulls her up on the bed. She scans her with the bike scanner and sends it over to Kingston, and anxiously waits for their reply.

It's early in the morning back east, but they respond quickly. They tell Alex her mother's nose and jaw are broken, but her skull is not cracked, although some concussion has been identified. She has a fractured right shoulder, six broken ribs, and severe liver and kidney bruising. It appears Robert had been kicking her. Seven of her once beautiful, even front teeth are all gone or broken off. She's very dehydrated and emaciated. Her heart is weak and damaged, and they think she may have had a minor stroke. Alex thinks, *that would explain the mumbling and the loose arm.* They say the liver and kidney damage is dangerous but could heal on their own with time. The minor stroke is a serious warning. There could be another one, much more lethal. They tell Alex how to set her mother's shoulder, jaw, and nose and recommend hydrating her as quickly as possible. Alex feels like she's back with young Tom. She looks for a bottle to get some liquid into her mother, but eventually holds her head up and spoons the water out of a glass. Her mother is half in and half out of consciousness. When she surfaces, she looks at Alex with such love and tries to reach for her face but cries out with pain. "Alex," she mumbles repeatedly. "Alex." Alex hopes that most of her bruises and pain will resolve in time. They have lots of time.

Chapter 36

HUNTING AND GATHERING

The house clean-up gives Alex a project while her mother recuperates. She's scrubbed every surface of the house, the furniture, the appliances, the floors. Anywhere where Robert's slimy fingers might have been. She's taped all the mattresses where they were slashed and flipped them to the other side. The furniture also needed to be taped back together. She finds decent slipcovers for everything in a once pricey home décor shop she would have never gone into in a lifetime. No one's eating slipcovers, so there's lots of choice. She meshes, retapes and replasters the holes in the drywall, then sands and repaints. Alex remembers watching her dad do that when he did the upgrade, and she thinks of him while she works.

She sweeps the floors of broken glass shards and straightens the cupboards, closets, and drawers. She leaves the gardening alone. She doesn't want anyone, particularly Robert, to know they're here. The house will never feel the same again. Robert returned the first night she rescued her mom and tried his code. When he couldn't get in, Alex heard him say on the speaker, "Fucking bitch." He doesn't know that bitch is Alex. She wonders, *could he possibly think my damaged and brutalized mother escaped alone?* An alert goes off when someone is outside, and she watches him on the exterior cameras when he shows up. He walks around the house's perimeter, looking for another way in. Her dad was thorough. There isn't one Robert would ever find. Her dad disguised it well. For weeks, Robert parks his bike in the driveway and stares at the house. He can't see lights or movement inside. He comes at different times of the day and night, probably hoping to catch someone coming or going. He'll think Alex's mom's emergency food was his last chance at survival. His appearance isn't as buttoned-down anymore. He hasn't shaved in a while, and his hair is growing. He often wears the same thing now. He's lost his menace, but it's still disturbing seeing him outside the house.

Alex's mother's minor stroke becomes more evident as her body heals. When conscious, she cries a lot, slurring, "I can't think straight." Her left arm is immobile. Between her paralyzed left arm and broken right shoulder, she has difficulty lifting herself out of bed, but they manage together. Alex picked up a portable chair to transfer her to the bathroom. Fortunately, her mother's face is not paralyzed. Small mercies, given the extent of the damage on that once beautiful face. Hopefully, a dentist has survived who can help her with her teeth when she's ready. Alex wonders, "How would I find this dentist, stick a poster on a telephone pole? Like searching for a lost cat?"

It takes months for Alex's mother's ribs, shoulder, and face to heal, but it happens. The swelling goes down, and her pain subsides. She can get up on her own. Alex starts rehabilitating her mother's shoulder and arms with frequent daily exercises. They work on her speech. Alex ducks out to dead houses up and down the street to get bread and basic food supplies to add to their frozen casseroles. They have yet to resort to the wafers. It's coming, though.

Alex continues to sleep with her every night. She watches her breath in her sleep, assuring herself her mother is still alive. Because of her mother's speech problems, they don't talk as much as before, but she improves daily and works hard at her exercises. Alex is so proud of her.

Instead, Alex talks, and her mother listens. She tells her everything that's happened since the attack in April. Her mother's eyes widen with interest at the story of finding the underground manufacturing plant. She mumbles, "Must have been scary." When Alex tells her she was almost a grandmother, she laughs out loud and says, "That would have been something." Alex says, "Maybe someday we can return to Alberta and visit the kids and Krista and Sal." Her mother looks at her, frowns, and says, "I don't think I could manage that trip, honey." Alex brushes that off and says, "You never know; we could connect to them in the future. Francis' I.T. team is working hard on getting communication back up." Alex's mom pats her hand in a mommy patronizing way and says, "You've always been so hopeful and optimistic. I love that." Alex says, "I got my mom back. Why would I be anything else?"

As her mother's speech improves, she tells Alex the story of Robert. She says, "I knew you wouldn't approve, but my friends and I were back and forth in each other's houses for years. We all had codes to each other's houses. If something had gone wrong, how else could we check on each other? It was our kind of security as we aged. We took care of each other. You lived on the other side of the country.

You had a husband and your own life. I was happy for you and could talk to you and see you on screen anytime I wanted. I had to live my life."

She says, "Giving Robert a code just naturally evolved. We saw a lot of each other, and he always said he liked my house better than his apartment. I didn't get invited to his apartment. He was in and out of this house a lot. He was good-looking, fun, and yes, I enjoyed the sex. It had been a while. I told him about your gift of the emergency wafers, but he didn't seem interested." She says, "After the world ended last April, he completely changed. We no longer had any restaurants to go to or friends to have drinks with. He was bored and anxious. Weeks would go by, and he wouldn't come to see me. When he did, all he talked about was running out of food and starving to death. He wasn't the fun Robert anymore, never stayed, and he was often just nasty and insulting."

She continues, "He then remembered my survival food and wanted to know where it was. Your warnings rang in my ears, and I knew I couldn't tell him where it was. I was certain he would steal it, and I would definitely starve to death. Then he got cruel. He would be verbally wounding and then would pull it all back, apologize and be sweet again. Sugar and salt. When he first asked about the food, I told him it was horrible and that I had thrown it out. He knew how expensive that would have been and didn't believe me. I insisted that was what I had done. He invited me over to his apartment in June. As I told you, I had never been there. He always kept that a big secret. He started hitting me there, asking about the wafers, and wouldn't let me leave. He would lock me to his bed frame when he went out. He became increasingly brutal and agitated, demanding where the food was. I stuck to my guns. I never told him. He didn't deserve that food. I couldn't get to the bathroom and was thirsty and starving. I disgusted him when I started messing myself, and he beat me even harder. He must have hated having that mess and smell in his pristine apartment. I don't know whether he drugged me with something, or I was just unconscious, because the next thing I knew, I was in the dark in that storage closet you found me in. I didn't know where I was. All I knew was he would come every few days and promise me water and food if I told him where the wafers were. Sometimes he would leave me some bread and water. Sometimes not. Then he would haul me out and kick me everywhere. There was no one to save me or hear me screaming. After a while, I just stopped screaming. I was sure I would die there. I hoped you were alive back in Ontario, but I couldn't connect with anyone on the day of the disaster or ever after. I would send you mental messages to be safe. I knew you would have lost Sam and Princie and been devastated, but I couldn't do anything to help you. I couldn't imagine you could come here, and I thought I would never see or talk to you again. Life had lost its worth." Alex sits beside her, holds her, and cries.

It's been several months since Alex got her mother home. She's up and about with much better arm and hand use. Her speech is almost clear, except when she's very tired. Her very bruised kidneys and liver are apparently healing. Alex scans her every week and sends it over to Kingston. They're amazed at her progress, particularly with her arm and speech. Alex says, "She has backbone." They say, "Like mother, like daughter."

A Victoria fall is always filled with heavy howling storms that churn the Pacific, make the windows creak, and take down big trees. Falling leaves crab their way across the road, and just for a minute, people think some small animal has survived, only to be disappointed when the wind flips the leaf over, revealing no beating heart. You remember you're on an island in the middle of the Pacific Ocean, no matter how big and solid it is. This fall is no exception. Because of the heavy rain and winds, bike excursions are limited.

Alex talks to Francis frequently and gets caught up on what they're working on in the Kingston underground and any advancements they're making. They're getting closer to an escape to the top. The mice are living much longer on their test trips above ground. She introduces Francis to her mom. They hit it off like teasing old friends, instantly at ease with each other. Francis has changed somehow. She seems happier and less stressed. Her face is softer. Miguel is often with her, and there's a noticeable warmth between them. They sign off one day, and her mother says, "I think Francis and Miguel are an item." Alex thinks, *what is it with mother's intuition?*

She's sprayed her mother's bike with the invisi-paint and has given her one of her extra invisi-suits. As her mother's body heals and loosens up, they ride out together and survey Victoria. Alex has to tell her mother to stop yelling out with joy as they speed through the streets. Her mother absolutely adores these invisible rides, world disaster be damned. She's so grateful to have her life back. The old life is gone, but she's ready for the new one. Her missing and broken teeth don't bother her. She still smiles with a wide grin, broken teeth and all. She puts on lipstick, mascara, and blush. She says, "What the hell. My daughter's with me, and I'm alive. I can't whistle through my teeth, but I never could. I have nothing to complain about." Alex thinks, *my indefatigable mother is back.*

Francis gives Alex a database of all the hospitals, clinics, and doctors' offices on the island. She also shares a list of where all the emergency wafers were sold. Alex had already been to a farm supply store and picked up a complete list of farms. She knows who owned them and what they grew. Working farms will be key to the island's survival.

When the weather's good, Alex and her mother work through Francis' list, starting at the top of the island. Sometimes they're away for days, staying in Smart Homes when they can find them. They're scarce in the remoter areas. Alex's tent isn't big enough for both of them, so they take some chances in less than safe houses without incident. They sleep in their invisi-suits just in case someone comes in. They're careful and Alex always has her guns with her.

Not much survival food was sold up island, and they had no luck finding any Libertas1 vaccine vials. Lots of other vaccination vials, but not that one. They document where the surviving farmers are but don't identify themselves yet. The farmers have their own food, at least. Alex will get back to them. She and her mom are a good team and work long days, but Alex has to pace her mom, as she tires easily. She's ready for bed at day's end. Her mother is very thorough when they work and misses nothing. She can find drugs in all the secret places people hide them. There aren't many dry days, but it keeps them busy all winter on the days they can ride. They notice various volunteers have set up emergency food camps up and down the coast. Alex assumes they're drawing from this past year's crops for supplies. They need to find out who's getting them the food or if any future farming plans have been implemented. They surreptitiously drop off the extra emergency food sleeves they find at these sites with a note explaining how to use them. They distribute them as they ride back down the island. Once they've finished their vaccine and food search, they plan to gather medical supplies in each town and hope to coordinate that. Since Alex can access every house, there's lots of stock in dead people's medicine cabinets. If no one is already doing it, Alex hopes to help survivors organize and return to farming. There's so much to do to restart their little world.

Decades ago, winters were mild in B.C. Midwest farmers and snowbirds vacationed there to get away from the miserable winter weather everywhere else in the country. No longer. It turns frigid in early November, with freezing winds blowing in off the Pacific. December brings heavy wet snow, and January invites howling glacial winds in from the Strait. It's frigid, damp, and miserable. Alex and her mother stay tucked in most days. Impossible to bike anywhere, let alone ride unnoticed. Their bike and foot tracks would show in the driveway and roads. They can't risk giving themselves away. Robert is still out there and comes back sporadically to check the house. They're acutely aware of the many people running out of food they can't help.

They work closely with Francis and her agricultural team, preparing future farming instructions for anybody alive who wants to listen and planning ways to reach them.

March comes, and the island begins to warm and turn green. Trees unfold and stretch their leaves. Almost overnight, crocuses and snowdrops, daffodils, tulips and forsythia, and all the wild ground cover that springs to life in Victoria pop out of the wet earth, seeking the sun. Given gardens sat untouched all last year, there's a lot of undergrowth and dead vegetation. These happy harbingers of renewal fight their way through anyway. Spring in Victoria comes early and is always glorious and reaffirming. The earth seems to have survived the disaster, just not the creatures that lived there. Things are regenerating. Francis reports the same for Kingston and the surrounding areas her drones can survey. The German site reports the same. They breathe a massive sigh of relief. One colossal question answered for this year, anyway. They still don't know if there's any permanent damage to growing things over the coming years. Alex thinks, *we need to get going on the farms. They're essential to our future.*

In early April, they have a dry day. Alex's mom is napping, so she rides out alone to survey Victoria and anybody left standing. She rides down to a food camp on Fort Street. She and her mother spent some time observing this camp in the late fall. The same woman is running it, and she has a smile and a hug for every despairing person showing up. She seems to have several people working with her. These people are here in need of a community and food, always food. They also get much needed human contact from Sue and her volunteers.

Along with vegetables, dried beans, and fruit, Alex sees this woman distributing the emergency wafers she and her mom left earlier. The woman has already added water to these, making them chewable meals and easier to distribute. This woman works long hours. She must sleep on-site, guarding her supplies. She has one of those faces and bodies that could be any race or a combination of many. She would be in her late 60s. Her face is weathered, like a desiccated mushroom. Hard to tell what she would have looked like in her youth, but she completely missed pretty, not even cute. She's just homely. She has thinning grey mouse-brown hair under her ever-present brown wool cap. When she flips it off, Alex can see she is bordering on balding. Alex thinks, *stress, probably*. The woman walks like a bulldog and maybe has bad knees. She has the most embracing happy face. Everything about her is a welcoming, warm, open door, saying, "Come on in."

The people who come to her are always laughing around her. She must be hilarious. Her sense of humor sustains these people with a sense of normalcy and love they thought they had lost. Everyone seems to love her. Alex wants to meet this woman.

Chapter 37

LEAP OF FAITH

Even at university, Francis was a loner. She was focused and disinterested in sharing her life, let alone her body. She was a tall, athletic beauty with lots of guys after her. Most fell away quickly, couldn't keep up, and she returned no play. For all of that, she had some relationships along the way, with a curated few. The men got serious. She didn't. She wanted to change the world all on her own.

There has been a new dynamic between her and Miguel since their baby discussion. He's flirting with her. She spots him looking at her across a crowded room, and when he catches her eye, he'll have a slight grin on his face and give her an affectionate wink. This makes her feel fifteen years old again with the hot rush of a crush on her neck and face. When he passes her, he touches her back or arm lightly. He'll bring dinner from the commissary to her apartment with a flower on the tray. He's subtle, but she feels this new, more intimate attention. They have always worked together as a team. The power dynamic has completely changed, though. They're in this together, and he carries as much responsibility as she does. She constantly thinks about the baby offer, but they don't discuss it. They still spend their evenings together, planning various versions of the future. A new intimacy has developed between them. They sit close together. She puts her hand on his to stress a point. He doesn't press. They touch, but not. He takes his time.

In January, the snow up top is a few feet deep. There's no sound except the wind soughing through the upper bare trees. Francis hopes the site selection team doesn't pick Kingston. Winter's too hard. She's an island girl. She doesn't like snow. The team is making their site presentation and recommendations in a few weeks.

It's a Friday night. It's been another demanding week, with the two of them constantly reassuring the crew that progress is being made. They check in on worksites, keep it light, invite people to talk, and let off steam. Some individuals need more care than others, and some are close to breaking. Some days, they feel the same, but lean on each other and get through the next twenty-four hours. They portray strength to the team but don't always feel strong.

Miguel has been kneading Francis' tight shoulders. They now comfortably do this for each other. He looks at her long neck, decides it's time to take the risk, and slowly drops his mouth to the nape, gently suckling her there. He hopes he isn't rebuffed. He feels her lean into it, and her head drops to one side in pleasure. He turns her around and softly kisses her. She returns the kiss. Francis is feeling electricity in every sexual part of her body. She hardly recognizes it, but it sure feels like more. She's ready. She whispers to him, "I'm not ovulating." He laughs and says, 'That's not exactly dirty talk, but I'll take it." He kisses her again, drawing her up against him, and says, "We could both use the practice." She grins and whispers, "Let's get naked." He laughs out loud and says, "That's my girl." And from then on, she was. They were lovers.

The winter goes by with no vaccine finds reported from Alex, nor much advance from either lab. Even if they could put it together, it would be almost impossible to test it safely with such a small group of people. Even if the mice continue to survive up top, someone eventually will have to be the guinea pig. A few suicidal people in the group would volunteer, but they need someone with the right mindset to take the first steps out. "That's one small step for a man..." and all that.

The medical lectures have continued three times a week with almost 100% turnout. Not including the medical professionals on the staff, they now have about 100 pseudo-pre-med students on the team. These underground survivors are eating this up. People enjoy the job-sharing program, and everyone has been generous with each other. There are a few holdouts, but that was to be expected. Each planning group provides regular updates, and they all feel they have a future above ground. They no longer feel doomed, just delayed.

The Site Location team sets up a group meeting in the big hall. Francis and Miguel have been prepped, but this is all new to the rest of them. The team presents several locations in Canada and the U.S. They provide show-and-tell drone photography and every site's pros and cons. Everyone's eyes are on the big screen. Could this be their new home? Then, with great fanfare and a piped-in drum roll, they make their final recommendation. It's Niagara on the Lake on the south side of Lake Ontario in Canada. It's just a few hours down the road. Lots of excellent farms, water, arable soil, and several vertical farms for the colder months. The climate is nearly perfect. It has mild winters and long, hot summers. It's not susceptible to hurricanes, tornados, or flooding. The housing options are extensive. There are plenty of Smart Homes ready for occupancy. They estimate there might be about 2-300 survivors left in town, probably considerably more in the greater region. That's enough to start a new society. They lay out all the options, put it to a vote, and all agree. Niagara it is. The room fills with applause. When it's safe to go up, they have a new home. There is a new sense of positivity in the room.

The team can now make demobilization plans for the time they can head up top and down the road. They'll need to take a lot of equipment with them, plus move over 100 people, depending on who stays. Even the choice of housing will have to be held democratically. The surviving residents in Niagara on the Lake will want first choice if they haven't moved already. They decide that an inventory will be put together of all the homes. There are tens of thousands of options. They'll hold a lottery for the most desirable. The survivors can stay put or change houses. There's so much planning to be done, and they get started immediately. Francis and Miguel haven't decided what they'll do with the invisi-material plant merchandise and equipment. Francis sees it as military equipment, which might come in handy in the future but could be more dangerous than helpful in the short term. They decide to leave it underground, locked up. They can always get to it if necessary.

It's now late March, and Francis wakes up at 5:30 AM as she always does. Something is different. She felt this way before, long ago. Overnight, her body has changed. She's pregnant. She rolls over, wakes Miguel, puts his hand on her belly, and says, "Congratulations." She then sends a silent ask to the universe, *please let this baby be healthy*.

The first anniversary of the disaster comes and goes. The test mice live on above the ground and have for months. The agricultural team is worried about missing the season. It's already late. It's time to ask for a volunteer to go up top. They think they could send whomever up in a hazmat suit and allow for a one-second outside breath and see how that goes. Francis now knows what it feels like for a general to send his young soldiers off to war. Many won't return. She and Miguel draft an application form, underlining the dire risks. They say they'll have the final word on the selected volunteer. They look at each other and press the post button on the Uni-site.

Five people come forward: three men and two women. Two of the men had made their intentions clear. They don't plan to stay, anyway. They want out. They haven't been involved in the work plans or much else. They really aren't on the team. If they lived, they would leave and not provide any follow-up information for the rest of them. They need to have the person live above ground for at least a month to see how they're doing physically. Regular scans and bloodwork need to be sent down. These two guys couldn't be counted on to stick around for a day, let alone a month. They could die down the road, and the underground team would never know. One of the other volunteers is mentally fragile, and they see it as a suicide attempt. They won't allow her to go. That leaves two candidates. Indira Banerjee is 39 years old and a very talented mechanical engineer. She'll be invaluable in their new life. She states in her proposal she wants to be part of the solution, and someone has to take the risk. It would be a huge risk to lose her. Jackson Abioye is on the agricultural team. He's currently the head chef in the kitchen. He's the 35-year-old son of West African farmers. He wants to get moving and contribute to the farming plans at the new site and ensure food supplies for the future. Both are too valuable to lose. All the volunteers' lives are valuable, even those who won't stick around. They interview them all again, ensuring they understand they must stay on top for a while and stay in touch. In the end, they eliminate the two guys and the fragile woman. They put Indira and Jackson's names into a box and draw them. It's Jackson. He's fearless and thrilled. Indira is gracious and probably relieved. Francis and Miguel are terrified.

Jackson's so well-liked in the unit that many of his friends try to talk him out of it. He's adamant. He's going. They don't tell the rest of the group when they send him up. The day of the test comes, they outfit him in a hazmat suit, and up he goes. If he makes it, a bot will bring him all his supplies. He rides a bike up the tunnel, the grass lid lifts, and he's above ground. It's like watching a reverse space landing, except this time, it's earth, not Mars. He raises his hands to the sky and says, "I'm back world."

No one's applauding. Yet. Everybody holds their breath while Jackson does the one-second breath test. He says, "Nothing, I'm okay." He then tries for five seconds. Francis, Miguel, and the lab staff stare at the screen. He says, "Still good." They check in with him and ask if he's still sure he wants to continue. He says, 'Hell yes." He then does one minute, then five minutes, then one hour. All good. Just after the one-hour test, disaster happens. He collapses to the ground and lies there, still. They watch with shock and horror. *Oh Jackson, please, please be okay,* Francis pleads in her head. The lab techs are frozen in front of the screen, watching, unbelieving. Their future disappears before their eyes. The bot camera zeros in on his mask. There's his beautiful black face, grinning. "Just kidding," he says. They could all throttle him if they didn't love him so much.

Jackson rides into Kingston and finds a Smart Home. They've given him a portable chip to get in. He's the first in the group to see the world as it is. He's been warned about the piles of sand when he finds the residents still in their beds. He steps back; he wasn't quite ready for that reality. All the warnings Francis and Miguel have been sharing over the past year are now real. He'd also been warned he'll be seen as a survivor with food. Therefore, he's in danger. He needs to lie low. He can't scout the town in his spare time. He's yet to see many vax survivors. The entire city is dead. It rings home to him now more than ever before. Everybody he ever knew is gone, a pile of sand. Francis and Miguel are very aware of the psychological impact of all of this on him. They both talk to him often during the day, ensuring he's mentally okay. He's very social and is lonely and bored without his kitchen and his mates. He spends a month there, mostly good-naturedly, complaining about the wasted farming time. Francis and Miguel assure him that missing one season won't end things. He sends in his health reports and scans four times a day. They'll be able to survive above ground.

Francis and Miguel have kept the team apprised of Jackson's progress and success. Great anticipation fills the halls of this underground home. They also share their baby news. It will be a boy and they'll be naming him Luis, after Miguel's dad. No one is surprised they're a couple. Everyone smiles as they pass each other through the halls.

Meanwhile, the site location team has put together complicated moving plans to get them to Niagara on the Lake. It's now late May, and it's time to head up top.

Chapter 38

TOMORROW BEGINS

Junie's captor wakes up and leaves the tent to have a piss. He comes back in and looks down at her on the floor. Junie is shivering and cramped but still thinks, *stay calm, don't upset this guy. He'll kill you. Stay alive.* She asks, "What's your name?" He says, "None of your business. We're not friends." He says, "Let's go back out to that farm and see what you can find to cook. Pick lots. I don't want to be going back and forth." He says, "I'll untie you, but don't think you can get away." He unties her feet first, and she stretches out her cramped legs. Then he unties her hands. Her wrists feel bloodless after the cord binding, and she tries to shake out her hands and arms. She says, "I really need to go to the latrine. Can we walk there? I promise I won't do anything." He says, "You can squat outside the tent. That way, I can keep my gun on you." He follows her out. She turns her back on him and squats. What he doesn't see her do is take the small gun strapped to her inner thigh and pocket it. She still has the gun in her bra. She'll wait for her chance. She thinks, *I'll probably have to kill this guy today. Not a good day.*

She grabs a large basket, and he walks behind her to the farm, poking her back with the gun to remind her of his presence. Although she knows this farm like the back of her hand, it was difficult finding things to cook in the dark and the rain the previous night. With daylight, she has more choices and takes her time filling the basket. He says, "I'm starving. Can't you hurry this up?" They return to the tent, and she prepares enough food for both of them. She looks over at him and asks, "Am I allowed to eat?" She's playing for time and opportunity. He's figuring out how to eat and keep his gun on her. He says, "Yeah when I'm finished." Once again, he wolfs down the food she prepared with his free hand. When he's done, he stays back from her with his gun still on her and says, "Eat. Then I'm tying you up again. Never believed in slavery, but it's looking damn good now." Junie swallows her rage at this comment. She no longer wants to save this guy's life. After she's eaten, he reties her hands behind her back and ties her feet back to the cot. She's back on the floor. He leaves, saying, "I'll be back for dinner. Have a nice day." He rides off. Junie tries everything to free herself from the cot, but it has enough weight to keep her stationary. She's stuck.

He returns late in the day. He unties her hands but keeps her ankles bound and says, "Make me supper, slave." With food in his belly, he's now cocky. He never takes his gun off her. As she cooks, she thinks about how to pull out her gun and overtake him without getting shot. She worries that when the food runs out, he'll tie her up and leave her to die. Her mind reaches out to Jacob, thinking, *don't give up on me, honey. I'm not done yet.*

Meanwhile, back at the Kracker's, Jacob has run out of places to look for Junie. His last hope is the Camps. He waits until dark. No one's on the roads, and he gets to the off-road without a problem. He knows the crazy biker is out there somewhere and constantly looks over his shoulder as he rides. He hopes she didn't run into him. As he approaches the encampment, he smells cooking. It smells a bit like Junie's cooking. There's something very wrong here. He hides his bike in the woods, stays under cover of the trees in the dark, and closes in on Junie's tent. There, with relief, he sees Junie. She's at least alive. Her head is down while she cooks something in a frying pan. There's something odd about the way she's moving. She's shuffling. He looks at her legs and sees they're bound. A scruffy looking guy sits in a chair across from her with his gun trained on her. Jacob doesn't know how she came to be here cooking for this guy, but it's not her choice, and she's in trouble.

Jacob knows what he has to do. He can't risk either he or Junie getting shot. He'll probably only have one chance at this, and he's never shot a gun. He'll get the guy's attention off Junie and onto him, without the guy seeing him. Then he'll take his shot. He takes a deep breath and lets out the most blood-curdling scream he can muster, then dives into the underbrush in case the guy takes a shot at him. The guy looks out into the dark and says, "What the fuck?" He then shoots blindly into the woods several times. Jacob hears the bullets ping past him hitting some trees. He lies flat out. He'll have to do that again. Junie knows immediately it's Jacob screaming and fears for his safety, but the guy's eyes are off her, and she takes her chance. As he turns his back to her, she shoots him. He slowly turns around looking at her, his gun is aimed at her. She thinks, *I'm done for now.* His mouth opens, and his eyes widen. Then his body crumples, and he drops to the tent's floor. The gun falls from his hand. She checks his pulse. It's over.

She worries that the guy's bullet found Jacob, and with her heart in her mouth, Junie calls out to him, "Jacob, are you okay?" There's only silence. She's heartsick, thinking if he's dead, it's her fault. Then a small voice from the woods asks, "Is he dead?" With immense relief, Junie says, "He is. Come here and help me untie this cord." Jacob comes out of the woods, suddenly sobbing. The last two days have been too much. Junie opens her arms and comforts him. "It's alright honey, it's alright, it's over. I'm okay. Thank you for saving my life." Jacob, still with tears running down his face, says, "You shot him." Junie says, "Yes, but you distracted him, and that was all I needed."

Junie and Jacob drag the body out into the woods and cover it with leaves. Jacob has now witnessed two murders in his new treacherous life. He doesn't care. He would have shot the guy himself, given a chance. They ride off together, Junie on the back of Jacob's bike. That night, Jacob plops himself down on Junie's bed and says, "I was so scared I'd lost you." Junie says, "Me too, honey, but we found each other again." He lies there quietly, staring at the ceiling, and dozes off. He's back in Junie's safe space. She pulls the duvet over them both. Sometimes boys still need to be little boys. This is one of those times.

After this, Jacob and Junie ride out at night and visit what they now consider their farm in Niagara on the Lake. They're safe in the Kracker's house, but the farmhouse isn't a secure lockdown, and they need to think about that. They decide to spend the winter in the Kracker's house and go back and forth to Junie's old farm at the Camps to gather what they can of the crops before winter comes, so they have something to eat besides the Nutri biscuits Jacob hijacked from the government food distribution depot. They wait a couple of weeks before revisiting the Camps. They find Junie's tent on the ground, with motorcycle track marks all over it. The mad biker had come back alright. They don't look toward the woods where the other guy's body is.

Junie introduces Jacob to everything she knows about farming as they harvest the crops from her little farm. He's a sponge, asking lots of good questions and eager to learn. Junie doesn't think the biker will be back. He'll think they're gone for good, and there's nothing else for him at the Camps. No food. Still, they keep their ears open, and Junie is always armed. Jacob starts carrying his father's gun all the time as well. They hate living like this, but it's their new reality.

At the Niagara on the Lake farm, there are acres of vineyards and orchards, but no open fields for wheat and bean crops, and these need to be seeded this fall. They clear a portion of the vineyard, pulling several acres of grapevine root stalks. Junie gets darker, and Jacob is sunburnt and freckled. He wears a broad hat, but his blonde hair still turns white in the sun. He grows a foot, and even though they wear gloves, their hands toughen. Jacob develops biceps, his chest broadens, and his legs fill out. His body is changing quickly with all this manual work. They're exhausted at day's end but make a lot of progress. It's late but by September's end, they're ready to sow their spring crops. They've scouted stores in the area where they might find seeds, but this is vineyard and orchard country, and they find nothing. Junie has a store of seeds for everything, and they draw on those without depleting them.

Junie says, "We'll have more next year after these crops come up." She worries about the absence of pollinating insects. Still, many of her crops are self-pollinating, so they should be okay. The inverted garden is a challenge, but there are many books on site, and they pore over them. They pick the fruit already there and ride around the village to see if anyone has set up any central sites for food. They don't find anyone, so in a sheltered area, they leave the piles of extra fruit with a large sign saying, "Help Yourself." When they return days later, they're gratified to see the fruit is gone. At least someone benefitted, and the fruit didn't go to waste.

By late November, winter blows in, and the snow's too deep to ride anywhere. They tuck into their safe, warm lair at the Kracker's and make plans for the spring. Junie had no children. She's enjoying every minute with young Jacob. In January, he comes to the kitchen for breakfast and says, "Morning," but it's a croak. Junie looks at him, feels his forehead for a temperature, and asks him if he's feeling okay. Jacob says, "Yeah, fine." Listening to him that morning, she realizes he's not sick. His voice is changing. He sounds like a man. Junie laughs out loud and says, "I won't know who I'm talking to anymore." Jacob tries a fake deep voice and laughs. He's changing in front of her eyes, growing up. Junie is not touchy-feely, but she compliments Jacob a lot about his bravery, his excellent mind, and how much she enjoys having him as a friend. His self-confidence blooms and grows with Junie. Even in these dire circumstances, he's happy.

By March, they can ride back to the Niagara on the Lake farm. It's too early for any crops, but they want to make the house more secure. More than anything, the doors need to be updated. They need the impenetrable ones. They take their measurements, read more books, and scout door manufacturers in the area. There's nothing they can't learn to do or take on in their minds. Jacob is loving his new life. He's learning new things every day, challenged, and never bored. He wishes Mr. Kracker could see him. He misses him.

There's always a new project. Finding new doors is easy. Getting them back to the farm is the problem. There are long-wheeled carts at the door manufacturer's, but it's four miles at least back to the farm. They put together a harness of cords they find, loop them into the cart, hook them onto Jacob's bike, and start a slow ride back.

They get a half mile down the street, rattling along with their doors, when a young black man comes running toward them, laughing. In a South African accent, he says, "I think I can help you." He introduces himself as Jackson Abioye and tells them a bit about himself. Jackson talks a lot, but he's a bubble of positivity. Jacob can't imagine this guy ever being down. He's so exuberant. Jackson tells them what's going on in Niagara on the Lake. He briefly shares the Kingston underground manufacturing plant story and how he and his team got here. He says, "I was the first one up. That was exciting." Jacob's eyes open wide, and he asks, "Weren't you scared?" Jackson says, "Nah, I couldn't believe my friends would send me to my death." Little did he realize Francis and Miguel weren't sure that wasn't exactly what they were doing. He tells them he's also a farmer and is looking forward to taking over a farm as they have. Junie and Jacob are wary. They don't want theirs taken over, particularly after their hard work.

Jackson says, "Stay here. I'll get a floater van so we can move those doors. We have someone who can help you install them. You're smart to upgrade, but it's been pretty safe here, and we've been here for almost a year." Junie and Jacob know that the mad biker is still riding around somewhere, so they aren't as confident. Junie is not sure she wants to bring Jackson back to the farm. Then he'll know which one they have. However, her Junie senses tell her she can trust this guy. She's not getting anything from him other than helpful. He speaks to both her and Jacob and doesn't treat Jacob like a kid. He asks Jacob, "How do you like farming?" Jacob grins back at him and says, "Hard work, but I like it." Jackson is always smiling, and it's hard not to like him. Besides Junie, he's the first nice person Jacob has run into since the attack. He renews Jacob's faith in humanity.

They load the doors and ride back to the farm. When Jackson sees what they've done, tearing out the vineyards and reseeding, he's amazed. He says, "You guys did a great job. What a lot of work, wow. Let us know if there's anything we can do to help you." Junie tells him they hope to help feed survivors, and he says, "Yeah, us too, that's great." He squints at her. "Was it you two who left the fruit downtown last fall?" Junie says, "Yes, we didn't want it to go to waste." Jacob says, "We have set up a food hall in town. I'll show you where it is. You can leave all your extra produce there. We have some people managing it." Junie says, "We need some help with the vertical farm, though. It's new technology to us." He says, "Sure, we have specialists now who can help you. I'll set that up for you." He tells them a town meeting is coming up in a few days and invites them to meet everyone else.

He says, oh yeah, we've got working SAT phones. I'll get you a couple.

When Jackson leaves, he says, "I'll drop off the SAT phones tomorrow. You won't know anyone to call but me, but that will change quickly. We have a good bunch of people who survived living here." Jacob asks, "Any kids?" Jackson says, "Yeah, a girl about your age and a guy around sixteen. I think you'll like them. I do." He says, "Oh yeah, five babies. We have a baby explosion."

Junie and Jacob's world has changed in one spinning day and a chance encounter. They decide to sleep in the farmhouse that night and try it out. They look at each other and laugh when they get in the house. Junie says, "Maybe we'll be alright." She's not a fool and knows the challenges that face them.

Chapter 39

CRIME AND PUNISHMENT

As Junie and Jacob worked their new farm before the winter set in, Peter regularly rode into Niagara on the Lake, combing the orchards and the vineyards for fruit. Thankfully, he did not find Junie and Jacob's farm. He had diarrhea all the time from all the fruit, but at least he wasn't hungry. There was something in the fruit that was calming him down a bit. He also found a stash of Nutri Biscuits hidden in the basement of a house he raided, and these got him through the winter. He was not ready to leave his apartment. His wife and son's remains are still there, and he can't figure out what to do with them. He can't get his head around burying them or spreading their sand somewhere. They didn't have a favorite place to do that kind of thing. He sleeps beside them in their bed, trying not to disturb the sand.

In mid-March, after a big melt, Peter rides into downtown Niagara on the Lake. He's surprised to find a market giving out food. A large sign on the street says, "Food. Come In." The market was formerly a grocery store, and now the shelves are filled with vegetables, grain, beans, and fruit. No more packaged goods. There are stacks of recipes and information sheets to show people what to do with the food and how to maximize their nutrition. A man and a woman in their late fifties manage the site and watch Peter hesitate, then come in. They have a warm parenting vibe coming from them. Peter feels oddly safe approaching them, goes in and asks if this is for anyone. The woman gives him a warm smile and an arm pat and said, "Yes, of course, help yourself and welcome. We haven't seen you before. I'm Sadie, and this is Rick." Peter shakes their hands and asks how long they've been there. Rick says, "About a year. It's a long story. We're part of a larger group. Some came up from Kingston, and we already lived here."

Rick asks Peter, "Where are you living? We haven't seen you before. Do you need any help with anything?" Risk senses Peter needs help with a lot of things. His body language is tense. Before the attack, Peter was reserved and didn't let many people in. Now, feeling the non-judgmental warmth of these two kind strangers, he tears up. He's talked to no one since the attack and the loss of his family. He hadn't realized how lonely he was. He thinks of Rick's question. "Need help with anything?" Peter thinks, *could you bring back my wife, baby boy, and my life?* He then finds he can't control himself and breaks down and sobs. He can't seem to stop crying. Sadie puts her arm across his back and says, "I know, honey, it's been awful for all of us. Cry as long as you need to." Sadie is used to people breaking down when they encounter her warm kindness. Everybody's a mental mess.

They invite Peter to stay for the day, get his bearings, and maybe relax. Rick sees how tightly wound Peter is and that he could use some company, at least. He looks like he's on the edge of a complete breakdown. Peter spends the day at the market, telling them about his dead wife and son, his gardening work, and his need for anxiety meds. They share their losses. Peter realizes he's not alone in his grief.

He asks Rick, "What do you think about all those bastards living in Smart Houses who survived this? Do you think they caused this?" Rick looks at Peter in amazement and says, "I don't know where you got that information, but everybody's dead except for those who got the vaccine." Many of my closest friends lived in Smart Homes. I assure you; they're piles of sand."

A cold realization settles on Peter. The day he shot Cora is hazy, but he now realizes Cora was probably a lone survivor. He shot her in a psychotic rage. He's a murderer. A feeling of shame and terror fills him simultaneously. He remembers there was one witness to it, that kid. He wonders what he was doing there and where is he now.

Rick says, "The team has set up a pharmacy down the street and collected drugs from every other pharmacy they could get into, plus people's houses. They have quite a stock. Why don't you wander over there and see if they have anything to help you? Tell them I sent you. Then come back to us. I have an idea you might be interested in."

Peter does this with his mind racing. He wonders, "What could happen to him if he gets found out? It's not like there are police or courts or even jails anymore. Where could that kid be, and what would he do if he saw him again?"

Two young females work in the pharmacy. Peter tells them Rick sent him there. He then names the drug he was taking and what it did for him. They say,

"Many people are stressed and anxious now. We have a P.T.S.D. epidemic." They continue, "We hope you understand, but to sustain and extend supplies, we are only prescribing partial doses and frankly trying to wean people off this drug because we'll run out of it. Our lab uses local vegetation to make a replacement that we can draw on indefinitely. You said that you noticed you felt a lot calmer eating all that fruit. Well, you weren't wrong." They provide him with a year's worth of his old drug, a much smaller dosage, and a list of things to eat. He thanks them and starts walking back to the food outlet. At the first block, he stops on the street and takes a pill. He can feel the old calmness wrap around his body like a warm blanket. It's the first time his mind has been clear for a long time. He thinks, *I have my sanity back.*

Rick and Sadie wait for him back at the old grocery store. People come and go, choosing food, chatting with them. Rick can see a visible difference in Peter's body. His shoulders have dropped, his face is looser and softer, and his hands aren't clenched. He says to Peter, "Better?" Peter gives him his first smile and says, "Yes, thanks, much better."

Rick then tells Peter about their agricultural team, led by Jackson Abioye. He suggests Peter move into town, choose a house, and join the team. His green thumb will be most welcome. Peter hesitates and says, "My wife's and son's remains are back in the apartment. I don't want to leave them." Rick says, "Find a nice container, even a cloth bag, and bring them with you. You'll find the right place for them eventually. No need to rush it." Peter thinks, *Yeah, I could do that. Bring them with me.* Rick tells him there'll be a town meeting in the next couple of days, and meanwhile, he'll introduce him to Jackson and get him working. They desperately need farmers. Peter reminds him his expertise was in landscaping. Rick says, "You worked with things that grow out of the ground. That's a skill we need." Peter wonders nervously if the kid might be at that town meeting.

Rick helps Peter select a house and move in. In a baby supply store in town, Peter finds a blue baby bag with fluffy white sheep leaping across it. He puts his family's remains in there and moves them into his first proper house. He places the bag on his wife's side of the bed and takes some comfort in their nearness.

The town meeting is held in the Court House Theatre building. There's still lots of seating, but many survivors are moving in from surrounding cities to avail themselves of the food. They'll have to move to a larger site soon. The mayor of Niagara on the Lake is a survivor, and he and Francis both take the stage and address the crowd. They bring them up to date on the farms, food availability, labor needs, service needs, the pharmacy, and several other housekeeping topics. People have a lot of questions, and they leave a lot of time for them. They talk about governance and decide to strike a committee to devise plans for how to deal with future offenses. They tell their audience, "We're not all good guys, unfortunately." Peter's stomach tightens while he thinks, *definitely not me*. A few people in the audience have the same thoughts about themselves.

Peter scours the room for familiar faces, one in particular. His mistake is he's looking for a very young teenager. Jacob has changed immensely and barely resembles that kid who saw him shoot Cora. Peter doesn't even remember looking for the kid after the shooting. His eyes skim over Jacob and move on, but Jacob recognizes him. Junie spots Peter at the same time and says under her breath to Jacob, "Keep cool. He doesn't recognize you. Don't look at him." Peter sees Junie and catches his breath. He remembers he threatened her with a gun while in one of his mad phases. They lock eyes, and a severe frown appears on her face. He thinks his short stint of a normal, somewhat happy life may quickly be over. She signals to him to meet her at the back of the theatre. He has no choice but to go. He remembers her shooting his gun out of his hand. He knows he can't screw with her.

He follows her outside when the meeting is over. Junie can tell this guy is no longer the crazed guy that came to her campsite. He's calm, together, and compliant. He's also extremely nervous. They find a quiet corner, and Junie says, "Tell me your story." She doesn't know what she'll do about running into him yet. Peter says, "How long have you got?" Junie says, "As long as it takes." Peter tells her everything, even his crazy conspiracy theory about people living in Smart Homes. He says, "I'm so, so sorry for terrorizing you. I was out of my mind without my meds, and I know how dangerous I was." He takes a deep breath and says, "I have another confession. I killed a woman while I was kind of out of my mind. I'm a murderer and don't know what to do about it." His face contorts, and he's crying into his hands. He says, "She'd survived, and I shot her dead. There was a kid there too. He saw me do it. He's out there somewhere and will show up somewhere and recognize me." Junie does not tell him she knows that. That would identify Jacob and put him in danger.

Junie asks him about his meds, and how stable he is. She must be sure he's no longer dangerous to their small group. He tells her what he's taking and what he's been cooking daily to ensure he's eating the right food to supplement his medication. The pharmacists gave him good advice. He's using his food as medicine and eating all the right things. Junie knows her food. She asks him what he thinks she should do. He says, "Give me a chance to prove myself. I can be part of our survival. I would owe you my life, even if I took someone else's. It would be my way of reparation if I can ever do that."

Junie says nothing. She does not want to act alone. She needs to talk to Francis. This won't be the first case of someone breaking the law they'll have to deal with. She says to Peter, "Give me a few days to think about this, and we'll talk again."

She says, "Meanwhile, keep up your good work and stay stable." Peter says again, "I'm so sorry for scaring you and your friend." Junie reminds him he returned and trampled her tent. Peter says, "I actually had a moment of sanity and, frankly, I was starving and came back to apologize and see if you would cook something for me. When I found you had left, I lost it."

Junie would like to believe him but she's no fool.

That night, both Junie and Jacob feel feverish and by morning, they're vomiting and very weak. A survivor comes by their farm to tell them many people are sick, and a virus is circulating in the village. Junie tells him to stay away and stay healthy. She tells Jacob she talked to Peter and will talk to him later. Jacob's so sick he doesn't care.

Junie has herbs for everything, makes up some soup, and insists Jacob drink it. She says, "It tastes vile, but it cures a lot of sicknesses." The two of them struggle through the next three days but eventually improve. Junie tells Jacob to stay at the farm in case he could still spread the virus. She masks up and heads into the village to see what's happening with everyone else. She learns the virus took its toll and too many people died quickly, mostly older survivors who were already weak. She goes to the food outlet and finds Peter working alone, wearing a mask, handing out food, and trying to console those who've lost friends. She asks him how he is. He says, "I didn't catch it. Don't know why, but I'm alright. I'm worried about Rick and Sadie, though." Junie says, "Go check on them. I'll hold the fort here." Peter says, "We need to keep the food outlet going. There are still lots of people who didn't get sick who need food." Junie says, "Good lad, and places her hand on his back." He looks forlorn and says, "Nothing is getting better." She says, "We're still alive. Be thankful for that. Now, go check on Rick and Sadie." He rides off quickly.

Just after Peter leaves, Francis shows up. Junie says, "Am I glad to see you. How are you and Miguel and Luis?" Francis says, "We're fine. It missed us. We must have had some protection from one of the many vaccines we've had over the years. How are you?" Junie shares their sick days and her soup treatment. Francis says, "You really need to be working with our lab. You're a damn medicine woman." Junie says, "I have a few tricks."

Junie goes on. "Have you spent much time with the new guy, Peter, and if so, what's your read on him?" Francis says, "I understand he was a mental mess when he first joined us, but our pharmacy folks stabilized him, and he's been a tremendous asset to the agricultural program. Jackson loves him. Why?" Junie says, "I don't really know how to deal with this, but I don't want it to be my decision alone. He murdered a woman back in one of his psychotic frenzies. I knew this because Jacob witnessed it. Peter confessed to me a few days back. He doesn't recognize Jacob. If he does, Jacob could be in danger." Francis says, "Wow, I'd hoped we wouldn't have to deal with anything like this again, and here we are." Francis says, "What are our choices, really? We can't try him and put him in jail. Before the attack, he would have probably been in psychiatric care, not jail. He wouldn't have been charged. We could ostracize him from the village, but that wouldn't help anyone and might set him back on a dangerous path."

Francis thinks about it and wanders about the food market. She looks at Junie and asks, "How do you feel about telling him you've talked to me? We're not happy about what he did, but we want him to be part of our future." Junie says, "He doesn't strike me as a natural killer, and he seems to be truly remorseful. He would need to promise to stay on his meds and follow the prescribed diet. He needs to understand that if we see him slipping, he'll be forced out of town." Francis says, "As for Jacob, you need to see what he thinks. Is he feeling charitable, and will he be able to keep his mouth shut for the rest of his life? He's still a teenager. Jacob is the key to this working out." Junie says, "and Peter staying on his meds and ultimately the right diet."

Junie wonders how Jacob will react to letting Peter live his life without recriminations. They'll be seeing a lot of each other in this small community. She returns to the farm and says to him, "We need to talk."

She spells out everything Peter told her and says, "Nobody's innocent here anymore. We're all potential killers. I have a gun and was ready to kill him if he returned and threatened our lives. I've worked with a lot of creeps on farms over the years. Not counting that guy who kidnapped me, I've shot two other men dead in self-defense. No one knows I did that. Now you do. You were ready to shoot my kidnapper. Who knows who else you might have killed if you had been threatened?" Jacob says, "I get that, and I understand Peter was out of his mind, but that woman wasn't threatening him." Junie says, "In his psychotic state, he thought both of you were part of a large conspiracy to kill everyone. He blamed you both for his wife and baby's death."

Junie continues, "Jacob, this is a different world, and the old rules don't apply anymore. People are hugely stressed, trying to stay sane and survive. Our world has been turned upside down, and nobody will react normally to what's being thrown at them. Francis and I believe Peter can be a big asset to our group if we forgive him and let him live his life." She pauses and asks, "Do you think you could do that?"

Jacob lowers his head, gets up, and walks around the room, running his hands through his hair. He goes to the window and stares out for a long time. Finally, he turns to Junie and says, "I want to talk to him."

Junie says, "He doesn't realize you were the kid who witnessed him shooting that woman." Jacob says, "I need to hear his story straight from him. I need to be sure I can trust him and that he won't ever stop taking his meds again." Junie says, "I agree. If the two of you are going to live the rest of your lives together in the same community, you need to be able to trust him." If you can't accept him, we'll have to ask him to leave, and who knows what will become of him then? Think about that."

Junie tracks down Peter the next day, working with Jackson and a couple of others. They're stripping out grape vines, which Junie and Jacob already know is brute work. They're covered with sweat and dirt. She calls him over and says, "I've talked to Francis and shared your story, but there's someone else you need to talk to. You've seen me with a young fellow. We share a farm just east of here. Peter, he's the kid who saw you shoot that woman." Peter's eyes open wide. He looks away and looks back at her and says, "I'm done, then. I'll have to leave." Junie says, "You scared the hell out of him, and he doesn't trust you. He wants to talk to you. Are you up for that?" Peter says, "Yeah, what have I got to lose but my future?"

That evening, Peter comes to their farm. Junie goes for a walk but still stays near the house. Jacob has his father's gun. He's grown so much he's almost the same height as Peter. He's still a lean young teenager, a whelp, but he has a man's voice and no longer looks like the scared kid Peter barely remembers. Jacob doesn't smile, opens the conversation, and says, "I need you to tell me what happened."

Peter says, "Of course, you were there. I was out of my mind. I must have scared the crap out of you. I'm sorry." He goes on, "You're right to be wary. I could be faking remorse just to live a normal life again. I could think I'm okay and stop taking my meds. I could go crazy again and kill someone, or a lot of people. I'm a dangerous risk. I get it."

He continues, "You lost your parents and other people you loved. I lost my wife and son. We're all in pain. Why should I be allowed to get away with murder? I've suffered from mental illness most of my life. I started taking meds around your age, never went off them, and lived a normal life. Loved my work, found my beautiful wife, we got pregnant, and had our little guy. Life wasn't perfect, but it was pretty damn good. Then, in one stroke, it all ended. I ran out of drugs in a month, couldn't find any replacements anywhere, and was desperate and started to lose it. I remember the day I shot that woman, and I remember there was a kid there, you, and I remember the rage I was experiencing. I thought all the people living in Smart Homes were part of a conspiracy that killed my wife and son."

Peter stands quietly, looking at Jacob, and says, "For the first time since the attack, and since I've been back on my medication, I feel normal again, like I can breathe. I have work, friends, and the beginning of a new life. I want to be part of the future of this community, to contribute. I cannot give that woman I shot back her life. I will regret that for the rest of my life. I can't stay here if you don't forgive me." His eyes fill, and he looks away.

Jacob has been quiet, listening, thinking, and deciding. He walks toward Peter, extends his hand, smiles, and says, "I think we can work this out. Let's put this behind us. We've all got a lot to do."

On that day, Jacob grew up.

Chapter 40

PLEASE SIR, I WANT SOME MORE

It's been a year since the attack in Victoria. Between the disaster and the latest virus, there aren't many survivors left to discuss it. Food supply is still a big problem. Alex worries it's almost too late to start or continue farming this year with farming amateurs. She and her mother continue their search and find emergency wafers and surviving farmers, but no vaccine vials. Francis' news of getting above ground is the happiest news of the year. The Kingston underground people can all start their new lives.

Francis and Miguel's pregnancy news is also pure joy. She and Miguel can't stop grinning on screen. Alex feels this baby boy will be her surrogate nephew and family. Francis tells her at least two other women are now pregnant. Alex says, "You better get your name into a reputable daycare soon with this explosion." Francis laughs. "Montessori, for sure." They're planning their move up and out in late May. Alex thinks, *lucky them. They can at least approach it with almost military tactics after all the operational planning they've been doing over the past year. They should be ready.* She's envious. They're not even close to anything like that in Victoria.

Vancouver Island might have 600 survivors, most of whom will be in Victoria and the rest spread around up island. Feeding and organizing that many people will be challenging. Finding people who want to farm or be involved in rebuilding their little society will be even more difficult. Many survivors are seniors who hadn't planned on working again before the attack. Other than the food tents, there's no evidence of people organizing their future. She wants to talk to the woman running the Fort Street food tent and the guy supplying it. That means she has to go in her civvies, no invisi-suit. Her mother insists on trimming Alex's hair and her putting on some makeup because she's so pale. Other than Taber, Alex hasn't seen much sun lately. Alex reminds her mother she's not applying for a job. Her mother reminds her she is. Alex gives in and puts on a bit of blush. Lipstick and mascara seem over the top. She now has a bit of grey hair threading through. It's been so long since she's really looked at herself. Alex is surprised to see herself aging.

She rides downtown in her invisi-suit early and parks her bike a few blocks away from the tent. There's an insurance office just up the street. She lets herself in, changes out of her suit, and checks there is a back door. She walks down the street and approaches the food tent. The woman she's been watching looks up, obviously doesn't recognize Alex, frowns briefly, then breaks out with a big welcoming grin. She says, "Hello. You're new. What do you need?" Alex is a bit taken aback by this question. She needs the world to right itself. She needs Sam back. This woman can't do that for her. Alex ignores the question and says, "I have food and shelter. I'm okay. I hope I can help you." She goes on, "My name is Alex Smith, and I live in town with my mother. We have enough emergency food, but I'd like to volunteer here if you'll have me." Alex thinks, *I'll do that for a week or two, and then I'll be better able to assess whether I can trust this woman.* The woman says, "Well, welcome, Alex Smith. You must have been hiding out for the past year. I don't remember ever seeing you before." Alex says, "My mother hasn't been well, and I've been caring for her." She doesn't go into details. The woman says, "Oh dear, is she improving?" Alex says, "Very much, thank you." The woman says, "I'm happy to hear that. You're lucky to have each other. There are so many unwell survivors with no one to care for them. We don't even know how to find them." Alex responds, "The situation is dire, for sure." The woman says, "Well, my name is Sue Blackthorn, and as you can see, I'm the chief cook and bottle washer here." Sue's diction is clear and articulate, and she comes across immediately as sharply intelligent. This woman can't be fooled. She's sure assessing Alex.

Alex looks around the tent. There are bins of every kind of vegetable, beans, and a wide variety of fruit. There are some drug store supplies and hygiene products that Sue or her volunteers have commandeered from somewhere. The stores carrying these items were stripped early. There are also handout recipes for the food being distributed to maximize the nutrition and extend its use. Alex notices her emergency wafers in one bin. Sue watches Alex looking at them. She says, "Some kind person has dropped off several supplies of these for us. We don't know when they do it. They seem to appear overnight or sometimes when we turn our backs. We call it ghost food. We're intrigued but grateful." Alex says, "How strange. I wonder who's doing that?" Sue looks hard at her. Alex feels like she can see right through her. She changes the subject and asks, "Where would I be most helpful?

Sue says, "Why don't you stick around here for a while? We'll be getting a shipment in about an hour, and we'll need to rotate the stock." Alex asks, "Who's supplying you?" Sue eyes her. She doesn't trust Alex yet. "A local guy" is all she says. Alex doesn't push. A few other people show up, and Sue greets them all with a hug. Some are volunteers, and others are here for the food. They all seem to know the routine. A solar van floats up, and a guy jumps out. Sue says, "Good morning, Del. How are you this bright morning?" He's not a smiley guy, but he greets her and gets to business unloading the van. He's in his early 30s, tall, thin, maybe East Indian, and bookish looking. He doesn't look like a farmer or like he's seen much hard labor. He doesn't look like he's much fun either. He pulls out baskets of every kind of vegetable and fruit. They unload the current baskets, so the newer supply goes on the bottom. Then they refill them. Alex is assigned to fruit today, and they've restocked in an hour. Sue gives her a roll of paper towels and some cleaner and says, "We wipe down everything several times a day. The barrel and pail rims are handled a lot, so we try to keep these as clean as possible." The last thing we need is to have an outbreak of some illness. All the diseases are still around. Flu, the common cold, HIV, hepatitis, STDs, and the variations of all the viruses that hit us in the past decades. They're all still with us. We have to be so careful. There are no vaccinations available. Smallpox could still take us all out. Alex goes to work, wiping down everything she can see that might need it, thinking, *I have to talk to Francis about this. Are her lab techs prepared?*

Meanwhile, people are lining up for food, and Sue's the official greeter. She shows them what she has and monitors what people take. She'll jokingly admonish someone who takes too much. Most don't try. The other volunteers all seem to know these people and help them load their bags. Despite the circumstances, there is lots of laughter and smiles. This goes on all day. Sue closes around six o'clock, pulls down the tent flap, and starts a final clean-up and reorganization of the product for the next day. She's closely supervised everything during the day, pulling out produce past its prime while circulating among the people, touching them, doling out hugs and silly jokes. She knows what she's doing, keeping these people sane. At the end of their shift, volunteers select their own produce. Sue says, "Dev won't be back for a few days, so we need to make do with what we have." She says to Alex, "Thank you. You worked hard today, and you were kind to my friends. Come back anytime." Alex says, "How about the day after tomorrow?" She doesn't want to crowd her and come every day. Sue smiles and says, "See you then." Alex already knows she'll be able to trust her. She now has to earn Sue's trust.

Chapter 41

NO GOODBYES

Alex doesn't like to leave her mother alone all day. Her mother has kept herself busy going through her clothes closets and deciding what she needs and doesn't need. Alex reminds her there is no one to donate to anymore or anywhere to dispose of these things. Her mother says, "Well, I'll box things up and get them out of the way. I won't be needing much of this anymore." She's right. There's no reason to dress up. Still, her comment gives Alex pause. She shares her volunteer day with her mother. Her mother says she would like to help too. Alex reminds her of their bigger plan to get this group organized. She's still sussing out whether Sue is the person to help with this. Alex suggests she should be the primary contact for now. Her mother says, "You're right. I wouldn't want to accidentally say the wrong thing. Better I stay out of it. I'm a bit tired anyway."

Her mother is sleeping a lot these days, and it worries Alex. She sees her energy levels fading, and she has a slight yellowish tinge to her skin. Alex scans her while she's sleeping and sends it to the medics back east. They get back to her with devastating news. "Her kidneys have never fully recuperated from the abuse and the severe bruising, and she's now struggling. You may lose her soon." Another gut punch. Alex sits down and tries to think about what she should do with this information, let alone do without her mother. She feels like she can't take any more loss. Alex had decided not to tell her, but her mother knows her own body, and when she wakes, she says to Alex, "Honey, I don't want to scare you, but I'm really not feeling well. I saw some blood when I peed today. I'm tired all the time and feel puffy. Look at my ankles." She takes off her socks, and her ankles are quite swollen.

There's nothing Alex can do about kidney failure. She can't do dialysis and she sure can't give her a kidney transplant. She tells her mother what the scan said. Her mother is quiet and says, "Well, honey, you risked your life and came all this way to find me, and you saved my life. I plan to enjoy what's left with you. If this is going to kill me, there's nothing either of us can do about it. We're big girls." Alex thinks, *you're one brave woman*. Her mother hugs her and changes the subject. "I'd love to ride along Dallas Road and up to Anderson Hill tomorrow if it's a dry day. Let's do that?" Alex's heart bursts with love for her mom. She's been through so much and still looks forward to tomorrow. Alex can't say she feels like that. The future scares the hell out of her, particularly without her mother. Alone again. Her mother's approach is to put one foot in front of the other and not look back.

Alex wakes early the following day, reaches over, and pats her mother's back. Her body is stiff, unmoving, and cold. She stole out in the night. She's gone. Too soon, too fast. Alex says to her, *I thought we had more time, months even*. She wraps herself around her mother's small, frail, dead body and lies there for hours. *Pull yourself together, Alex,* she thinks. *Don't fall apart.*

She has the medics scan her one last time to see if they can give her a post-mortem reading on the cause of her death. They tell her it appears her heart just stopped. Alex thinks, *so has mine*. They say, "Kidney failure would have been an awful death. This is better." Alex says, "Yeah, better." Francis is on the screen with tears in her eyes. She says, "Anything I say right now won't help. You were both so lucky to have had each other. She was a life gift. You'll have her close in your memory forever. Now you need to let yourself mourn." Alex says, "You know, finding her was the culmination and victory of this trip. I had almost a year with her. I've lost her again, but she would have wanted me to get back to living and go on and not sit around crying. I will cry. Lots. But I have work to do here."

Alex allows herself all the sadness a person can stand. She goes through all the stages of grief except denial. She can't deny her mother is gone. She thinks, *after seeing so much death, I accepted its inevitability, but this is my mom*. She rages in anger at the life-ending damage Robert did to her mother. She thinks, *he stole her from me with his brutality*.

She needs to confront him and goes to his apartment. His bike is there. That makes her nervous, but she needs to do this. She climbs the stairs, slowly opens his door, and takes a wrist reading. Nothing. He's not here. His apartment looks a lot different from the last time she was here. It's disheveled, with dust on surfaces, and his furniture is out of place. He's eaten his way through her mother's food in the freezer. There's not a shred of food left. His bed is tangled and unmade. It doesn't take her long to get to the bathroom. She finds his desiccated carcass in a bloody, tumbled lump in the corner of his shower.

There's a big blood spray on the shower wall and scraps of something she doesn't want to look too closely at. Brains? His revolver has fallen from his hand. He's blown the top of his head off. He couldn't take it anymore. Alex has seen so much death in the past year; this doesn't even shock her. He was probably starving. She was surprised he hadn't found Sue's food tent. It's not that far away. She wonders why he didn't just take the 'kill pill.' Guns still seem to be the weapon of choice for suicide for men. Alex is relieved she didn't have to kill him. She knows she would have.

She rechecks the bankers' boxes in his closet. The jewelry and money are still there. He couldn't trade those for food. She doesn't want her mother's jewelry. It has no value to her, and he's handled the pieces. She checks his computer and finds the source of his income. There are dozens of compromising nude pictures of women, mostly in their 60s and up, obviously posing for him. Having a bit of fun, they probably thought. Of course, her mother is there. He was successfully blackmailing these women, given his jewelry and cash stash. She guesses last year's April debacle happened before he tried to blackmail her mother. The cash would have been untraceable. There was another file on his computer. Pictures of a woman with a small boy. It looks like him. They're smiling and happy. Something awful happened to this guy that turned him. She'll never know what, but it appears he was once an ordinary happy little loved, and loving boy. Alex looks back at the bathroom where he lies and asks. *What happened to you, Robert?* She deletes everything on the device and takes it with her. Alex looks at the bed her mother was tied to, then closes the apartment door. She rides down to the Dallas Road pier and tosses the device into the sea. Those women's secrets are buried forever. Alex doesn't even feel anger anymore, just sadness for everyone. Especially herself. She's feeling very sorry for herself. She rides slowly back home.

Alex has to figure out what to do with her mother's body. She leaves her in her bed for now and starts sleeping in her own bed again. Her mother's body has quickly dried into a carcass. It's not her mom, just an old container of once was. Her dad's ashes are with his parents in a graveyard across from Royal Roads. Although she briefly considers it, she can't just take her mother's body there and leave her to blow away with the wind, nor is she up to grave digging. With her personal fear of the ocean, dropping her into the sea doesn't sit right either. In the end, Alex takes her mother's body down to the beach along Dallas Road, sets a beach fire, and turns her body into ashes. No one disturbs a single beach fire in the middle of the night, especially these days. She sits on a log on the stony cold beach and warms her hands over the fire that was her mother.

When the fire dies down, she gathers her mother's ashes and rides to Anderson Hill. She has Sam's and Princie's small sand container with her as well. She scatters them all on the hillside there in the moonlight. When the sun comes up, it will warm them, and the wind will spread them out for wildflowers to use for nourishment. She sits on the bench overlooking the Strait in the cool of the dark night. She and Sam used to sit here all the time. They got engaged here. Their life ahead of them. She can come back and visit anytime. Their memories live on and will drive her.

Alex goes home and digs out an old pair of runners, sprays them with some invisi-paint, and they dry quickly. It's almost four in the morning, and she goes for a long run. It's the first time she's gone running since the day before the attack. She's out of shape, but her body remembers and rises to it. She runs every night after that. It makes her feel alive.

Chapter 42

NEW GROWTH

Sue watches Alex walk down the street toward her tent and says to her, "I thought we'd lost you." Alex says, "I'm sorry. My mother died two weeks ago, and I needed time to process that." Sue says, "Oh honey, I'm so sorry. What happened?" Alex says, "Kidneys, then her heart stopped." Alex doesn't want to share the details right now. She says, "She wanted to come and help here but never got the chance. She was a fighter; you would have liked her." Sue says, "I wish I'd met her. I like her daughter." She asks, "Are you sure you're okay to be here?" Alex says, "Sue, we've all seen so much death. I'm almost inured to it. There's so much work to do. We can't waste a second worrying about the past."

Alex dives in. "I have some ideas and ways I can help you, help all of us, beyond what you're doing here. We need to talk privately, and I need your complete discretion." Sue eyes her and says, "Interesting. I'm intrigued. People are coming in, so let's sit down and talk at day's end. Yes, I can keep a secret."

They work throughout the day. Volunteers and people looking for food come and go. It's a busy hub. Most Victoria survivors have found Sue. Her food supplies are dropping, and she expects a shipment from Dev tomorrow. Alex considers what she should share with Sue. Certainly not the invisi-suit and bike. She thinks she can safely share the wrist implant that gets her in anywhere and the life reader. That's what will be valuable to Sue.

Sue's volunteers come from all walks but are primarily people who had a bit of money and could afford the vaccine. They're survivors twice, first cancer and now this. There's an unspoken agreement. Nobody talks about their various cancers. They all had it and were all saved from it with the vaccine. 'Nuf' said. Alex evaluates these people for potential farming volunteers. Many are seniors who wouldn't want to take up a challenge like that. There are only about 15 people here today. It's a small slice of the survivor population but still a good cross-section of who remains.

There are a few people in their 20s and 30s, several in their late 60s and 70s, and one teenage black kid with a pink hair stripe. Alex gets a kick out of him, still splashing some style. There's one person she's particularly taken to. Georgia is a transexual woman, a big woman in a big man's body. They chat throughout the day and share their lives. What they did when they did it. That horrible April morning of the attack, Georgia was a high school math and science teacher, prepping for the first-period trig class and thinking about some after-class tutoring for a couple of struggling kids. She told Alex how much she loved her job and seeing the satisfaction and new confidence in a teenager's eyes after mastering a difficult concept.

She talked about her youth. She'd been a little girl stuck in a boy's, then a man's body for a lifetime, and she wanted out. Watching her body grow and turn on her as a teenager had been devastating. She'd thought about it all her life but waited until her early 40s to make the change. She worried the most about losing her job. She loved teaching. Happily, she was embraced, encouraged, and welcomed into her new world of femininity by the school administration and her very savvy students. Nothing fazed them. They thought it was cool and brave. They really liked him or her, no matter what sex she wanted to be. Not all their parents were okay with it. Their kids loved her, though, and excelled in her classes, so they kept their thoughts to themselves. The rest of the world was definitely not on board. Too many people still choose to remain ignorant about the reality and science of being born with your sexual identification not lining up with your exterior body. She has a short pixie cut she's been hacking away at for the last year. She doesn't wear makeup, but nobody does. Nobody wears jewelry much anymore, either. She wears women's clothing, casual and comfortable pants, and tops. Stylish but conservative. She hadn't had breasts installed, nor did she feign them with a stuffed bra. She still has estrogen meds but says they don't suppress her testosterone much. Her voice is still deep, and she still has to shave. She says, "I'm a big guy. Can't hide that. I just want to be recognized as the female I've always been." She considers herself lucky to be alive and contributing. Alex likes her spirit.

They get to the end of the day, and Sue and Alex finally have private time together. Sue has done her final clean-up and sits down with a sigh. Alex says, "Are you ready?" Sue lifts her eyebrows and says, "Sounds like we're about to take off. What have you got?" Alex says, "I'll start at the beginning, or the end, depending on your viewpoint." She shares the story of her previous research work and her journey from home to Kingston, across the country, and back to Victoria. Alex talks about camouflage rather than invisibility as it relates to Kingston. She tells her about Diya and touches on her time with the kids and Krista and Sal and their farm and tells her a bit more about her mother's cause of death. She tells her about the highway murders. She tells her about her wrist implant and how it allows her access to any house, building, or computer. She tells her she is the one supplying her with the emergency wafers and that she has access to many more.

Sue laughs out loud at that bit of news. She says, "You know, on your first day, your eyes went right to that basket. I had a feeling you had something to do with those wafers." Alex tells her about her work with Francis on their agricultural future and her aspirations to get volunteers to work with the surviving farmers. Hopefully, they can take over some farms to create a more significant food source. She talks about possibly working with Dev to do this if he's willing. Alex talks about Francis' team working on communication solutions and medical work. Sue has remained mostly silent through all of this, nodding in agreement with the island's needs. Alex wonders if she believes her. She's been blabbing on for a long time. When Alex finishes, Sue looks down at her knees, looks back up, takes a deep breath, and then says, "Wow. I sensed something different about you but didn't envision this." Alex says, "I'm just a regular woman like you, trying to make the best of a horrible situation. I was lucky enough to get some gadgets from Francis' team to ease the way across the country. We need food, drugs, and some form of communication, but most of all, farms, and a food source beyond what Dev is doing. We have to work together to get the world back operating again as much as possible. Can you help me?"

Sue says, "I'll do whatever I can. I have met most of Victoria's survivors over the past 8-9 months. I have a pretty good idea of who might be a potential farm volunteer. We'll need to talk to Dev. He works out of UVIC and manages a vertical farm alone. That's how he's stocking me with fresh veg and fruit. We discovered each other when he started dropping off food on the street. People were taking it all. It needed to be managed. I intercepted him one day, and we came up with a plan. He helped me set up the tent and get some baskets, and we've embellished it with recipes and some signage. We got to know each other, and we've been working together ever since."

Sue says, "Dev was born here. His grandparents were from Delhi, and his parents have been in Canada since they were very young. He visited India once as a student and was appalled by the noise, smells, crowds, and poverty. He hates that it's part of his culture, that India has become the pariah of nations and he hates being Indian. He's a reverse bigot." Alex asks, "He shared all that with you?

Pretty darned personal." Sue says, "It was easy to see, the way he talked, always assuming there was a racial slight in anything said. He was becoming a pain in the ass, and I told him that." He stopped talking like that, to me, at least." Sue says, "He needs to get over it and get comfortable in his skin. He needs to be proud of himself and his culture, even if the states would have liked to blow India off the map. She tells Alex Dev is very introverted and shy, has a Ph.D. in botany, and probably envisioned his future in a research lab, making unusual things grow. He wouldn't have imagined himself feeding downtown Victoria with his vertical farm for the rest of his life.

Sue goes on, "He might not be the best person to reach out to surviving farmers, let alone teach people how to farm. He's not the friendliest guy on the planet. He also might not appreciate a non-farmer and an ex-product researcher like yourself telling him how to do his job. Hell, you've probably only got a B.A. He's a bit of an academic snob." Alex thinks, *great. He's an unhappy guy she needs to help them launch the farm program, and he'll probably disregard her altogether.* Sue says, "Approaching one or two surviving farmers might be a better way to do that. Let's first talk to Dev and strategize an approach he might be more accepting of. Maybe ask for his advice rather than his leadership. He'll be here tomorrow. I'll arrange a meeting with him. I suggest you tell him everything you told me before asking for his help."

Sue asks Alex to show her how her wrist implant works. Alex thinks she's checking out her story and still doesn't believe her. There's a Smart Home just across the street. They walk over, and Alex reads it. She shows Sue the implant reading blue. No one's alive in there. She then holds her wrist against the entry code system. The door slides open. Alex invites Sue in to check it out. Sue says, "I don't need to go in. They were my neighbors and friends. I've seen enough piles of sand, thank you." She looks at Alex and her wrist and says, "Amazing, this changes the game." They talk long into the night and start to make plans. They become fast friends and collaborators. Sue says, "You should get home and get some sleep. I bed down here most nights. Yes, I have a gun, but if someone wants to steal a tomato in the night, I don't plan to shoot them. I'm just making sure someone doesn't walk away with everything. I wash up after the morning volunteers arrive." She points across the street. "That's my house over there." Alex takes in Sue's substantial and lovely rambling house. It sits well back from the road with a large lawn up front that, of course, hasn't been mowed.

Alex can see where she had extensive landscaping around the house once. It's all in need of a clipping now. Sue had money. Alex says incredulously, "That's yours?" Sue says, "Yes, I was in tech before all this happened. It paid well. My husband's over there, still a pile in our bed. He was an eye surgeon. He gave vision to lots of people in this town. I don't sleep there much. Besides, I have a new job now." Alex asks, "Kids?" Sue says, "Two boys, married with kids, one each." She puts her head down and says, "All gone." Alex touches her shoulder and says, "We've all experienced great loss." There's nothing more she can say. Sue smiles at Alex, shakes her head, and says, "We march on." Alex says, "Yes, we do."

Alex says, "I'd like to get your food operation moved into somewhere more substantial that you can also lock down. Did you actually sleep outside all winter?" Sue laughs. "I'm not an idiot, of course not. I said I don't sleep there much, but I do when the weather is bad, too often in Victoria." Alex thinks, *definitely not an idiot.* She's confident she's chosen the right person to help lead them into the future.

The next day, Dev arrives, and before he unloads, Sue takes him aside and sets up a meeting later at her house. She points at Alex but doesn't introduce them. He eyes Alex warily across the space. He's string thin with thick dark hair badly in need of a trim, but still looking lustrous. Alex thinks, *I've always been envious of thick black hair. If he had a woman in his life, she would have insisted he trim his eyebrows. They are a singular snake across his forehead.* His nose is prominent. He has a light beard. Must have one of those shavers that constantly keep men's beards at the three-day growth length. His mouth is his best feature. He has full lips and gleaming white even teeth when he smiles, which isn't often.

Once they've been introduced and sit down together, Alex repeats a shortened version of the story she shared with Sue the previous night. She doesn't mention the water and soil testing she's been doing for Kingston because he might want to see the setup, and of course, that's on her invisi-bike. She needs this guy's agricultural intelligence, but he sure isn't a likable character. He does not smile, and his eyes drill through her in judgment. Alex knows he has the massive responsibility of stocking Sue's food camp, perhaps forever. Not the future he had envisioned. That wouldn't make anyone happy.

When Alex finishes sharing her story, she tells him she and her mother had already scanned the island for surviving farmers and know where they are. There are three of them, and they'll all need help soon. He knows all three and has provided research and educational support to all the farmers in B.C. This is a big break. Only one of these survivors has a farm less than 50 miles from downtown Victoria. Alex suggests it would be good to approach these three, determine their needs, and see where they can help. She also suggests they need to get other closer farms reactivated and reseeded. She presumes they'll need more bean crops for protein. She says to him, "You have the brains and the research. We need your help." She also asks, "We're vulnerable with only you operating your vertical farm. Would you be willing to train an assistant?" She waits for him to shut that down. He says nothing. He turns his back on the two of them and looks out the window. Sue and Alex exchange looks and shrug at each other. Alex pushes on and says, "We should probably try to get outlying survivors to move into town. It would be easier to service them." Dev still says nothing and looks at her. Sue says to him, "What do you think, Dev?"

A slow smile builds on his face. It changes his face entirely. He's almost good-looking. He says, "I've been thinking we needed to get organized and was hoping someone else would do it. I'm a scientist, not an organizer. Alex, it sounds like you are, and I'll do everything I can to help. You're right, it's up to us, but it won't be as easy as you imagine." Alex says, "I saw Krista and Sal's farm in operation. I know how complicated it is. Why don't we think in baby steps? First, we need volunteers."

They are over the first hurdle with Dev. He's on board and will be a tremendous asset. Sue lists about 30 people she thinks might be suitable candidates for farming. She only knows them as her volunteers or as drop-ins at the food tent. She doesn't know where they live. They have to wait for them to show up.

Meanwhile, Alex and Dev ride up to the three farms with the surviving farmers. Alex has snagged an excellent bike that's not invisible for these trips. Dev brings the agricultural authority she doesn't have, so they think these ideas are all coming from him. That's okay. They are greeted by various stages of relief from all three. None of them really knew what happened but lost their family and friends and pets and, a few of them, livestock. They've been torn between continuing their work and wondering if anybody's left to eat their food. Alex and Dev talk to them about needing their help. Farming is a tight community. They all know each other and have connected since the disaster. They're open to any ideas. Everybody was waiting for someone to develop a plan.

Over the month, Sue meets with all her prospects as they drop in. She put up a sign "Wanted. People to assist with farming. Must be capable of manual work and possibly willing to move out of the city." There's little manual work left in farming. It's all done by bots, but they still need fit people. She gets a sign-up from almost all her candidates. They're eager to be doing something. That's an excellent start. Georgia is one of them. She laughs and asks if she can wear gingham.

The food tent and farm organizing work keep Alex occupied. She's still in mourning for her mom, her husband, her friends, the kids in Taber, and even her dog. Everyone's been robbed of hope and getting through each day is like climbing a mountain.

Dev and Alex bring the three farmers down to the city to figure out how best to go about the next steps and visit the closer farms. They're all very familiar with every farm on the island, what they grew, their challenges, and their probable needs. They talk about the possibility of them moving in further and taking over another farm or farms. None of them want to abandon their farms but see the wisdom of this thinking. They also like the idea of serving a community of living people. There are few survivors left up island. They leave them with this and settle them in a nearby Smart Home so they can continue talking.

Training the volunteers is their next challenge. Each farmer has different needs. Alex and Dev ask, "What if you suspend everything, consider moving in further to another farm and take the summer to train the new people? They would see most of the planting and harvest cycle if we got started now." Getting people to turn a lifetime work habit around can be challenging. They finally agree, and each takes over two farms closer to town. They plan their crops to cover more nutrition needs, particularly beans for protein. Trainees are assigned, and Alex and Dev check in on them regularly. As expected, some personalities don't work out, and there's drop off. A few don't like the work. They get through the summer with Dev's guidance and surprising patience. Turns out he's an excellent teacher and well-liked by the farming apprentices and the farmers. They have some good yield from the farms, and Dev and Georgia start deliveries to the other food sites on the island. They have to overcome the same drawback Krista and Sal had, finding a grain mill. There isn't a grain mill on the island, so all grain has to be milled on individual machines. It's a minor problem. There aren't that many people to feed.

Dev brings Alex into his vertical farm. He's growing everything here; his fruit crop is varied and impressive. He needs an assistant, though. They review the farming apprentices and discuss who he feels he could train and work with. Alex suspects he's a hard taskmaster, so the right temperament is critical.

He surprises both Sue and Alex when he chooses Georgia. Dev likes her for her scientific mind and her discipline. Georgia's thrilled. She brings out the best in

Dev, almost in a motherly way, and he opens up with her like the rare blooms he researched. He's not in a lab, but he's happy. Georgia is a quick study and brings her own ideas to work. She makes Dev proud of himself and turns him into a happy Indian. She also makes him laugh. Every day she comes up with "Reasons to love being an Indian." He responds with, "Reasons to love being a girl." The dark humor between them sustains them. They're so good for each other. She trims his eyebrows and gorgeous dark hair, and they laugh a lot.

Chapter 43

PEOPLE ARE STRANGE

"People are strange, when you're a stranger, faces look ugly when you're alone. Women seem wicked when you're unwanted, streets are uneven when you're down. The Doors, 1967

After a bumpy start, Dev and Alex become good friends, working long days and nights together and supporting nervous farmers and trainees. Georgia and Dev are so kind and patient with the trainees. It's coming together.

About a month in, Alex senses a slight problem. Dating wasn't a big thing in Dev's old life. He was too busy in his lab and thought he'd get around to finding a wife later. After the attack, he thought his chances were gone, until he met Alex.

Dev hasn't talked to many women for the last year, he never talks to the people who come to the food tent. Sue and Georgia are both are too old to be girlfriend prospects. He has his eye on Alex. After visiting a farm, Dev takes Alex's hand as they walk, smiles at her and says, "Things are turning out." Alex thinks quickly, *how do I get out of this one without offending him?* She disengages her hand gently from his and faces him, putting her hands on his forearms. She says, "Dev, I'm still in love with my husband. I always will be. I know he's dead, but that's the way it is." She watches his face fall. Dev is embarrassed and thinks, *I went too far, shouldn't have done that.* He says to her, "I'm sorry, I didn't mean to assume." She keeps it light, laughs, and says, "Are you kidding, I'm flattered. She says, "Dev, I know I'm irresistible, but I'm not the one." She says, "An adorable brunette volunteers at the food tent regularly. Have you seen her?" He says, "Sofia? Yes, I've seen her. She's helped me unload a few times, but she never speaks or makes eye contact."

Alex says incredulously, "And you do? Try harder. Approach her. Say hi, anything. She's probably shy. You're a single, smart, cute guy. Use it." Dev soaks up Alex's compliment and, just like that, she's given him someone else to consider.

She dodged that bullet without offending him. Georgia encourages this new flirtation between Dev and Sophia. In the back of Georgia's mind, she knows someone has to have kids. Maybe these two. She could be the grandmother. One step at a time. Currently, Dev and Sophia barely look at each other. They have a way to go.

Alex thinks, *I'm not a farmer, just a catalyst*. The gears turn, crops are harvested and distributed, and several newly minted farmers are happy at work. It's time for her to step away from that. Alex and Sue have moved the food distribution operation inside a nearby community hall. Sue can lock it up at night and sleep in her own bed. Alex is now gathering drugs and medical supplies from locked-up houses and has set up a supply warehouse. Much of it is stale dated now, but they throw nothing out. She knows most meds last much longer than their printed best-before date. They also gather all vaccine vials they find in freezers in pharmacies and hospitals. These are for flu and innumerable other afflictions. Again, they're beyond their best-before date, but it's all they've got right now. At the very least, Francis' lab people can try to replicate them. Like Taber, Vancouver Island has suffered from the latest round of virus infections, and many people have succumbed. They try to distribute all they can find of the latest anti-viral drugs.

Alex and Sue hold weekly meetings at the convention center. There's more space to share information with a larger group. They post invitations in central points all over the city, hoping they'll catch people's attention. Alex and Sue are always the speakers at these meetings. Alex wonders if they have any hidden leaders out there in the crowd. They've yet to show their hands.

Her invisible gear remains invisible, and Alex doesn't tell anyone she has it. It's her ace in the hole. She still uses the insurance office up the street to change before she comes into work. She always carries her suit with her just in case she needs it. To look a bit more normal, she's had to find new casual clothes other than her black cat woman outfit. When she leaves work, she goes back up the street to the insurance office, changes, and privately rides home in her invisi-suit. Alex has been bringing produce home from the outlet and cooking up some decent dinners for herself. It's like a science project, and she now knows why Sam enjoyed doing the cooking. She thinks, *he'd be mighty proud of me*.

One volunteer, Freddie, seems to take more interest in Alex than she'd like. Freddie is late 40s, about 5' 8", stocky but not fat, just a thick build. He shaves his head, but you can tell he's bald up top but not on the sides. He has meaty features, a broad nose, full lips, and a wide face. A generalization, but he looks a bit like the skinhead thugs who made all the trouble at the U.K. football games. He's probably not a good drunk. It seems more curiosity than male/female interest, but he's relentless in his questions. "So, you show up, and suddenly you're the queen? What's that all about?" Alex says, "Just a volunteer, Fred, nothing else." Or "So, you and Sue are pretty close. Do I sense a romance?" Alex rolls her eyes and says, "We're not lesbians, Fred. Don't get excited. We're just widows and friends." Or "Where do you live?" Alex dismisses him and says, "None of your business."

After a while, she notices he's following her when she leaves. He keeps his distance, but he's definitely following her. When she ducks into the insurance office to get changed, she often finds him standing outside the building, staring in. She's even seen him checking the whole exterior. She wonders, *is he thinking of breaking in?* One time, she watched him knock hard on the door. She was now across the street, invisible in her suit and watching. She hears him say, "Come on, Alex, I know you're in there." Alex can see it agitates him when she doesn't answer the door. She thinks, *don't know what this guy's beef is, but he could be dangerous.*

Alex finds out several months later. They've locked up for the day, and Alex rides up the street. She now uses her alternate visible bike for this part of the trip. Freddie rides up beside her. "Feel like going for a ride?" He asks. "Maybe see if we can find a beer somewhere?" Alex says, "No thanks, Fred, I'm tired." She tries to ride off, and he blocks her. He says, "You think you're pretty hot, don't you?" This makes Alex laugh. Her skinny, pale, going gray self is the last thing from 'hot.' She says, "Freddie, knock it off. Leave me alone." He then says, "I know where you live." Alex receives this as a threat. He thinks she lives in the insurance office up the street." She says, "Yeah, I know you've been following me. Stop doing that." He says, "You're not very safe there." Alex thinks, *Okay, another threat.* She says firmly, "Fred, get out of my way. I want to get going." She watches his neck redden and his jaw tighten. He wants what he wants. He's a bully. He then gets nasty. "You're a snotty little bitch, aren't you?" He dismounts and starts toward her. He has one of those rolling walks that always seem to go along with clenched fists. He reminds her of a tank, ready to thunder over everything in his way. She asks herself, *what the hell is his thing with me, other than I don't want to have anything to do with him?* She doesn't know his intentions, but she's not interested in getting beat up by this guy. She's had enough of him." She says to herself, *okay, Freddie, good night,* and zaps him. He won't remember any of this. He'll wake up in the street around 1:00 in the morning and wonder how he got there. She hopes it rains. She returns to the insurance office, knowing she has to change to another interim house. She changes into her invisi-suit and rides her invisi bike home, thinking, *I have to talk to Sue about this.*

The next time Freddie's in for food, Sue asks him, "Can we have a word?" She's in earshot of Alex, and Alex hears her say, "If I ever hear that you've harassed, followed, or threatened anyone I know, you'll be cut off. No food. Do you understand?" Freddie frowns at her and asks, "What are you talking about?" Sue says, "Call me a mind reader," and walks away from him. Alex doesn't look at him, but she knows he's watching her. He doesn't remember their interaction last week, but he might remember approaching her as she left that night. He knows his intentions have somehow been exposed. He wonders, "How did I end up on the pavement that night? Must have fallen and knocked myself out." That's all he can figure. He doesn't challenge Sue, grabs his food bag, and storms off.

He continues to come to the food tent but doesn't look Alex in the eye. She greets him coolly but doesn't give him any time. She acts as if it never happened. All he knows is he doesn't trust Alex. Something weird is going on with her. He doesn't like her at all.

He can't risk being cut off from the food supply, but he goes back to his apartment, simmers, and plans Alex's demise. He has a long history of hating women, particularly those with some authority. He waits a while and then tries to follow her home again. Meanwhile, he's been sidling up to young Sophia and trying to chat her up. Sophia doesn't like his attention but doesn't know how to tell him to move off. Alex catches Sue's eye and nods toward him. Sue wanders over his way and says, "Remember our chat, Freddie?" He lifts his hands and says with a greasy grin, "I wasn't doing anything," in mock shock. She says, "And you won't be. Last warning." Now he's really pissed. He thinks, *who appointed this ugly old cow the president here?* He leaves, spitting angry. Alex says to Sue, "He's dangerous and I think capable of doing damn near anything. We'll need to keep a sharp eye. Make sure there are always two of you when you lock up and get one of the male volunteers to escort you to your house if I'm not around." Sue says, "That punk doesn't scare me. Don't forget, I'm armed and would have no problem protecting myself." Alex says, "I've had to kill a few people on this journey. You don't want to carry that with you, no matter how despicable the person is." Sue says, "Don't worry about me. Watch your own ass. He's not done with you."

They've posted a search for pharmacists, lab techs, I.T. experts, doctors, dentists, nurses, and radio and T.V. technicians around town and bring it up at every meeting. Alex is particularly interested in finding someone who can guide her through operating a radio station or T.V. station. These would have just shut down and should still be engaged with their satellites. She thinks, *if we can find the right buttons to push, maybe we can broadcast again. There's always a button.* A few nurses responded to their posting: one dentist, who'll be very busy, and two retired doctors. All want to help where they can, but none of them are young. They don't have the luxury of medicine 101 that Francis and her team have back east. They set up a small medical practice, but they're all in their 70s and tire easily. Patients line up, and the days are long. They need help. Alex and Sue talk to the medical volunteers about a training program for basic dentistry and medical emergencies. None of them show any interest in that. They retired before all this happened, and they sure don't want to be the only doctor, dentist, or trainer on the Island. Alex and Sue try to express how much they're needed, no matter how difficult it is for them to get back to work. This hasn't been a 'step-up' group other than the farm volunteers. Their new society isn't going very well.

No one's talking about babies; they have more urgent issues now. Alex doesn't bring it up.

About a month later, Alex arrives early and finds their food site tossed, with food all over the floor and baskets overturned. Sue picks up the pieces, throws out no longer usable food, and slogs her way through the chaos. Alex asks, "Any idea?" Sue says, "Yeah, guess who?" Alex says, "He's a bastard. What do you want to do?" Sue says, "Well, he's cut off and gets no more food. He'll deny doing this and will cause a problem when this happens. I'm pretty tough and will deal with him. We need to be in a Smart Building with no exterior access when it's locked down. I have my eye on a couple of sites near here. We'll go see them as soon as the volunteers come in. We'll move tonight. I have a floater van in my garage. We should be able to do it in a couple of moves. Freddie could show up armed when he's really hungry. I'm prepared to shoot him if he does." Alex thinks, *wow, this broad doesn't mess around.* Alex tells Sue, "You know I also have a pretty good gun?" Sue says, "Yeah, but I know you don't want to use it again. If it comes to it, I'll take care of him."

After they close up the damaged site, they work hard and get everything moved, leave directional signage for everyone, and are now in a very secure building. They don't share the threat with the volunteers. Just say a few things were knocked over while they moved. They don't want to scare them. It's not long before Freddie shows his hand. After work, Alex rides back to her new interim change house, and it's late. She checks behind her and sees a bike in her mirrors. She pulls off into a random house, takes a quick reading, all dead, and rides into the garage, with the door just closing behind her as he cruises by looking in. He knows where she is. That's okay. She quickly slips on her invisi-suit, leaves by the back door, and stands across the street. Freddie is off his bike and circling the house, looking for an entrance. She hears him muttering, "No one knows you're in here but me, and you're never coming out, you little bitch." Alex thinks, *so, he wants to kill me. This disaster sure has spawned a bunch of psychopaths, or am I just having bad luck?*

The house wasn't a Smart Home, and he kicks in the door easily. With the door ajar, she can hear him rage, "Where are you, you bitch?" She watches this drama from the curb. Freddie finds her bike, lifts it up, and tosses it into the street. The front wheel lists to the side. Alex thinks, *well, I'll be walking to my interim house.* She's pretty sure he's tearing the house apart, thinking she's hiding somewhere in a cupboard or under a bed. He finally charges out, yells, "Fuck!" and rides away. So, Sue was right. She has to watch her ass. Well, everything actually, she has to watch everything.

Alex's interim change house is a couple of miles away. She walks there, grabs her invisible bike, and rides home. Life's getting interesting.

Freddie goes back to his apartment and steams. He has very little food left. He's been intercepting people who have picked up food a few blocks from the distribution site. Sue and Alex have yet to catch him at it. Everybody's advised to travel in twos.

After this started happening, Alex was out in her invisi-suit, foraging through houses looking for drugs they can use. Every house has something. Some have extensive supplies of things they can use. It's a nice day, and she takes a break down near the harbor. There was an old hotel here once. She thinks it was called the Empress. It's been gone for decades, way before her time. The rising sea affected its underpinnings, and it had to come down. There's just a lawn where it once stood. One of their volunteers, Paul, she thinks his name is, strolls up the street, enjoying the sunshine and the harbor. He has the food bag he always brings, and it looks like he just restocked. Alex can't believe her eyes, but Freddie rides up on his bike beside him and calls out to him. Paul turns around and calmly says, "Oh hi Freddie. Beautiful day, huh?" Freddie continues to ride slowly alongside Paul, who's on the sidewalk. Alex sees Freddie look around to see if anyone's around. There isn't anyone on the street other than her, and they can't see her. She hears Freddie order Paul to give him his bag of food. He's holding his arm as if he might have a gun. Alex can't see for sure. Paul looks at Freddie and says, "What are you doing?" Freddie says, "Taking the food." Paul says slowly, "I don't think so." Alex watches in surprise as Paul quickly punches Freddie in the gut and efficiently takes him down to the ground with his arm twisted behind his back. Freddie cries out in pain. Paul takes Freddie's gun and tosses it into the harbor. He warns Freddie it will hurt a lot more if he hassles anyone else. He picks up his bag of food, turns around and calmly walks away, like he does this every day. Alex thinks, *Jesus! He might as well have been whistling to himself. It's just another day in paradise. The world has gone mad.* Freddie lays there for a while, waiting until Paul is out of sight, and then gets up and speeds away.

Alex rides back quickly to tell Sue what just happened. Sue laughs out loud. She tells Alex that Paul was a security guard for the Lieutenant Governor. He would have been ready for a Freddie. Paul comes in about a week later and says nothing. He's his usual friendly, warm, calm self. He says to Alex, "All okay?" She grins at him and says, "all okay, Paul, thanks for asking." Sue drifts by and gives him a quick arm squeeze. He knows that somehow, they know. None of them ever speak of it again.

Freddie goes strangely quiet.

Chapter 44

TALK TO ME

Sue and Alex have talked to the volunteer doctors, nurses, and dentists about the survivors' training classes. Everyone realizes the need, but none feel up to it. They're tired enough already. Alex reminds them that if even one of them topples over with a heart attack, the rest of the survivors are in jeopardy. Some basic skills have to be passed on. After much convincing, they finally agree to a limited program in their fields. Alex passes on Francis' medical training curriculum. They're impressed. She reminds them that giving the survivors these skills might save a life or make the afflicted person more comfortable. Alex reiterates, "We can't afford to lose anyone. There aren't that many of us." The medical volunteers adjust their work schedules, and Alex and Sue explain it all at the next town meeting. When they ask for a 'hands up' of who might be interested in attending, all hands go up. Alex thinks, *finally, we're getting some hard-won participation from this group.*

A couple of months into the town meetings, a kid waits for Alex at the end of the session. He's about 18, black, about six feet, and slim. He's carefully selected his clothes to look casually sloppy. It's a curated 'look.' He has a short 'fro' and has added a pink streak along one side. He must have a barber's clipper at home. He's a nice-looking kid, and she likes his pink stripe. Alex thinks with humor, *must look edgy in the middle of a disaster.* He has an easy smile and is shaving whatever beard he might have. He has the loose, effortless movements of an athlete or a dancer. He's comfortable in his bones. He's polite and confident for his age, which surprises her. She has seen him volunteering at the food tent, but they've never talked.

He says, "Hi, my name is Donnie. Can we talk?" Alex says, "Sure, what's up?" He says, "I know you've been asking for help with the T.V. station and the radio station. I worked at the T.V. station in the summer and know a bit about how it works. I've been over there, and we should be able to bring it to life. I used to watch everything they did." Alex has never been much of a hugger, but she grabs this kid and squeezes him. He barely endures it but doesn't move away. He keeps his arms at his sides and smiles. "Why didn't you come forward before?" she asks. He says, "I wasn't sure I remembered it all, but I was there yesterday, and I think I know how to do it." He says, "There are also military radio lines we can hook into; I've done that many times." Alex says, "Let me guess, you have a bunch of gear in your parent's basement, right?"

Donnie says, "I have a radio station set up in my bedroom." Alex says, "I don't even know you, Donnie, but I already love you." He says dismissively, "Whatever." She thinks with amusement, *ah yes, the teenager slaps me down.* She says, "Don't get excited, kiddo, just a turn of phrase." He says nothing. She asks, "Have you connected with anyone?" He says, "Yeah, a couple of Russians, some guy from Denmark, a woman from California, and a kid from Australia. When I need a translator, I use my app. I can never seem to get them again, but I haven't been setting up times to reconnect. I need to try that."

Donnie says, "Do you want to come over and see if we can get anyone on my radio station after the meeting?" Alex jumps at the chance and says, "Yes!" His house is up the hill on Kings Road, just above Bay Street. It's a straight climb on the bikes. She notices he's installed several aerials on his roof. "Is that for your radio station?" she asks. He says, "Yeah, the higher the aerial, the better the reception, and it depends a lot on what's going on in the skies. You can't depend on it." His house is very tidy, considering a teenager has lived there alone for a long time. There's a piano in the living room and several guitars leaning against the walls. Various pieces of equipment are hooked into the instruments. He has quite a setup in his bedroom, a wall of radio gear. He says, "I just leave it on all the time in case someone's trying to call out from somewhere." Alex asks, "When do you sleep?" He says, "I can sleep anytime. It doesn't matter to me." They hang out together for about a half hour with nothing happening on the radio.

While they wait, Alex asks, "Do you play all those instruments?" He says, "Some of them, guitar and sax mostly. My dad was the musician. He could play anything." She says, "Tell me about your family?" He says, "It was just my dad and me. My mom died when I was little." Alex says, "That's tough. Do you remember her?" He says, "Sorta. I was almost six when she died. She took me to the playground across the street. I remember that. Oh yeah, she taught me how to ride my bike. We went skiing once together. I was cold and fell a lot. I didn't like it. We went inside and had hot chocolate instead." Alex says, "She sounds lovely. What did she die of?" He says, "Some virus. She got it working at the hospital. She was a nurse." Alex says, "You and your dad must have been pretty sad." He says, "Yeah, but we had each other. I miss him." Donnie's eyes well up, and he looks away. Alex knows he won't want her to hug him again, but this kid needs a good cry and a hug. He's been alone for over a year.

He quickly pulls his face together and says, "What about you?" Alex thinks, *what do you know, empathy? A kid who cares what other people are feeling.* She says, "My dad died when I was twelve. It was just my mom and me. My husband and my dog died from the attack. We didn't have any kids. My mother just died a few months ago. She's why I came back here. I'm alone too, and, like you, I really miss her." They sit together in silence. Two orphans. Nothing left to be said.

A voice suddenly blasts out from the radio. Alex isn't sure of the language. Donnie has hooked up a translator app to his gear. Alex thinks, *I love techy kids.* The language pops up as Cantonese and starts translating. "Hello, anybody out there? Respond if you're listening." Donnie answers, "We're here in Victoria, B.C., on the southwest coast of Canada. Where are you?" The person answers, "Guangzhou, southeast China. How are you?" Donnie says, "We're surviving. We have food. How about you?" The voice says, "It's very hard here. Our survivors are starving. There's very little food. It's all been taken." Donnie says, "What are you going to do?" The voice says, "I think I'll go to Vietnam. There are farms close to the border. Maybe I'll find some food there." Donnie says, "What's your name?" The radio goes silent. They've lost him. Literally. Donnie says, "Most of the calls are like that. We often get cut off, and there's no way to call back." Alex asks, "Are they all starving?" He says, "Yeah, most of them say that."

She looks around his room. The walls are layered with bookshelves loaded with books. He's a reader. She asks him how he's been spending his time since the attack. He tells her he was in third-year med school and wanted to be an exploratory surgeon in integrated micro biometrics. *Of course, who wouldn't?* Alex thinks facetiously. Donnie says, "I'd already hacked into all the course material up to the doctorate level, and I've completed most of it. That's off the table now, obviously. The attack has set medicine back so far." Alex says, "The reservoir of knowledge is still there. We can start over. It's still a possibility in your lifetime." He says, "We can't even communicate with the world now. We're back in the stone age with medicine. We've barely discovered fire." Alex says, "So you won't send any little yellow submarines into someone's digestive tract. You can still be a tremendous help medically. Could you assist any of our doctors or nurses here?" He says, "Those old crocks? They know very little about modern medicine and wouldn't appreciate an 18-year-old bringing them up to date." Alex thinks, *a budding scientist has been nipped in the bud.*

She changes the subject and asks, "Are your dad's remains here?" He says, "No, he was a nurse, like my mom, and was working when it happened. I went to the hospital and found his name tag on his clothes with all the sand inside." She asks, "Did you bring him home?" He says, "No, I didn't know what to do. I left him there. It was just a pile of sand, not my dad." Alex asks, "Where's your mom?" He says, "We sprinkled her ashes in the ocean. She loved the ocean, especially on stormy days." Alex asks, "Do you want him with her?" He says, "I dunno, I guess." She says, "Then let's go do that." Donnie asks, "Do you have a boat?" Alex says, "Yeah, I stole it, and it's docked in the Oak Bay Marina." He says, "Never mind. I have a motorboat. We can go out with that. We don't have to go very far." They go to the hospital, and he finds his dad's pile of sand. They put it in a pillowcase. Alex thinks, *I've been putting people's sand into trusty pillowcases this entire trip.* They ride down to the marina. It's late, and no one's around. His family motorboat bounces in its slip, and they get in. They don't motor out very far, just beyond the seawall. Alex looks at him. "Do you want to say anything?" He says, "Yeah." Then he goes quiet for a long time, staring out over the water. They sit there in silence in the dark, bobbing around in the boat. Alex thinks, *I can wait.* Finally, Donnie says, "Thanks for everything, dad. I love you. Say hello to mom." Short and sweet. He spreads his dad's sand out over the water. It's a calm evening. It all quickly sinks. Alex doesn't know whether that did Donnie any good or not. He's quiet as they putter back to shore. She wishes she could fix all the broken hearts she keeps encountering.

Alex says, "I promised Sue I'd work on the drug warehouse with her tomorrow. Can we meet at the T.V. station the day after and see if we can get that happening?" Donnie says, "Yeah, when?" she says, "How about ten? I'll meet you there." He says, "Okay." Alex goes into mother mode and asks, "What are you eating for dinner tonight?" He says he's made up a bunch of veg casseroles and thawed one of them. She thinks, *of course, he's a young scientist. Why wouldn't he cook?*

The next day, Alex shares her Donnie time with Sue. Sue says, "He's a brilliant kid, started university when he was 15 and aced all his courses." Alex says, "He could be very useful to our medical team if only I could talk him into it. He thinks they're old and out of touch. He thinks I'm old." Sue says, "Remember what you felt like at that age? Twenty-five seemed ancient. He's a good human being. I think he'll come around."

Alex contacts Francis as well and shares her Donnie radio experience. Francis says, "Yes, our team has been making lots of connections with people worldwide by radio, but as your Donnie said, it's patchy." They've made better headway with the SAT phones and have been able to patch into a few satellites and have connected. We all have SAT phones here now and our screens are working. Alex says, "You're kidding? Can I call you?" Francis says, "Let's see if we can connect. Try right now. Here's my contact information." Alex goes off screen, grabs her SAT phone, and dials up Francis. There's that gorgeous face and lovely island accent at the other end. Alex says, "Oh my god, Francis, this is life-changing." Francis grins widely and says, "I wasn't sure we could connect, and I didn't want to disappoint you. I'm so glad it worked. We're on the right track." Alex asks, "Do you think I can hook up with Krista?" Francis says, "All you can do is try, although they may be hooked into a different satellite than the ones we've connected with."

Alex asks her how the move to Niagara on the Lake went. Francis says, "So many stories, and of course, things never go as you would expect." We're getting a lot of pushback from the surviving locals. They don't like this cocky young team coming in and trying to take over. Of the few survivors, there are still a lot of clicky old Niagara on the Lake people living here, mostly in their late 70s. They don't want to do anything. They complain. They're not adjusting to the new world order well. It's a process. Hardly any farmers survived, so taking over the farms has been easy. We have to change the crops. They were mainly growing grapes here. We couldn't possibly drink that much."

Francis says, "We've met an interesting duo. There's a Jamaican woman here with a young teenage local boy. They took over a farm a while back and are doing a great job. I quite like her. Her name is June, and he's Jacob. He calls her Junie. She seems to have taken him under her wing. He's a nice kid, and they're getting along well with the team. Everyone has adopted Jacob, and he's enjoying the attention. They're a welcome addition to our family."

Alex asks Francis how she's feeling. She's due in early December. Francis shows Alex her big belly. "I'm a waddler, apparently. So far, so good, no problems. Miguel is so excited. Now that we're in a town, he brings home baby stuff daily from the shops." Alex asks, "What kind of house did you choose? There are some beauties there." Francis says, "Yes, and we chose a nice one, but it's new and practical and won't need much work for a while." We didn't go for the big splashy historical mansion. We have too much to do setting up this new life. Neither of us is into cleaning a big house, nor are we particularly handy." Alex says, "Tomorrow, we'll try to bring the T.V. station back to life." I'll report back. She immediately tries Krista and Sal on her SAT phone. No one picks up, it's not connected, or it's sitting somewhere in a drawer, abandoned.

The next day, Alex meets Donnie at the station. He's already sitting at the media control panel. He says, "It's still live. There should have been an automatic video stream that kicked in after the attack, but it must have been cut off somehow." She reminds him that all screens went dead, probably worldwide." He says, "Yeah, I'm trying to figure out why. That shouldn't have happened. The main satellites wouldn't have disconnected. It could be a simple fix. She asks if he minds bringing the I.T. team from NOTL to this discussion. He says, "That would be great. They probably have the answer." She has the bike screen with her, calls up the I.T. team, introduces them to Donnie, and tells them what they're trying to do. They say this problem has puzzled them, and they couldn't figure it out without access to a T.V. station. There isn't one in NOTL. They also think it should be a simple flip of a switch.

Alex says, "May I put in my very non-techy two cents? Has anybody tried shutting down the station and turning it back on again? Technical advice down through the ages." They all say they're concerned they won't be able to reconnect to the satellite if they do that. Alex says, "Well, we currently have nothing. I'm willing to risk it." Donnie says, "I'm not." One tech person says, "Go for it." The other says, "I'm with Donnie." Alex says, "There are two T.V. stations on the island. How be we risk this one, and then we'll know?

She says to Donnie, "Shut down the power in the entire station. There must be a panel somewhere." He says, "I know where it is. I already checked it. I'll do it, but this is a very unscientific approach." She says, "Go for it anyway." He disappears. All the station panel lights go off. Everything goes off. They wait in the dark for ten minutes. The only light is from Alex's screen, with the tech guys' faces wide-eyed, exchanging glances. Alex says, "Okay, fingers crossed, turn it back on again." Suddenly, the room lights up. Two different backup streaming videos appear on two of the many screens on the wall. The studio fills with sound. It's 'old school technology,' but Alex and Donnie look at each other and yell. Alex stands in front of a camera, Donnie flicks on the corresponding key, and there she is, on screen. She races next door to a house, lets herself in, and turns on the screens. There's the station backdrop. Hallelujah!

When she returns to the station, Donnie and the two tech guys are screaming with excitement at each other. "We did it!" Alex is thinking, "Well, um guys, it was me that suggested you just turn the damn power off, but, oh well." She says, "Okay, we should put out a broadcast right now. Lots of people won't even have turned their screens off. If they had this channel on, we should pop up on their screen." Donnie says, "Go for it. What are you going to say?" Alex says, "I'll just wing it." She stands in front of the screen with the station's picture of the harbor on it. Donnie aims the camera at her.

Alex says, "Hi there, those who might be watching. We have great news. As you can see, we're live here in the station down on Government Street. Your fellow volunteer, Donnie, got it up and running with help from our tech friends back east. From now on, we'll be able to provide you with regular updates and weather reports from the boat radios. We think the station has a library of videos we can stream to you when nobody's on air, which will be most of the time. We'll have to check that out. I'll come on at six every night to update you with any news. Not sure what that might be, but we'll think of something. If any of you have any suggestions or want to join us, please, let us know. You can do a musical performance or a comedy act or tell a story or some theatre. Whatever, we would love to hear from you at the next meeting." Alex signs off with, "Until tomorrow."

Alex sees her pale, dragged-out self up on the screen. She thinks, *I look tired. I may have to incorporate some makeup, a curling iron, and better clothes.* Donnie turns off the camera. He says, "There were 4,562 watchers for your broadcast, but all that tells us is those screens came on. Most of them will be in dead houses." Alex says, "Let's see if the numbers change tomorrow." Donnie says, "I'm going to spend the day here and see what they have in their library and how all the rest of this stuff works." Alex says, "You're a wizard." He says, "They're only in the movies, Alex." She deadeyes him and says, "You've got to stop taking me literally." He laughs. She says, "Have fun with your new toy." His head is down, going over the control boards. He barely notices her leave.

Alex rides straight to Sue and tells her the good news. She hugs Alex and says, "You're really pulling us together. Thank you." Alex tells her about the SAT phones working in some places. Sue excitedly says, "Let's try ours. Give me your contact information. My wrist phone's back at the house. I'll go back and call you from there." She rides off, and Alex waits and thinks, *if we can get these working in town, we have communication.* A half-hour goes by, and nothing. Alex thinks, *she should have made it home by now and found the phone.* Another half-hour goes by. Alex thinks, *very weird. If she can't call me, she would have just come back here.* Her phone rings just as she mounts her bike to ride up to Sue's place. It's Sue. Sue grins back at Alex and says, "Sorry, a volunteer stopped me on the way out and needed to talk. You know my people come first." Alex says in total exasperation, "Sue, for Christ's sake, very noble of you, but we're communicating on our SAT phones. I can see you!" That's Alex's news broadcast for that night.

Alex rides back to the station and tells Donnie the news about the SAT phones. He says, "Wow, it's all happening fast. That's so great." She asks, "Do you have a SAT phone?" He rolls his eyes and says, "Of course. Adults!" Alex thinks, *guess I'm one of those.* She says to him sarcastically, "Forgive me for being one. Give me your contact info." She keys it into her phone.

She rides up to UVic to tell Dev and Georgia. They scream. Alex wouldn't have ever imagined either of them screaming, but there they were, yelling their heads off with exultation. She keys in their contact info. She's building a contact list, just like the old days, before the world changed. Alex calls Krista and Sal again. No joy.

Before her next broadcast, Alex takes the time to put on some makeup. Not much, some lipstick, blush, and mascara. She curls her hair. Her mother had great clothes. Alex chooses a red sweater and navy pants from her closet and checks herself out. She thinks, *Almost the old me. Not as bad as I thought.* She walks into the station, and Donnie looks up. "Holy crap, Alex, do you ever look different!" Alex says, "Thanks, I think. They might not recognize me with lipstick on." He says, "Seriously, you look great. You should wear makeup every day." Big compliments from an 18-year-old kid with pink hair. She goes on air with their big SAT news, posts her and Sue's contact information, and says, "If the line is busy, it means we're talking to one of you. Don't give up. You can drop by the food site and leave your contact info for anybody who wants to pick it up. I'll repeat this message every night. I have picked up a boat radio that provides weather reports. It looks like we're in for rain. What a surprise. There'll be a 20-m.p.h. wind tomorrow, and the rain will clear by mid-afternoon. Temperatures will reach highs tomorrow of around 65 degrees."

Alex continues, "Donnie's found about 10,000 movies, podcasts, etc., and we'll broadcast these continuously. He'll create a weekly broadcast list with times posted in the conference center. I hope more of you have tuned in tonight. We look forward to your input and ideas and seeing you at the next meeting." Once she's signed off, Donnie says, "The numbers were up by about 50 watchers. They're talking to each other." They continue their broadcasts nightly. Alex chatters aimlessly for about fifteen minutes and gives the weather forecast. She repeats what she's said before, assuming more and more survivors are tuning in. When she arrives at the next meeting and walks in, there are about 250 people there. They break out in applause as she goes up to the stage. This embarrasses her; she didn't expect it. Alex says, "Thanks, folks, but your screens are back up, and SAT phones are working because of the expertise of our own Donnie Klassen and the I.T. team back east. I hope most of you know that's what we've achieved this week. It's been a huge step ahead. How many of you have tuned in to your home screens?" Most put their hands up.

Alex says, "Now, we'll really need some help. We need performers, musicians, lecturers, artists, comedians, storytellers, and anybody with something to share. We don't care how good or bad you are. We want variety. I can't carry this all by myself." She goes on, "I'm also hoping a few people might want to try their hand at co-hosting the nightly 'news.' There's a sign-up sheet at the back of the room. Don't be shy. Hell, I even put on lipstick and mascara. You can at least play your accordion or whatever you do." This brings a laugh.

Amazingly, this small crowd, so reticent so far, comes up with a wide variety of acts, some very professional. Alex puts Donnie in charge of scheduling them. She thinks he's having a bit of a laugh. She and Sue's SAT phones constantly ring for the first couple of weeks. "Hi Alex, just checking that it works. You're looking great, by the way." "Hi Alex, I have an idea for a performance. Can I run it by you?" And so on. Sue gets the same calls. The town is coming alive. Even the doctors, nurses, and their one dentist seem happier. People are booking appointments with them now rather than showing up and standing in unhappy lines.

The medical emergency training classes are going well and highly attended. They use Francis' medical team's format and omit little. Nobody will take out anyone's appendix, but they know how to deal with a broken bone. They often talk about emergencies they won't be able to fix. They need to prepare for these. There'll be situations where they can only make the person comfortable. Many are aging. That's an issue. There are already a couple of people with apparent early stage senility. They talk about how to deal with that. Keep them safe, fed, and sheltered. There'll be bedridden people, eventually. Aging goes on, and it's a bitch.

Chapter 45

ENDINGS AND BEGINNINGS

In early December, Miguel calls Alex with some distressing news. He says, "Francis doesn't want to worry you, but she went into false labor and is bedridden right now." Alex says, "Well, I am worried. How's the baby?" Miguel says, "He seems to be okay, he's in position for lift off, but I'm worried about Francis. Her blood pressure is high, and she isn't feeling well. The medics would like to perform a C-section and get him out early. You may know there's a high risk of stillbirth at her age." Alex asks, "What does Francis think?" Miguel says, "She knows the risks of surgery on her belly in our limited circumstances here, but our medics say they're confident it would be okay. She sees the baby as the future and wants to save him at all costs." Alex says, "Even her life?" Miguel says, "Even her life." Alex says, "I'll check in with her later today. I know she'll worry about the baby after losing her first one." Miguel says, "Right now, I'm more worried about Francis."

Miguel calls Alex hours later and tells her they had to make a fast decision. The baby's heart rate was falling, and the medics went ahead with the C-section. He says, "So far, Francis is very weak but fine, and Luis, our wailing baby boy, is here." He holds him up to the screen. He has a wrinkled little newborn face, all snuffles and clasping little fists. Miguel says, "He has all his fingers and toes and is a healthy six pounds, two ounces." Alex asks, "How's his heart? That was her first little girl's problem." Miguel says, "Yes, and he's healthy." Alex says, "Congratulations, dad. He's gorgeous. Scary, but you have a brand new baby boy. Francis is strong and healthy; she'll be up and about in no time."

It's not to be. The next day, Miguel tells Alex that Francis is struggling. Her stomach incision is infected, and she's hemorrhaging. They have a very limited blood bank, and she's receiving infusions. Alex waits frantically for the next report. The thought of losing Francis is too much. There's nothing she can do but wait. Miguel says he's staying by Francis' bedside, and two women have taken over the care of Luis for now. He's in good hands and thriving. They bring him back to Miguel at night, and he rocks him while he sits with Francis. He's chief diaper changer and bottle feeder now. His heart has never been so full of love for this new little life or so distraught as he watches Francis struggle. She's always been so strong and fit. He can't believe she can barely open her eyes to talk to him. When Luis cries, Francis softly calls out, "Matty?" She thinks Luis is her lost little girl.

Weeks go by with Francis rallying and then weakening. Miguel lies by her side and gets up at night when Luis cries, needs changing, feeding, or cuddling. Sometimes Francis is awake enough that he can lay Luis in the crook of her arm. She looks down at him sleepily, not quite conscious, not quite aware her baby boy is in her arms. Miguel is on edge every minute.

One morning he's heating a bottle and hears Francis call out to him. He races in. Her eyes are clear. She whispers, "Is that our son in the bassinet?" Miguel can't help himself and weeps in relief. Francis has never seen him cry. He brings Luis to her, and she cradles him, looking up at Miguel with a wide smile. She says, "I may have left town for a while. What happened?" Miguel fills her in. He says, "You almost died. I couldn't imagine life without you." Francis reaches out, hugs him, and says, "I'm back. It's all going to be okay." Within a week, Francis is up, tired, but mostly back to normal. She calls Alex and says, "Sorry to scare the hell out of everyone." Alex says, "Yeah, please don't do that again."

Alex thinks, *is this what life will be like from now on, death, near death, and more death?* Her body seems wired to a new tuning fork of constant watchfulness, vibrating in the slightest breeze of danger.

Winter passes, and they enter their second spring after the attack. Francis and Alex talk daily. They each have a town they're trying to rebuild, and they share their challenges, successes, ideas, and frustrations. One day in early spring, Francis says, "Alex, I want to talk to you about something." Alex thinks, *oh, oh, this sounds like bad news.* Francis says, "I want you to think about this. We need to get the country as reconnected as possible, not just our little villages. That means testing the SAT satellites, connecting those with SAT phones to each other, and getting the few T.V. stations back up and running. Our guys are hacking into more and more communication satellites daily. We need someone to do the cross-country trek and try to connect with the remaining survivors. You've been successful in pulling Victoria together. You're a born organizer. You have the invisi gear to do it safely. Would you consider taking this on and coming home? It would be a long and dangerous trip. Every stop would require connecting with people; they may not all be meeting. It could be like starting over in each city. It's a huge job, but you're the one I think could do it. Should do it." She goes on, "Besides which, we need an editor for our newspaper." Alex says, "Aaah, an end goal. That could be interesting."

Alex doesn't know what to think. She hadn't considered ever leaving Victoria again.

Alex says to Francis, "We're just getting Victoria on its feet; there's still so much to do." Francis says, "From what you've told me, you've been doing a fine job delegating. You should have been a CEO." Alex says, "Not my game." Francis says, "Think about it. Talk it over with Sue. I think she'll give you wise counsel. I'll leave it with you. No hurry. The world is waiting." Alex says, "Yeah, no pressure." Alex thinks, *this is a huge ask*. She's not ready to talk to Sue about it and doesn't want her to think she's abandoning her. Alex doesn't know what to do.

She sleeps fitfully. She really doesn't want to go. Victoria is her home. Even with her mother gone, it's still home. She can stay here and continue working with Sue on food and drugs and with Donnie on communication. Their meager medical team needs to be sat on until a few assistants are trained. Thanks to Dev and Georgia, farming and food distribution are up and running. It'll never be the old Victoria, but they can build a new one.

Alex's mind is racing. She compares staying and leaving. If she goes, she leaves Sue high and dry. She'll have to take another treacherous boat trip across the strait. Not appealing. She's not a techie. She'd need to lean on the tech people back east and Donnie if she could even connect with him off the island on their SAT phones. Visiting all the major cities in the country and trying to pull together a communication strategy with whoever remains is no small feat. Some of those cities are big. She could easily just get ignored. Not all the T.V. stations will be as easy to get up and running. She can't seem to connect with Krista and Sal. She's sure whoever's left in Calgary, the tech center will have figured something out. Newfoundland and Labrador are no go's. She won't be crossing the Atlantic to get there.

Then Alex flips it over and asks herself, w*ho really needs her here?* Sue was doing just fine before she came along. She knows the city needs to elect a manager. She doesn't want that role. The medical situation is a problem, but it isn't anything Alex can fix. It is what it is. She has had to make a lot of big decisions on this trip. This is another one. In the morning, her head is clear.

She waits until the end of the day to get Sue alone. Several people have come forward to co-host the 6:00 broadcast. It turns out they have a town full of hams. That's alright. Alex asks Sue to stop fiddling with the food and sit. Sue does this, puts her hands on her knees, and says, "Give it to me." Alex lays it all out for her, saying she doesn't want to leave her. Sue holds Alex's hands and says, "Alex, this is your future. We were all just wandering around lost, and you pulled us together. You have done more than anyone could ask here. The rest of the country needs you." Alex says, "You make me feel like a soldier going off to war." Sue says, "Well, it's one way to look at it." Sue continues, "I love you like a daughter. I will miss you so much. But because of you, we can now talk on our phones. It's not the end. I can talk to you until I die. Every day if I want. Hopefully, I can cheer you on, make you laugh, and let you know how our little crew is doing here. How cool is that?" Alex says, "Maybe I was hoping you would talk me out of it." Sue says, "It's your decision, honey. Stay. We would love to have you here forever. Or go. Help the country get back on its feet." Alex looks at her, starts crying, and says, "I'll miss you so much."

They agree they need to get a town manager in place before Alex leaves, but they decide to keep her exit quiet for now. At the next town meeting, they say they're looking for a town manager, a good generalist with excellent people skills. They decide to be democratic and run an election. Four people step forward, put their bona fides out there, and they have a vote. A well-known guy who ran a very successful non-profit business sourcing housing for people wins. Sue and Alex like him. If he doesn't work out, they can always have another election. Democracy lives.

Alex drops by the T.V. station to see how Donnie is doing. He's running a variety show here. He's rehearsing two tap dancers. They tap and twirl their way around the studio. It's hilarious. Donnie isn't looking entertained. He says to them in a flat voice, "That's great. How about next Tuesday at noon, and we'll see how it goes from there?" They're thrilled. They leave, and it's just Donnie and Alex.

He deadeyes her and says, "You're leaving, aren't you?" Alex says, "How did you know?" He says, "I've been watching you hand off many things. I don't know what you'd be doing if you stayed." She tells him what the plan is. He looks up at her and says, "Bring me with you?" Alex is stunned and immediately says, "Sorry, kiddo, that won't work. It's too dangerous." Donnie says, "We would have each other's backs." He goes on, "Besides which, you need me. Someone has to set up those T.V. stations. You don't know how to do that."

Alex responds feebly, "I would talk to you and the tech people; I could figure it out." Donnie says, "But if I were with you, you wouldn't have to worry about that, and your trip wouldn't be wasted." Alex thinks, *he's got a point*. She says, "People kill in broad daylight. There are too many desperate survivors who'll do anything for food." Donnie says, "Like who?" Damn, he wants an example. She decides not to tell him about killing the two highway guys. She says, "Remember Freddie." He says, "Yeah, he was a creep." She asks, "Seen him lately?" He says, "No! Did someone take him out? Seriously?" She says, "I don't know where he is, but Sue had cut him off at the food site, and he was harassing some people for their food." One of our volunteers dealt with him, but it's dangerous out there, Donnie. I couldn't put you at risk. You're too young and have too much ahead of you." He says, "Like what? Stay here and rehearse tap dancers? Not my permanent gig, thank you. I want to do something bigger medically. I want to meet the team in Niagara on the Lake. I could be so much more useful there. Besides, I can help you get across the country. You need me. Come on, Alex. Take me with you." She says, "Can I sleep on it?" He says, "Sure, but decide yes."

Again, Alex talks to her dear friend Sue about this. She needs someone else's opinion besides Donnie's. Sue says, "He's right, you know. He'll be wasted here. He needs a bigger universe. It wouldn't hurt to have a road companion." Alex says, "Again, I was hoping you would talk me out of it." She talks to Francis about it, and she says, "You would have to kit him out in all the invisi gear and share all that with him. Can you trust him to use his discretion? He would have to keep it all to himself even when he comes back here. Only two of our crew know about the invisi fabric. How old is he?" Alex says, "Around eighteen." Francis says, "Eighteen-year-old boys, and he's still a boy, aren't renowned for keeping their mouths shut. They like to brag." He's right about bringing technical skills to the stations. You don't want to waste your time because you can't figure it out." Alex says, "Yet you asked me to do it." Francis says, "Someone has to get out there and try. You could find other Donnies to help you in the cities you visit, and you always have our tech team. It's a tough call, Alex. You know the kid better than I do."

Alex knows she risks Donnie striking out on his own if she turns him down. That would be way too dangerous. In the end, bringing him with her seems the best choice.

The next night is a community meeting night at the Convention Center. It's teeming rain, and Alex is running late, switching between her house, the interim house, and the convention center. Her SAT phone goes off. It's Donnie, and he's speaking fast and frantically. His face on the screen is panicked and his eyes are filled with tears. "Alex, you need to get down here now. There's been a big explosion. I don't know who survived. There's blood everywhere. Please come now." He breaks off in a sob. Heart in her throat, Alex races down to the site. It's a disaster. Donnie is pacing in front of the building, what's left of it, his eyes wide with shock. He's visibly trembling.

There are no fire trucks, ambulances, sirens, or even gawkers. It's strangely silent as the building smolders in the early evening, with shredded walls, roofs, and debris everywhere. Donnie says, "I've checked the space. There are no survivors. You may not want to go in there. It's hell." Alex reaches out and touches his arm, and goes in anyway. There are parts of bodies all over the room, mangled arms, legs, and heads. It's gruesome. She quickly moves through the space, looking for survivors. Donnie was right. No one came out of this alive. Alex thinks 150-200 people are gone. They'll never know exactly who. The explosion ripped apart their small community and decimated it. She goes to the front, looking for signs of Sue. Her familiar brown wool cap lies on the floor with what looks like half her head inside. She's almost grateful her face is gone. Her body is nowhere to be seen. Alex crouches on the floor beside the cap and wails softly to herself, *no, no, no.* There'll be no Sue at the other end of the SAT phone, no lifetime of connection and friendship, no Sue ever again. It's unbearable.

She knows who did this.

What remains of the building isn't safe. Alex surveys the room to assure herself no one's left alive. She finds Donnie and says, "Let's go back to my house." She asks, "Are you okay to ride behind me?" Donnie nods. She decides not to stop at the interim house tonight and change. She can explain all the invisi-suit stuff to him later. She has yet to tell him he can leave the Island with her. She's not sure what to do now but she knows she has to be the strong one tonight.

Once home, she calls Dev and Georgia and tells them what happened. They both go silent and then ask what they can do. Alex says, "Frankly, I don't know. I'm still in shock. We'll have to clean up the bodies as much as possible, but I can't face that tonight. The building isn't safe. I have Donnie with me. We both need to process this." They say, "Call us in the morning, and we'll be right there."

Alex sits down, puts her head in her hands, and says sadly to Donnie. "I wonder if we can resurrect what's left of this town after this. Donnie looks at her and says, "Yeah, there aren't many people left." Alex says, "If we leave together, we'll feel like we're abandoning the few people left here. It'll weigh on us." Donnie says, "Yeah, I get that, but isn't there a bigger need to try to pull some of the country back together by helping more people get organized and connected?" Alex says, "Big needs, small needs, they're all needs. We'll have to do our best to leave the few people remaining here set up as safely as possible. At least they have food." Donnie says, "In the long term, they were all doomed anyway, don't you think?" Alex thinks, *There's the directness of youth. Everything is black and white.* She says, "No. I have hopes for younger people here, and Dev and Georgia are still alive. There might be another 300 people out there on the Island who weren't at the meeting who can carry on. Maybe those few remaining aren't doomed entirely." Donnie says, "If they get sick, they are. Our entire medical crew went down in the explosion. I couldn't do much for them, even if I stayed." Alex says, "Unfortunately, that applies worldwide right now. Not much medical aid left."

She changes the subject and asks him if he's ready to talk about the trip. He asks, "Does this mean you're taking me with you?" Alex says, "Yes, that's what I mean." After one of the worst days of his life, Donnie manages a smile. Alex says, "There's a lot I need to share with you. If you come with me, you can never, I mean never, tell anyone what I'm about to tell you." He says, "Holy shit, you killed Freddie!" Alex says, "No, I did not kill Freddie, although I'm pretty sure he caused the explosion tonight. He's still out there. This is something much different. I have a long story to tell you. Don't talk. Just listen." She rolls it all out to him. He stays mute. She includes Francis' concern about his ability to keep his mouth shut.

Donnie finally speaks. He says, "My dad talked a lot about some very personal things he heard and witnessed in his work at the hospital. It was always expected that was between us. It was his way of unloading. I knew they weren't stories I could ever tell my friends. And I didn't. I was going to be a doctor. Discretion is essential. I completely understand why Francis wouldn't want this known. It could endanger people's lives if the wrong person got their hands on this gear. This is between you and me, Francis, and Miguel when I meet them." Alex says, "Well, we'd be stopping in Taber to see Krista and Sal. They also know." He says, "Of course. Anyone else you 'didn't' tell?" Alex says, "No one else, smart ass. Sue didn't even know it all." He says, "Can I try on the suit?" Alex says, "Sure, here's some glasses so you can see it. It's a one-size-fits-all, except for little kids, so it should be okay. Slip it on and go look at yourself in the bathroom mirror. It's freaky." Donnie does that, and she hears him in the bathroom. "Holy shit, I half didn't believe you." Alex says, "Welcome to my invisible world."

She says, "Why don't you bed down in the spare room tonight, and we'll deal with the explosion site tomorrow, if you can face it. I want to honor those people and clean up as much as possible." Donnie says, "I don't know if I can sleep. I can't get the image of the bloody room out of my mind." Alex says, "I know. I think I'll sit here for a while and think about what to do for the remaining people." He says, "Let's do that together." They talk long into the night, and he finally dozes off on the couch. She covers him with a duvet. She doesn't sleep.

The following day, she calls Dev and Georgia and tells them she's going down to the site to clean up the bodies. They meet her and Donnie there, and the four of them stand across the street from the ruined structure, a small team in their desolation. Four very lonely survivors in their ever-shrinking world. Alex says, "As gruesome as it sounds, we should get every garbage bag we can find. There's probably a supply somewhere. We'll put on some rubber gloves and bag what we can find. Dev says, "We're honoring our friends. Let's think of it that way." What's left of the bodies has quickly dried. There are leg and arm bones, some torsos, and a few heads. Alex picks up Sue's hat, shakes out the now dried brains and tucks her hat into her shirt, close to her heart. Georgia weeps silently while she works, and Dev and Donnie keep their heads down while they pick up body parts and bag them. It's the worst thing any of them ever imagined themselves doing in their lives, but they do it. Alex is worried about the safety of the remaining building and wants to get everybody in and out as quickly as possible. They can hear the building creak. After a few hours, they stack the bags inside and walk out. No hearse is coming to pick up the bodies, no funeral, no last goodbye.

Alex says, "Thanks to all of you for rising to this. They would have done it for us." Georgia says, "Dev and I talked all night about what we can do now. There are still survivors; some are probably outside the distribution building right now, waiting for food or to volunteer. They won't know this has happened, and we must get to them. We also need someone to take over the site's management with Sue gone.

They hear a great groan, then watch the building shiver and collapse to the ground as it implodes. A huge cloud of dust rises in the air. The world doesn't need more human dust. They got out just in time. They stand in silence, just staring at the rubble. Alex feels like they should be singing Amazing Grace or something. Not their thing. Instead, tears roll down all their faces and they are quiet. The sadness in unbearable.

Alex says, "Donnie and I are going down to the station to do a broadcast and tell everyone what happened." She also says, "I think it was Freddie who did this, and he's still out there. We all need to be careful. He's most likely to turn up at the food site now that he thinks we're all dead." They ride off to their separate locations. Once Alex is done with her broadcast, she and Donnie join Dev and Georgia back at the food distribution site. Only about five people have shown up, and they're of course shocked to hear the devastating news, particularly the loss of Sue. Everyone's crying. To their great relief, Sophia walks in. She falls apart like the others at the news. Alex takes a giant leap and asks Sophia if she could take over for Sue and manage the site. Sophia looks at her and says, "I would be honored." Sophia and Dev don't know it yet, but her new position working directly with Dev will bring them a lot closer.

Alex has already decided to never leave Sophia alone there. She's sure Freddie will turn up. For the next week, she and Donnie stay with Sophia and hand out food to the few remaining people that show up. The heavy sadness hangs on them and everyone who comes to the site. They are rudderless now. Alex feels they're being watched, but Freddie hasn't shown up. Several days after the explosion, he doesn't disappoint and sidles in. He has a smirk on his face. He's obviously surprised to see Alex and says, "You're still here?" Alex says, "Yeah, Freddie, why would you think I wouldn't be?" Freddie doesn't even have the good sense to deny it, and she hears him say under his breath, "Fucking bitch." He says, "I hear your building blew up?" Alex says, "Where did you hear that? Nothing blew up." She's laying a trap for him. He's so proud of his work; he needs to brag. He says, "Yeah, I heard there were bodies everywhere, even your best friend Sue." Alex lies, "Sorry, Freddy, Sue's fine, not blown up. I talked to her this morning. I don't know what you're talking about." Freddy falls into the trap and says, "I heard her brains were in that stupid hat she wore."

Alex tries to remain calm. He must have gone into the site after the explosion. Otherwise, he wouldn't have seen Sue's cap. He's just admitted he did this.

Alex thinks of Sue, saying she would not think twice about taking him out if he threatened her or her people. She was brave and sure of herself. Alex makes a big decision and says to Freddie, "Let's go for a walk. I want to talk to you." The others look at her with alarm, and she says, "Don't worry, I've got this." Freddy smiles in a smarmy self-congratulatory way and says, "Finally coming around, are you? Sure, we can go for a walk." Alex says, "Let's just stroll around the corner." She can tell he's uncertain and doesn't know what she's up to, but she's just a small woman, and as soon as they are out of sight of the rest of the people, he already knows he'll first beat the crap out of her and then kill her. His hate for her is so strong he can think of nothing else but to eliminate her. He hasn't even examined this feeling. It just is, and he needs to satisfy it.

They wander off and are out of sight. Alex has her small gun in her hand in her pocket. She keeps her distance from him but senses he's building to do something. She can see it in the bulging veins in his neck. He turns on her quickly with his fist raised, and she just as quickly shoots him. He falls to the sidewalk, lifeless, eyes still open. Alex feels no guilt, turns to him, and says, "That was for Sue and all our friends." She leaves him there, walks back, and speaks quietly to Donnie, Dev, and Georgia, out of earshot of Sophia. She says, "I just killed him. We need to move his body out of sight." The three of them look at her, shocked. Donnie says quietly, "Holy shit!" Dev says nothing. He stares at her. Georgia finally speaks up, "Okay, where is he? I can probably do this on my own." Georgia and Alex return to Freddie's body, and Georgia, using the strength of her male arms, moves him easily out of sight to the backyard of the house he died in front of. She looks at Alex and asks, "Are you okay?" Alex says, "Yep, I'm okay." Georgia says, "Good girl. Sue would have been proud of you." They all view Alex in a new light.

They spend the next month trying to get the rest of the survivors organized as much as possible. With no medical help, they need to rely on what they've learned in the medical classes over the past few months. It's not enough, but they can do nothing about that. Alex finally gets up the nerve to tell them she and Donnie are leaving and why. This is received with great silence, and Alex fills with guilt. Dev finally speaks and says, "Alex, you and Donnie will be of more use to the country trying to help people get organized and expand communication, that's for sure. There really isn't much more you can do here. We'll carry on. I'm eternally grateful for what you did organizing all of us. It is what it is." He's graciously letting her off the hook. Alex thinks, *yeah, but I wish it were different.* Dev goes on, "None of us will survive any longer if you stay." Georgia says, "Am I selfish if I say I want you to stay?" Alex reaches out to her and gives her a long hug. She says, "Georgia, the town manager went down in the building and someone has to take the lead here and keep an eye on all the components of Victoria working and improving. I think it should be you. Are you up for it?" Dev jumps in and says, "Of course she's up for it." Georgia looks over at Dev and Alex and says, "That's a huge responsibility but you're right, we need an overseer. If you could do it, so can I. I'll do my best." Alex says, "The world hasn't ended. It's just had a setback and has overcome those before. I'll miss you both so much."

Alex gets Donnie all the gear he'll need for the trip, a few changes of clothes to wear underneath his invisi-suit, a good little tent, long enough for his frame and his bike, and an inflatable mattress and blanket. They have better camping gear here than when she first went shopping. She can cover his tent with the extra invisi fabric if they have to sleep rough. They'll find a new bike for him in Vancouver and spray it, and with the help of the tech team back east, hook his helmet up to hers. They'll need three times the number of wafers to feed a teenager on the road. Most of the frozen food in the Smart Houses will be inedible by now, so they'll be eating flavored wafers, like it or not. Donnie's so excited. It's Christmas in April for him. He runs all the T.V. station technical stuff by Dev and Georgia, and they get it. Thankfully.

Alex says a hard goodbye to Dev and Georgia. Georgia tries to make it easy, gives her a long hug, and says breezily, "Call me tomorrow when you get to the other side. I need to know you both didn't sink in the sea." Alex laughs and says, "We'll be fine. Donnie's a nice kid. Seeing who he becomes as he grows up will be exciting."

It's a chilly May morning in Victoria, overcast, with not much wind. Alex and her young companion head down to the marina. She's two years older than when she left, but so much older. They take the same boat she sailed over with. The crossing will be less scary with Donnie at the helm. He at least knows what he's doing. He also understands her unease with the ocean and agrees to poke their way back through the islands to the mainland. She thinks, *There's that empathy again. He'll be a good leader some day. We'll be fine together.*

They leave their lovely imperfect island behind, along with the mountains, their living and dead friends, and soon the sea. *Leaving Eden*, Alex thinks. She reflects sadly. *Nothing's resolved. My husband is dead, my mother is dead, and Sue and so many survivors are now dead because of illness and the madness of humanity. It has to get better, or we're all lost.* Their remaining friends on the Island may not survive past the current generation, or just a few may scratch through. Alex can't fix that. She knows she won't be back.

With their backs straight and eyes forward, they motor out of the harbor and across the strait, looking east.

They each have challenges and colossal life changes ahead of them. But that's another story for another time.

Made in the USA
Columbia, SC
06 January 2023

74453411R00176